BERLIN

W9-BVK-243

POTSDAM

POLAND

SCHWERIN

Elbe

Oder

BERLIN

BRANDENBURG   POTSDAM

WARSAW

Elbe

Neisse

Oder

LEIPZIG

DRESDEN

WEIMAR

Elbe

PRAGUE

Main

CZECHOSLOVAKIA

NÜRNBURG

Danube

AUGSBURG   PASSAU

Danube   VIENNA

MUNICH

INZELL

GARMISCH

AUSTRIA

R K

THE
RUNNER

ALSO BY CHRISTOPHER REICH

NUMBERED ACCOUNT

THE
RUNNER

CHRISTOPHER
REICH

Delacorte Press

Published by
Delacorte Press
Random House, Inc.
1540 Broadway
New York, New York 10036

Delacorte Press® is a registered trademark of Random House, Inc., and the colophon is a trademark of Random House, Inc.

Library of Congress Cataloging-in-Publication Data

Reich, Christopher.
The runner : a novel / Christopher Reich.
p.   cm.
ISBN 0-385-33366-8
1. World War, 1939–1945—Fiction.   I. Title.
PS3568.E476284 R86 2000
813'.54—dc21   99–089058

Manufactured in the United States of America
Published simultaneously in Canada

March 2000

10 9 8 7 6 5 4 3 2 1

BVG

For my parents, Babs and Willy Reich, with love

THE
RUNNER

CHAPTER

1

AT NINE O'CLOCK, ON A WARM JULY evening in the Bavarian Alps, Erich Seyss stepped from the doorway of his assigned barracks and walked briskly across the grass toward the burned-out stable that housed the prisoners' latrine. He wore a shapeless gray uniform that carried neither rank nor insignia. No cap adorned his head. Only his arrogant gait and undaunted posture remained to identify him as an officer of the German Reich. In the distance, the sun's last rays crowned snowcapped peaks with a hazy orange halo. Closer, and less angelic, twin barbed-wire fences and a succession of spindly-legged watchtowers surrounded a five-acre enclosure, home to three thousand defeated soldiers.

POW Camp 8, as it was officially designated by the United States Army of Occupation, sat in a broad meadow on the western outskirts of Garmisch, a once chic resort that in 1936 had played host to the Winter Olympic Games. Until three months earlier, the compound had served as the headquarters of the German Army's First Mountain Division. Like Garmisch, it had escaped the war unscathed—weathered, perhaps, but untouched by a single bomb or bullet. Today, the assembly of stout stone buildings and low-slung wooden cabins housed what Seyss had heard an American officer refer to as "the scum and brutes of the German Army."

Seyss smiled inwardly, thinking "the loyal and proven" was more like it, then jogged a few steps across the macadam road that bisected the camp. In contrast to his relaxed demeanor, his mood was turbulent, a giddy mix of anxiety and bravado that had his stomach doing somersaults and his heartbeat the four-hundred-meter dash. To his left ran the prisoners' barracks, a row of stern three-story buildings built to sleep two hundred men, now filled with a thousand. Farther on hunched a weathered cabin that housed the radio shack, and ten meters past that, the camp commander's personal quarters. Barely visible at the end of the road was a tall wooden gate swathed in barbed wire and framed by sturdy watchtowers. The gate provided the camp's sole entry and exit. Tonight, it was his destination.

In ten minutes, either he would be free or dead.

He had arrived at the camp in late May, transported from a hospital in Vienna, where he had been recovering from a Russian bullet to his lower back. The wound was his third of the war and the most serious. He'd suffered it in a rearguard action against lead elements of Malinovsky's Ninth Army, maintaining a defensive perimeter so his men could make it across the Enns River and into the American zone of occupation before the official end of hostilities at midnight, May 8. Surrender to the Russians was not an option for soldiers whose collar patch bore the twin runes of the SS.

A week after his surgery, a chubby American major had showed up at his bedside, a little too solicitous of his good health. He'd asked how his kidney was and confided that a man didn't really need a spleen. All the while, Seyss had known what he was after, so when finally the major demanded his name, he gave it voluntarily. He did not wish to be found in two months' time cowering in his lover's boudoir or hiding beneath his neighbor's haystack. Peeling back his hospital smock, he had lifted his left arm so that the SS blood group number tattooed on its pale flank could be read. The American had checked the group number against that written on his clipboard, then, as if declaring the patient cured, smiled, and said, "Erich Siegfried Seyss, you have been identified by the Allied powers as a war criminal and are subject to immediate transfer to an appropriate detention facility, where you will be kept in custody until the time of your trial." He didn't provide any specifics as to the nature of the crimes or where they were alleged to have taken place—on the Dnieper, the Danube, the Vistula, or the Ambleve, though Seyss acknowledged it might have been any one of those places. The major had simply produced a pair of handcuffs and locked his right hand to the bed's metal frame.

Recalling the moment, Seyss paused to light a cigarette and stare at the fiery silhouette of the mountains surrounding him. He considered the charge again and shook his head. *War crimes.* Where did the war end and the crimes begin? He didn't loathe himself for acts from which other, lesser men might have shrunk. As an officer who had sworn his loyalty to Adolf Hitler, he had simply done as he'd been told and acted as honorably as circumstances did or did not allow. If the Allied powers wanted to try him, fine. He'd lost the war. What else could they do?

Dismissing his anger, Seyss cut behind the hall, then traversed a dirt infield littered with bales of firewood. Dusk brought quiet to the camp. Prisoners were confined to their barracks until dawn. GIs freed from duty hustled into town for a late beer. Those staying behind gathered in their quarters for heated games of poker and gin rummy. He walked slower now, guarding the shambling pace of a man with nowhere to go. Still, a sheen of perspiration clung to his forehead. He ventured a glance at the wristwatch taped high on his forearm. Three minutes past nine. Tonight everything would hinge on timing.

Fifty feet away, a lone sentry rounded the corner of the latrine. Spotting Seyss, he called, "Hey, Fritz, get over here. Time for bed check. What're you doing out?"

Seyss approached the GI, pleased he was precisely on schedule. "Just have to make a pee," he answered in English. "Plumbing's messed up and gone to hell. No hard feelings, though. It was Ivan's doing, not yours." Born of an Irish mother and a German father, he'd grown up speaking both languages interchangeably. He could recite Yeats with a Dubliner's impish brogue and quote Goethe with a Swabian's contemptuous slur.

"Just give me your pass and shut up."

Seyss retrieved a yellow slip from his pocket and handed it over. The pass cited an irregularly functioning kidney as grounds for permission to visit the latrine at all hours.

The sentry studied the slip, then pointed at his watch. "Bedtime, Fritz. Curfew in five minutes."

"Don't worry, Joe. I'll be back in plenty of time for my story. And don't forget a glass of warm milk. I can't sleep without it."

The sentry handed him back the pass, even managing a laugh. "Just make it snappy."

Seyss said "yessir," then moved on toward the latrine. Americans were easily seduced by foreigners who could speak their language and he'd been quick to take advantage of their garrulousness, using any pretext to ask carefully disguised questions about the camp's security. What he'd learned was useful to a man with an eye bent on escape. Twenty-four soldiers were posted on night watch—one in each of the eleven towers that ringed the camp, ten walking the area perimeter and three in the camp commander's office located just inside the gate. Only seven of the 150-man camp garrison had been in Germany longer than three months. The rest were replacement troops—green soldiers who had never fired a gun in anger. Most interesting, Colonel Janks, the reed-thin martinet who commanded the camp, had forbidden the use of the klieg lights mounted in the watchtowers except in emergency situations. He had cited a paucity of diesel oil as the reason, but word around camp said otherwise. Janks was selling the oil for dollars on the black market.

Stepping into the latrine, Seyss took a last drag on the cigarette, then threw it into the slit trench running the length of the stable. Despite the absence of a roof and the steady breeze sweeping the building, the stench was ungodly. He smiled grimly. At least he wouldn't have to bear this particular hardship any longer.

Two weeks earlier, the camp doctor, Peter Hansen, had given him word that his presence was required in Munich. Individuals whose intentions could not be questioned, he'd said. Powerful men whose decisions would govern the Fatherland's future. *Kameraden.* As to the identity of the patriots who had requested Seyss's presence, Hansen provided no more information. Nor could he explain the nature of their interest in him. *Kameraden* was all he had said. And that was enough. He was, however, able to supply several items necessary to effect an escape: a wristwatch, a dagger, and, of course, the pass. The rest Seyss managed himself.

Inside the latrine, he acted quickly. Removing his tunic and his pants, he turned both inside out, then put them back on. A pool table's green baize darkened by paint from the camp motor pool had left the garments the same olive drab as an American infantryman's uniform. He ran to a corner of the stable, fell to one knee, and dug at the ground. The earth was loose and came away easily. A minute later, he found what he was looking for. He stood and brushed the dirt off what appeared a dented bedpan, then placed it on his head. His "helmet" was, in fact, a camp soccer ball, deflated, cut in two, and painted the same dull green as his tunic.

Seyss poked his head out of the latrine. The sentry was turning left, past the last barracks. He would continue to the southwest corner of the camp before doubling back to meet up with the officer of the watch and conduct the nightly bed check in Fox, Golf, and Hotel Barracks—or Fichte, Goethe, and Hegel Haus, as some closet intellect from Wittenberg called them. He would not return for at least eleven minutes. Dr. Hansen's Swiss watch had timed his movements for the past twelve nights.

Seyss moved as soon as the sentry disappeared. Thirty yards away stood the camp storehouse, and fifty yards beyond that, the kitchen of the American officers' mess—his destination. Leaving the latrine, he set out across the soccer field. He kept his shoulders pinned back and his head held high. Fifty feet above his right shoulder stood a watchtower, and in that watchtower, an untested twenty-year-old with a hankering to fire the Browning .30-caliber machine gun he hadn't shot since his last day of training.

A voice yelled at him from the tower. "Jacobs, that you?"

Seyss shuddered, but kept walking. He raised an arm in greeting, but his gesture failed to satisfy whoever was in the tower.

"Is that you, Conlan?" came the voice. "You're the only prick that walks like he's got a spading tool up his ass."

Seyss knew he had to respond. Emboldened by the fact that he must at least look like a GI, he lifted his head toward the parapet and yelled, "Shut the hell up! Don't you know Jerry's sleeping?"

No response came from the tower. Reflexively, he bunched his shoulders. The initial burst would strike his back dead center. Finally, the voice answered, "Miller, that you?"

Seyss waved him off and a moment later was swallowed by the shadow of the camp storehouse. He jogged to the far corner and peeked around it. It was a forty-yard dash across open terrain to the rear of the camp kitchen. Every tree inside the compound had been cut down to improve the guard towers' fields of fire. Walk it and he risked being engaged in conversation by a tardy sentry or a clerk on his way to the radio shack. The doctor's pass would do him no good then. He had no choice but to run. Pulling up his trousers, Seyss swept the "helmet" from his head and dropped it to the ground. At the western end of the camp, a pair of sentries disappeared inside Hotel Barracks. Bed check in Hegel Haus.

A glance to his left. The main road was deserted.

Steeling himself, he remembered a maxim he'd been taught at the officers' academy. In battle, the intrepid soldier must follow Nietzsche's maxim to "live dangerously." Only in this manner could victory be achieved. It was one of the quaint catch phrases the older professors quoted to convince their students that war was the natural offspring of the German intellect and thus a legitimate undertaking.

"Live dangerously," he whispered, his lips curled with irony.

And taking a deep breath, he ran.

He ran tentatively at first, his steps short and ungainly. His stitches had been removed two days earlier and he'd had no choice but to wait until this moment to explore the gravity of his injuries, or, more important, the extent of their healing. Any moment, he expected to be leveled by some demon pain kept hidden by his inactivity. None came, so he lengthened his stride. The shadow of a watchtower threatened from the corner of his eye, but he could see no movement from its parapet. In the alpine night, he was a fleeting shadow. He pressed harder, enjoying the soft stamp of grass under his feet. His legs felt strong and limber. The legs of a runner, he reminded himself. The legs of a champion. And then, he was there, hugging the kitchen wall.

Seyss flattened his back against the building. Sliding to the corner, he peeked to his right. Vlassov's two-horse rig was parked in front of the kitchen. The black marketeer came every Sunday night at eight-thirty hauling a bounty of souvenirs pilfered from a dead army: battle flags,

Walther pistols, Schmeisser machine guns, you name it. And, of course, all manner of military decoration. Rumor had it the souvenirs brought top dollar among Allied soldiers who had never seen battle. A Luger fetched seventy-five dollars. A Mauser automatic rifle twice that. He wondered how much an Iron Cross would bring.

Seyss darted to the center of the kitchen and fell to the grass. The cabin was built on cement foundations sixteen inches above the ground, a protective measure to guard against the flooding of the Loisach River, which cut through the meadow a hundred yards to the south. He slid under the wooden frame and crawled toward the front of the kitchen. Here the earth was muddy, soaked by the runoff from an afternoon thundershower. He moved more slowly now, carefully freeing each knee and elbow from the mire. His hands were slathered with red clay. He rubbed his thumb and forefinger together, savoring its gritty texture, and the memory of another day filled his mind.

He saw himself settling in the blocks, spreading his hands in the fine ocher dirt. Laying his fingers along the starting line, he cocked first one leg, then the other behind him. Suddenly, the crowd murmured as one, the communal sigh of 100,000 spectators, and he knew it was Jesse Owens, the American, two lanes to his right, standing down. He lifted his head and the world collapsed to the narrow lane stretching before him to eternity, and there just visible, the white ribbon that would wrap him in his country's glory. He felt himself rise in the blocks, his body quivering with anticipation, his being an instrument of physical expression. *Macht zur Sieg.* The will to victory. And then the snap of the starter's pistol. The explosion of the crowd as he sprang from the line. The dark blur flashing past his right where no one had passed before, the instant knowing that all was lost, that the race was the American's, and that Germany's White Lion was defeated.

He opened his eyes and the roar of the crowd faded, replaced by the sawing of summer locusts.

Seyss dragged his body forward. He could hear voices coming from above him. The bellow of an American's voice stopped him. It was Janks, the camp commander.

"I don't care if that sword belonged to Hermann Goering himself, I will not give up two fifty-pound bags of flour for it. The most I can offer is one bag of flour, a carton of condensed milk, and a sack of Louisiana rice. Take it or leave it."

"Eggs," said Vlassov. "I need eggs."

"No eggs, friend. Eggs are for Americans only. I'll give you some peaches instead. What do you say?" Janks sounded anxious, still new to his role as war profiteer.

"Yes, it is okay," Vlassov said after a moment. Seyss guessed he was a Czech, one more Slav with no home to go back to. The Americans referred to them as DPs—displaced persons.

Tucking a shoulder under his chest, he tried to roll onto his back. Maybe he could catch a glimpse of the dealings through a crack in the floorboards. The crawl space was too narrow and he returned to his prone position. A beetle skittered up his arm and onto the back of his neck. He raised an arm to knock it away, but froze as his hand brushed the floor. He clenched his teeth, willing the insect away. Its legs tickled his flesh, then it was gone. He scooted a few inches forward. The confinement was suffocating him. *Hurry up*, he urged Janks and Vlassov. He felt his breath coming faster, panic approaching step by step. No one escaped out the front gate. The idea was insane.

Listening to Janks barter away the prisoners' food supplies, Seyss felt his fear ebb and fury take its place. A sack of grain for a pistol. Two boxes of chocolate for a silver wound badge. A gross of K rations for a general's cap. Small wonder the camp population was half starved. Finally Janks said it. Fifteen loaves of bread for an Iron Cross. Twenty loaves plus a carton of Lucky Strikes if it had oak clusters. At the mention of the Iron Cross, Seyss's hand moved to his own neck. It was bare, of course. His own decorations had been confiscated at the hospital in Vienna. Held as evidence, he'd been told. That small and beautiful piece of metal for which he'd spent his blood was this evening deemed worth a few loaves of bread and a carton of cigarettes. Seyss was in no mood to appreciate such grotesque irony.

"What's next?" asked Janks. "That it? We done here?"

"That is all, Colonel," said Vlassov.

"Good. Load up your wagon and get the hell out of here."

As the footsteps tramped above him, Seyss slid his wrist toward his eyes and focused on the watch's tritium hands. Eight minutes past nine. Bed check was well under way. Had the officer of the watch reached his barracks yet?

He crawled forward until he was under the porch that extended from the southern side of the kitchen. A cool breeze lapped at his face. Vlassov lumbered back and forth carrying his evening's wages. After his fourth trip to the wagon, he reentered the kitchen and spoke to Janks. "All done, Colonel. I see you next week."

"Till next week, Mr. Vlassov. My boys will open the gate once they see you in your wagon. Go on, now."

Vlassov grunted a good-bye and walked out of the room. The kitchen door opened and closed. Seyss slid from beneath the porch and raised himself to one knee. Vlassov was standing in the dark, smoking his customary cigarette before mounting his wagon and leaving the camp. Seyss stared at him a moment. He had been taught to hate the mongrel Slav, to disrespect this man without a homeland, this *untermensch*. But all he saw was an opponent. A man who stood in his way.

Placing the blade of the dagger in his mouth, he grasped the railing, and sprang onto the porch. He landed silently. A single step and he was upon Vlassov. Spinning him round, he clamped a hand over his mouth, then plunged the dagger into the base of his throat. Vlassov grunted, bucked once, and was still. Maintaining his grip on the knife, Seyss peeled off the Czech's reefer jacket one arm at a time. He removed the dagger and gently lowered the body to the ground. A clean kill.

Seyss checked his watch. Twelve past the hour. The officer of the watch had reached his barracks by now. At any moment, the whistle would sound announcing that a prisoner was missing. Three short blows, a pause, then three more. The gates would remain locked until Janks gave the all-clear. Urging himself to hurry, he plucked Vlassov's cap off the porch and placed it on his own head, sure to tuck his lank blond hair under the visor. He had put on the Czech's jacket when the kitchen door opened. Colonel Janks stepped onto the porch, slowly extending his neck like a cautious turtle. No doubt he'd heard Vlassov's dying snort and decided to see if something was amiss. Spotting the Czech's body, he took an involuntary step forward. When he raised his head, he was looking at Erich Seyss.

Seyss moved reflexively, shoving the colonel against the door while slapping a hand over his mouth. Janks stared into his pale blue eyes and for a moment, Seyss saw his own fear mirrored in the American's face. He considered delivering Janks a blow to the head, leaving him unconscious. No one would care about a dead Czech, but an American officer killed by a German POW? The whole army would be after him. Then he heard Janks's plaintiff voice offering Vlassov twenty loaves of bread for an Iron Cross and his reason evaporated.

"Tell me, Colonel," he whispered, "how many loaves of bread for an SS officer's dagger?"

Janks's eyes tightened in confusion. "But you weren't—"

Before he could complete his thought, Seyss rammed the blade into his chest. He withdrew the knife and stabbed him again. Janks's eyes bulged. He coughed, and a skein of blood decorated Seyss's cheek. Seyss could feel it warming his skin, rolling down his face, brushing his lips. He tasted the blood of his enemy and his heart beat madly. He took a deep breath, willing the demon to pass, but it was too late and he knew it.

Smiling, he let the wildness take him.

When he was again himself, he pulled at the dagger but it was either impaled on bone or so slick with blood that it would not come free. He dropped Janks's body, then knelt beside it, searching for the pearl-handled Colt automatic that the colonel displayed so proudly on his hip. Vain Americans. Every last one wanted to be like Patton. He removed the pistol from its holster and shoved it into his pocket.

Fighting to maintain his nerve, Seyss stepped off the porch and mounted the wagon. Vlassov's jacket was slick with blood, but in the dark it appeared only to be badly stained. He gave the reins a brief tug. The two bays raised their heads as one, then turned to the left and walked toward the gate. Passing through the shadow of the watchtower, he glanced up and saw the nose of a .30-caliber machine gun drooping over the parapet, and behind it a baby-faced soldier aligning him in its sights. Ahead, a dirt road ran through the meadow before veering left and disappearing into the veil of forest that descended from the mountain. A GI approached the wagon, cradling his carbine in one arm. Seyss hunched over the reins to shield the jacket. His right hand delved into his pocket for the comforting heft of Jank's pistol. He could only hope it was loaded. Lowering his eyes, he whispered "Good night."

"Yeah," grunted the guard. "See you next Sunday." He patted the bay's rump, then turned to the gate, dragged it open, and waved the wagon through.

The whistle blew when he was fifty yards down the road. A moment later, klieg lights doused the wagon. Several gunshots rang out. But no figure could be seen at the reins.

Erich Seyss was gone.

The White Lion was free.

CHAPTER

2

THE CAFÉ DOWNSTAIRS WAS PLAYING Dietrich again. "Lilli Marlene" for the third time this morning and it was still before ten. Glad for the distraction, Devlin Judge slid his chair from his desk and stepped onto the balcony of his fifth-floor office. The music was clearer now. Dietrich's dusky voice bounced off the cobblestones and wandered through the canyon of apartments and office buildings, mingling with the cling-clang of bicycle bells and the hot sweet scent of freshly baked croissants.

Humming nervously, Judge let his eyes wander the rooftops of Paris. A bold sun splashed the landscape of ocher tile and verdigris, its lustral rays erasing a lifetime of soot and grime. The Arc de Triomphe stood guard at the end of the block. Through the fine morning haze, the towering limestone plains looked close enough to touch. If he rose on his toes, he could catch the crown of the Eiffel Tower. Normally the sights made his heart jump. Today he found the view mundane. His work, too, refused his attention. Since arriving three hours earlier, he'd been unable to concentrate on anything except the uneasy buzz that had taken firm, unremitting possession of his gut.

Today was the day. He didn't need a damn thing to make his heart race faster than it already was.

Ordering himself back to his desk, he pulled on his reading glasses, tugged at his cuffs, and with a resigned sigh, picked up the leather-bound diary he'd been struggling with all morning. The faded blue script spoke of a dinner in August of 1942 given by Adolf Hitler at Wolfschanze, his battlefield headquarters in east Prussia. Hitler had ranted at length about the chronic shortage of labor in the country's largest factories and had ordered shipments of foreign workers to the Fatherland increased. *Sklavenarbeit* was the word he employed. Slave labor. The information would be useful tomorrow when Judge sat face to face with the diarist himself and listened to the fat man's confident denials. In open court, it would prove damning.

The prospect made Judge smile for the first time that morning.

Selecting a bookmark from a neat stack two inches deep, he inscribed a number at its head and inserted it into the diary. He sighed. No. 1,216, and still nearly three years of the war to go. Copying the numerals to his legal pad, he transcribed the pertinent details in the painstaking print he'd developed over five years as an attorney. Neatness brought clarity, and clarity, order, he reminded himself. There was no room for confusion in a proper legal argument. That went for the simplest case of larceny. It counted double for the most important trial in the tenure of civilized mankind.

Devlin Parnell Judge had not come to Europe simply as an attorney but as a member of the International Military Tribunal, the august legal body established by the Allied powers—Russia, Britain, France and the United States—to try the leaders of the Third Reich for war crimes. The acts were so heinous, so original in their barbarity, that they warranted a new and unique classification: Crimes against humanity.

Judge had been assigned to the Interrogations Division. They were the hard-eyed boys, charged with drawing incriminating statements from the accused so that their silver-tongued colleagues could make mincemeat of them on the stand. It wasn't the first team, but he was happy all the same. Every lawyer in Manhattan, including those who worked alongside him at the U.S. Attorney's office, wanted in. The war crimes trials would make front-page news and the men who stood before the bar would be as famous as Ruth or DiMaggio. Though he'd lobbied hard for the spot, Judge's motivations had little to do with career advancement. Nor were they shaped by any altruistic bent. Only as a member of the International Military Tribunal could he uncover the details of what had happened to his brother, Francis Xavier, an ordained Jesuit priest and army chaplain killed in Belgium seven months before. More important, only as a member of the IMT could he have the power to make those responsible pay.

Today was the day.

The phone rang and Judge pounced on it.

But it was only a driver from Motor Transport confirming his pick-up tomorrow morning. Was six o'clock all right? They needed an hour to get to Orly and an hour on top of that for the flight to Mondorf-les-Bains. The major would be at the Ashcan by nine o'clock sharp. Judge said he'd be ready and hung up the phone.

The Ashcan was slang for the Palace Hotel in Luxembourg, a fading five-star princess pressed into service as a maximum-security prison. Inside its peeling stucco walls resided fifty of the highest-ranking Nazis in captivity. Speer, Donitz, Keitel: the shameless *bonzen* of the National Socialist Workers' party. And, of course, Hermann Wilhelm Goering, Hitler's jovial prince, and the man with whose interrogation Judge had been charged.

He continued reading, the historical significance of his work granting him a resolve he couldn't otherwise muster. Ten minutes later, he decided further progress was futile. Off came the glasses, down went the diary. He simply couldn't concentrate. Better not to work at all than to risk bad product. Rising from his desk, he closed the balcony doors behind him. The music was no longer a distraction, just a nuisance. Germany's most famous expatriate singing the English lyrics to Hitler's favorite tune. Why did the song make him so homesick?

Pacing the perimeter of his cramped office, Judge plucked a dozen law books from their scattered resting places and returned them to the shelves. He was not a tall man, but the beam of his shoulders and the girth of his neck conspired to ensure that he was never ignored. This strength was also apparent in his back, which was broad and well muscled, the result of a youth hustling barrels of Canadian whiskey at the local speakeasy. His hands, too, were thick and compact, at odds with his well-manicured nails and the wedding band he still wore only to pretty them.

He had a gambler's sly face with flashing brown eyes and a smile that promised trouble. His black hair was cut short and parted with a razor slash. And this guileful mien set on a fighter's frame lent him a smoldering ambiguity. At El Morocco, he was made to wait even with a reservation in hand. At the Cotton Club, he was immediately shown the best table in the house. But Judge had no problem reconciling his physical contradictions, for in them he read his own secret history. He was the neighborhood rascal masquerading as the law. The reformed sinner who prayed louder than the rest, not so that God might better hear him but to drum out his own undying doubts.

Finished replacing the heavy legal tomes, he scanned the office for anything else out of place. The bookshelves were packed full, spines arranged by height. A dozen legal pads rose high on a credenza. As usual his desk was immaculate. A chipped porcelain mug stuffed with a bouquet of sharpened pencils decorated one corner. An army-issue day calendar rested in the other, its officious red script declaring the date to be Monday, July 9. Tucked behind a green-visored table lamp stood two small photographs—his sole concession to lending his office of six weeks a touch of home.

One showed a tall, portly man with wavy dark hair sporting the bold pinstripes of the Fordham Rams, his insouciant smile and practiced slouch betrayed by the serious grip with which he held the bat to his shoulder. Judge picked up the frame and wiped away a day's accumulation of dust, then returned it to its place. His brother, Francis, hadn't been much of a ball player. He was a klutz with a glove and slow as an ox. But give him a fastball and he'd knock it out of the park. Anything else, forget it. He'd go down swinging in four pitches. The words *full count* were nowhere in his lexicon.

The second photo was smaller, worn and creased from a thousand days in Judge's wallet. A smiling four-year-old greeted the camera, dark hair parted and combed like his father's, eyes opened wide with excitement as if life was something he couldn't get enough of. Judge dusted that photo, too, returning his boy's smile with equal parts longing and pride.

He'd brought a few other reminders of home with him to Europe— a sterling fob watch gifted him by his old boss, Thomas Dewey, back when Dewey was just a special prosecutor and not yet governor of New York State; a small ornately sculpted crucifix that had belonged to his brother, and a photo of his parents, deceased these ten years—but these he stored in his drawer. An attorney's eyes were best kept on his work, he'd been taught, and personal mementos little more than crutches for the unfocused mind.

Satisfied that his office was in presentable shape, he contemplated returning to his desk. Eyeing the low-backed chair, he took an unconscious step backward, as if it were electrified. Even on good days, he wasn't a patient man. Today he was downright skittish. A hand fell to his wrist and he began turning his watch round and round. He couldn't remember when he'd acquired the habit, only that it was a long time ago. What was waiting but a genteel form of torture?

The latest batch of documents had arrived yesterday at noon. Forty-seven filing cabinets stuffed with three thousand pounds of official government correspondence, property of the Reich Main Security Office at Prinz Albrechtstrasse 8, Berlin headquarters of the SS, or *Schutzstaffel*—Hitler's private black guard. Judge's spies upstairs in C&C—Cataloguing and Collating—told him these were the papers he'd been waiting for: movement orders, casualty lists, after-action reports chronicling the daily battlefield history of the SS's elite divisions. Somewhere inside was word of who had killed his brother. It was just a question of finding it.

Today was the day.

A sharp knock at the door interrupted his vacillating. A short, rumpled officer with thinning gray hair and wire-rimmed spectacles entered the office. His uniform was similar to Judge's. Dark olive jacket, khaki shirt and tie, with light slacks to match. "Pink and greens," in the military vernacular. Like Judge, he was an attorney and carried the insignia of the Judge Advocate General's Corps on his lapel.

"I think you'd better come with me," said Colonel Bob Storey, chief of the IMT's Document Control Division. "We might have found our pot of gold."

"What is it? Do you have a name?"

"Just come along. You'll have plenty of time to ask questions later."

Judge grabbed his coat and dashed out of the office. The hallways of 7 rue de Presbourg bustled with civilian and military personnel. Not a

day passed without a mother lode of documents being discovered somewhere in Germany. Last week, 485 tons of diplomatic papers were found
in a cave in the Harz Mountains. The week before, the archives of the
Luftwaffe Central Command turned up in a salt mine in Obersalzberg,
Austria. Anything remotely dealing with activities that might be con-
strued as war crimes was sent here. Given the scope of the Nazis' atroc-
ities and their propensity for documenting their every act, that made for
a hell of a lot of paper.

Judge followed Storey at a close distance, the two marking a brisk
pace. He was troubled by his older colleague's ambivalence. If they'd
found a pot of gold, why wasn't he more excited? After all, Bob Storey
had been his partner in this thing from day one—his cheerleader, his
unofficial commanding officer, and more recently, Judge believed, his
friend.

He'd approached Storey his very first day on the job, asking his help
with a personal matter. His older brother, Francis Xavier, had been
killed last December at Malmedy, he explained. Might Storey keep an
eye out for any documents that might shed light on the facts surrounding the incident? It was a tale every American knew well, emblazoned on
the country's collective memory by headlines of fire and vitriol.
"Captured GIs Massacred in Malmedy." "A Hundred Soldiers Shot in
Cold Blood." And, perhaps, most eloquently, "Murder!" Storey agreed
immediately.

These were the details: On the morning of Sunday, December 17,
1944, a column of American troops, primarily members of B Battery of
the 285th Field Artillery Observation Battalion, found themselves driving south on a two-lane country road in eastern Belgium. The day was
sunny, the temperature above zero. Little snow covered the ground.
The men traveled in a convoy of thirty vehicles—jeeps, weapons carriers, heavy trucks, and two ambulances—reaching the village of
Malmedy at twelve-fifteen. The area was safely under American control.
Route markers had passed through earlier in the day and several other
units had followed the same path without incident an hour before. But
as B Battery passed through Malmedy, word came that German patrols
had been spotted a few miles to the southwest. (Though the massive
German counteroffensive that came to be known as the Battle of the

Bulge had been launched the day before, no fighting had been reported in this particular sector.)

B Battery continued as planned. A few miles outside of Malmedy, after passing through the Baugnez Crossroads, an intersection of five country roads, the convoy suddenly came under direct fire from a column of German tanks less than half a mile away. At least five vehicles were hit and their occupants killed or wounded. The rest halted immediately, many seeking protection in a gully next to the road. The rapidly approaching German tanks kept up their fire, both with machine gun and cannon. Two minutes later, a Panther tank plowed B Battery's lead jeep off the road. In the face of a vastly superior force, the American soldiers—among them, Father Francis Xavier Judge, SJ—surrendered.

The German column was, in fact, the lead element of *Kampfgruppe Peiper* or Task Force Peiper, a fast attack force of 115 tanks, 100 self-propelled guns, and 4,500 men charged with breaking through American lines and dashing to the Meuse River. While the main element of the *kampfgruppe* continued past the Baugnez Crossroads, a detachment was left behind to deal with their prisoners. One hundred thirteen GIs were herded into the surrounding fields and disarmed. A few minutes later, the Germans opened fire on the unsuspecting prisoners. After the shooting ceased, two German soldiers walked through the field shooting the wounded Americans. Amazingly, of the 113 Americans assembled in the field south of Malmedy, forty escaped by playing dead and fleeing into the surrounding woods as opportunity permitted.

That much Judge knew. He'd compiled the information from the existing record: interviews with the massacre's survivors, statements of captured German troops who'd fought as part of the task force, as well as descriptions of battlefield actions given by officers who had been nearby at the time. Yet seven months after the act, he was still unable to identify the officer who had given the order to fire.

Judge closed the door to Storey's office, refusing the offer of a seat. "So, what have you got?"

Storey drew a manila file from his drawer and slid it across his desk. "Good news and bad news, I'm afraid."

"How's that?" Judge spun the file around so that it faced him right side up. A pink routing slip was attached to the cover. He read to whom the file belonged and shook his head. His efforts had narrowed the list of suspects to three men, and if he didn't know them personally, he was intimately familiar with their records. "He was my long shot. Guy was an Olympian, for crying out loud. You'd think he'd know something about fair play. What clinched it?"

"Go ahead. Read. But Devlin, I'm warning you, it's tough going."

Judge paused before opening the cover, offering a prayer for his departed brother. Inside was a single document, two pages in length, immaculately typed on SS field stationery. It was an after-action report filed by one Lieutenant Werner Ploschke. Judge ventured a halting look at Storey, then took a deep breath and read.

"At 13:02 hours on 17 December 1944, a convoy of American jeeps and trucks was spotted passing through the junction of N-23 and N-32, proceeding south on the Ligneuville–St. Vith road near the town of Malmedy. Lieutenant Werner Sternebeck engaged the enemy immediately. Two Panther tanks fired six rounds each from their main guns. Four American vehicles were destroyed. Five others were damaged while taking evasive maneuvers. Sternebeck drove his tank to the head of the American column and fired his machine gun over the heads of the Americans to gain their immediate surrender. Kampfgruppe commander Major Jochen Peiper ordered all gasoline siphoned from the ruined cars and those vehicles in working condition confiscated. Hereafter, he continued his advance with the main element of the attack group and left the area.

"Major Erich Seyss, now in command, ordered all American soldiers into the adjoining field where they were disarmed and searched for items of intelligence value. Forty-six pairs of winter boots and eighty heavy jackets were remanded to field quartermaster Sergeant Steiner. Seyss then ordered Panthers 107, 111, 83, and 254 and Tigers 54 and 58 brought alongside the field. All guns were trained on the prisoners. At 14:05 hours, he commanded gunners and rearguard infantry to fire on the Americans. The shooting lasted seven minutes. Exactly two thousand two hundred forty-four rounds were expended. Afterward Seyss entered the field along with Sergeant Richard Biedermann and administered the coup de grace as necessary."

Judge put down the paper. There it was, then. Everything he'd searched for. Everything he needed to secure a conviction. Seyss was already in an American lockup somewhere. As an SS officer, he'd been subject to automatic arrest when he was captured. It was just a matter of time, then, until he was brought to trial. But if Judge had been expecting a few pangs of gratification, he was disappointed. No surge of adrenaline warmed his neck. No flush of victory colored his cheeks. All he had was a name, some papers, and the knowledge that in a year or so, somewhere in Germany, the floor would fall from beneath a gallows and Seyss would die. The law had never felt so sterile.

"I suppose this will nail it," he said, trying hard to add a cheerful lilt to his voice. "We won't even need to bring in any of our eyewitnesses. Seyss's comrades signed his death warrant. It'll be the hangman for sure."

Storey nodded curtly. "There are some pictures, too."

Judge grimaced involuntarily and the corrosive drip in his belly started all over again. "Oh? Whose are they?"

"German. They're rough, so don't feel you have to look. I thought it my responsibility to inform you. Naturally, they'll form part of the prosecutorial record."

Good news and bad news, he'd said.

Storey handed him a sheaf of photographs an inch thick. Eight-by-tens. Judge mumbled "Thanks," then began shuffling through them. He could feel his heart beating faster, his throat tightening involuntarily. It was the way he felt in court when his lead witness impeached his testimony under cross-examination. The first few showed sixty or seventy GIs scattered across a plowed field. Some of the soldiers were stripped down to their skivvies, others fully clothed. All of them were dead. The photographer abandoned landscapes for portraits. Judge stared at the faces of a dozen murdered GIs. One still arrested his eye.

An American soldier lay naked from the waist up in the snow, a string of perfect holes diagonally traversing his torso from right to left. One arm was outstretched, as if waving good-bye. A crater crusted the open palm. Quite a shot. The face was frozen in surprise and terror, mouth ajar, eyes opened their widest. Still, he was easy to recognize. The thick black hair, the cleft chin, the inquiring nose—a snooper's nose, Judge had called it—the scar above the eyebrow, and of course, the eyes—wide and accusing. Even in death Francis Xavier Judge was taking his younger brother's measure.

Seyss ordered all machine gunners to open fire on the prisoners . . . 2,244 rounds were expended.

Judge stood perfectly still, the text of the after-action report echoing in his head. Silently he yelled for Francis to run, to fall to the ground. He saw his brother raising his hands in the air, could hear the prayer issuing from his lips, *Yea, though I walk through the valley of the shadow of death, I will fear no evil, for thou art with me; thy rod and thy staff they comfort me.* He witnessed the look of worry turn to fear, then horror, as the first shots cracked the winter cold. *Damn you, Francis. Hit the deck!*

He flipped to the next photograph and his frustration flamed to anger.

The picture showed an SS officer wearing a camouflage uniform standing in the field, jackboot planted firmly on a GI's back. One hand was fastened round a lock of hair, lifting the head, the other bringing a pistol to the nape of the doomed soldier's neck. The officer had blond hair and his face was streaked with dirt. An Iron Cross hung from his neck. Another was pinned to his breast. A hero. Four silver diamonds on his collar patch indicated his rank as major. Another man stood behind him, laughing.

Seyss entered the field along with SS Sergeant Richard Biedermann and administered the coup de grace as necessary.

Judge dropped the pictures onto the desk, turning away from Storey and closing his eyes. He'd thought his tireless digging had inured him to the loss of his brother, that his intimate knowledge of the manner and circumstance of Frankie's death had somehow deadened the wound. He was wrong. The German's recounting of the massacre—so factual, so cold, so *trivial*—coupled with the frank photographs ripped open his hurt and christened his pain anew.

"You all right?" asked Storey.

Judge tried to answer, but didn't dare speak. His throat was suddenly unnavigable, his legs growing weaker by the second. Somehow he managed a grim nod.

Storey patted him on the arm. "Like I said, there's some bad news, too."

Judge shot Storey a withering glance, ignorant of the tear rolling down his cheek. What could be worse than seeing a photo of your only brother, the last member of your family, slaughtered in a desolate field in a foreign land?

"Bad news?"

"It's Seyss," said Storey. "He's escaped."

CHAPTER

3

THE JEEP SPED DOWN THE Champs Élysées, past outdoor cafés crowded with servicemen and cinemas advertising American films. Flags of every color and nationality sprouted from parapets and doorways the length of the boulevard: the Stars and Stripes, the Union Jack, the Hammer and Sickle, and everywhere, *le bleu, blanc, et rouge*—the French Tricolor. Swatches of bunting, memories of V-E Day, adorned an occasional balcony. The marcelled crepe was faded, perhaps, wilted by summer rain, but no less proud because of it.

Judge sat in the rear of the jeep, one hand clamped to the chassis, the other atop a compendious olive file square in his lap. The open air was a tonic for his woozy head. Everyone knew you didn't mix booze and the same should be said for emotions, he thought. Anger, remorse, frustration, loss—Christ, he'd downed a shot of every one. A glance at the file sobered him. Stenciled across its cover were the letters UNWCC—United Nations War Crimes Commission—and inside was every fact, rumor, and half-truth the commission had gathered about the wartime doings of Major Erich Siegfried Seyss, late of the Waffen-SS. The latest addition had been made only an hour ago.

Crossing the Place de la Concorde, the jeep rattled over a sea of cobblestones as it circled the Obelisk, the ancient masonic symbol that celebrated Napoleon's victory over the British in Egypt, and later served as the model for the Washington Monument. An easterly gust carried a taste of the Seine: brine, moss, and the hint of caprice. The Invalides stood away to his right, a majestic stone armory seated at the head of a grass avenue five football fields in length. The Little General himself was interred somewhere inside its cool walls.

Everywhere Judge looked in this town he was surrounded by history and all of it had to do with war. He wondered if it was foolish to allow personal animosity to prevent his taking part in what promised to be a seminal historical event of his time. He shook his head. War. Empire. Revenge. Scale them down and what did you have? Anger. Avarice. Pride. History was only personal grievance writ large.

TWO DOORMEN CLAD IN MAROON topcoats waited at the base of the steps leading to the Hotel Ritz. Judge jumped from the back of the jeep, the dossier tucked high under one arm, and set off up the broad stairs. Bob Storey pulled him close as they entered the lobby.

"I've already spoken with Justice Jackson and made a plea on your behalf. He's as fair a man as I've met, but he can be brusque. Remember, we're damned lucky he's even here. Luckier he's seeing us. Let's take that as a good sign. Just be polite and let him do the talking."

Justice Jackson was Associate Justice of the Supreme Court—Robert Jackson, chief American prosecutor for the coming war crimes trial and the de facto organizer of the International Military Tribunal. He was in Paris for the day, on his way to Germany to scout locations for the war crimes trials. Judge had met him once, a brief powwow in D.C. to give thanks for his appointment to the IMT. He remembered the firm handshake, the steely gray eyes, the softly spoken words, and the sense of mission they had successfully imparted. It had been one of the proudest days of his life.

"Fair, I have no doubt," said Judge. "Reasonable, that's another question."

"These days you're a soldier first and a lawyer second," cautioned Storey. "Fair is more than you have a right to expect." His face softened and he winked. "As for reasonable, well, that's plain out of the question."

The lobby was marble and mirrors and velvet furniture encrusted with gold leaf. Judge spent a moment adjusting his tie and combing his hair. He pulled at each cuff, ensuring that one inch of cotton protruded beyond the sleeve and no more. He was damned if he'd make a lousy impression. Only the Lord could see your heart, he'd been taught. Everyone else judged you by your appearance. His uniform was impeccable. Tailor-made from Brooks Brothers. Gabardine, and not the cheap stuff either: Super 100 all the way. It had cost nearly a month's salary after alimony. Giving himself a final looking over, he headed to the elevator.

A soldier, first, eh? If Jackson saw it that way, he didn't have anything to worry about.

"THE WAR CRIMES TRIALS ARE a watershed, Major," said Robert Jackson from his position at the head of a mahogany conference table. "A defining moment in history. For the first time, we are treating war as a crime and the aggressors as criminals. We are showing the world that waging aggressive war will no longer be tolerated. The trials aren't just a symbol of superior might but of superior morality."

Judge nodded, saying "Absolutely, sir." He was seated to Jackson's right in the drawing room of a palatial suite on the hotel's second floor. Storey sat next to him and Judge could sense his hand poised above his arm, ready to calm him should the verdict go against them. He was trying hard to heed Storey's advice and let Jackson do all the talking. Normally it would have been an easy task. He wouldn't have dared interrupt a man of Jackson's stature. Head of Antitrust at Justice, attorney general under F.D.R., then a slot on the highest court in the land. It was the career Judge had dreamed about. Today, though, it took his every power of restraint to stop from reaching across the table, grabbing the old man's tie, and telling him to hurry up, goddammit, and get on with it.

"When you joined our little outfit, Major, you made a commitment," Jackson continued. "Not just to your fellow members of the IMT but to your country and, dare I say, the entire civilized world, to see our view of morality driven home. Walk out and you'll be doing us all a disservice."

Judge didn't miss the threat tucked inside Jackson's words. There was no question but that his own career would be at the highest risk. His request had been simple enough: an immediate transfer to the unit charged with tracking down Erich Seyss; command of the investigation, if possible. The prognosis didn't look promising.

"1 appreciate your concern, sir," he said. "Naturally, I'll take up my position again as soon as I've located Seyss and returned him to custody."

"Will you?" Jackson smirked from the corner of his mouth. "Kind of you to let me know. Tell me, do you have the vaguest idea when that might be?"

"No, sir." Judge had forgotten that a Supreme Court justice could be sarcastic, too.

"And any notion where Seyss has gone?"

Again Judge said no. Storey had given him the details of the escape earlier. Seyss had killed two men, including the camp commander, then traipsed out the front gates in full view of the camp guards—two sentries on the ground, two in the towers, each manning a .30-caliber machine gun. Twelve hours later, no information had been received about his whereabouts.

"I phoned the military police unit up in Garmisch earlier this morning," Judge volunteered. "The preliminary investigation is just being finished up. Counterintelligence is being brought in and so is CID, but Third Army HQ hasn't assigned the case yet. The officer of the day stated they're looking for someone properly qualified."

Jackson took the news skeptically, shifting his gaze to Storey. "That so, Bob? From what I understand, Janks is the first officer to be killed by a German since the surrender. You'd think George Patton would have had a dozen men assigned to the case by now. Third Army, that's his command, isn't it?"

"Manpower's tight," said Storey, shoulders bunched in apology. "We're losing a ton of GIs every day. Half are shipping out for home, half to R and R depots on their way to Japan. On top of that, CIC is getting set to run an important operation in ten days' time. A real big deal called Tallyho. Funny, the names they come up with."

But Jackson wasn't smiling. He darted his eyes between Storey and

Judge, as if trying to guess what kind of scheme the two of them were working. "Tallyho?"

"It's a zonal effort," continued Storey, "a big shindig cooked up to pull in the Nazis who've eluded our nets to date. Most are SS men slated for automatic arrest who never got around to turning themselves in. All in all seventy thousand troops in four army groups are scheduled to take part. Like I said, it's a big deal."

Judge was impressed by the depth of Storey's knowledge. The chief of the Document Control Division was privy to more information than he'd imagined.

"And Goering?" asked Jackson, returning his crocodile eyes to Judge. "Who's to handle him in the interim?"

For once Judge had an answer prepared. "Begging your pardon, sir, but the trials won't start for a few months. If I'm gone for a week, I'll still have plenty of time to conduct a thorough interrogation of the prisoner."

"And what exactly makes you think you'd be of assistance, Major?"

Judge cleared his throat, encouraged by the opportunity to plead his case. "I spent ten years as a police officer before coming to the bar, first as a blue jacket, then as a detective. My last four years were with Homicide."

"In Germany?" Jackson cut in, raising his head. He was smiling.

"No, sir," Judge answered, matching the friendly expression. "In New York. Brooklyn, actually."

"Ah, no doubt that explains why you're familiar with the geography of southern Germany. Know your way around Bavaria, do you? Have you ever been to Garmisch, Major? Or to Germany, at all, for that matter?"

Jackson wasn't just sarcastic, he was mean. "No, sir. This would be my first trip. However, my German is fluent. I'm familiar with German customs."

"I know all about your Teutonic heritage, Judge. However, the quaint tales your mother told you as a child have little application to the tracking down and capture of an accused war criminal. Seyss is an experienced combat officer, and I see from his file, a native of this particular region." Jackson sighed deeply and Judge could feel the meeting coming to a rapid and unsatisfactory conclusion. "Naturally, Major, I know of your personal interest in Seyss. It was one of the reasons we took you onto the IMT in the first place. What happened to your brother was terrible. And *I am* sorry. But tragedies like these occur all too often in war. If they didn't, none of us would be sitting here today, would we?"

Judge had heard the last few words coming and had whispered them under his breath along with Justice Jackson. "No, sir."

"Good. Then you'll understand when I turn down your request for a transfer. Hermann Goering must be convicted on all counts. He's far more important than some two-bit SS hoodlum. We're not set to prosecute Seyss and his colleagues until next year. He's a small fry in the scheme of things. Surely your brother would understand that. He was a Jesuit, after all. It's a question of logic, pure and simple. Love Aquinas, the Jezzies do." Jackson leaned forward and tapped Judge's forearm. "Do a good job with Goering and I'll make you a lead prosecutor on the secondary trials. I'm certain Seyss will be in custody again by that time. How's that?"

Judge bridled at the touch. What did Jackson think? He'd trade his brother for a promotion on the IMT? "Sir, I beg you to reconsider."

"The decision is final. A transfer is out of the question." Jackson slammed his hand on the table like a gavel, then rose, tugging the pickets of his vest. "Give my regards to Hermann. Did you know they call him Fat Stuff? I hear it drives him crazy."

Judge rose with him and when he spoke his voice had lost its harness of respectful reserve. "This morning we received irrefutable evidence that Erich Seyss ordered the massacre of our boys at Malmedy. It's the kind of proof a prosecutor kills for: a report written by his own men implicating him at the scene of the crime. Of course, I'm aware of my responsibilities to the court and to my country, but Francis was my brother. My responsibilities to him come first."

"Please, Major, let's not make this more difficult than it has to—"

Finally, it was Judge's turn to interrupt. "I've spent my entire adult life as an officer of the law," he argued. "I've been trained to pursue those who break the law and taught to use my brains and my reasoning to ensure they don't do it again. For the first time, I can use what I've learned to provide some measure of justice to someone close to me. If I don't do everything within my power to bring in the man who killed my brother—the animal who murdered seventy *American* boys in cold blood—all my years as a cop, all my time before the bar, will have been for nothing."

"Hogwash," countered Jackson, calling his tone and raising it a note. "With all due respect to you, Major, and your brother, you don't have a snowball's chance in hell of finding Erich Seyss. You'll be wasting everyone's time, especially your own. Now if that's all, you're excused."

"No, sir," Judge retorted. "That isn't all. If I do not receive this transfer, I plan to resign my commission effectively."

"And do what precisely? Find him yourself? Alone you won't get out of Paris for a week. And if you did, what then? Do you have a car? Gasoline?" Jackson laughed gruffly. "Read your enlistment papers, son. You joined the United States Army in time of war. You serve at your nation's leisure. You don't have the power to resign."

Judge looked to Storey for backup, but his older colleague had moved to the window, and stood looking down upon the Place Vendôme, shaking his head. Suddenly Judge knew he'd gone too far, that he'd let his desire to serve his brother's memory overrule his common sense. This was after all, an associate justice of the Supreme Court he was talking to. Still, he couldn't give up now.

"Dammit, sir, all I'm asking is to give Erich Seyss the chance to learn the full and proper measure of the law. You said yourself you wanted me to help drive home our new morality. Fine. Let me start with him. If it were your brother who Seyss killed, wouldn't you want to do the same?"

Jackson's eyes widened—with anger, surprise, and maybe, Judge hoped, even understanding—then he turned and stalked out of the drawing room. "I'll be back in a minute, Major. Sit down and try not to make a nuisance of yourself. Bob, come with me."

JUDGE POURED HIMSELF A GLASS of water from a crystal carafe, then collapsed onto a yellow couch, exhaling deeply. Taking a sip, he could hear Jackson's and Storey's voices behind the bedroom doors, raised in a not altogether friendly conversation. A frank exchange of views, the papers would say. He just hoped Storey was arguing in favor of his transfer, not against a court martial. Someplace back there, he'd passed insubordination in a hurry. His only consolation was that Francis would have done the same for him.

Closing his eyes, he remembered the last time he'd seen his brother. August 2, 1943. Frankie's departure to England. The two of them saying good-bye, alone among a crowd of ten thousand packed onto Pier 4B at the Brooklyn Navy Yard. Francis was wearing a GI's olive drab fatigues, captain's bars pinned to one lapel, the Savior's cross on the other. He was staring at ten days of rough seas, tight quarters, and lousy chow, not to mention the Nazi wolf pack breathing down his neck, and he'd never looked happier.

"Hey, kid, don't go being a hero," Judge said, mimicking Spencer Tracy's rough-and-tumble voice while patting his brother on the arm. Francis couldn't get enough of Tracy. *Boys' Town*, *Captain's Courageous*, *Woman of the Year*—they were his favorite films.

"That's God's decision," Francis replied stoically, "not mine."

"Hey, Frankie, I was joking. Whatcha gonna do, anyway? Throw Bibles at Hitler?"

Finally a smile. "If it would stop the war a day sooner, I surely would."

Francis was taller by four inches and outweighed him by a good seventy pounds. If the Roman Catholic Church had mandated a vow of hunger, he'd have never made it through seminary. Judge came in for a last hug. He kissed his brother's cheek and let himself be drawn close. He knew he should be the one going. Francis was forty-three years old. He couldn't see past the hem of his cassock without his glasses, and he cried like a baby at the pictures. This was him all over. Drawing the hardest duty and smiling about it.

"I love you," Judge said.

Francis stared at him long and hard, confused by his brother's sentiment. The fact was, the two had never been especially close. Too much sermonizing on Francis's part. He'd been talking fire and brimstone since he was twenty-three and Judge thirteen. Repent all sinners, lest ye be cast into the abyss. Love was couched threefold behind expectation, responsibility, and since Judge's divorce, indignation. As Jackson had said, he was a "Jezzie." One of Ignatius Loyola's Soldiers of Christ. What could you expect?

"Don't worry about me, Dev. I'll be just fine." And then, as if to prove his point or, looking back, maybe his invincibility, he'd removed the leather lanyard from his neck, yanked off the crucifix and handed it to Judge. "Remember, Dev, the Lord looks after his own."

Judge opened his eyes, calling back the photographs he'd seen that morning. Francis lying prostrate in a muddy field, a dozen bullet holes his final benediction. Seyss's boot in a soldier's back. *No, Frankie, not anymore he doesn't. Nowadays, you have to look after yourself.*

JACKSON AND STOREY REENTERED THE drawing room an hour later. If a solution had been reached, their grim demeanor gave no clue of it. Judge stood, wanting to make a final plea, but Jackson spoke before he got a chance.

"Believe it or not, I do appreciate your dilemma. You made a persuasive case for yourself. And if I don't recognize the law behind your argument, I do recognize the sentiment. Never underestimate the value of emotion on a jury. Or passion. Sometimes a tear is all it takes to topple the soundest defense—though I'll thank you to leave my brother out of it, if there's ever a next time."

Judge no longer had a problem following Storey's advice to keep his mouth shut. Any lawyer could recognize the preamble to good news. One thing bothered him. Why the hell did Storey look so glum?

A knock came at the door and Storey rushed to open it. A messenger wearing sand-colored puttees, crash helmet under one arm, handed over a yellow envelope, asking Storey to sign a receipt. Storey scribbled his signature, then handed the envelope to Jackson, all the while avoiding Judge's inquisitive glare.

"I believe this is yours," said Jackson, thrusting the envelope toward Judge.

Judge tore open the telegram. It read: "Per verbal orders supreme commander armed forces Europe. Major Devlin Parnell Judge, JAG, is forthwith and immediately transferred on temporary duty to the Office of the Provost Marshal, United States Third Army, General George

S. Patton, Jr., commanding. The duration of the transfer shall last no longer than seven days and will end at midnight, 15 July 1945. Every member of this command is to provide this officer with all assistance he requests. Signed, General Dwight D. Eisenhower."

Judge wanted to smile. He'd gotten his transfer to Patton's Third, and with Eisenhower's blessing, no less. But something in the telegram bothered him. Reading it a second time, his eyes tripped over the words that left stillborn his excitement. "The duration of the transfer shall be seven days." *Seven days!* It would take him a day just to travel to Bad Toelz and get acquainted with the setup. The transfer was hardly better than being turned down altogether. If ever he'd won a Pyrrhic victory, this was it. So much for Storey's downcast look.

"I can't have you traveling all over Europe at your discretion," explained Jackson. "This will put a rush on things. Do your work, find him, and get back. I hope I'm making you happy."

Judge kowtowed as decorum demanded. "Yes, sir, I appreciate your efforts on my behalf. Thank you."

Jackson ambled to a dresser and poured himself a tumbler of scotch. "By the way, you should feel right at home in Bad Toelz. The provost marshal is a fellow named Mullins. Ring a bell?"

"Would that be Spanner Mullins, sir?"

"If Spanner is some kind of nickname for Stanley, yes, it would. Your former precinct commander is delighted to have you aboard. Said Tallyho is pinching his resources in a terrible way. He asked if you might be granted a longer stay, but I had to turn him down. Told him you were too good a man to lose indefinitely."

Judge mumbled "Thank you" again. He was happy to be reporting to Mullins but hardly surprised. Half of New York City was in Europe. His commanding officer at Interrogations was John Harlan Amen, the former district attorney for Brooklyn. Telford Taylor, a prominent Park Avenue attorney who'd recruited him out of law school was also working under Justice Jackson, and now who should turn up but Spanner Mullins, commander of the Twentieth Precinct during his ten years as a New York City cop. He'd heard his former boss was attached to Patton's staff. He should have figured it would be in the provost marshal's office.

"I'm flying to Nuremberg tomorrow morning," said Jackson. "If you want to hitch a lift, be at Orly Airport at nine o'clock. Seven days, Major. Next Monday, I want you at the Ashcan in Luxembourg beginning your interrogation of Fat Stuff. Is that clear? Oh, and Judge, one last thing. You're going to Patton's command. Make sure your shoes are shined."

BACK IN HIS OFFICE AT 7 rue de Presbourg, Bob Storey locked the door and rushed to his desk. Unlocking a cabinet near the window, he removed a scuffed black telephone, pulling the cord behind it so he could set the apparatus on his desk. Lifting the receiver, he dialed a five digit number in London.

A woman answered after three rings. "Personnel."

"I need to speak to Walter Williams, please. It's his nephew, Victor."

"Thank you. I'll put you right through."

Two minutes passed until a deep, gravelly voice came onto the line. "That you, Bob? We secure?"

"Yes, Bill, the line's clear," said Storey. "We've got a rather interesting situation developing over here. A war criminal's escaped and one of Jackson's boys wants to go after him."

"A lawyer? You're kidding?"

"I believe we all practiced the trade at some time in our life. Unlike us, this one did the exciting stuff before joining the bar."

Storey had spent the first part of the year on a mission for his friend "Bill." Traveling behind Russian lines, he'd accompanied a team of Red Army jurists as they dealt with suspected war criminals. Usually, the accused were brought before the court at dawn, tried by lunch, and shot by dusk. It wasn't the exercise of justice. Just power.

"Is that right?" asked Bill. "Don't leave me hanging."

"This man happened to be a peace officer in his other life."

"We call them policemen outside of Texas," Bill laughed. "Give me the details."

Storey relayed the news of Seyss's escape, Judge's interest in the German officer, and his success in obtaining a transfer to Patton's Third

Army, Office of the Provost Marshal. He even recited the text of Eisenhower's orders verbatim. A photographic memory was one of the attributes that had made him such an attractive find.

"And when is Judge leaving?"

"Tomorrow morning," said Storey.

"Well, you were right to let me know, Bob. Many thanks. I'll make sure we keep an eye on him. After all, we wouldn't want the boy causing us any trouble."

CHAPTER

4

A PERSISTENT RAPPING ON THE bedroom door roused him from his slumber.

"Herr Seyss, it is time to wake. You are to dress and come to the salon at once."

"*Sofort,*" Seyss answered, his voice immediately clear. Right away.

Lifting his head from the down pillow, he squinted into the darkness and willed the room into focus. Slowly, reluctantly, it obliged: the armoire where he'd hung his clothing, the night table where a basin of water had been set for him to wash; the damask curtains drawn to block out the morning light. And with it, memories of the night before.

Free from the camp, he'd abandoned the wagon and headed into the forest. His destination was a logging road that ran along the crest of the mountain—a two-mile run uphill. His exhilaration at being free wore off after the first incline, leaving his legs trembling and his lungs afire. Hardly his nation's greatest hope. To stoke his resolve, he seized on his shame at having nearly botched the escape, but over the last half mile, that too faded. Anger carried him over the crest of the mountain, his ire at the pitiful condition he'd been left in by Janks and Vlassov and the entire Allied war machine.

He spotted the Mercedes right off, tucked in a copse of birch trees so that only its chrome snout was visible. A pair of headlamps flashed once and two men dressed in formal business attire climbed from the cabin. "Hurry, Herr Sturmbannführer," one whispered. "Into the trunk. The Olympicsstrasse is only clear until eleven P.M."

Nearing them, Seyss took a closer look at the car: A 1936 Mercedes touring sedan, black with spoke hubcaps, whitewall tires, and on its mesh grille a crimson badge displaying the letter *B* in ornate white Gothic script—the symbol of Bach Industries, Germany's largest armaments manufacturer. He'd thought he recognized it; now he was sure. He'd ridden in this very car a hundred times before the war.

At last, he knew who had summoned him. Only one further question remained: Why?

That had been six hours ago.

Seyss walked to the night table and splashed water in his face, then on his chest and neck. Drying himself, he crossed the room to open the curtains. Sunshine flooded the bedroom. He unlatched the window and a wave of hot air swept over him. It was not six in the morning, but six in the evening. He had slept eighteen hours without waking.

THREE SETS OF CLOTHING HUNG inside the armoire. He chose a pair of tan trousers and a white shirt. Putting them on, he stared at his body in the mirror. His face and forearms were colored a rich mountain brown but the rest of him was ghostly pale. The scar from the Russian's bullet had left an ugly pink weal four inches long above his waist. He could count his ribs easily. His arms, though, had kept their tone. Once he'd done thirty-seven pull-ups to win a battalion fitness contest. He was less pleased with his posture. A late-opening parachute had compressed three veterbrae in his spine and left him slightly askew, tilted an inch or so to the left. His hair had turned nearly white in the mountain sun but his face was too slim, shadowed by the haunted scowl he'd seen on so many other soldiers and sworn never to adopt himself. Once women had found him handsome. They'd told him he had a kind mouth and soulful eyes. Moving closer to the mirror, he struggled to find a hint of the compassion they'd seen. He couldn't.

After buttoning his shirt, he grabbed a loden blazer and gave himself a final looking over. His shock was immediate and overwhelming. Staring back at him was a civilian. A man who would never again don his country's uniform. A man who had lost the war. Cheeks scrubbed, hair combed, clothes just so, he looked more like a country squire than an escapee from an American prison camp. The thought came to him that he was betraying the comrades he'd left eighty miles away in a barbed-wire pen. He dismissed it. Any man who'd suffered even a little of war knew never to question his luck. Good fortune was like a weekend pass: never too soon coming and always too soon gone. Besides, Seyss didn't imagine he'd be taking a vacation anytime soon.

THE DRAWING ROOM OF THE Villa Ludwig hadn't changed since the war began. Louis XV sofas upholstered in burgundy chintz crowded every wall. The Bösendorfer grand, ever polished as if for that evening's performance, shared its corner with an immortal Phoenician palm. And sagging from the walls hung the same succession of dreary landscapes by Caspar David Friedrich. A mausoleum for the living, observed Seyss, as he entered the marble-floored chamber.

"Erich, so wonderful to see you," declared Egon Bach, rising from a wing chair. "Sleep the great healer? You're looking fit, all things considered."

Every large family has its runt and Egon Bach, youngest of the seven Bach children, claimed the title. He was very short and very thin and his cropped brown hair, cut a full inch above the ear, spoke volumes about his love of all things fascist. It was his vision, however, that had kept him from active service. His tortoiseshell spectacles carried lenses so thick that his obsidian eyes stared at you from the end of a drunken corridor. But Seyss had never heard him complain about his physical shortcomings. Instead, Egon had joined the family business and used his position as sole heir in the executive suite to bring him the glory a battlefield never would. Whatever enmity he'd felt at being left out of the match he'd channeled into his work. Last Seyss heard, he'd been appointed to the firm's executive board, the youngest member by thirty years.

"Hello, Egon. I apologize for keeping your father waiting."

"Don't apologize to Father," he said in a sprightly tone. "Apologize to me."

"*You?*" Seyss shook the smaller man's hand, finding the grip cool and clammy. "You called me down here?"

A self-satisfied smile. "I've been running the firm for a year now."

Seyss had difficulty imagining the diminutive man, two years his junior, running the behemoth that was Bach Industries. A little like Goebbels governing the Reich. "I hadn't heard your father had retired."

"He hasn't—at least not officially. The Americans have him under house arrest. The past year he's suffered a series of strokes that have left him soft. He'll be dead before fall."

Don't smile, Egon, or I'll cuff you, thought Seyss. "And how is it that *you* escaped the Allies' interest? They're a thorough bunch."

"Thorough but pragmatic," answered Egon, sensing his anger and taking a wise step to the rear. "We've managed an arrangement. I've been declared necessary to the rebuilding of Germany."

"Have you? Bravo." Seyss raised an eyebrow, but decided not to delve any further into the subject. The Bachs had always brokered some type of arrangement going with whoever was in power. Monarchs, republicans, fascists. It came as no surprise that Egon had worked out something with the Americans. Approaching the window, Seyss peeked from the lace curtains. Fifty meters away, two American soldiers stood guard at the entry to Villa Ludwig's driveway. "Where were they when I arrived last night?"

"On duty, of course. Otherwise I would have met you myself."

An arrangement indeed. Enough to clear the Olympicstrasse of military police for an hour but not to rid himself of a permanent guard. Things were more complicated than Bach had let on. "And your family? How did your brothers make out?"

Egon removed his glasses and as he polished them with his tie, his defenseless eyes crossed. "Fritz was killed at Monte Cassino a year ago. Heinz was in your area, the Dnieper Bend in the Ukraine. Apparently his tank took a direct hit. It was one of ours: a Panzer IV from our Essen *metalwerke*. A shame." The creep sounded more concerned about the failure of the equipment than the death of his brother. "You knew about Karl. Seven kills before he went down over the Channel."

"I'd heard, yes." The Bachs might be an arrogant bunch but they were brave. Three of four sons lost. The Führer could ask no more of any family. "My condolences."

Replacing his glasses, Egon retrieved two beers from the cherry-wood side bar. "To fallen comrades."

"May their memories never be forgotten."

The Hacker-Pschorr was warm, but still Seyss's favorite, and its bitter aftertaste resuscitated memories of his time with the Bach family. In this room, he'd listened to Hans Frizsche, the voice of the German DNB, announce the Anschluss with Austria, and a year later the annexation of the Sudetenland. In this room, he'd received the orders canceling his leave in August of 1939. In this room, he'd lowered himself to one knee and asked the only woman he'd ever loved to marry him. For a moment, he allowed himself to drift with the tide of his bittersweet memories. Before he could stop himself, he asked, "And Ingrid?"

"At Sonnenbrücke taking care of Father." The Bachs owned homes in every corner of Germany. Each had a name. Sonnenbrücke was their palatial hunting lodge in the Chiemgauer Alps. "She always wanted to be a doctor," added Egon. "Now's her chance."

"And Wilimovsky?"

Egon shook his head brusquely. "Shot down in the East a year ago. Pity for a girl to be widowed so young, though it's the boy I'm worried about. Just six." Suddenly he froze, his voice ratcheting up a notch. "Not interested, are you? *Or have you been all along?*"

Seyss met Egon's salacious gaze, but his thoughts were with Ingrid and the time was a crisp fall day in 1938. They had been seeing each other for a year and he had arrived that morning to spend his weekend pass at Villa Ludwig before continuing on to an infantry training course at Brunswick. Against her father's will, she had decided to study medicine. With the Jews forbidden to practice, there was a growing shortage of doctors and she was anxious to break from her family. Even now, he could see her as she fell onto the couch in that exaggerated fashion that infuriated her father, a perfectly assembled mess of platinum hair and ruby red lipstick.

"I've decided to get a flat of my own," she had said, after they'd had a cup of tea.

"What for?" he asked. "You have plenty of room here. Besides, your father won't permit it."

"I want us to be alone. You could come see me anytime you like. I'm sick of Fritz or Hilda barging in. Egon watches us through the keyhole."

"Don't be silly. You're just eighteen." He, being twenty-one, and the embodiment of wisdom.

"Almost nineteen," she replied coquettishly, tracing the looping silver script embroidered on his left sleeve. LAH. Leibstandarte Adolf Hitler. "An officer assigned to the Führer's bodyguard shouldn't have to ask my father's permission every time he wants to see me."

Erich considered the dilemma. He didn't like to admit that he was a stickler for rules and regulations. Earlier in the day, they'd argued about her makeup and clothing. Adhering to the party line, he had found himself saying that too much lipstick was un-German and that pants demeaned her femininity. He'd even declared that an SS man couldn't be seen with a "trouser woman." At that, Ingrid had broken out laughing, and after a moment, he had joined her. He knew what he had said was ridiculous, but an uncontrollable part of his nature compelled him to defend the party's philosophy. He was, above all, a good National Socialist. Truth be told, he adored her tight blouses and soft curls. The idea of spending the night alone with Ingrid Bach was overpowering.

"I think the museum quarter would be the best place to start looking, don't you?"

Ingrid screamed with delight and pulled him close. Guiding his hand to her breast, she kissed him in a very un-German fashion.

"I said, you're not still interested?" Egon repeated.

"Of course not," snapped Seyss, his attention again riveted to the here and now. He felt angry with himself for allowing his emotions free reign. Tucking in his jaw, he adopted the dry tone taught all SS officers. *Sächlichkeit*, it was called. The ability to view one's circumstances with rigid objectivity. "Please pass along my regards to her and the boy."

"I'll be sure to." Egon laughed rudely. "Though I'm not certain she'll be too pleased. She never quite recovered, you know."

"It was a different time," said Seyss, answering his own accusations as well as his host's. "One had obligations."

"As a party member, I understand. As Ingrid's brother, I take a different view. You hurt her badly."

Seyss finished his beer and set down the empty glass. Five minutes listening to Egon's nasal bray and he remembered all over again how much he hated the impudent bastard. He was sick of the small talk. He'd risked his life to be here and killed two men in the process. It was time to get down to business.

"How did you find me, anyway?"

"It was easy once I realized you'd be on the Allies' list of war criminals. Still, I'd have thought you'd have learned to follow orders in your time. It was a foolish thing, killing the camp commander. He was with us, you know."

"It was necessary."

"It was rash. One more Nazi on the run means nothing to the Americans. But you had to murder an officer. Damn it, man, what were you thinking?"

Seyss tightened the muscles in his neck as his temper flared. What could Egon Bach know about the need to avenge your comrades? To cleanse your soul with the blood of your enemy? About the beauty of looking into a man's eyes as he died by your hand? The smaller man's anger fired his impatience to learn the reason why he'd been told to come to Munich. But he'd be damned if he asked.

To temper his restlessness, he clasped his hands behind his back and made a slow circuit around the room. His eyes fell to a patch of wall where a replica of Alfred Bach's golden party badge, the highest honor the Nazi party bestowed upon civilians, used to hang. In its place was a photograph of Alfred Bach with Edward VIII, the English monarch who had given up his throne to marry an American divorcée. Shocked, he took a closer look at the other pictures hanging nearby. The color photo of Adolf Hitler thanking Alfred Bach for the handmade armchair he'd been given for his fiftieth birthday had been replaced by one of the elder Bach in the company of Charles Lindbergh, the famed American flyer. Another showed Alfred Bach shaking hands with Winston Churchill, circa 1912.

"It's not wise to wear your allegiance on your sleeve," chimed Egon from across the room. "These days, it's difficult to meet anyone who voluntarily joined the party, let alone someone who actually voted our Führer into power. We're a nation of amnesiacs. National socialism is dead, Erich."

But Seyss wasn't interested in an apology for Bach's cosmetic renunciation of the party. "And Germany?"

"The Fatherland will never die. You and I won't allow it. What did Herder say about our country's geist—its spirit?"

" 'It shall flourish so long as a single German lives,' " quoted Seyss from an ancient textbook.

"Exactly. Hurry up, then. We have a quarter of an hour until our guests arrive. I imagine you're starving."

As Seyss followed Egon Bach into the hallway, he paused for a last look at the drawing room. A spray of chrysanthemums decorated a nook previously reserved for a national socialist banner. The bronze bust of Hitler cast by Fritz Todt had been replaced by a replica of Michelangelo's *David*. And, of course, there was the matter of the photographs.

The room had changed.

It was Erich Seyss who hadn't.

CHAPTER

5

DOWN, DOWN, DOWN, THEY WALKED, through a white-tiled cata-comb lit by stuttering bulbs in steel mesh cages, a passage so narrow and dank that Seyss nearly succumbed to his recently acquired claustropho-bia. Now, three hundred thirty-seven stairs later, they had arrived. Barring their path was a gray steel door large enough to have locked down the boiler room of the battleship *Bismarck*. Above it, the words "Luftschutzbunker 50 Personen," were painted in perfect black script. Air raid shelter. 50 persons.

Egon leaned his shoulder into the door and gave a shove. "A little dramatic, perhaps, but necessary. Hard for my colleagues to visit the main house."

"You mean they couldn't fit into the trunk of the Mercedes?" Seyss asked dryly.

Egon did not laugh. "Go on, then. These are not men one keeps waiting."

Seyss's first thought was that he'd never seen a shelter decorated so opulently. The underground refuge was done up like the lobby of the Adlon in Berlin: navy carpets, teak coffee tables, sleek sofas. All that was missing was the Babylonian fountain spewing water from an elephant's trunk and an unctuous maître d'hôtel eager to show them to a table.

Two older men stood waiting in the center of the room. Greeting them, Egon turned to Erich and said, "I believe you know Mr. Weber and Mr. Schnitzel."

"Good evening, gentlemen. It's been some time." Seyss delivered a firm handshake to each man, punctuated by a curt nod and crisp click of the heels. He had worked with both during the war and if they weren't friends, they were certainly well acquainted. Robert Weber was vice chairman of North German Aluminum, the country's largest metals company. Arthur Schnitzel, finance director of FEBA, a monolithic chemical concern.

"You're looking well, Major," said Weber. "May I offer my congratulations on your escape."

"Yes, congratulations," cawed Schnitzel, "though we could have done without the theatrics."

Seyss answered with a clipped smile, staring daggers into the old man's gray eyes until he averted his gaze. During his tenure as SS Reichsführer Himmler's adjutant for industrial affairs, his brief had been to ensure that manpower requirements necessary to run their plants at full capacity were met. He was Himmler's golden boy in those days, in charge of negotiating contracts between Germany's most important industrial concerns and the SS main office for the transport, and delivery, of foreign impressed labor, mostly Jews and *mischlings* from Poland and Russia. Suddenly it was clear why they were meeting in an air raid bunker and not in Egon's living room. Like him, Weber and Schnitzel were wanted by the Allied powers for war crimes. Slave labor, no doubt. Not everyone could be declared "necessary to the rebuilding of Germany."

"Gentlemen, this isn't a coffee-klatsch," said Egon, flitting between them at his usual frenetic pace. "We have much to discuss and little time. Help yourself to brandy and cigars, then let's get started."

Schnitzel and Weber poured themselves generous snifters of VSOP, then took their places on a maroon velvet couch. Seyss sat across from them, choosing an antique armchair. Nothing like a little discomfort to focus the mind on matters at hand.

"Germany is in ruins," declared Egon Bach as he slipped down between Schnitzel and Weber. "We have no electricity. Sewage is kaput.

No mail has been delivered since April. We no longer have a government, a police force, or even a soccer team. Coal is more expensive than
caviar and cigarettes are worth more than both of them together.
Verrückt! Crazy!"

"We are a divided people," said Weber, picking up the baton.
Dressed in a severe black suit, monocle in his eye, he was the embodiment of his native Prussia. The Allies have split the country into four
zones of occupation. The British have taken the Ruhr and the North.
The French, the Rhineland and Saar. The Americans control the center
from Bavaria to Niedersachsen, and the Russians have stolen the East."

"Our industry is in ruins," continued Schnitzel. "Frankfurt,
Cologne, Mannheim—all leveled. Young Bach here lost seventy of his
ninety plants. Sixty percent of his production capability wiped out." A
short white-haired man who had lost his right leg at the Somme in 1916,
Schnitzel wore his crutches and neatly pinned trousers more proudly
than any medal. Friends and enemies alike knew him as the Stork. "I'm
hardly better off. Fifty-five percent of my factories have been damaged
beyond repair."

"But salvageable," added Weber. "None of our companies have been
forced to stop production completely. Give us five years and we can
bring our output back to what it was before the war. The key to the
revival of Germany is the rebuilding of our industry."

"*If we are permitted to do so,*" said Egon. "The Allies have forbidden
us to reconstruct our plants. They want to dismantle the forges, blast
furnaces, and steel works, that survived the war and cart them off to
France and England, even, God forbid, to Russia. A crew of American
engineers is scheduled to dismantle our fifteen-thousand-ton press next
week. They'll probably ship the damn thing to New Jersey and use it to
make guns for their battleships."

Perched on the edge of his seat, Seyss listened with a rapt silence.
The recounting of his country's pillage stoked his anger as a breeze fans
a fire. And though he said nothing, his mind was churning. What could
be so important that Weber and Schnitzel had risked arrest to see him?
Why this lengthy preamble? Why the persuasive pitch to their voices,
the pleading gleam to their eyes? There was no need to convince him.
He was a soldier. He did what he was told.

He'd imagined that he'd been summoned from Garmisch to help a *kamerad* escape the country—Bormann, perhaps, Eichmann, maybe even the Führer. There were rumors Hitler was alive, that the corpses in the Reich Chancellery belonged to his double and Eva Braun's sister. Clearly that wasn't the case. The conversation was more concerned with the state of the economy than any military objective. Confused, he was left with the same question as when he'd jumped into the back of Egon's Mercedes nearly twenty-four hours earlier. What did they have in store for him?

"Rumor has it they're going to flood the coal mines," Weber was saying. "Send our soldiers to France as forced labor."

"A permanent end to our war-making ability," lamented Schnitzel. "Germany is to become a pastoral state, an agrarian economy."

"Think of Denmark," said Egon. "Without Tivoli Gardens." Standing, he walked to a side table where a scale model of Grosse Gertie the Bachs' monstrous 200-mm cannon, rested. He picked up the field gun, admiring it from every angle as if it were a Fabergé egg. "The Allies have confiscated our weaponry. It is against the law for a German to possess so much as a side arm. We're not even allowed to keep the grease from our stoves, lest we use it to manufacture explosives. We will be left nothing with which to defend ourselves."

Weber plucked the monocle from his eye. "And that, Herr Seyss, is our problem. We haven't gathered here today to bemoan our financial losses. We have larger issues at heart. Look around you. The Americans are withdrawing their troops from our country and sending them to the Pacific in preparation for the invasion of Japan. The war has bankrupted the British. There's an election in a few weeks' time and talk is Churchill is for the dung heap. You can imagine where that will leave us and our agrarian economy."

Seyss nodded, quick to draw his own inferences.

"You've fought against the Russians," said Egon. "What do you think Mr. Stalin will do with the tanks and cannons that now line the Elbe? Do you think he will send them back to Mother Russia? Of course not. He will move them to our border and he will wait. He will wait for the Americans to go home and for the British to withdraw. He will wait until our factories are no more and our presses are dismantled and the lot of us are in the fields milking Holsteins and tending flocks of sheep with our thumbs up our agrarian asses. That is what he will do. And then he will attack. I give him two days until he is at the Rhine."

Weber lectured Seyss with the butt of his monocle, his voice crackling with a fevered intensity. "Today we live as a conquered people. But the Americans are like us. They are not an evil race. Each day, they work to make sure we have enough to eat and that our sewers no longer back up and that we can have a few hours of electricity. The Bolsheviks are not cut from the same cloth. They are from the East. *Untermenschen.* Subhumans. The descendants of Genghis Khan. It would be better to die than to submit to their will!"

Weber sounded like an editorial from *Der Strumer*, thought Seyss. Unfortunately, everything he said was true.

"I agree that Stalin is a bastard," burst Seyss, no longer able to bottle his frustration. "I agree that the dismantling of our industrial capacity poses a grave threat to our nation's ability to defend itself. And that we cannot permit our mines to be flooded. But, gentlemen, what do you wish me to do about it? I am a soldier, not a politician. Tell me to take an enemy ridge, I can assemble my men, put together a plan, and attack. Ask me to convince the Americans not to make Germany an agrarian state, I don't know how I can help."

"The two aren't as far removed as you might think," said Weber, eyes bright.

Egon Bach lifted a calming hand. "We understand your confusion. Just hear us out. At first we, too, were skeptical as to our ability to color the final outcome. But the situation is too important to let fate run its course unchallenged."

"Then tell me what you want me to do." Despite its size the room was beginning to close in upon him. A pallor of smoke hung in the air. Even with bulbs burning in four lamps, the shelter seemed to be growing dimmer and dimmer.

Egon raised both hands in front of him, patting the air. "In due time, Erich. In due time."

Seyss sat ramrod straight. He knew the longer the preface, the more dangerous the mission. *Sächlichkeit*, he thought, drawing a heavy breath. *Discipline.*

"Thirteen years ago, my father convened a group of gentlemen unhappy with the complexion of Germany's politics," said Egon. "The Depression had silenced our country's factories. Our own firm was on the verge of collapse. Father's guests shared the same bleak prospects. Krupp. Thyssen. Rocher. Men who had constructed the steel works, rolling mills, foundries, and shipyards that power our nation."

Egon paused, sweeping his owl's head to look each man in the eye. He was a mesmerizing little creep, Seyss would give him that much.

"Father recognized that only one man could save them. Adolf Hitler, leader of the National Socialist Workers party. Hitler would rearm the nation and lead us to war. And though war wasn't a pleasant prospect, as a businessman he recognized it was the only solution to their problems. But in November of 1932, the Nazi party was in danger of collapse. They had lost thirty-five seats to the Communists in the most recent elections. Worse, they were all but bankrupt. Goering came to Father and confided that without an immediate cash infusion the party would be unable to pay the mountain of bills it had run up in the election. A failure to meet their obligations would be catastrophic. Ernst Roehm and his storm troopers were threatening to rebel and throw Hitler out. If that happened, President Hindenburg would have no choice but to seek a chancellor from the left. An entente with the Communists was even possible, God forbid.

"Father proposed that his colleagues join him in a new league of industrialists. Not a luncheon group who would waste their time quibbling about quotas and tariffs over seven-course meals at Horchers but one that would focus their efforts on influencing the proper political direction for the Fatherland. He had even thought of a name for his secret assembly of coal barons, steel magnates, and iron makers. The Circle of Fire."

"The Circle of Fire," repeated Schnitzel, the words rolling off his tongue in a cloud of blue smoke.

Egon's grateful smile was like a doff of the hat. "Father's solution was simple. First they would pay the Nazis' debts. Then, as one, they would travel to Berlin and demand that Hindenburg make Hitler chancellor. The old man was a landowner like them. He would listen. The rest, as they say, is history. Two months later, on January thirtieth, 1933,

Hindenburg named Hitler chancellor of Germany. Bach Industries was saved."

Seyss smiled inwardly, recalling a phrase every schoolboy knew by heart. *Wenn Bach blüht, so blüht Deutschland.* When Bach prospers, so prospers Germany. So much for destiny and the will of the people.

"Over the past weeks, we have brought the Circle of Fire back to life," said Egon. "Friends, colleagues, even former competitors who share our worries have joined us. Why, you ask? For one reason and one reason only. To ensure that Germany remains intact long after our occupiers have departed."

If Seyss had been alone with Egon, he would have thought the younger man joking. *To ensure Germany remains intact.* That kind of bluster was his trademark. But when spoken in the company of Schnitzel and Weber, men as hardened by the war as any veteran of the front, his words adopted a gravitas usually denied by his youth.

The Stork laughed and the tension in the room dissipated. "That's when the answer came to us. Germany must become indispensable to the Americans."

"Indispensable?" asked Seyss.

"Indispensable," repeated Schnitzel, smiling. "An ally."

Seyss smiled, too, but in disbelief. *"An ally?"*

"Yes," said Schnitzel. "Their soldiers dote on our women and children. Many of their families come from the Fatherland. Why are you so shocked?"

Seyss clamped his jaw shut, eyeing the Stork as if he were mad. "The Amis have just spent the past three years beating the living shit out of us and you expect them to turn around and give us a kiss on the cheek?"

Weber coughed once, a rude honk that passed for a laugh in Prussia. "Of course not. We'll have to give them a kick in the ass first."

Exasperated, Seyss raised his hands, then let them fall. "If the German people are to become the Americans' ally, who's to be our mutual enemy?"

The three men found the remark humorous, their conjoined laughs rumbling long and low like distant thunder.

"Relations between the Americans and the Russians are touchy," said Weber, when their mirth had been exhausted. "The Red Army has limited the Americans' and Brits' access to Berlin, yet the city is to be governed by all three powers. The first American troops will arrive in two days to take up their permanent station. How long before they are at each others' throats?"

Schnitzel's cheeks glowed with excitement. "Stalin has overstepped himself in Poland and Czechoslovakia. He has promised free elections yet he's seen to it that his puppets are in place in both countries. He has violated the agreement he made with Mr. Roosevelt and Mr. Churchill at Yalta four months ago. We have it on good authority the Americans aren't pleased."

Seyss shrugged his shoulders. "So? Do you expect Eisenhower to cross the Elbe because Stalin has thrown up a few roadblocks and taken a little more land than agreed upon?"

"Of course not," the Stork retorted. "We expect you to give him a much better reason."

"Me?"

"*Yes, you,*" hissed Egon, and the room fell silent. "Terminal. It is the Americans' code name for the conference to be held in Potsdam in a week's time. There, the provisions governing reparations—measures which will include the settling of our borders and the emasculation of our industrial might—will be settled. The new American president, Truman, will attend, as will Churchill and Stalin. It would be a pity if something should happen to flare the tensions between these three great Allies. Personally, I can think of only one thing. And it is a soldier's job, not a politician's."

A soldier's job.

Seyss stood and paced the room's perimeter. So there it was: another foray behind enemy lines. He should have known it was something of the kind. Why else single him out? He spoke Russian like a commissar. His English was his mother's. He'd spent practically the entire war roaming unfriendly territory. Strangely, he felt relieved, the burden of ignorance lifted from his chest at last.

"What exactly do you have in mind?"

Egon Bach drew a cigar from his pocket and lit it. "Sooner or later, the flame of democracy will ignite the cradle of communism. We want you to provide the spark."

CHAPTER

6

THE HEADQUARTERS OF THE United States Army of Occupation, military government of Bavaria, was located in the barracks and classrooms of the former SS academy at Bad Toelz, a sleepy hamlet perched on the banks of the Isar River twenty miles south of Munich. The academy was impressive: a three-story stone edifice painted a rich cream with steep gabled roofs that ran in a continuous square around a parade ground the size of Ebbetts Field. Stands of mature poplars stood sentry at each corner of the parade ground. A flagpole rose from its center, the Stars and Stripes snapping to attention in the warm morning breeze.

Devlin Judge hopped from the jeep as soon as it had pulled to a halt, and followed his driver into the building. Marching up a few stairs, he came to a wide corridor running in either direction as far as the eye could see. The place was as busy as Grand Central Station. A steady stream of soldiers zipped back and forth as if drawn by a magnetic force. To a man their uniforms were impeccable, their posture equally so. This was Patton's command all right. "Spit and polish" and "blood and guts."

Judge walked for two minutes down the hallway. A broad black stripe ran down the center of the flagstone flooring. Every fifty feet, a pair of soldiers knelt low vigorously maintaining its sheen. His escort turned right leading him up a broad winding staircase. A different word was painted across the base of each step. *Entschiedenheit. Mut. Lauterheit.* Decisiveness. Courage. Integrity. Brocades of black cloth were draped like bunting from the walls. Between them painted in Gothic script were the names of the SS's elite divisions: *Das Reich. Viking. Totenkopf.* All over Germany, Allied soldiers were working to efface all traces of the Nazi party from the landscape. The swastika had been outlawed in every shape and form. Yet here it looked as if Patton were maintaining a shrine to the worst element of the German army: the SS.

At the top of the stairway, the two men turned right again and continued to the end of the hallway where a brace of military policemen in gleaming white helmets and matching Sam Browne belts stood at attention beside an open door. Hanging above the door was a small red flag with four gold stars. Instead of entering the office, though, Judge's escort continued past it, stopping at the next door down. A hand-lettered sign announced United States Army of Occupation, Provost Marshal. He knocked once, then opened the door and allowed Judge to pass before him.

"Get in here, Detective," boomed the familiar voice. "On the double." Rising from his desk—all six foot four of him—Stanley Mullins crossed the room, arms open in greeting. "Hello, Dev. I can't tell you how sorry I am about Father Francis. A loss to us all."

"Hello, Spanner. Long time."

Mullins pulled him to his shoulder, whispering in his ear, "It's Colonel Mullins, these days, if you'd be so kind. The boss is a bit of a stickler."

Judge accepted the outstretched hand and gave it a firm shake. "Colonel Mullins it is, then."

Mullins bobbed his chin, but failed to provide the expected wink. "Good to see you, lad. You did the right thing coming to visit."

So far as Judge knew, Mullins had never set foot in the old country, yet there was no mistaking the lilting brogue. He wasn't just tall but thick, and the twenty pounds he'd put on since Judge had last seen him gave him not only the girth of an oak but the solidity, too. His hair was thinning, more salt than pepper, parted expertly and slicked into place with a handful of brilliantine. His complexion was ruddier than Judge remembered, the blue eyes a tad more suspicious. He was Irish at first sight, but God forbid you joked about his love of a good pint. Come from five generations of coppers, Mullins didn't touch a drop. Not a tee-totaler, mind you, just a man who appreciated control. And control was what was written all over him. In his uniform with the creases sharp enough to cut butter and the blouse bathed in enough starch to stand at parade rest. In his stride, the long, precise steps, each premeasured, each perfectly executed. And mostly, Judge thought, in his posture, a bearing so rigid, so upright, that even standing still, it conveyed its own kinetic aggression.

"I remember you joined up a couple years back," said Judge, when Mullins had stopped pumping his hand. "What's it been?"

"Three years and then some."

"St. Paddy's Day, wasn't it?" Mullins had thrown an Irish wake to mourn his leaving the force. Judge had received an invite but didn't attend. By then, Brooklyn was off-limits. "I wanted to stop by and send you off. I'm sorry."

"Nonsense, lad. You had more important things to do than bid your old boyfriends farewell. I've been keeping track of you in the papers. Assistant United States Attorney Devlin Parnell Judge—Brooklyn's very own gangbuster. Tell me, Dev, what's your streak up to these days? Twenty-six? Twenty-seven?"

"Something like that." Actually, it was twenty-nine. Fifty-eight out of sixty cases won over a four-year period. A career built on the backs of corrupt city officials, shady building contractors, and union thugs. He'd earned the moniker Gangbuster for putting away Vic Fazio, a small-time hijacker looking to muscle in on Lepke's turf of murder for hire by accepting contracts to knock off total strangers, men and women outside the rackets.

"Fair number without a loss," Mullins grinned suspiciously. "Not paying off the bench, are you?"

"What? And have you lose faith in me? Never."

Mullins laughed, wagging a finger. "There's my straight-shooter. Just remember, I knew you before you converted."

"Yeah, I remember," said Judge. "You won't let me forget." He laughed, too, but less brightly, thinking it was the debts you could never repay whose reminder bothered you most.

Mullins draped an arm over his shoulder, steering him toward his scarred headmaster's desk and the pair of wooden school chairs set before it. "Well, lad, I'm pleased to set eyes on you again. You waited a damn sight long enough to get into the game. Frankly, I was beginning to wonder."

Judge chose to ignore the implicit chastisement, the hint of duty unfulfilled. It was a delicate issue, even now that he wore an olive drab uniform and a campaign cap. The fact was that Thomas Dewey, special prosecutor for the state of New York, an appointee of the president of the United States, had asked him personally to stay on. The army needed bodies, he'd said, not minds. And certainly not minds as astute as Judge's. If he wanted to help his country, he should start at home. Clean up New York City. It had practically been an order.

Bodies, not minds.

The recollection of the words and the urbane attorney who had uttered them sent a proud shudder along Judge's spine. For a kid raised on the streets of Brooklyn, it was the compliment he'd always dreamed of receiving. So he'd stayed. But as the war dragged on, year after year, as his promotions came faster and the cut of his suits improved, a voice inside him protested that he liked the size of his office a little too much, that he spent too much time adjusting the dimple in his Windsor knot, and that he grinned too eagerly at the sight of his name in cheap newsprint.

Judge settled into a chair, dropping his briefcase to one side. He explained about his appointment to the International Military Tribunal four months earlier, his more recent discovery that Erich Seyss was responsible for Francis's death, and his push for a transfer to the unit looking into Seyss's escape. "I hope you don't mind my forcing myself on you."

Mullins looked up from the nickel cigar he was unwrapping. "No, you don't, lad. You don't mind at all. And bully for you. You've got family to answer to. I imagine your wife's proud of you. Teresa, wasn't it?"

Judge laughed softly, surprised by the acuity of Mullins's memory, then remembering that he'd been at the wedding. "Maria Teresa O'Hare. Italian and Irish split down the middle. A half breed like me." He smiled apologetically. "We're not together anymore."

Mullins struck a match and fired the cigar. "What do you mean 'not together'?"

"We divorced two years ago."

"Oh?" Mullins's countenance ruffled behind a cloud of blue smoke. Divorce wasn't in an Irishman's vocabulary. "I'm sorry to hear that."

"We were drifting apart for a long time before that. She wanted the job on Park Avenue, you know, white shoe firm, the athletic club, weekends in the country. I chose the other road—Dewey, the U.S. Attorney's office, working weekends. It was the only law I knew."

Mullins pulled the cigar from his lips and leaned his bulk over the desk, the inquisitive blue eyes not settling for an excuse when the truth was so close at hand. "Was it the boy, God rest his soul?"

Ryan? It figured that Mullins had the temerity to come right out and ask. Whether it was the gossip in him or the father confessor, Judge didn't know. But he couldn't deny the sympathy in his voice. For all his faults, Mullins cared for the men under his command as he would his own sons. "I don't know. Yeah, maybe. When he left us, we couldn't use him to patch over our differences any longer. Anyway, neither of us tried too hard after that."

Mullins lowered his eyes, sighing loudly, then landing both fists softly on the desktop. "Aye, the polio. Nearly killed Mr. Roosevelt, too. Poor boy, hardly stood a chance. He's with the Lord now. At least we can take comfort in that." He drew on his cigar and sat back in his chair. "I am sorry about Father Francis. He was the good egg, wasn't he?"

And this time, Judge felt the barb. *The good egg.* He being the bad one: the violence-prone urchin on his way to the state reformatory until Spanner Mullins had intervened. His self-pity angered him until he recognized it for what it was. Mullins's none-too-subtle way of letting him know who was in charge.

"Yes, he was," Judge answered equably. "Francis was always the good one."

"And this bastard, Seyss, you say he's the man responsible?"

Judge patted the briefcase by his side, happy to be on the safe side of reminiscence. "Eyewitness evidence written in the Germans' own hand."

"I imagined as much. Else you wouldn't be sitting here before me."

Suddenly, Mullins was out of his chair, stubbing out the cigar while circling the desk and motioning for Judge to join him. "Off your duff, then, lad. The boss wants to say his hellos before his noontime ride."

"Patton?"

"Who else?"

"SO THIS IS JUDGE? He doesn't look like such a mean sonuvabitch to me. Show him in, dammit. Show him in!"

General of the Army George S. Patton, Jr., strode across the room with the energy of an untamed stallion. Resplendent in tan breeches and black riding boots, pearl-handled revolver at his side and cigar clenched in his teeth, he was the personification of American victory: brash, arrogant, and with a shower of stars on his uniform—Judge counted twenty-four in all—more than a little overwhelming.

"Got here in a hurry, I see," he said. "I admire a man with a fire under his ass."

Judge was sure to give the extended hand a firm shake. "It's an honor, sir,"

Patton patted him on the arm while shooting Mullins a questioning glance. "Sure this is the right man, Colonel? I'm not certain he's quite the ferocious bastard you advertised."

Mullins smiled broadly, locking his arms behind his back. "That he is, General. Just give him a little prodding. Believe me, he's tougher than a bulldog and at least half as smart."

Patton roared, and kicked the white bull terrier sleeping at his feet. "Hear that, Willie, you yellow bastard?"

"Willie" for William the Conqueror, Judge remembered. The dog whimpered and buried his head under his paws.

The three men were standing in the center of Patton's palatial office. At the far end of the room sat a broad pine desk framed by the Stars and Stripes and the colors of the United States Third Army. Behind the desk, a French window rose from the polished wooden floor to the molded ceiling, which itself was a masterwork. Painted in the center of the ceiling was a trompe l'oeil watercolor of Apollo in his golden chariot parting the clouds and casting a bolt of lightning from what appeared a height of a hundred feet, but was only about fifteen. The twin runes of the SS—flashes they were called—adorned the collar of his tunic. It was a suitably pagan image, thought Judge, but by then Patton was talking again.

"I appreciate you stepping away from your duty in Luxembourg and giving us a hand. The war crimes trials are an important event. A soldier finds his glory on the battlefield. The place for a lawyer is a courtroom. I'm sure it wasn't an easy decision. If you want out, say so now. I don't want you quitting midstream."

"No, sir," said Judge loudly, responding to Patton's infectious bravado. "My only regret is that the transfer is temporary. I'll be with you for seven days. I hope that proves to be enough time."

"Hell, Major, in thirty-six hours, I turned the entire Third Army on its axis and motored a hundred miles through the shittiest piece of weather you'd ever laid eyes on to relieve my good friend, General McAuliffe, at Bastogne. If I could keep forty thousand men moving for three days in a blizzard while under enemy fire, you can find one lousy German in seven."

"Yessir." There it was again. The booming voice. The willful nod. Give him a machine gun, point the way, and he'd be over the top in a second, screaming like a banshee as he stormed an enemy pillbox. Patton had that strong an effect on a man.

The general looked older in person than he did in his photographs. He was a tall man, bald save a crust of white hair. His face was ruddy, possessed of a wind-kissed hue that spoke of hours spent outdoors. His eyes were a hard agate blue, measuring their range of fire from concrete gun slits. His mouth was cast in permanent disapproval. The first words you'd expect to see it utter were "fuck" or "shit" or "piss," and you wouldn't be disappointed. Older, Judge thought, but damned fit for a man of sixty.

Clamping the cigar in the corner of his mouth, Patton wrapped an arm around Judge's shoulder and guided him to the side of the room. "Mullins tells me this is a personal matter between you and Major Seyss?"

"Seyss was the scene commander at Malmedy. He issued the order to open fire."

"And your brother, the priest, he was there?"

"That would be Francis Xavier. He should never have been at the front."

But Patton didn't appear to hear. Eyes wrinkled in distaste, he stared at the floor, slowly shaking his head. "Hard to believe a man of Seyss's caliber could do such a thing. He ran for his country in the '36 Olympics, you know? The Boche called him the White Lion. He was a national hero."

Judge wasn't sure if Patton was appalled by Seyss's behavior or trying to defend it. Patton was an Olympian, too. He'd represented the United States in the modern pentathlon in the 1912 Games in Stockholm. Maybe that explained the prideful note in his voice.

Patton shook off his reverie with a grunt, and strode to the center of the room. The time for intimacy was over, his buoyant manner restored. "I take it you know the details of Seyss's escape. Frankly, I'm livid. We can't have the German people getting the idea that they can kill our boys and get away with it. An officer, no less. I won't have it, understand?"

He began a slow march toward the door, one hand patting Judge's back. "Need anything, call me. Don't worry about going through proper channels. That's all bullshit. If there's a problem, I want to hear from you directly. And if you can't find me, talk to Mullins. Is that clear?"

Judge said yes.

Patton spun to face Mullins, jabbing the cigar at his beefy chest. "And, Colonel, remember what the order from Ike said. Be sure to extend Major Judge our every courtesy and convenience."

"Yes, General."

Judge caught a sarcastic glance passing between them and the thought came to him that despite their alacrity, these two proud men might be peeved at having an investigator from outside their ranks foisted upon them. Patton's encouraging hand and enthusiastic voice erased the idea as quickly as it had appeared.

"Now, Major," he barked, "draw a weapon from the armory and get the hell out of here. I don't want to hear a goddamn word from you until you've found Seyss."

Judge got the message loud and clear. Patton was there if needed, but only in the strictest of emergencies. Firing off a salute, he followed Mullins from the room.

"Just one more thing, Major," Patton called from behind his desk.

Judge froze, craning his head through the door. "Yes, sir?"

"Don't bring me the sonuvabitch. Just kill him."

7

BACK IN MULLINS'S OFFICE, Judge collapsed in a chair opposite his new commanding officer's desk. Taking a moment to polish his reading specs, he gave the office a quick once-over. Parquet floors, battered desk, American flag in one corner, regimental flag in the other, and in the center of it all, flashing his leprechaun's smile, Stanley "Spanner" Mullins. The words to a favorite Gershwin tune played in his head. *"Seems like old times just got new again."*

Opening his satchel, he withdrew the UNWCC dossier and slid it across the desk. "You seen the file on this guy?"

Mullins brought it toward him, admiring its heft. "Looks as if Herr Seyss has been attracting the eye of our colleagues in Washington for some time."

"Yeah, too long."

Setting an elbow on the desk, Judge went over the file's contents. Seyss had first appeared on Allied radar in the fall of 1942, he explained, as a junior officer attached to Einsatzgruppe B, operating out of Kiev on the Russian front. The Einsatzgruppe, or action commandos, were the bad boys. Professional murderers. Following the wake of the German army's advance, they methodically rounded up Jews, Gypsies, Communists—just about any minority deemed unsuitable for incorporation into the Thousand Year Reich—and killed them. He turned up a second time in Poland in the spring of '43, just in time to lead a company of storm troopers on a raid into the Warsaw Ghetto. Eighteen months later, his shadow fell across Frankie's path in the Ardennes. Looking back, there wasn't much question of the outcome. Francis hadn't stood a chance.

Mullins ran a cracked fingernail across the cover page. "Says here he's a local boy, born and raised in Munich. Twenty-one Lindenstrasse."

Judge had noted the address, too, and was anxious to visit the place. "Any idea where that is?"

"None. But, Jesus, lad, didn't you get a look at the place flying in? The city was eighty percent destroyed. Even if he still has a home, odds are he won't go near it."

Maybe, thought Judge, but it was as logical a starting point. Helping Mullins flip the page, he continued where he'd left off. "Seyss's father was a factory owner. Nothing about the mother. No word if either of them made it through the war. He had one brother, a queer who got himself a one-way ticket to Ravensbruck in '39."

"They killed him because he was a nancy boy?" Mullins gave a startled guffaw. "A bit rough, wouldn't you say?"

Judge simply shook his head. One more incomprehensible crime among a thousand others. What frightened him more was the allegiance Seyss continued to show his government after they'd killed his brother. A true believer, he thought, and the recognition drew goose bumps up and down his arms. Rising from his chair, he circled the desk to better view the file with Mullins.

A color photograph of Erich Seyss taken upon his arrest was stapled to the inside cover. Seyss faced the camera squarely, dressed in a charcoal tunic with a pointed black collar, an identification board bearing his name held in front of his chest. He was almost handsome. A harder version of an East Coast blue blood, Judge thought. Bringing the mug shot closer, he memorized the features for the hundredth time: the line of the hair, high on his forehead with a fragile widow's peak. The set of the lips, thin and determined. The frank gaze, yes, especially the gaze. A man couldn't disguise his eyes. They were pale, almost translucent. Even in his prisoner's attire, Seyss looked sure of himself.

Not cocky, like the hoods who worked for the Dutchman or Luciano, but resolute. And something else, too. A word popped into Judge's head. Remorseless.

A true believer.

Drawing the file toward him, he removed the photograph and set it to one side. He returned his attention to the stack of papers, choosing a two-page report and handing it to Mullins. It was a translation of the after-action report filed by the First SS Panzer Division on December 17, 1944. "Here's our evidence."

Mullins read the report without comment, pausing only to remove his half-smoked cigar from the ashtray and relight it. Judge read the report along with him. When he'd finished, he knew that, like Francis, he, too, had a higher calling.

"Brutal bastard," sighed Mullins, chomping the cigar in the corner of his mouth. "If I were you, Dev, I'd take the general's advice. Kill him and be done with it."

Judge looked queerly at Mullins, as if he hadn't heard correctly. "That's against the law, Spanner."

Mullins beckoned him close with a curl of his finger and a crooked smile. "This is Germany, lad. There is no law."

Start at the beginning, Mullins had taught him. So he did.

"What about the murder of this Colonel Janks?"

"I'm afraid General Patton didn't tell you some of the seamier details surrounding the murder. Seems our man Janks was not the straightest of arrows. Word is, he had an operation going on the side. The second man killed, this Czech fellow, Vlassov, was his partner. The two had a sweet deal running: Nazi souvenirs for victuals."

"You're telling me Janks was starving the prisoners to line his own pockets?" Judge supposed he shouldn't be surprised. For the past two years, Manhattan had been overflowing with souvenirs from the Pacific—samurai swords, Japanese flags, family photographs taken from the wallets of the emperor's dead soldiers. It figured that sooner or later wares from Germany would make it back to the States.

"But mum's the word," said Mullins. "This sordid business doesn't make the late Colonel Janks any less the patriot. Our job is to teach Jerry not to mess with his American overseers."

Judge cracked a wry smile. Agree or not, he understood the harmful effect of negative public relations. "You been up to that camp? Easy to sneak out of?"

"Not yet," said Mullins. "But it's not Sing Sing, if that's what you mean. A few of Seyss's comrades are still vacationing there. Brace them, if you have to. Maybe one will have some interesting news for you."

"Bracing" was cop slang for physically intimidating a suspect to make him talk. Basically, it meant beating the crap out of a man until he confessed. Under Mullins's tutelage, Judge had become a master practitioner. But after a few years, he'd sworn off it. He'd always harbored the quaint notion that a man was innocent until proven guilty, and that brains were more powerful than brawn.

"That's a start, anyway," he said. "What kind of help can you throw my way?"

"Last count we've got twelve teams fanned out over our zone of occupation, at two hundred officers and three hundred enlisted men whose primary mission in life is to hunt down these Nazi bastards. Officially, they're part of CIC—counterintelligence. Only ten were policemen back home and fewer than that speak the lingo. Why do you think I'm so glad to see you?"

Before Judge could offer a sarcastic aside, a short, prim officer bustled into the room. Sporting a pencil-thin mustache, hair slick with brilliantine, he looked like a poor man's Errol Flynn—a little fatter, without the dashing chin and with a right eye that wandered aimlessly.

"Afternoon, Mullins," he said, before turning to Judge and offering a hand. "Hadley Everett, Division G-Two. I coordinate the intelligence ops around here. MIS. CIC. SIS. Glad to have you aboard."

Judge spotted the twin stars pinned to each epaulet and rocketed from his chair to a position of rigid attention. "General Everett. It's a pleasure, sir."

"At ease, Major." Everett eyed him up and down, as if Judge were a bum asking for a dime. "Not many men wangle a transfer from Ike. Impressive. I just hope you're up to the task."

News spread quickly, thought Judge. He couldn't help noticing the oversized ring on Everett's finger. A West Point grad. Ringknockers, they were called. The military's equivalent of a Harvard man—Judge's natural nemesis in the U.S. Attorney's office. Summoning his powers of equanimity, he smiled. "Well, sir, I certainly wouldn't want to disappoint General Eisenhower."

"Good thinking. Still, if you need any help finding your way, don't hesitate to shout."

"Thank you, sir, but I think I can manage."

Judge's work gathering information about Hermann Goering's activities had brought him into contact with members of each of the branches Everett had mentioned. MIS stood for military intelligence, the group responsible for gathering information about the strength and intentions of enemy forces. Their goal was to determine who would attack, where and when. Interrogation of prisoners, behind-the-lines espionage, and photo reconnaissance fell into their bailiwick. Now that the war was over, they were out of a job.

CIC, or counterintelligence, was concerned with the security of American forces in the field. Their mission was to identify all organizations or groups of people among the civilian populations who might be hostile to American forces. In occupied Germany, that meant tracking down war criminals and other Germans targeted for automatic arrest.

SIS stood for signals intelligence—the eavesdroppers and code breakers.

Judge didn't like this showboat telling him what to do, so he went over to the offensive. "I take it Seyss's photo has been wired to all police units around the zone."

"Not all of them, I'm afraid," replied Everett. "Wires are still down in some places and it's an extremely busy time for us. Tallyho and all. But I've been instructed to provide any resources we can muster."

That was double-talk if he'd ever heard it. Only time would tell if Everett was as good as his word. "I'd like to suggest that we dispatch couriers with copies of the photograph to every CIC unit and military police detachment in our zone. We'll start at the army level and work our way down through regiment, division, and so on. Enough copies should be made to give our counterparts in the British, French, and Russian zones."

"You can forget about the Russians," said Mullins. "Ivan doesn't play ball."

"Rather," said Everett, running a finger along his mustache. "Best to steer clear of our Soviet comrades. Go on, then, Major. I'm keen to hear what else you have in mind."

Judge relaxed a notch, happy to see that Everett was receptive to his plan. "Seyss is no different from a criminal on the run. He may be on his home turf but if we get the word out that we're after him, and if we offer some kind of reward, someone, somewhere is going to recognize him. As General Patton pointed out, he was an Olympian. That can work for and against us. On the one hand, a good portion of the population may recognize him. On the other hand, if he's considered a hero, they may be hesitant about turning him over to us. Regardless, we get the word out that we're serious about catching this bastard."

"Oh, we're serious, boy-o," chimed in Mullins, and Judge knew lack of support from that quarter wouldn't be a problem.

He continued. "Let's put the picture on the front page of *Stars and Stripes*, *Yank* and every German-language newspaper that's being printed right now. How much can we offer as a reward?"

Everett rubbed his chin, one eye on Mullins, the other drilling a hole in the floor. "What do you think would do the trick, Colonel?"

"Five hundred would do nicely."

"One problem," Everett countered. "Germans aren't allowed to hold our currency. I'd say give them cigarettes but that would make us appear to be condoning the black market."

"Five hundred's too much," said Judge. "Everybody and his uncle will be saying he's seen Seyss. Make it a hundred bucks' worth of goods at the local PX."

"Done," said Everett.

"What's the status of the local constabulary?" asked Judge. "Any help in getting the word out?"

"It varies town by town," responded Mullins, "but don't expect much. Nearly every policeman was a Nazi. The men who've taken their place are hardly your Eliot Nesses."

"Part of the glories of denazification, Major," explained Everett, who'd taken up perch in the doorway on his way out of Mullins's office. "All the qualified men we need to rebuild this damned country are off-limits. Nazis one and all. We're left with the dregs."

Judge frowned. They might be "the dregs," but they were certainly preferable to the alternative.

"Good luck, then, Major," said Everett, gifting him with a lazy salute. "Remember, General Patton wants some good news about Tallyho to tell the president when he arrives in Berlin next week. I'm sure he'd enjoy informing him that Seyss is under arrest. Or dead. I do hope seven days is sufficient."

It wasn't, but Judge didn't have a say in the matter.

"Off your duff, then," said Mullins, slipping on his jacket and making a beeline for the hallway. "I'll show you to the armory, pick you out a nice forty-five like we carried back home in the mighty two-zero. Your office is downstairs. You have three peckerheads all your own to boss around. We wouldn't want Ike to think we're not helping you to our utmost."

There it was again, the edge to his courtesy.

"And my driver?" Judge asked, following close behind. "I'd like to get out to Lindenstrasse this afternoon."

"Coming tomorrow morning at six. As I recall, you're an early riser."

"Tomorrow?" Judge swore under his breath. His seven days had been cut to six.

Mullins shot him a nasty glance over his shoulder. "I'll hear no complaints, thank you very much. It's no easy task finding someone who knows his way around this part of the country on such short notice. Besides, you should be pleased. Your chauffeur's got himself a Silver Star. We got you a hero to make sure you don't get into any trouble."

Judge gritted his teeth and picked up his pace. You had to run if you wanted to keep up with Spanner Mullins.

8

ERICH SEYSS WAS A CONNOISSEUR of destruction. He had only to hear a shell's whistle to know its caliber, to catch a rifle's report to guess its bore, to lay eyes on a ruin and know who and what had devastated it. Staring at the ravaged facade of a three-story building in a squalid, bombed-out district of south Munich, therefore, he needed only a few seconds to recreate the action that had rendered it a teetering, gutless wreck. Sustained machine-gun fire had chiseled a thousand pocks into the building. Fire from a phosphorous grenade had garlanded the windows with wreaths of impregnable soot. Any fool could see where the tank had rammed through the bottom floor, leaving the house lopsided and in need of a crutch.

Seyss imagined the American troops scrambling up the road, each squad providing covering fire for the next, as slowly, inexorably, they took up position around the house. He could hear the tap-tap-tapping of small arms, the thudding of the machine gun, the muffled roar of the grenades, and above them all, the screams of the wounded. City fighting was slow, sweaty, and unimaginably loud. The mere recollection left his mouth dry and sticky. Sometime during the pitched battle, an artillery piece had been brought to bear. A 75-mm Howitzer, by the size of the hole rent in the wall high on the second story. That was the end, of course. The boys defending the house would have had no choice but to give it up and move down the road to the next parcel of land worth dying for. One more piece of Germany swallowed by the relentless green tide.

Seyss poked his head round the stack of empty ammo crates that for the last twenty minutes had served as his blind, glancing a last time up and down the street. Satisfied that no unfriendly eyes were watching the building, he crossed the road and jogged up the front path, neatly threading his way through a field of debris. He paused by the entry long enough to read the address inscribed on a soot-encrusted brass plaque. Twenty-one Lindenstrasse. He offered an unfeeling smile. Home.

Hurrying inside, he made a quick tour of the ground floor, through the salon, the living room, the kitchen. His eyes scanned what floor remained for boot prints, cigarette butts, any sign of a recent visit. He saw nothing to alarm him. At times, he was forced to tiptoe across the coarse spars that had supported the flooring. Hearing a strange flutter, he froze and glanced up. Through the torn floorboards, he glimpsed the ceiling of his bedroom three stories above him. The tail of his curtains gently slapped the wall, then fell back.

Twenty years had passed since he'd lived at Lindenstrasse. At the age of eight, he'd been sent away to school, first to the state military barracks at Brunswick, then to the SS Academy at Bad Toelz. Home had always been simply a way station between postings. If he'd expected an onslaught of nostalgia, he was mistaken. His only sadness was at the condition of the house itself. Nearly all the flooring had been torn out, probably to use as firewood. It went without saying that the furniture, paintings, carpets, and assorted bric-a-brac that had made up his home was gone. Even the wallpaper had been rudely torn off. The house was nothing but a husk.

"Father?" he called, sotto voce. "I'm home."

His whisper died inside the barren shell and he laughed silently. He had no idea where his father might be, nor did he care. Six months had passed since he'd last seen him, a lunchtime visit on his way to the Austro-Hungarian border. There he'd sat, Otto Seyss, gray and paunchy, proud holder of National Socialist party number 835, one of the oldest of the *alte kämpfer*, loudly proclaiming over his ersatz coffee and ersatz sausage that the retreat of the German Army on all fronts was a ruse. *A ruse!* And that, any day now, Hitler would unleash his secret weapons under construction at the rocket laboratories at Peenemünde and the war would be over—*snap!*—like that. The Allies forced to surrender, the Russians driven back to Stalingrad, the German Army once again victorious, with all Europe its prize. Seyss had branded his father's talk of secret weapons a sham, arguing that the war had been over for two years already, and that he should get the hell out of Munich as soon as possible if he wanted to survive the coming fight. His father had responded accordingly, calling him a traitor and a coward. The same things he'd called his wife six years earlier when she'd declared herself unwilling to support the tyrant who had shipped her youngest son to a detention camp. Only that time, he'd punctuated his remarks with a vicious right hook that had sent his wife home to Dublin for good with a shattered jaw.

Seyss returned to the front door before venturing upstairs and scanned the road in both directions. Lindenstrasse was deserted. The once-noble town houses had been picked clean and abandoned, the entire neighborhood left to its decaying self. Not a GI or a German was in sight. Reassured, he made his way to the main staircase. Remarkably, it was intact, except for the banister, which was nowhere to be seen. He climbed quickly, taking the stairs two at a time, stopping only when he'd reached the top.

The third floor was composed of three rooms. His parents' bedroom occupied the northern half. The southern half was divided into two rooms for Seyss and his younger brother, Adam. He glanced into Adam's room, imagining a lanky, argumentative boy with a crop of honey-colored hair and his own blue eyes. He stood still for a moment searching for some reminder of his loss, waiting for a sliver of remorse, hoping even, but none came. Adam was just one more casualty of the war. That he had never donned a uniform or picked up a rifle mattered little.

Seyss continued down the hallway and entered his own room. Crossing to the opposite wall, he lowered himself to one knee. A carpet of glass, mortar, and dust an inch deep covered the floor. He cleared a small circle, then hooked his fingers under the heating grate, gave a firm tug, and laid it to one side. Delicately he inserted his hand into the rectangular void. His fingers crept to the right, to the shallow shelf he had carved as a boy to hide his collection of French postcards, sepia-toned photographs of "adventurous" French women. A wall of dirt tickled his fingertips. Confounded, he reached farther into the hole, but froze when he heard the whine of an approaching engine. After a moment, another engine joined it, then another. An entire fucking armored column was advancing down Lindenstrasse!

Seyss slid his hand from the hole and lifted his eyes above the windowsill. Two jeeps and an armored personnel carrier crammed full of troops were a few hundred meters away and closing. Egon had warned him that the Americans would make the search for Janks's murderer a top priority. In light of the extraordinary information he possessed, Seyss had been foolish not to heed the admonition. For three hours last night, Egon had discussed the most intimate details of Terminal: the Allied leaders' meeting place in Potsdam, their daily schedule, proposed security measures, even the addresses in the leafy suburb of Babelsberg where Churchill, Truman, and Stalin would reside during the conference. The intelligence was far better than any soldier could expect and, *if accurate*, had come from the highest levels of the American command. Seyss made it a point to question such things.

Outside, the growl of the motors grew louder. Seyss pressed himself against the wall, darting a glance out the window every few seconds. One hand dropped to his waist, but the Luger he sought wasn't there. His only defense against inquisitive Americans was the *persilschein* folded neatly in his breast pocket. Issued by the occupational government, the document declared that one Sgt. Erwin Hasselbach was free of any ties to the Nazi party and eligible for all manner of work. Signed by a major general in the Third Army, it was what passed for identification these days. The document got its nickname from a laundry detergent called Persil. Hold a *persilschein* and you were clean.

Seyss looked out the window again. Damn! The little procession was continuing along Lindenstrasse as if rolling along a streetcar track. His heart was beating very fast now. He was sweating. Embarking on a mental reconnaissance of his home, he plotted his escape should the soldiers, in fact, be charged with his arrest. Move now and he could make it to the ground floor in time to get out the back. His eyes shot to the exposed vent. What lay inside was imperative for his coming journey. His passport to Potsdam, as it were.

Clenching his fist, he forced himself to wait a second longer. No fugitive in his right mind would return to his home. It was the first place any policeman would look. Ergo, no policeman would think he'd be stupid enough to go there. Ergo, no policeman would waste his time checking the place, especially once they knew that his home was situated in a suburb of Munich that had been razed from the map.

Daring another look, Seyss noted that the vehicles showed no sign of slowing. If anything, they were moving faster. One by one, they rumbled past, leaving only spirals of dust in their wake. He wanted to laugh. He always did when he got out of a tight scrape.

Returning to the floor, he delved his arm into the heating vent. This time he reached in as far as he could, meeting the curtain of dirt and pushing through it. His fingers touched a blunt metallic object. Taking hold, he worked it brusquely through the earthen shaft until it passed through the rectangular opening and sat on the floor by his feet.

The sterling silver box was the size and width of a hardbound book. Embossed on its cover were twin bolts of lightning, in fact, ancient runes that denoted the SS or Schutzstaffel, the private army organized by Heinrich Himmler and others in 1923 to act as Adolf Hitler's personal protection squad. Beneath the runes, engraved in a neat cursive script, was Seyss's name. Once the box had held his medals.

Commanding himself to relax, he removed its cover and sorted through the contents, cataloguing each item even as he slipped it into his pockets. One folding buck knife, SS issue, sharpened to a razor's edge. One billfold, contents a thousand Reichsmarks. Two dog tags taken from dead GIs. And finally, wrapped in a sheet of wax paper, a sturdy white card with a black stripe running diagonally across it from top to bottom. Typeset in Cyrillic, not Western, lettering. The government-issue identification of one Colonel Ivan Truchin, late of the Russian NKVD or secret police.

Seyss ran a finger along the card's edges, marveling at its immaculate condition. Few Russian soldiers were issued official pieces of identification. Fewer still managed to keep them in any kind of decent condition. A document issued by the Comintern itself, one bearing the signature of Lavrenti Beria, now that was a rarity, indeed, and spoke to Colonel Truchin's importance to the revolution. Seyss gingerly slid it into his breast pocket. His ticket to Terminal. Nothing else would have brought him back to his house.

But Seyss wasn't quite finished. A last foray into his adolescent hiding place yielded a canvas web belt, black, tattered, unremarkable except for its surprising weight. Around a kilo, if he wasn't mistaken. Cut into the belt were ten oblong pockets. In each rested one hundred grams of gold smelted from the SS private foundry near Frankfurt. The slim ingots had been labeled "nonmonetary" gold because of their lesser purity—.95 versus the Reichsbank's standard of .999. It was difficult and costly to purify gold extracted from candelabras, wedding rings, eyeglasses, watches, dental fillings, and the like. Each ingot bore the imprimatur of the Third Reich: an eagle holding a wreathed swastika in its talons.

Seyss cinched the belt low around his waist, tucking in his shirt over it, then patted himself down to make sure the belt wasn't visible. Egon had provided him with two thousand American dollars, an amount well in excess of his needs. Still, Seyss preferred to be prudent. Egon Bach's intelligence was *spitzenclasse*, but his planning was too meticulous, cut through with the fanciful ambitions and precise timetables of an armchair general.

Seyss was to lead a squad of men into the Soviet zone of occupation, travel two hundred kilometers along the main corridor to Berlin, and pierce the guarded enclave of Potsdam. Former members of Seyss's command had been tracked down and recruited. Good men, all. Contacts had been established along the route of travel—in Heidelberg, Frankfurt, and the German capital itself. He would have access to safe houses, revised intelligence, and most important, Soviet weaponry, transport, and uniforms. Once in Potsdam, however, he would be on his own. He knew the objectives. How he chose to fulfill them was his choice. Only five days remained until the conference began and Egon had made it clear he must act soon afterward. Something about ensuring that the last wishes of a country's leaders not be respected.

The rest, Egon had said, would take care of itself. Dominos, he'd laughed. One falling onto the back of the next.

Reviewing the carefully laid-out plan a final time, Seyss selected those elements that would be of use and discarded the rest. While impressed by Egon's logistics, he was also wary of them. Information flowed two ways. To his mind, the operation was already too big. He worried that Weber or Schnitzel, or one of their cronies among the Circle of Fire, might find the details of such a plan helpful in bartering his freedom from his American overlords. Then, of course, there was Egon, himself. His uneasy arrangement with the Americans left Seyss nervous. Very nervous indeed.

One last item remained inside the box. A photograph of a young couple standing in front of a sparkling fountain. Out of habit, he turned it over to read the date and place inscribed, though he hardly needed a reminder. September 3, 1938. Nuremberg. God, he looked magnificent, his uniform just so, his jackboots buffed to a high polish. So did Ingrid. Like the princess she was and would always be. He skimmed his thumb over her face, imagining the feel of her cheek. Staring into her eyes, he saw only the heartache that was to follow—his abrupt good-bye, the canceled nuptials, the failure even to explain himself—and he was accosted by a wave of shame. *Sächlichkeit*, he reminded himself. *You gave her up for the Fatherland.* He'd practically memorized Darré's letter. "The Office of Race and Resettlement therefore denies your application for marriage on grounds of violating section IIC of . . ." He winced at the memory, though his belief in the verdict was undiminished, then continued his recital. ". . . so that the purity of the Fatherland may not be further diluted."

And with that recollection came another, not of Ingrid but of Egon, which given his current circumstance was perhaps more appropriate. The time was November 1940. A gray Friday morning in Munich. The two men were standing in the grand entry hall of Bach Industries headquarters following an armaments production meeting. Egon was raised high on his tiptoes, red in the face, lecturing Seyss with a rude forefinger.

"All you had to do was ask your superior officer for an exception," he railed, "and you would have been permitted to marry Ingrid. She's devastated, Erich. What is one-eighth, anyhow? She's a Bach, damn it. The Führer has seen the family tree worked up by RuSHA. You know yourself he overlooks this type of thing when it's *crucial* to the Fatherland. I'll ask him myself for an exception. He'll only be too happy to oblige."

Angered by Egon's transparent artifice, Seyss managed a curt "No, thank you." Egon was arguing on behalf of the family *konzern*, not Ingrid. Somehow he thought an alliance with the "White Lion" might save the firm from future difficulties. Rubbish! Whether Seyss might obtain an exception was beside the point. It was a question of principle. An officer did not knowingly harm his own country. Blood was blood, and any foreign strain beyond an eighth was deemed to tarnish the country's bloodstock. It was all there in the Nuremberg decrees.

"You're a coward, Erich," Egon spat, after a minute. "You're much too afraid of the state you serve. I admire your devotion, but there comes a moment when a man stands up for what is his. If you loved Ingrid, you'd be married today."

And then something inside of Seyss broke. One minute he was standing at perfect attention, the next he was whipping Egon across the face with his leather gloves, sending his glasses flying, forcing him to a knee. "Shut up!" he railed. "Shut up! What do you know about courage or sacrifice? You, little Egon Bach, who fights his war from a quilted leather chair and a mahogany desk? You are a Jew, understand. Not a German. *A Jew.* You have no right to judge me."

And saying the words he finally believed them. Egon was a Jew. And so was Ingrid.

"I'm sorry, Erich. I'm sorry. Calm down, damn it!"

Seyss redirected his arm in midflight, slapping the gloves against his thigh instead of Egon's simpering face. The lapse of self-control was regrettable, a sign that his heart was not yet wholly subjugated to his Führer's will. Pulling the soft black leather tightly over each hand, he breathed easier. Egon's glasses lay next to his boots. Seyss bent, polished them with a handkerchief, and handed them to his newest enemy. "Next time, think before you talk."

Nearly five years later, he hadn't forgotten the incident or the stare of unvarnished hatred that had greeted his parting words. And neither had Egon. He would bet on it.

Giving a wistful nod, Seyss slid the photograph into his breast pocket behind Colonel Truchin's identification. The room had grown warm and stuffy. A fly zigged and zagged through the air, its incessant buzz a drill in his ear. He replaced the cover and returned the box to its hiding place. He began to feel antsy. The railway station was a good hour's walk and he didn't want to miss his train. His *persilschein* was good for a one-way ticket home, listed for purposes of the mission as Heidelberg. Yes, he decided, he must leave now. Kneeling, he fitted the heating grate into place. And as his fingers pressed the metal into the floor, he experienced an odd sensation on the back of his neck, rather like a feather tickling the base of his scalp.

Get out, a familiar voice whispered. *You've been here too long.*

He was at the window in a second, venturing a lightning glance down the street. No cars approached. No one was visible. He turned his ear into the wind, listening. Nothing. He breathed easier, happy that this time his instinct had misled him.

Then he heard it.

A lone motor trawling down Lindenstrasse.

And he froze.

CHAPTER

9

DEVLIN JUDGE EMERGED FROM THE bachelor officers' quarters at 6:00 A.M., eager to begin his search for Erich Seyss. The air was cool and damp, the dawn mist rapidly burning off to reveal a cloudless sky. Birds chirped everywhere in the verdant canopy that shaded the streets of Bad Toelz.

A lone jeep was parked at the curb. Seeing Judge, a lean, compact soldier jumped from behind the driver's wheel and brought himself to attention. "Morning, Major," he called. "First Sergeant Darren C. Honey at your service."

Judge returned the salute. "I needed you yesterday, Sergeant. Where were you?"

"I apologize," said Honey. "Roads in this country are all crapped out. It was all I could do to get here last night. Colonel Mullins personally brought me up-to-date on the case."

"Did he?" Judge fended off a smirk. Instead of sending Honey to him, Mullins had briefed him himself. He wanted there to be no question who was in charge of the investigation. "So I take it you know who we're looking for and why?"

"Yes, sir. And if I might take this moment, I'd like to offer my condolences. I'm sorry about your brother."

Judge dismissed the remark with a grateful smile. "So, Sergeant, did you volunteer for this snipe hunt or did Mullins shanghai you into it?"

"Volunteered, sir." Honey's face darkened as if his integrity had been impugned, and he puffed out his chest that much more because of it. "Word came down General Patton needed help tracking down a fugitive. That kind of work is right up our alley. Thirty-second CIC in Augsburg, that is. We call ourselves Nazi hunters. It's our mission to find the krauts who haven't turned themselves in yet. This is the first chance we've had to go after one who killed some of our boys."

Judge smiled at his escort's unvarnished enthusiasm, thinking the little guy would fit in pretty good on a stoop on Atlantic Avenue. Even with his helmet, Honey was shorter by a head. He had a card sharp's blue eyes and a smile as wide as his southern accent. At first glance he looked the model soldier. Eisenhower jacket buttoned snugly over a khaki shirt and tie, olive drab trousers bloused neatly into polished jump boots. But his .45-caliber side arm was all cowboy, slung low on the hip and ready for the quick draw.

Judge threw his briefcase into the back of the jeep, then pulled a slip of paper from his pocket. "Twenty-one Lindenstrasse, know where it is?"

"Spent four months in this part of the country. Guess I'd better." Honey waved away the paper, circling the jeep and hopping in behind the wheel. "That part of town got hit up and down. B-17s took out a rail yard near there and infantry tore it up taking the city."

"So I've been told, but that's where Seyss grew up. I'm hoping we can talk to a neighbor, get a feel for what kind of guy he is. Who knows? Maybe we'll get lucky and find him sleeping in his old bed."

"Sooner find a rooster warming an egg," cracked Honey, tipping back his helmet as if it were his Sunday Stetson. "And if you'll pardon me, I can tell you what kind of guy Seyss is already. Major in the Waffen-SS. Made it through six years of the war in one piece. He's a survivor, sir. He won't go near the place. Dollar to a dime, he's in Italy as we speak."

Judge climbed in beside the driver, fixing him with a no-nonsense stare. If you believed that, you wouldn't have volunteered. "Now, let's get the hell out of here."

Honey fired the engine and brought the jeep round in a wide arc, accelerating down the narrow streets and out of town. Settling back, Judge recognized a curious tingling in the hollow of his gut. The spark of a new case. The thrill of not knowing what lay around the corner. The petty excitement he'd given up when he'd left the force. All of these were heightened by his presence in the enemy's homeland, and for a few minutes he was genuinely happy. But soon, those sentiments faded, dragged down by the leaden weight hanging from his web belt. He glanced at the .45-caliber Colt Commander snuggled in its scarred leather holster. Nine bullets in the cartridge and one in the snout. When expecting action, release the safety and cock the hammer. That way you don't have to put your full weight on the trigger to fire the first shot. It was all coming back now.

"Looks like you've been overseas a long time," he said, eyeing the twin rows of multicolored ribbons that adorned Honey's chest.

" 'Bout my whole life," answered Honey. "I shipped out in November of '42. Operation Torch—the landings in North Africa. Hitched a ride to Sicily, then got put ashore at Anzio. Tell you the truth, I'm ready to get home."

"Where's that?"

"Place you've never heard of. Harlingen, Texas. Queen of the Rio Grande Valley."

"You're right. Never heard of it. But what do I know? I'm from New York City."

"Yes, sir," said Honey, shooting him his best shit-eating grin. "Kind of shows."

Judge accepted the rebuke with a laugh, then returned his eye to a sturdy angle iron rising perpendicularly from the center of the front bumper. For the last fifteen minutes, he'd been trying to figure out what the devil it was. Stymied, he pointed to it and asked Honey for an explanation.

"Werewolves," the Texan answered. "Krauts who don't want to surrender. They've taken to stringing wire across the roads at night. If you're on a motorcycle or riding in one of these jeeps with your windshield down a string of concertina can take your head right off. They haven't killed anyone yet, but they've blinded a couple and given a few more a decent haircut. That iron cuts the wire nicely."

Judge felt an anxious twinge in his gut. "Are there many of them?"

"Werewolves?" Honey shrugged and his hand brushed against the butt of his pistol. "Rumor is there might be a horde of them holed up in the mountains south of here. I doubt it myself. Tell you the truth, most krauts are as tired of this whole damned mess as we are. Still, every once in a while we find one who doesn't want to come in of his own volition."

"Sounds dangerous," he said.

Honey shrugged off the suggestion. "These days, it isn't the Nazis who're so bad. It's the wives or girlfriends who're protecting them. Just last week, a pretty young fräulein came after me with a pitchfork." He nodded his head for emphasis. "She wasn't joking. No, sir."

A distinctive ribbon of red, white, and blue stood out among the fruit salad on Honey's chest. Judge recognized it as the Silver Star Mullins had mentioned, a citation given for extraordinary gallantry in combat. Shifting his gaze, he traded the varied hues of Honey's ribbons for the gray expanse of road stretching in front of them. He was in Germany now, on occupied soil in another man's country. Less than two months ago, over 6 million German soldiers had been ordered to lay down their arms. It made sense that a few were upset at no longer being the vaunted "supermen" that Hitler loved to crow about.

For a while, the two men rode in silence. Honey kept his eyes pinned to the road, driving the jeep as if they were in a cross-country rally: powering into turns, braking at the last moment, accelerating on the straightaway. Judge clamped one hand to the dashboard and the other to his seat for fear he'd be bounced out of the vehicle. Seeing the speedometer reach sixty, he swallowed hard. He'd never enjoyed driving, and, in fact, didn't even carry a license. Growing up, he'd been too poor to own a car. Nowadays he was too busy. To ease his anxiety, he reviewed the measures he'd put into effect the previous afternoon to bring about the rapid apprehension of Erich Siegfried Seyss.

First, he'd dispatched motorcycle couriers to the headquarters of the six U.S. Army groups stationed inside the American zone of occupation in Germany. Each courier carried a photograph of Erich Seyss and a letter signed by General George S. Patton stating his unequivocal desire that Seyss be captured. Instructions were given to copy the photograph and distribute it to all elements of military intelligence, as well as to every unit of military police down to platoon level.

Next, he'd had the same picture transmitted via wire to the editorial offices of *Stars and Stripes* in Paris and Rome, *Yank* in London, and the four largest German-language newspapers—*Die Mitteilungen*, the *Frankfurter Presse*, the *Hessiche Post* and the *Kölnischer Kurier*—which together boasted a circulation of 3 million copies. In twenty-four hours, every GI from Sicily to Stockholm would wake up with a picture of the White Lion on the front page of his favorite paper. And on Sunday, when the German papers appeared, so would a large number of Erich Seyss's compatriots.

But Judge hadn't stopped there. He'd spent an hour pleading his case to Radio Luxembourg, an American controlled pan-European station, until they'd agreed to broadcast a description of Seyss and a rundown of his crimes during their nightly four-hour German-language program. Radio Berlin, controlled by Stalin's forces, was less amenable.

Finally, he'd arranged for jeeps mounted with sixteen-inch loudspeakers to patrol the sector's largest cities blaring Seyss's name, his description, and most important, the news that a hundred-dollar reward was being offered for information leading to his arrest.

The net had been cast.

The jeep crested a small hill offering an unimpeded vista of the surrounding countryside. Fields of saffron hugged both sides of the road, seas of blazing yellow swaying in a gentle breeze. Beyond them, brown hillocks furrowed for cultivation rolled toward the horizon. The burnt carcass of a Tiger tank rested like a desecrated shrine atop a nearby rise. A hundred yards away slouched its target: a barn holed by shell fire, its shingled roof hanging in tatters. Stranger than the scenery, though, was the rancid smell that queered the warm wind. Judge had expected Germany to smell more like gunsmoke than sour milk.

A few minutes later, the jeep rolled into the outskirts of Munich. What from above had looked like a dead city was, in fact, very much alive. On every corner, American military police supervised lines of gray-uniformed POWs clearing debris from clogged roads. Men and women dressed in little more than rags stumbled over rubble palaces, searching for splintered wood, broken pipes, and cracked bricks—anything that might be salvaged. Their hooded eyes all flashed the same message of hate and resentment, as if defeat were a shameful illness passed on to them by the Americans. Worst, though, was the smell. The sour odor he had noticed in the countryside had blossomed into a ripe, eye-watering stench. He yanked a handkerchief from his pocket and covered his nose, trying hard not to breathe too deeply.

"Better get used to that perfume," said Honey. "We reckon over thirty thousand people are buried under all this . . ." He motioned a hand at the wreckage all around him. "This crap. And summer's just getting started. That stink's going to get worse before it gets better."

Judge remained mute, the sight of so much destruction, so much suffering, robbing him of the ability to speak. Reflexively he clawed at his wristwatch, spinning it round his wrist. He needed a distraction. Anything. He imagined Brewers' Row left a pile of rubble. Schaeffer's, Rheingold's, Pulaski's Biergarten, all razed to the ground. The ill-formed pictures made him sick to his stomach.

"It's okay, Major," said Honey, eyeing him sympathetically. "If it didn't get to you, you wouldn't be human."

Judge sat up straighter, propping a shoe against the chassis. He wanted to ask something dreadfully stupid like "Why?" or "To what end?" He saw Francis dead and frozen in the Belgian mud and his pity vanished. In its place blossomed an all-encompassing hatred of Hitler and Germany and the wretched system that could bring such destruction to pass. "Bastards deserved it."

"That they did," replied Honey. "All the same, it's pretty lousy."

Judge didn't care to meet his driver's earnest gaze. "Just get us to Seyss's house. Twenty-one Lindenstrasse."

HONEY STEERED THE JEEP THROUGH the crowded streets, slowing occasionally to consult the road map spread across his lap. They crossed a bridge, then rumbled past a brick wall fronting a mound of rubble and mortar piled as high as a streetlamp. On the wall was a large poster of a voluptuous woman in a tight dress flashing them a welcoming eye while slapping her behind. The word *Verboten* was stenciled in bold letters across her shapely form.

Honey cocked a thumb at the tempting *fräulein*. "Ike's number-one rule: no fraternizing with the enemy. That's a sixty-five-dollar fine. One week's salary gone, no questions asked. No talking to them, no drinking with them, and certainly, no frattin' with them." He grinned like a naughty teenager. "Of course, you're a married man. No need to explain General Eisenhower's rules to you."

Judge played along with Honey's sarcastic banter. "Don't count me out just yet. This ring is just for show. Keeps the girls at the office honest. I've been divorced going on two years."

"Divorced? Sorry to hear that."

"Don't be. There comes a time when it's best just to break things off. End everyone's suffering. Know what I mean?" He attempted to smile, but felt like he was sucking on a lemon. For some reason, Honey's words roiled him, coming off as condemning instead of conciliatory. Judge gazed combatively to the sky. Somewhere up there, Francis was having a last laugh at his expense.

"An unholy of unholies," he'd taken to saying, while berating his brother from the end of a Jesuit fingertip. It was the argument they'd never resolved. The one issue they could never get around. To Francis Xavier, man and woman, once married, did not divorce. Not when they'd brought a boy into the world. And certainly not when they'd sat together and watched that boy die. Holy bonds, he'd said. Ties that cannot be undone.

Judge stared off at some broken landmark, wishing that a snap of the fingers could rid him of his guilt. Not about the divorce, mind you. What alternative was there when the sight of your spouse brought back every mistake you'd ever made, every sin you'd committed, and the price levied in a young boy's blood to rectify them? When three years had passed since husband and wife shared a smile or a joke, never mind a conjugal bed? No, Judge didn't have a shred of guilt about the divorce.

It was Francis who haunted him.

A hundred times before he'd shipped out, Judge had urged himself to apologize to his older brother. Say fifty Hail Marys. A hundred Our

Fathers. Whatever that all-knowing, self-righteous son of a bitch wanted him to do to make amends. Francis was his only blood relation. What did it matter if Judge prostrated himself before the altar of fraternal obedience? But no, that hadn't been his way. In his universe, Francis was the only person not allowed to win an argument. The only one to whom an apology was impossible.

Judge forced a bluff laugh, even as he cursed himself for being a stubborn ass.

Honey welcomed the smile with visible relief and took up where he left off. "Another thing, Major: Stay away from the black market. Germans aren't allowed to hold U.S. dollars. Their own currency ain't worth a damn so they'll trade just about anything they've got for some cigarettes or stockings." He leaned closer, as if to confide a secret. "And remember, the going rate for a carton of Luckies is fifty bucks."

Judge was getting the idea, all right. Over here, rules didn't count for much. Mullins had said it better. *This is Germany, lad. There is no law.*

Five minutes later, Honey pulled the jeep to the side of the road and pointed at a three-story concrete scarecrow, the last structure left standing on the entire block. "Thar she blows. Number twenty-one Lindenstrasse."

Judge put his hands on the dash and stood, staring hard at the building. It was a typical Wilhelmine affair: steep mansard roof with dormer windows, solid terraces fronting the windows on the second floor, colonnaded entry. Or at least it used to be. The place had taken some thumping. Fire had gutted half of it. One corner was demolished and there were enough holes in the place to make it look like a Swiss cheese.

"Believe it or not, this used to be quite a neighborhood," said Honey. "Not your Sutton Place, but definitely your Upper West Side."

Judge shot Honey an annoyed glance. "I thought you were from Texas?"

"Got a sister in Manhattan. I visited her once."

"Just once?" Judge was beginning to think there was more to Honey and his Silver Star than met the eye. "Well, Sergeant, what do you say? Shall we have a look-see?"

But Honey was already out of the jeep, drawing his pistol and cocking the hammer in a single fluid motion. "I was about to suggest the same thing. If I'm not mistaken, I caught somebody peeking at us from an upstairs window. How much you care to wager it's Mr. Seyss himself?"

Judge jumped to the ground, drawing his pistol and hustling across the street. "Didn't you say something back there about a rooster and eggs?"

"Me?" Honey spun, slowing long enough to offer Judge his already familiar grin. "What the hell do I know about chickens? In Texas we got steers."

And then they were inside the house.

CHAPTER

10

JUDGE FOLLOWED HONEY TOWARD THE house, his stride lengthening to a jog, then a run. He bolted up the steps through the front door, and reaching the foyer, slammed into his driver's back.

"Slow down," cautioned Honey, pointing to the absent flooring. "You don't want to end up down there."

Judge stepped to the edge of the white-tiled foyer. Large bites had been torn from the wooden floor, revealing a latticework of spars none more than six inches across. Here and there, the ceiling of the basement was visible. Mostly, though, he could only see darkness and wonder how far it was to the cellar floor. He cast an ear upward, straining to catch a footfall.

"Go to the back door and don't let anyone by," he ordered Honey, flicking the pistol toward a dim corridor leading to the rear of the house. "Odds are, whoever you saw up there is a squatter, someone looking for a place to stay, maybe scrounge some firewood. Let's talk to him. I doubt it's Seyss, but who knows, maybe he's seen him around, maybe he knew him before the war. Understood?"

Honey nodded enthusiastically, not believing a word. "Got it."

"And Sergeant," Judge added, his voice tighter than expected. "Go easy with that firearm."

"Yessir." Honey offered a smile, but his voice was absent its friendly tone. "But I'll thank you not to tell me how to handle my pistol." Sliding by Judge, he mounted a spar and walked nimbly toward the rear of the house.

Judge followed a second later, finding the going more difficult. The narrow beam looked like a tightrope. Below him, stars of light reflected off puddles dampening the basement floor. He guessed the distance to be twenty feet. A long, hard fall onto concrete. Eyes glued to the spar, arms flung to either side of him, he proceeded, moving faster as his confidence grew. Reaching the stairs, he took off at a devilish clip. A single flight betrayed his poor conditioning. He'd given up cigarettes five years ago, but his lungs felt tired and unfit. Too many all-nighters stoked by coffee, chops, and a bourbon constitutional.

He paused on the first-floor landing to suck down some air and listen for footsteps. Nothing. He stood for a moment, poised to set off, arm cocked, pistol brushing his cheek. Six years after he'd turned in his shield, the gun fit in his palm snug as a preacher's Bible. Hammer cocked, safety off. It was all coming back to him.

Charging up the second flight of stairs, he enjoyed a sudden spurt of adrenaline. This was what he had loved about being a policeman: the cornering of a suspect, the apprehension of a fugitive, the cathartic rush of delivering a guilty soul into the legal system. Too often, though, the arrests didn't translate into convictions. Charges were dropped for lack of evidence. A two-bit hoodlum skipped bail. A lazy prosecutor bungled the case. Judge couldn't stand seeing his work undone, so he became an attorney.

He climbed the final flight of stairs slowly, letting his breath come back to him. A dusky corridor greeted his arrival on the top floor. He picked out a voice humming softly in the room down the hallway to his right. He dropped the .45 to his side, his finger caressing the trigger's smooth slope, the weapon's strangely animate heft promising retribution, if not justice. A masculine form flitted across the doorway, then disappeared from view without glancing in his direction. A silhouette backlit by the morning sun. Strange, thought Judge. He'd pounded up the stairs like a wounded bull elephant. Why wasn't the guy curious who else was in the building?

Abandoning any pretense of stealth, he took the hallway in three long strides and crossed the threshold into a sun-filled room. A harsh morning glare hit him squarely in the eyes, forcing him to squint. A legion of dust stirred in the air. The room reeked of charred wood and mildewed paint.

The man stood at the far wall, a thin strap stretched between his hands, concerned for all the world with measuring a gaping hole sited high between the two windows. He wore baggy gray trousers and a blue workman's coat, a dark rally cap pulled low over his forehead. Horn-rimmed spectacles obscured his eyes. He was still humming.

"*Hände auf dem Kopf,*" Judge shouted. "Hands on your head. Turn around slowly."

The man jumped at the sound of Judge's voice, spinning rapidly, doing as he was told. When he saw the pistol pointed at him, he jumped again. "Please," he blurted. "I'm a friend."

"Walk slowly toward me," said Judge. "Now!" It was the first time he'd spoken German since arriving and the crisp, officious words settled him to his task.

"My name is Licht," the man said, his tremulous voice pitched high. "I am with the city building authority. Bureau Five, Section A. I'm attached to Colonel Allen's office." He smiled weakly, then lifted a hand from his head to gesture at the flaking walls. "The whole thing will have to come down, you know. Fire, shelling . . . Christ, even the joists are kaput. Dry rot, I'd say. Bet the fools living here didn't even know. It will never do for an officers' club."

But Judge wasn't listening. His attention was riveted on the man's face, and his hands, too, lest he make any sudden move.

"Shut up and take off your cap. Drop it to your side."

Licht hesitated a moment before complying. The cap dropped like a rock to the floor, and to Judge's anxious ear, it made about as much noise. A shock of black hair fell across Licht's brow. He brushed it back and stood straighter, venturing a nervous smile. Judge studied his features, careful not to lose eye contact as he drew the photo of Erich Seyss from his breast pocket. Holding it level with the snout of his pistol, he compared one face to the other. The animal who had ordered his brother's death, to the frightened building inspector standing ten feet away.

Chin. Lips. Nose. All were more or less the same, but he couldn't be sure.

"Now your glasses. Take them off and get away from the window."

Licht took a defiant step forward, fear hardening to obduracy. "I won't go anywhere until you put that gun down. I've already told you who I am. If you'd like to see my papers, I'll be happy to oblige. The war's been over two months. It is time for this nonsense to stop." And as he spoke an interesting thing occurred. The sun crept an inch higher on the yardarm and a shaft of light caught Mr. Licht of the Munich Building Authority, Bureau Five, Section A, squarely in the face, piercing the lenses of his spectacles and firing the luminous blue eyes poised behind them.

Judge had never before seen eyes that color.

"Please take off your glasses," he repeated.

His voice was calm, quiet even, but his heart was racing at full throttle. Slipping the photo of Seyss into his pocket, he took a step to the rear, wanting to guard a safe distance between them. He had him. Sturmbannführer Erich Siegfried Seyss. Germany's White Lion. Francis Xavier Judge's killer.

As Judge stared at this man, a feeling unlike anything he'd experienced took possession of him. His neck flushed, his stomach hardened, and he had an urgent need to blink very rapidly, not to drive away tears but to ease the crescendo of hatred bursting in his ears. He was no longer looking at Licht, the building inspector, but at Seyss, the SS major who enjoyed burying his boot in the back of wounded Americans as a prelude to firing a bullet into their brains.

"Take off your glasses!" he shouted, his calm a distant memory.

Seyss shrugged, then removed the black frames, folding them and sliding them into his jacket. "If you wish."

Judge stared into his face. He had no illusions about getting some measure of the man, of fathoming even for an instant what powered this unfeeling beast. He only wanted to read his expression when he emptied his entire clip into his gut and left a string of bullet holes across his torso mimicking the wounds that had killed Francis.

"Major Judge, everything hunky-dory up there?"

Honey's voice, vaulting from the ground floor, surprised him. Seyss's eyes flicked toward the hallway and Judge gripped the pistol harder, expecting the SS man to leap at him.

Yes, you murderous bastard, there are two of us. This is the end of the line.

But Seyss did not move. If anything, he looked more relaxed than before, as if Honey were exactly the person he'd been waiting for. Inside, though, Judge knew he was sweating.

Lowering the pistol so that the barrel was aimed at Seyss's chest, he ratcheted his finger a notch. The trigger passed its first safety, and in the silence that had enveloped the room, the click was audible. His arm tensed reflexively, muscles readying to arrest the pistol's violent kick. He heard Mullins whispering to him conspiratorially, "This is Germany, lad. There isn't any law." Patton barking, "Don't bring me the sonuvabitch. Just kill him."

No, Judge told himself. He would not follow that route. Down there lies darkness. Down there lies the past. Interrogation rooms sour with stale sweat and spilled blood. Shattered cheekbones and broken noses that mapped the swiftest route to the truth. His own unsleeping history.

And suddenly, the tide of anger crested, reason asserting itself over revenge.

"Honey," he shouted over his shoulder. "Get up here on the double. We've got our man." Then speaking to Seyss in German: "You're very good, Seyss. But I'm afraid that wasn't a measuring tape you were using, it was your belt. You're under a—"

Seyss moved before the last word had left his mouth, springing at him as if from a starting block. Judge pulled the trigger, but Seyss was already upon him, hand locked on the gun's snout, using his leverage to wrestle it from his grip. The gun went off, once, twice, missing its mark high and wide, the roar splintering the large room. A fist pummeled his gut and Judge doubled over, losing hold of the gun, hearing it clatter to the floor. He threw out his left arm to push Seyss away, bringing his right hand up for his chin, but the German was no longer there. A lightning hand flashed under the punch, fastening on to his tunic. Seyss ducked low, spun a half circle and flipped him over his shoulder. Judge landed on his back with a grunt and a moment later, Seyss was on top of him, knee pinning him to the ground, grinning wildly. He scooped up the pistol with his right hand and laid the barrel squarely against his forehead.

"What the hell's going on up there?" shouted Honey. "Major, you okay? Answer back!"

Seyss placed a finger on Judge's lips and whispered, "Say yes."

"*Gehen Sie zum Teufel*. Go to hell."

"Everything is fine," called Seyss, his English flawless, the accent if anything too flat. "Stay put and we'll be down in a second."

He pressed the gun harder against his forehead and Judge could see he was deciding whether or not to kill him. It would be a rash decision. Seyss needed him to get out of the house. Otherwise, he'd be locked in a shoot-out with Honey. Suddenly the pressure abated and Seyss lifted him to his feet. He was very strong for a lithe man.

"Now, Major Judge, you are going to accompany me down the stairs. Be nice and you'll go home to see your lovely wife in America."

Seyss pushed Judge down the hall, holding him in check with a ferocious arm lock. Judge considered trying to warn Honey but abandoned the notion. He had to assume that Seyss hadn't fooled him. It was time to see what that Silver Star was worth.

The two men made a slow descent down the stairs. When they'd reached the second-floor landing, Seyss shoved Judge against the wall and clamped a hand over his mouth. Sliding the pistol from his prisoner, he pointed it downward and fired a bullet through the floor. Before Judge could move a muscle, the pistol was back in the ribs. Seyss kept his eyes on the stairs below as the bullet's report faded. His ruse to draw Honey out failed. Not a sound came from the ground floor. No one appeared.

The two men continued down the stairs.

"So you know for the next time," Seyss said amicably, "should one of us German bastards resist, the proper procedure is to shoot him."

"I'll keep that in mind," said Judge. "Give me my gun. We'll go back upstairs and do it over again. I don't usually make the same mistake twice."

"I'm sure you don't, though I must say your uniform is a little light on ribbons. New to the game, are you? If I hadn't heard you speak English, I would have taken you for a German. Or are you? Perhaps a Jew smart enough to have left before the war?"

They descended another step.

"My mother came from Berlin," he answered. "From Wedding."

Judge kept his eyes in front of him, measuring where he might tumble to give Honey a clear line of fire, or if he should simply sacrifice himself and jump. It would be easy enough. There was no banister to prevent his fall. If he had any assurance Honey would kill Seyss, he wouldn't think twice about it.

"Yes, Wedding. Of course. I should have picked up the accent. Home to the working classes. Hotbed of communism. If you don't mind my saying, your uniform is a tad natty for a son of the revolution. What were you back on civvy street?"

Another step down.

"An attorney."

"Hmm," Seyss intoned, as if impressed. "Does your army normally send attorneys after fugitives, or is that a privilege reserved solely for war criminals?"

Judge hated him the more for having a sense of humor. "Believe it or not, I used to be a policeman. Guess I'm a little rusty."

"You'll find no complaint from me." Seyss moved the snout of the gun to Judge's jaw and turned his face so he could better see him. "Now that you mention it, you look like a copper. Jaw a little too square, nose a shade too curious. You would've done well in the Gestapo. They only use their weapons once their prisoners are in custody."

"Oh? That sounds like standard SS training. Or was Malmedy a special occasion?"

Seyss smirked and shook his head, not answering, and Judge regretted not killing him when he'd had the chance.

They had reached the first floor. Seyss hustled Judge to the head of the stairs, then just as quickly backed him up, thrusting his head into the corridor behind him, looking left, then right. There was still no sign of Honey and Judge began to grow nervous wondering just what the feisty Texan had in mind. The rotting crossbeams that latticed the ground floor presented a decided problem. Once down the final flight of stairs,

Seyss would have to give up his hostage. Two men couldn't tiptoe across the beams together. He hoped Honey realized the same thing. Now was the time for him to act, to bargain, to take a damn shot. Who cared if he hit Judge, at least he'd have an open target.

Abruptly Seyss forced him to the edge of the landing, whispering in his ear, "I'm sorry, Major, but your services are no longer required. It has been a pleasure. Bon voyage." And with that he pushed his hostage off the stairs.

Judge stumbled into the void, turning as he fell, throwing out an arm toward Seyss. One hand brushed the German's trousers, catching the cut of his pocket, tearing it while tugging Seyss dangerously close to the edge. Seyss dropped to a knee, butting his palm to the wooden landing to arrest his forward momentum. His pants ripped and a pair of dog tags tumbled free. But Judge's flailing was in vain. He hung for an instant, paralyzed, then dropped to the basement.

He never made it.

With a sickening thud, he struck an exposed spar, the wind leaving him in a great rush. He'd landed in a sitting position and a fraction of a second later, his momentum plunged him down. Slipping off the beam, he threw his arms around the splintered spar and arrested his flight.

Yet, even as he fell, Honey showed himself. Judge caught his shadow peeking around the salon wall, heard his voice yelling "Halt!" Then a dozen gunshots exploded inside the stairwell. Seyss had gotten his shoot-out, all right. Shards of plaster burst from the wall and fluttered onto Judge's head. Five seconds later the gunfire had subsided.

Honey called, "You okay?"

Hanging from the crossbeam, Judge answered, "Forget about me. Go get that sonuvabitch. Now!"

The sound of Honey's boots thumping up the stairs was his only response.

Gasping for breath, he dug his nails into the soft wood and attempted to swing his legs up to the beam. A thousand needles jabbed his abdomen, stopping his motion midway and threatening his grip on the beam. Grunting, he dropped his legs and adjusted his hands, interlocking his fingers. His muscles quickly caught fire. A glance below provided little reassurance. He had been wrong about its being twenty feet to the basement floor. It was twenty-five at least. He'd be lucky to survive with two broken legs.

And the thought of the failure to capture Seyss, a defeat crowned not only by his own incompetence but by his death or injury, spurred in Judge a sudden, tireless fury. Crying out, he gave his legs a mighty swing and brought an ankle over the beam. Another grunt and he'd pulled himself flat onto the spar.

Honey appeared at the top of the steps a moment later. Seeing Judge, he ran down the stairs and helped him off the beam and into the foyer.

"He's gone. Dropped out the back window."

Judge eyed him through a veil of frustration and self-loathing. "Why didn't you go after him?"

"Didn't think I could catch him, if you want to know." Honey shot him a downcast look, as if disappointed at Judge's lack of gratitude. "Besides, you take care of your own first. There'll be another day."

"Yes, there will."

Judge limped out the front door of Lindenstrasse 21, staring into the blue German sky. A spasm fired in his back, and, grimacing, he swore to do everything within his power to haul in Erich Siegfried Seyss.

CHAPTER

11

INGRID BACH WOKE TO THE SHARP report of rifle fire cascading down the valley. Opening her eyes, she stared at the ceiling and waited for the next shot. *Crack!* She flinched. There passed a comma of silence, raw and empty, then the gun's echo whistled over the treetops and departed the meadow. *Damn the Americans*, she thought to herself. *Will they ever stop hunting my precious chamois?* The question dissolved like a wisp of smoke. They would stop when they left the country. Not before.

Ingrid lay still for a few seconds longer, treasuring the last calm she would have until late that evening, then rose from her bed and padded to the window. Last night's forecast had called for cloudy skies and showers. People used to joke that the only thing more inaccurate than the weather forecast was a bulletin from the front. Drawing the curtains, she peered from the window. The sky was frosted blue, without a single cloud. Forecasting hadn't improved, but at least the war was over.

Opening the window, she thrust her head into the morning sun. The air was crisp and breezy, a tinge of warmth hiding deep in its folds. The hooded peaks of the Furka and the Wasserhorn loomed close above her shoulder, silently guarding the entrance to a narrow valley that in summer exploded in a palette of greens and in winter hid under a blanket of snow. One hundred yards from her window curved the shore of a crystal blue lake, its surface scalloped by a freshening wind. Her perfectionist's eye caught a streak of exposed wood on the gazebo in Agnes' Meadow where she had been married. She would dig up a can of paint in the garage and touch up the eaves, first thing.

Having thus begun her list of items to accomplish during the day, Ingrid closed the window and walked purposefully to her bathroom where she made her toilette. A hundred strokes of her mother's sterling hairbrush, a cold-water rinse for her face and neck, then a few dabs of makeup. She was disappointed to see her favorite lipstick, Guerlain's *Passion de la Nuit*, was nearly exhausted. The rouge and mascara her husband had spirited from Paris had run out months ago.

Once the lodge had been full of luxuries from all corners of the ever-expanding Reich: Russian furs, Danish hams, Polish vodka, and, of course, French fashions—dresses, scarves, cosmetics. All of it had gone to keep the household running.

Finished applying her lipstick, she moved closer to the mirror to give herself a final looking over. As usual, she was overwhelmed by her plain appearance. Her eyes were a common blue, neither pale nor particularly colorful. Her nose was a shade long, dignified with a barely perceptible cleft at its tip. "Patrician," her father had called it and it was his greatest compliment. The summer sun had sprinkled her cheeks with freckles. Her one mystery and sole asset were her lips, which were full and well formed and naturally crimson. Not at all typical for a woman of Aryan extraction, she'd been informed by a professor of eugenics from Humboldt University, just before he tried to kiss her. What was it, then, that men had found so attractive? Certainly not her hair. Cut to drape her brow and fall to her shoulders, it was as thick and straight as a sheaf of summer wheat, but unfortunately hardly its color. Once kept a striking platinum blond by Munich's finest coiffeurs, it had gone a tepid yellow, her horrid brown roots all too apparent. One day soon she would muster her courage and do battle with the bottle of peroxide in the medicine cabinet.

Ingrid dressed quickly, slipping into a black wool dress that had belonged to one of the maids. She would have preferred beige slacks, a burgundy cashmere sweater, and a silk foulard at her neck, but grease, paint, and sweat did little to enhance the creations of Chanel and

Ballenciaga. Leaving her bedroom, she descended the main staircase to the great hall. The vast chamber was as quiet as the grave, her every footstep echoing lugubriously off the vaulted ceiling and paneled walls.

In better times, Sonnenbrücke had boasted a staff of ten housemaids and four manservants, not including the chef. Ingrid could see them now: Sophie dusting the family portraits; Genevieve polishing the silver; Herr Liebgott working his magic in the kitchen. All but one had left when the war ended. The Bachs were pariahs. Living reminders of Germany's bloody fall from grace. Only Herbert, the family's longest-serving retainer and majordomo, remained. At eighty, he had nowhere else to go. These days, Ingrid relied on herself to keep Sonnenbrücke in order.

Reaching the ground floor, she continued across the hall and passed through the butler's panty into the kitchen. Three months ago, she would have found it abuzz with activity, even at this early hour—a smoked stag hanging from a curing hook; copper kettles boiling with freshly made spätzle; mountains of red cabbage piled on the cutting board. This morning, the cavernous room was empty save for an elderly man, head in hand, seated on a stool next to the sink.

"Herbert?" she called. "What is the matter?"

The leonine gray head lifted. *"Kein mehr Brot,"* responded Herbert Kretschmar. "No more bread." Despite the Bach family's precipitous change in circumstance, he still wore the traditional black frock coat and striped flannel trousers of a professional butler. "What will we serve Master Pauli for breakfast?"

Ingrid rushed to the bread larder. A smattering of crumbs dusted the cutting board. "But the ration was for three loaves."

"Last week we received only two. We are four mouths, even if your father does not eat so much. I should have foreseen the circumstances. Forgive me."

Ingrid touched his shoulder. "No, Herbert, it's my fault. I should have traded for more. We only have two days until we can draw our next rations. We will make do." She injected a cheery lilt into her voice. "Come, let's fry our little angel a sausage for breakfast. We'll tell him it's a special treat."

Opening the meat locker, she found a last sausage dangling from a small hook. She laid it on the counter and cut it into six slices. From the vegetable nook, she retrieved a potato and set it in a pot of water to boil. A half cup of homemade blackberry jam remained. There was still some flour, a bowl of cherries and a few apples. They would have enough for today. But what about tomorrow? What if the rations continued to come up short? They couldn't go on eating potatoes forever. Throwing a dash of salt into the pot, she felt her hands cramp with fear.

Keep moving, an urgent voice counseled. *Keep moving and your problems will stay behind you.*

Heeding the advice, she concerned herself with putting breakfast on the table. But even the busiest hands couldn't divert her mind from its persistent nagging. Providing for the house had been Papa's province, then her husband's. She'd had little experience handling such things. With embarrassing acuity, she remembered her last trip to their banker, Herr Notnagel in Munich. "I'm so sorry, Frau Gräfin," he had said with suffocating kindness, "but neither you nor your father any longer possesses the least right to your family accounts. Everything has been placed in your brother's name." The Lex Bach. A decree from the Führer deeding all assets of Bach Industries to her only surviving brother, Egon. Effective August 2, 1944. Egon's reward for informing Adolf Hitler about her father's vocal dissatisfaction with the continued prosecution of the war.

She'd been left with Sonnenbrücke, the family's hunting lodge tucked away in the southeastern corner of the country, where she'd lived since Allied bombers had begun encroaching on the Reich's frontiers. It was more hotel than home: twenty guest suites and ten bedrooms all with private baths, two dining halls, a grand ballroom, winter garden, countless salons, six staircases, a free standing smokehouse and seven dumb waiters. All of it done up to look like one of mad King Ludwig's ridiculous castles.

She drained the copper pot and cut the potato in two, enough for Herbert and Pauli. She was not hungry. Setting the table, she inventoried what remained within the lodge that she might trade for black market goods. She'd sold the last of the Gobelin tapestries months ago. A dealer in Munich had offered two thousand reichsmarks, knowing it was worth ten times that. She'd accepted. To cover the staff's salaries, she'd been forced to part with several prized oils, portraits from the family gallery that had been painted by the famed British artist John Singer Sargent. Only one thing of value remained: her father's wine cellar. At last count, four hundred sixty-six bottles of vintage French wine lay in the damp tomb beneath the kitchen. Petrus, Lafite-Rothschild, Haut-Brion—*les vins nobles de Bordeaux.* She would not consider the glass displays full of her precious Meissen figurines and vases. The delicate blue-and-white porcelain was her single vice. Collected since childhood, each piece held a treasured memory. It was Pauli's sole birthright.

It would be the wine, then.

She informed Herbert of her decision, then hastened from the kitchen and mounted the servants' stairs to the first floor. Checking her watch, she saw that it was nearly eight o'clock. Time to wake her son.

Pauli was already out of bed, sitting on the floor running a miniature tank back and forth across the carpet. He was a sturdy child with tangled blond hair falling short of determined blue eyes. Since the war had ended, he'd been plagued by nightmares. A rumor had circulated at school that the Red Army was crossing Czechoslovakia to invade southern Germany, roasting German-born children on spits, then feeding them to its troops. She had told him such stories were ridiculous, but like any six-year-old boy he had an energetic imagination.

Kneeling, she gave Pauli his morning kiss and asked him how he had slept. "Fine," he said cheerfully. "Next year I will join the Pimpfen and then I can fight the dirty reds. The Führer will be proud of me."

The Pimpfen was the entry level of Hitler Youth. A boy joined when he was ten and stayed until he was fourteen. The Pimpfen, the Hitler Youth, the Volksturm—children were taught to fight before they could read. Killing had been deemed a virtue instead of a sin.

Running a hand through his ivory locks, she explained again that the war was over. There would be no more Pimpfen, no more Hitler Youth. For a child who had never known peace, the concept was difficult to comprehend.

"If the war is over, why isn't Daddy home?"

Ingrid lifted his chin until he met her gaze. It was frightening how he resembled his father. "Don't you remember what I told you, sweetheart? Daddy isn't coming home."

Pauli threw his eyes to the floor, grabbing his tank and running it furiously up and down his leg. She let him play like this for a few moments, then escorted him to the bathroom and helped him brush his teeth and wash his face. She picked out an outfit for him, and as he dressed she heard him singing the words to an anthem she knew too well.

Die Fahne hoch, die Reihen fest geschlossen,
S.A. marschiert in ruhig festen Schritt.
Kameraden die Rotfront und Reaktion erschossen . . .

He went on, the words to the Horst Wessel song, the Nazi's sacred anthem, spilling as effortlessly from his lips as the Lord's Prayer used to spill from hers. When would he finally take to heart that the war was over and his daddy wasn't coming home?

Shuddering involuntarily, she ushered him out of the room and downstairs to the kitchen.

BREAKFAST WAS A ROUSING SUCCESS. Pauli screamed with delight at the steaming plate of sausage and potatoes accompanied by a glass of fresh milk. Herbert sat beside him, entertaining the master of the house with stories of hunting parties of old. Ingrid studied them both, nibbling a fingernail, worrying.

For six years, she had managed to outrun the privations imposed by the war. She was rich. She had powerful friends. *She was a Bach.* Finding and paying for goods on the black market was not a problem. But six months after Egon stole the family business, a new reality imposed itself. The upkeep of Sonnenbrücke—food, electricity, staff, medicine—was devastatingly expensive. By January, she was broke.

She'd visited Egon at the Villa Ludwig soon afterward to ask for more money and it seemed he'd been waiting for the request. Yes, he'd smiled cloyingly, he'd be happy to lend her some money. Say, five thousand marks, should she accompany a visiting dignitary to dinner and ensure he had an enjoyable evening? "Whatever's necessary, Ingrid. I'm sure you and Field Marshal Scherner will get along famously. After all, *'it is what you do best.'* And to underscore his meaning, or knowing Egon, just to be rude, he'd pinched her rump and blown her a harlot's kiss. Furious and utterly humiliated, she'd slapped him across the face and sworn never to speak with him again.

But the sight of Pauli wolfing down his meager meal made her question whether she'd been rash, if pride had taken precedence over necessity. Momentarily she was paralyzed with fear. What would happen when she could no longer barter for fresh butter and chickens and red cabbage on the black market? The wine would only take her so far. One month, perhaps two. Then how would she feed Pauli? With more sausage stuffed with sawdust? Bread leavened with sand?

She stood so abruptly that Pauli let go a frightened cry.

Keep moving, a fevered voice inside her commanded. *Don't look behind you!*

Forcing a smile to her face, she told him she must look in on Grandpapa and fled the room. She ran up the back staircase, loosening the serving apron from her neck. Reaching the first-floor landing, she rested her head against the wall. Deep breaths did little to ease her anxiety. It wasn't fair that she should be expected to support the household—to do the cooking, the cleaning, the mending, and the caring for her father and her child. She was a Bach, dammit! There were others to do those jobs.

Keep moving! responded the voice, but now it sounded as scared as she.

I can't, she whimpered. *I don't want to.* Then came the scariest rejoinder of all, the one that haunted her more as each day passed and her family's circumstances worsened. *Why? If there's nothing to look forward to, why?*

Frightened by her dark thoughts, she drew herself upright and wiped at her eyes. Somehow her tears eased her anxiety and when she reached the door to her father's bedroom, she had regained not only her composure but her confidence. She rested for a few seconds, gathering her breath and finding her courage. Her fingers danced through her hair, guiding stray locks to their place as if by intuition. Closing her eyes, she offered a brief prayer that today would be a good one for her father. Then she knocked and opened the door.

The room was dark. The labored huff and sigh of her father's breathing rose from the bed. Alfred Bach was still asleep. She drew the curtains, then rolled up the blinds and threw open a window. Sunlight burst into the room as a gust of wind invigorated the still air.

"Good morning, Papa," she said, giving his shoulder a gentle squeeze.

The old man's eyes fluttered, then opened. "Good morning."

Ingrid smiled. He said good morning no matter what time of day one greeted him. "How was your sleep? Did you see Mama in your dreams?"

"Good morning," he said again.

Ingrid kept her smile in place, but her heart sank. Illness had shrunk him. The outline of his frame hardly showed under the duvet. "Good morning," she whispered.

Every so often her father had moments of clarity. *"Aufhellungen,"* the doctor called them. The term denoted a clearing of the clouds. On those days, Papa would be himself again, barking orders left and right, complaining about his arthritis, cursing that nincompoop Hitler's decision to delay the invasion of Russia so that he could take a vacation in the Balkans. She had hoped today might be one of those occasions.

Alfred Bach lurched forward and Ingrid's hands dropped to the sturdy restraints hanging from the bedside. "Ingrid, my darling daughter," he said, "how I love you."

She released the ties. "I love you, too, Papa."

"How is Bobby?"

Always the questions about her husband. "He's fine."

"Is he coming to the party?"

Ingrid smiled coyly. Lately, her father had gotten it into his head that every day was his birthday. "I'm so sorry, Papa, but Bobby cannot come. His squadron is stationed in the East. He's probably flying right—"

"No, no," interrupted Alfred Bach. "He must be on his estate. He's a *graf*, after all. Don't forget that. His responsibility is to his land. A man must keep his eye on things."

Alfred Bach loved his son-in-law's vast tracts of land in eastern Pomerania almost as much as the title that had accompanied them. Graf Robert Friedrich von und zu Wilimovsky. And, of course, she was the *gräfin*, though her claim to the title was dubious now that the Red Army had seized her husband's estates.

They were a pair, the Wilimovskys and the Bachs. Two of Germany's fabled family's, one destitute and ruined, the other soon to be.

She'd known Bobby her entire life. He was a dark, willowy boy—she'd never been able to think of him as a man—who loved sleek boats, fast cars, and faster airplanes. But he was no playboy. God, no. He'd neither drunk nor smoked. To her chagrin, he hadn't even liked sex very much. He'd proposed at midnight, New Year's Eve, 1939, at the Bristol in Berlin, Reichsmarschall Goering standing close by as his second. Maybe it was the Champagne or his dancing brown eyes or the fact that earlier in the day she'd learned she was carrying a child. Whatever the reason, she'd said yes, then and there. She had loved Bobby very much. But she'd hadn't been in love with him. At least not then—and if she was to keep to the morning's theme of unblinking introspection—maybe not ever.

Erich had stolen that from her. Not the ability to love so much as the capacity to trust that was love's necessary antecedent. She saw him now as he always visited her, dressed in his formal evening attire, blond hair swept sternly from his forehead, bronzed skin glowing in contrast to his blackest of black uniforms. A gold medallion hung from his neck, an award bestowed by the Führer that very evening to honor the Fatherland's finest athlete. A year after his defeat at the Olympic Games, Erich Seyss had regained his country's adulation, winning three events at the European Championships, all by decisive—or as Adolf Hitler lauded in toasting him—"Germanic" margins.

He wasn't the handsomest man she'd ever seen, perhaps not even in the room that night, but he possessed about him a stillness, a composure that was its own attraction. He smiled reluctantly, as if humor were a commodity in short supply. He had the gift of patience, of making others come to him, and not speaking until one wasn't sure whether he'd even heard a word you'd blathered in that first gush of hellos and congratulations and generally shameless fawning. But the most alluring of all his qualities was his confidence, unalloyed and unspoken. To everyone who saw him that night in Berlin, seated on the dais to the Führer's left, he was, of course, the new Germany. The Fatherland reborn.

And when he appeared at her side late in the evening, not only smiling but bowing as he requested the next waltz, his diamond-blue eyes riveted upon her as if she was more valuable than any medal, she broke her every coquette's precept and agreed immediately.

He was a wonderful dancer.

That had been eight years ago, Ingrid realized, almost to the day.

"Bobby won't be coming to the party tonight," she said to her father. "But I've invited all your friends. The Mellars, the Klinsmans, the Schroeders."

A drawer in the nearest cabinet housed her father's medication. Lidocaine to be injected twice daily. Aspirin. Morphine for the days when his pain was unbearable. She had no medicine to sharpen his mind. She administered the lidocaine and made sure her father had swallowed his aspirin, then went downstairs to prepare a light breakfast for him.

She saw the car as she passed the front door on her way back to his room.

A large American sedan swept up the driveway, a red flag fluttering from its front bumper. A pair of motorcycles preceded it and a jeep came to the rear. Setting down her father's tray, she moved to the window. In the meadow, Pauli was rushing toward the vehicles, all gaping mouth and scraped knees. Visitors were rare. Apart from the squad of soldiers stationed at the head of the driveway, ostensibly to keep her father under house arrest, and the ever-present GIs running about the woods slaughtering her chamois, only a clutch of friends came to Sonnenbrücke. With petrol so scarce, it was simply too much of an excursion.

The motorcade halted directly before the front door. The petite red flag bore three gold stars. She was to receive a general officer. She prayed he would not bring bad news. She wasn't sure she could bear anything more. Self-consciously, she prettied her hair and ran a hand over her dress. One part of her was aghast at her appearance, another proud of it. Damning her misplaced vanity, she let her hair fall where it might, then opened the door and stepped onto the brick portico. She recognized the officer stepping from the rear of the sedan at once. Leslie Carswell, the general who commanded the troops keeping an eye on Papa. She'd met him during the interrogations conducted to establish whether her father was fit for trial. He was tall and distinguished with trim gray hair, wiry eyebrows, and a craggy face you could hang climbing ropes on. Older, but not bad-looking. A southerner, if she remembered correctly. Like so many Americans he refused to walk like a soldier, sauntering casually across the driveway as if taking a Sunday walk.

"Miss Bach, a pleasure to see you again," he called, extending a hand.

"Good day, General. To what do I owe the pleasure?" Casting a glance over his shoulder, she noticed that his driver and the other members of his retinue were staying in their places. Odd.

"A social call, ma'am."

"Oh? I didn't realize American men were permitted to mingle with the Hun."

"The Hun?" Carswell slapped a hand on his thigh. "Why, with that lovely accent you sound as English as the queen herself."

Ingrid smiled politely. She had no illusions about Carswell's ability to influence the conditions of her father's incarceration. One call could land Papa in an eight-by-ten cell, illness or no. "Papa insisted all the children learn English fluently," she responded. "He was a great friend of Mr. Churchill's."

"I'm all for bettering relations between the fine German people and us Americans. In fact, that's the reason for my visit. I was thinking it might be useful for us to have a discussion about what your father was doing during the last months of the war."

"He was ill," she shot back defensively. "You know that."

Carswell chuckled as if there'd been a misunderstanding. "Before that, I mean. Some of the boys in Intelligence had a few questions about the extent of his resistance. Not many of Hitler's top dogs went against him and lived."

"Father talked, that's all. He may not have liked the Führer but he certainly wasn't going to compromise production. His first loyalty was to our soldiers."

"And did you agree?"

"War is a man's business, General. The opinions of a twenty-five-year-old woman don't hold particular sway."

Ignorance relieved her of complicity. What she did not know, she could not be responsible for. It was a hand-tailored excuse, worn thin these six years, and lately she'd begun to see through it altogether. One could not simply close their eyes and pretend nothing was happening. Ignorance was just a different kind of guilt.

"That may be, Miss Bach, but I'd be most interested to hear them. Have you by any chance been to the Casa Carioca in Garmisch? It's quite a nice establishment."

Taking in Carswell's wolfish grin, Ingrid suddenly realized why he'd come. He couldn't care less about Papa's opposition to the Führer. He wanted to bed her. Many women were allowing themselves to be taken as mistresses to American GIs. In exchange for their company, they received cigarettes, stockings, chocolate, even perfume—all of it ready currency on the black market. She had no illusions how they earned their keep. "Mistress" was just a diamond-crusted word for whore.

"I'm sorry, General, but I just couldn't. Someone must look after Papa, and my son still doesn't know what to make of your GIs camped on our driveway. Maybe another time."

Carswell was ever the gentleman. Tipping his cap, he said he'd come again next week, if only to inquire as to her father's health. "And Miss Bach, if there's anything I can help you with . . . anything . . . do let me know."

Ingrid remained outside as the motorcade circled the marble fountain and accelerated up the driveway. To her everlasting shame, she even found herself waving.

Papa's wine would only last so long.

12

"Here he is, then, the luckiest man in Germany."

Stanley Mullins swept into the hospital room in a swirl of self-importance, taking up position at the end of Judge's bed. "I don't know if a cracked rib will get you a Purple Heart, lad, but I can surely put in a request."

Judge prodded the swath of bandages wrapped around his torso and winced. The only medal he deserved was one for monumental ineptitude. "Just get me out of here, Spanner," he said. "We need to get up to Garmisch pronto. Seyss is in Munich and the only people who might have an idea why are his buddies in that camp. The sooner we talk to them, the better."

Mullins tapped a finger to the side of his nose. "Got the scent of him, do you? There's my bloodhound. Let me have a word with the docs. They seem to think you need a few days to mend."

Judge was up on an elbow, shaking his head before Mullins could finish his words. The typescript of his orders scrolled before him like the news wire at Times Square. *Temporary duty. Seven days. To expire at midnight, Sunday, July 15th.* He was down to five days and he'd scared off the prey. It wasn't quite the start he'd been hoping for.

"Relax, Dev," soothed Mullins. "Word's out that Seyss is in town.

We've doubled the patrols, set up two dozen roadblocks, and instituted spot identification checks at random points all over the city . . . all per your very own instructions."

The key word being "random," Judge thought, disgustedly. There was no time to get a new description of Seyss out to the troops patrolling the city. Most hadn't even had a chance to see his photograph. They'd be stopping every blond male over five feet tall. A black-haired, bespectacled six-footer would pass unnoticed, untouched, and unhindered. Still, Judge knew it was better than nothing, so he kept his complaints to himself.

Mullins motioned for him to scoot over and sat down on the bed beside him. "Before I track down the nearest sawbones, Dev, I wanted a word."

Judge sat up stiffly. "Yeah?"

"Now tell me honest, are you feeling okay?"

"I've been better, but there's no reason to keep me tied to a bed."

Mullins's watery eyes brimmed with concern. "You're sure? You know my rule about sending out a man when he's less than a hundred percent. It's the only way I can look after you."

"It's a rib, Spanner. Not even broken, just cracked. But thanks for asking."

Mullins tapped a finger to his forehead. "And up here? Everything as it should be?"

"Sure."

"Good. Good." Mullins smiled, but something in his regard changed. His worries about Judge's well-being answered, he'd moved on to more important matters. "I don't mean to pry, lad, but what happened back there at Lindenstrasse? One second you're telling Sergeant Honey you've got your man, the next, Mr. Seyss has a gun in your back, you're doing a swan dive off the stairs, and he's making his escape."

"I found him upstairs pretending to be some sort of building inspector. I called for Honey and then he . . ." Judge averted his eyes, praying he wasn't turning some awful shade of crimson.

"He what?"

"He . . ." Judge was robbed for words. He'd been asking himself the same question since Honey had hauled him off the rotted spar earlier that morning. *What happened in there?* and its unspoken corollary, *Why didn't you kill him?* Hearing the words issue verbatim from Mullins's lips, he flushed anew with shame and humiliation. For behind them loomed a matter of far greater import: What if his failure to shoot Seyss wasn't a question of atrophied reflex but of atrophied nerve? "Dammit, Spanner, he was just faster than I was. He jumped me and got the gun. What am I supposed to say?"

"Dev, you were in the same room with the bastard. Did you forget what he'd done to your brother?"

"Of course not," Judge retorted. "What? You expect me to shoot him on sight? Last I heard, it was up to the courts to decide a man's punishment."

Mullins inched closer, his imposing bulk every bit as threatening as Judge's stormy conscience. "It's just that from that distance a man's body is like the broad side of a barn. How could you miss? Safety off, hammer back. A funny thing for the Academy's honor graduate to forget."

"That was eighteen years ago, but if it makes you happy, I didn't forget."

"Well, then, lad, if it's not the technique, the problem must lie elsewhere." A ruddy hand fell to Judge's shoulder delivering the brunt of Mullins's exasperation. "What happened to the young thug I took off the streets? My own Jimmy Sullivan, you were. Tell me true, Dev, when you handed in your detective's shield, did you toss in your balls along with it?"

Judge knocked the arm away, while somewhere inside him a band snapped. "Go fuck yourself, Spanner."

Mullins's face colored and when he spoke his voice was barely a whisper. "You can call me Spanner once you've brought in Seyss. Until then, you'll be wise to remember your manners. It's Colonel Mullins to you."

Judge was fed up with Mullins's games. "Then you can tell the colonel to go fuck himself, too."

Mullins smiled. "There's my lad. Just wanted to make sure the spirit hadn't been siphoned out of you. There's hope yet."

The former lieutenant from Brooklyn's Twentieth Precinct rose and sauntered from the room, mumbling he was off to find a doctor who could sign "the lad" out. Judge dropped his head on his pillow, wondering if Mullins's words contained a grain of truth. Since coming to the hospital, he'd been replaying his confrontation with Seyss over and over. He kept seeing Seyss lunge at him, feeling that twinge of hesitation when his finger froze up and he'd allowed the Nazi swine to get the better of him.

What happened to the young thug I brought in off the street? My own Jimmy Sullivan, you were.

Judge tried without success to shake off the question. He wasn't one to dwell in the past. He didn't like recalling those days. Frankly, he had an aversion to looking back. Too many close calls, too many unexplained coincidences. It made him uncomfortable to realize how narrowly his success had been won. But the bite of Mullins's words whisked away his hesitance and transported him to his youth—to the only day that really mattered. May 24, 1926. And its memory was so sharp, so crystalline, he shivered, even as he sat sweating in his lumpy hospital bed.

It was the cry he remembered most. The old man's scream when they'd hit him with the blackjack.

Dev and the boys had been hanging around the Maryann Sweet Shop all day long, drinking egg creams and playing quarters in the back alley when the parade went by. A hundred Italian men and women dressed in their Sunday best marching down Pulaski Street—black suits, fedoras, every man a mustache, every woman a shawl—all of them gathered around a ten-foot-tall papier-mâché mockup of blessed Saint Maria Teresa Whoever they carried on their shoulders.

"Look at 'em," Artie Flannagan had joked. "Just off the boat."

"Not a real American among 'em," said Jack Barnes.

But it was Moochy Wills who'd encapsulated their feelings most eloquently. "Fuckin' wops!"

The escapade was Moochy's idea. Follow the patron of the society home, give him a sock to the head, and nab the money from the collection plate. The guy would be carrying a hundred, easy. Italians weren't lazy like the Irish. Stupid, maybe, but not lazy.

Twenty years after the fact, Judge could still feel his initial stab of reluctance: the sharp ache in his gut, the sudden loss of breath. He'd acted up before. Ditching school, crashing speakeasies, once even helping some wiseguys unload a few dozen cases of hooch down at Sheepshead Bay in the dead of night. But this was different. This was robbery. He knew it and still he didn't say a goddamned word.

So they did it, just like Moochy said. They marched behind the parade until it dispersed. They waited outside the tiny *ristorante* while the faithful ate and drank and raised the roof, and when the party was over, they followed Il Padrone home to his apartment in Flatbush. Judge could see them all as if he were watching the scene unfold on the silver screen. Moochy, Jack, Artie, and Dev, perched on the stoop of that run-down tenement. And, of course, Il Padrone. He was an older guy, fifty and slight, wearing a silver sash around his chest decorated with a score of Italian words. Seeing the three strapping teenagers so close, he flinched, then shaking off his fear, offered a smile and a tip of the hat. *"Buona sera,"* he said. Good evening.

"Yer in America," answered Moochy Wills, raising the blackjack over his head. "Learn to talk fuckin' English."

The rest happened fast. Moochy bringing down the jack on the old guy's neck, the bony hand flailing the air, hopelessly working to defend himself. Artie and Jack, and yes, Dev, too, throwing in their best kicks, not looking where their work boots struck. Then Moochy clearing them away, wanting the guy for himself, clubbing him over and over until blood poured from his forehead and he'd collapsed to his knees. All of them laughing hysterically, shouting "Fuckin' wop!" over and over.

And that cry! It wasn't pain, not even fear. It was worse. It was disappointment. This didn't happen in America. This was why he'd left Palermo or Naples or wherever the hell he was from. That cry!

Out of nowhere, Artie Flannagan yelled, "Jesus, the cops!"

The boys had been so focused on clobbering the old man, none of them had noticed the patrolman twirling his nightstick at the corner of Seventeenth and Newkirk. He was a bear of a copper with a jaw like a steam shovel and a voice to freeze the hair on top of your head. Seeing the old man prostrate on the sidewalk, he shouted for the boys to stop right there and took off toward them with the stride of a thoroughbred. Judge remembered thinking that a big guy couldn't move that fast. It was impossible.

Moochy grabbed the money from the Italian's coat and hightailed it down the street. Artie and Jack followed. But Dev didn't budge. His legs refused to move. He stood rooted to the spot, listening for the immigrant's pathetic whining. Thing was, the Italian had stopped making any noise whatsoever a minute before.

His sentence was three years at Boys' State. Two for the crime and one on top for not cooperating with the court—that is, not ratting out his friends.

The arresting officer, Patrolman Stanley Mullins, presented himself to Judge's family as they left the courtroom.

"Yes, sir, you've got a bad egg, there, Mr. Judge," he said, looking down from his lofty promontory. "A shame he should get into this kind of trouble at so early an age."

There was nodding all around. A sob and a sniff from the ashamed mother. A cuff to the head from Dev's father. A smirk from Francis, the seminarian.

"Still, I do believe there's some good inside the boy," Mullins went on. "It takes a man to stand up for his friends. A bigger man yet to know when he's done something wrong and 'fess up. Aye, there's a wee vein of gold in this one. And, if you don't mind, sir and madam, I'd like to help you find it."

Mullins spoke to the judge and had the sentence reduced to two years' probation. For his part, Dev had "come 'rounds" to the precinct house on Wilson Avenue every Tuesday, Thursday, and Saturday for two years. He didn't learn a thing about police work. His duty consisted of shoveling out the stables at the rear of the station and taking boxing practice with the precinct team. The larger men beat the tar out of him. But only for so long. Young Dev had always been a quick learner.

And he had another job, too—one Mullins hadn't told his parents about. Every Monday and Wednesday afternoon at three-thirty sharp, Dev showed his face at the back door of the F&M Schaefer Brewing Company, engaged since the adoption of the Volstead Act in the production of root beer soda and "near beer." And for three hours, he would haul fifty-gallon barrels of their finest from vat to garage, loading them aboard Mack Bulldog trucks with side panels curiously advertising Hoffman's Moving Services. His pay was a dollar an hour—a princely sum, even if he never saw a dime. Every cent went to a newly promoted sergeant of the watch who stashed it in a cashbox inside his desk. Nine months later, Dev and Sergeant Mullins trundled off to the home of Signor Alfonso Partenza, president of the Società Benevolenza di Santa Maria Teresa, unemployed day worker and father of ten.

"A donation to the cause," Mullins told Signor Partenza, offering a new calfskin billfold that held the stolen sum of $216. "The least we could do to make your sore neck feel the wee-est bit better."

"Grazie," Partenza answered, grateful but not so trusting that he didn't count the money. This was America, after all. Not so different from Italy.

All this came back to Judge as he lay in the silent room, grimacing at the ache of his ribs, his tailbone, and most of all, his own unsettled mind.

What happened to the little thug I took off the street?

Still here, Judge answered, finding the fighting voice inside of him. Maybe a little rusty, but still here. And next time, he'd follow Seyss's advice. Shoot first and ask questions later.

A knock on the door saved him from further brooding. Darren Honey walked into the room, helmet under one arm. "Jeep's downstairs. Ready when you are."

Judge peeled back the sheets and with a grimace swung his legs over the side of the bed. "You reach my pal in Paris, get him working on those names?"

Honey dropped a hand into his helmet and removed a green polyethylene bag holding the dog tags he'd retrieved from the basement of Lindenstrasse 21. "Colonel Storey said he'd contact Graves Registration pronto. It's going to take him a couple of days to figure out if these two were killed or just POWs. He said to tell you, though, that they weren't at Malmedy."

"So, what do you think Seyss was doing with those tags?"

"I don't think Seyss would risk going to his house for some souvenirs. Normally, if Fritz goes home, it's to get some money or see a girlfriend, maybe get something decent to eat. You got a closer look at him than I did. Did you see him carrying anything else?"

"No. Not a thing."

"Cheer up," continued Honey, his smile back in place. "Seyss is in Munich. He knows we're after him. Let him be the nervous one. The way I see it, it's his turn to make a mistake."

Judge colored. He couldn't tell if Honey was being rude or just tactless. Before he could say anything in his own defense, Mullins returned with a physician in tow. The doctor examined him and pronounced him fit for travel. Fifteen minutes later, he and Mullins were standing outside the hospital waiting for Honey to draw the jeep around.

"Good luck, then," said Mullins, offering a shake of his meaty paw. "If our German friends in Camp Eight don't feel like talking, remember what I taught you. You were a fair practitioner in your day."

"Yeah," said Judge, looking away. *Your own Jimmy Sullivan.* "I'll keep in it mind."

Mullins grabbed his chin and brought their faces close together. "Serious, lad. You let him go once. Now it's my name you're ruining, too."

CHAPTER

13

THE DRIVE TO CAMP 8 TOOK two hours, a steady climb through fields of summer corn and rolling hills laced with tumbling brooks. The afternoon sky was a pale blue, scratched with hazy cumulus. Few cars traveled the narrow country roads but traffic was heavy nonetheless. Dozens of pushcarts freighted with all manner of household items—chairs, dressers, mirrors, and, of course, clothing—trudged along both sides of the highway. Each was accompanied by a shabby flock of women and children, sometimes even a man. Some were Germans returning to their homes, others foreigners shoved about by war's merciless tide. The estimates out of Washington said that over 6 million of these displaced persons were on the move across Germany. The flotsam of Hitler's folly.

Judge kept his eyes on the road. Unwilling to admit to Honey, or himself, how Seyss had gotten the drop on him, he remained silent. Large divots had been clawed from the pavement by the treads of angry tanks and the jeep's incessant jarring down and out of these furrows racked his already sore frame. After an hour, he grew numb from it, seeing his persistent discomfort as a hair shirt of his own tailoring. How Francis would welcome his kid brother's newly discovered piety! The irony brought a grudging smile to Judge's lips.

Occasionally, the jeep sped by an abandoned Sherman tank, half-track, or six-ton truck parked at an odd angle, half on, half off the road. In the pell-mell drive to capture enemy territory, the vehicles had been abandoned where they'd broken down.

At ten o'clock sharp, they reached the gates to Prisoner of War Enclosure 8. A spit-shined corporal, M-1 carbine slung over a shoulder, pointed the way to the command post. Honey brought the vehicle to a halt outside a stone-and-pine cabin that reminded Judge of the low-rent place in the Catskills where he'd stayed on his honeymoon. His wife had called it Grossinger's without the class. It was the first salvo in their battle over the direction of his career, but he'd been too young, too much in love to notice.

A few hundred German soldiers milled around the playing field across the compound from the CP. Their tunics were filthy, their faces gaunt. Most huddled in small groups sharing a common cigarette. From their ranks drifted the smothering stink of dirt and sweat.

Entering the CP, Judge and Honey were met by the camp commander.

"Morning, gentlemen," said Colonel William Miller. "I've been so looking forward to seeing you. Come with me." He was shorter than Judge, bald and bespectacled, with the hint of a drinker's belly. He had analytical brown eyes, a wispy mustache, and a pasty complexion that testified to a longtime love affair with his desk. A parson's son, thought Judge; a lifelong conformist enjoying his first chance to whip those of little faith into line.

Miller whisked them toward a pair of chairs set before his desk. "Please sit down. Make yourselves at home."

Judge took a last look at his notes and smiled graciously before beginning his questioning. The primary investigator's report had been succinct if unenlightening, consisting of a description of the crime scene and an unimaginative recounting of the escape. No effort had been made, however, to ascertain how Seyss had obtained the murder weapon, appropriately an SS officer's dagger, or how he had managed to traipse across three hundred yards of open space unseen.

"Colonel Miller," he began, "we're not interested in Colonel Janks's illicit activities. Whatever worries you may have about that matter, please put them to rest. We're here to talk about how Erich Seyss managed to get out of this camp. Do you have any idea how he got his hands on the dagger?"

"No idea," Miller declared gravely, his eyes shifting like a pendulum between Judge and Honey.

"Was Seyss allowed out of the camp at any time?"

"No."

Judge offered Honey a resigned glance. Monosyllabic responses were ideal under cross-examination, but Miller was a friendly witness— at least in theory. "Are *any* prisoners allowed out of the camp at any time?"

"Most leave every day. We organize work details to help out in Garmisch. Some of the prisoners work on farms, getting the harvest in. Others help out in the kitchens of hotels and restaurants in town, washing dishes, sweeping the floor. I can provide you a list of the establishments. Menial jobs, mind you, and the prisoners are under constant guard. A detachment of soldiers accompanies every group."

Now they were getting somewhere. "How many?"

"Two or three GIs for each crew of ten prisoners."

Honey chuckled. "Excuse me for saying so, Colonel, but isn't that like a couple of hens guarding a pack of foxes?"

Miller colored, but to his credit did not respond.

Judge took up the questioning. "But Seyss never left?"

"Major Seyss was a class-one war criminal awaiting transfer to an appropriate holding facility. He was confined to the camp at all times. Besides, he was under medical supervision. He was in no condition to work."

"Just to escape, eh?" added Honey.

Judge went on before Miller could protest. Honey was, after all, a noncom, and had no business speaking to an officer so disrespectfully. "And how are the prisoners searched when they return to camp?"

"They're patted down."

"Patted down?" brayed Honey, and this time Judge silenced him with a reproachful look. It was clear that anyone could have smuggled in a dagger. Work crews outside the camp for eight to ten hours a day supervised by a couple of postadolescent GIs. Judge was surprised the prisoners weren't equipped with an entire arsenal by now—steak knives to begin with. "When you mention Seyss's medical condition, you are referring to the bullet that took out his spleen?"

"He saw the camp doctor daily. A local physician from Garmisch named Peter Hansen. It's army policy to use natives whenever possible. Naturally, we were quite interested ourselves in speaking with Dr. Hansen. Unfortunately, he's no longer at home."

Judge made no comment, choosing to conceal his disappointment in a quest for further details. "And was Hansen a member of the German military?"

"Yes, sir. I believe he served in the army."

Honey tapped Judge's arm. "A full-blooded Nazi no doubt."

Judge shifted his attention to Miller. "Was he, in fact, a member of the Nazi party?"

Miller stared into his lap and coughed. "Yes, sir, I believe he was."

Seeking clarification, Judge raised a hand. "I thought General Eisenhower had outlawed the employment of former Nazis in any capacity. Isn't that the basis of our denazification program?"

"General Patton thinks differently," Miller retorted. "He's encouraged us to use whoever's available. He said being a Nazi is no different than being a Republican or a Democrat."

Judge wanted to shout "What?" but out of respect for his ribs, kept his outrage in check. "One more question: Was Dr. Hansen searched upon arriving at camp each day?"

Miller retained his strict posture. "No, sir."

"You outrank me, Colonel. A 'sir' isn't necessary."

Miller flushed, but Judge saved him from his embarrassment, suggesting that they retrace the prisoners' steps the night of the escape. Mercifully, Honey kept quiet.

Outside, Miller led Judge and Honey around the back of the command post to a trail running alongside the north fence. They passed one barracks after another, stopping at the fourth down the line.

"We count them at morning and at dusk," explained Miller. "Seyss was assigned a spot in this Barracks F." He pointed to the cream stone building with a riding crop. "PFC McDonough reported seeing Seyss at five minutes before bed check. Seyss said he was on his way to the latrine. McDonough confirms seeing him enter. He'd been given a pass from Dr. Hansen allowing him use of the facilities at any time. His kidneys were also badly damaged."

"Dr. Hansen said so?" ventured Honey, a smirk lurking close behind his lips.

The three men were standing at the entry to Barracks F.

"So he left from here," said Judge. "He went to the latrine, then made his way to the kitchen." His outstretched arm pointed to a stable fifty yards to their right, then rotated counterclockwise ninety degrees, stopping at a stained pine building two hundred yards farther on. "Where he killed Colonel Janks and Vlassov, mounted Vlassov's wagon, and drove through the gate."

Judge walked to the center of the road that bisected the camp and turned in a full circle. Against a backdrop of green meadows rolling to snowcapped peaks, he counted eleven watchtowers rimming the perimeter of the camp. He continued to the latrine where again he stopped and turned round, as if taking his bearings. His gaze skimmed the grass, tracing the path Erich Seyss had taken to the kitchen. He began walking. Every few steps he paused to look to his right and left, checking if one of the watchtowers had a clear view of him. When he reached the supply shed at the rear of the kitchen, he raised his hands in the air and exclaimed, "I give up, Colonel! Seyss was in the direct line of sight of at least three watchtowers the entire way. Would you care to explain to me how a prisoner could cross such a wide distance without being seen, or as I would have hoped, detained, questioned, and returned to his bed?"

"It was a moonless night," Miller countered defensively. "We've spoken with the soldiers manning those towers. They didn't see a thing. We certainly don't keep the compound lit after dark."

"No, no," said Judge, irascible because of his discomfort. "I don't buy it. Either he didn't come this way or he wasn't dressed like his buddies. Or . . ." And here he stopped and fixed Miller with his most hawkish gaze. "Or he had help on the inside."

The accusation hung between the men for several seconds, ripe with unpleasant implications. Then Miller stepped forward. "We did find something odd a few days ago," he offered sheepishly. "Maybe you'd care to take a—"

"Please, Colonel, yes, we'd like to see it."

Miller shuffled off to his office and returned carrying what appeared to be an olive drab mixing bowl. "This turned up behind the shed."

Honey plucked the rounded object from Miller's hands, swept off his cap, and fitted it to his own head. "It's a helmet, for chrissakes. What did he use? A soccer ball?"

"Yes," Miller stuttered, "but we don't know if it belonged to Seyss or if he used it during the—"

"Give it here, Sergeant," ordered Judge. Handling the "helmet" he scraped away some of the paint, revealing strips of chipped brown leather. "For argument's sake, I'll just assume he was wearing fatigues as well."

Judge stalked past Miller to the porch where Janks and Vlassov had been murdered. The gates to the camp stood sixty feet away, no farther than the distance from the pitcher's mound to home plate. Approaching them, he craned his neck to take in the guard towers crowding either side. Two soldiers manned each parapet. Judge's eyes, however, were drawn to the perforated snout of the .30-caliber machine gun, and next to it, the bald countenance of a klieg light. He lowered his gaze to the gates themselves and the sentries walking back and forth before them. Ten to one, these kids were itching to give their guns a workout. Had Seyss been stopped that night, he would have been cut to ribbons.

The man we're after is a gambler, he thought. *Brave, daring, and more than a little reckless.* But then Judge had learned that firsthand this morning.

Turning, he tossed the ball to Miller. "I'm ready to interview the prisoners now."

JUDGE'S FIRST IMPRESSION OF Sergeant Willy Fischer was that he looked the way a tank driver should: short and wiry, with a shock of black hair and a pack mule's stubborn glare. Fischer had spent the war attached to the First SS Panzer Division. From December 1944 through May of this year, he had served under Erich Seyss. He was being detained at the camp for his participation in the Malmedy massacre, though on a lesser charge than his commanding officer. On Judge's orders, he'd been removed from the camp population the previous afternoon and confined to an empty larder in the supply shack—what passed for the cooler at POW Camp 8. Since then he'd been fed a warm dinner and an American breakfast of scrambled eggs, toast, and bacon. No explanation had been given for his confinement. Judge wanted him confused.

"*Guten Morgen,*" Judge said loudly, doing his best impression of a German officer. "I'm sorry we couldn't find a bed for you, but at least you had something to eat."

"Good morning to you." Brushing the dust from his uniform, Fischer took a step toward Judge. His dark eyes raced over the uniform, trying to ascertain who exactly this man was. Judge saved him the trouble, introducing himself as an inspector with the military police and saying he needed his assistance with an important case. "It concerns your former commanding officer."

"I'm sorry but he's not here any longer," Fischer said wryly. "I believe he checked out a few days ago."

"Know where he went?"

"Baden Baden, if I'm not mistaken. He usually goes this time of year to take the cure."

Despite himself, Judge laughed. He hadn't expected a man who'd spent three years trapped in an iron sarcophagus to have a sense of humor. A clerk shuffled into the room with a school chair in each hand. When he'd left, Judge shut the door and gestured for the prisoner to take a seat. "Cigarette?"

"*Ja. Danke.*"

Judge tossed him a pack of Lucky Strikes, then handed him his Zippo lighter. He wasn't sure how exactly to handle Fischer. What point was there in threatening a man who'd survived the war only to face the gallows? The man would cooperate only if he felt it would benefit him. "Where's your family?"

Fischer remained silent for a long while, smoking his cigarette and staring at his inquisitor. Judge imagined he was asking himself how far to go, examining his conscience for signs that he'd suffered enough as it was. Finally, he said, "Frankfurt."

"Does your wife know you're here?"

"I've written her." Fischer shrugged as if to say he didn't have much faith that the letters were being delivered.

"Give me her address. I'll make sure they have enough ration stamps, someplace warm to sleep."

"What? No Hershey bars and stockings?"

Judge played the jolly good fellow. "How could I forget? I'll throw them in, too."

"You're a generous man. A pack of cigarettes, a couple of decent meals and the word of an American officer that he will look after my family." Fischer pursed his lips as if appraising the offer, while a bemused expression tightened his features. He stood and tossed the lighter to Judge. "Seyss is gone. Leave him."

"I'm afraid I can't do that."

Fischer pointed an accusing finger at his interrogator. "Do you know what the Ivans do to members of the SS when they catch them? They take a bayonet and insert it . . ." He left off. "Forget it. I don't talk about the man who saved my life."

And you, Judge wanted to say. *What did you do to the Russians when you caught them? Shoot them, starve them, send them to a factory to work until they dropped dead of exhaustion.* Three million Russian soldiers had perished under German captivity. But if Judge was seething, he did not let his anger show.

"You didn't fight the war to end up in prison for the rest of your life. Help me find Seyss and I'll see the courts go easy on you."

Fischer scoffed and retreated to a dark corner of the room.

"Tell me how you helped him get out of the camp."

"Helped him?" Fischer laughed to himself. "No one helps the major."

"The time for heroes is over," Judge said crossly. "It's time to think about yourself. Your family. Tell me where Erich Seyss is."

Fischer ambled back to his chair and sat down. After a last drag, he threw his cigarette on the floor, then ran a filthy hand over his mouth. "I am a German soldier," he said, answering a question only he had heard.

Judge met his hard gaze. "The war is over."

Fischer shook his head, then dropped his eyes to the floor. "Too bad, eh?"

JUDGE STOOD OUTSIDE THE LARDER, his back to the wall, willing himself to maintain his composure. An hour of questioning and cajoling hadn't gotten him anywhere. What upset him was not Fischer's flippant cynicism but his own misreading of the prisoner. His years in law enforcement had taught him that there was no honor among thieves. His mistake had been to assume that a defeated soldier would act in the same manner as a captured criminal. He had not reckoned on the inculcated loyalty of the German military. Unless he could convince the second POW that Seyss had wronged him, he'd have no chance in securing the man's cooperation.

Honey stood next to him, arms crossed, eyes too insistent by half. "There's another way to make Fritz talk."

Judge shook his head and walked toward the second larder. "I know."

CORPORAL PETER DIETSCH SAT CROUCHED in the corner of the barren room, clasped hands protecting his mouth as if at any moment it might betray him of its own volition. Like Fischer, Dietsch had served under Seyss's command in the Ardennes and later in Russia and Austria. Like Fischer, he had been a member of a tank squad, his occupational specialty that of gunner. But Dietsch had not volunteered for the Waffen-SS. He'd been transferred into the First SS Panzer Division from a Wehrmacht replacement battalion in November 1944. A conscript. Judge could only pray that Dietsch's loyalties didn't run as deep as Fischer's.

"Good morning," he began, speaking German, of course, but casually this time. No more baying like a Prussian bloodhound. "Enjoy your breakfast?"

Dietsch eyed him warily before standing up and saying thank you very much, he had indeed. He was a tall, gangly boy, nineteen according to his *soldbuch*. His blond hair was shorn to the scalp, his nose too big for his face, and his chin too small. He was the runt who took his beatings and didn't complain.

Judge explained why he was there. He wanted to know if Dietsch could shed some light on Seyss's escape or if he knew where Seyss had gone. Dietsch vehemently denied any knowledge of the escape or of his whereabouts, then launched himself into an impassioned defense of the heroic soldier. It was the same crap that Fischer had spewed, but Judge let him have his say. He wanted to give Dietsch plenty of chances to convince himself of his loyalty.

"I have a hard time listening to you speak so highly of the man who got you into this trouble," said Judge when the boy finally stopped speaking. "If it weren't for Seyss ordering you to open fire on one hundred unarmed American soldiers, you wouldn't be sitting here looking at a hangman's rope."

"When attacking there is no time to take prisoners," answered Dietsch. "The Führer himself issued the orders."

"So Hitler was with you in Malmedy? Because if he wasn't, I'm afraid it's your commanding officer who is responsible for giving you that order."

"Of course Hitler wasn't there," retorted Dietsch.

"That's right. It was Seyss who ordered you to pull the trigger. It was Seyss who turned you from an honorable soldier into a cold-blooded murderer."

Dietsch lowered his eyes. "Yes. Fine. It was Seyss. So what? What do you want anyway?"

Judge leaned forward and put a comforting hand on the boy's knee. "For you to talk to me. Help me learn how Seyss got out of here. Tell me where he went."

Dietsch glanced up. His blues eyes had gone glassy, shedding the defiance they'd harbored only a moment before. Judge could see that not only did he know something but that he was going to talk. The tension in the room vanished, as noticeable as an abrupt drop in atmospheric pressure. Instead of pressing, though, he sat back and let the boy come to him. He wouldn't repeat his mistake with Fischer. He took out another pack of cigarettes and put it on the floor between them. After a moment, Dietsch bent over and picked it up. "You mind?"

"Help yourself."

Dietsch fumbled with the pack, taking an eternity to get the cigarette into his mouth. He smoked like the schoolboy he should have been, puffing earnestly, staring at the skeins of smoke rising in front of his big nose as if he were contemplating Kant's *Critique of Pure Reason.* And just when Judge's patience was deserting him, he spoke. "I want out," he said. "My wife is eight months pregnant. I must see her. At least a visit."

Judge almost felt sorry for him. The kid would talk himself into a phone call if he let him go on. "Forty-eight hours," he said. "A two-day pass to visit your wife and you'll be accompanied by a guard at all times . . . if you have information that can help me."

Dietsch laughed. "I didn't know he'd made it until yesterday evening. I asked myself why else would they throw me in the cooler?"

"Tell me everything."

"Forty-eight hours?"

Judge nodded.

Dietsch shot him a glance that asked if he could trust him, then sighed and began speaking. "We thought he was crazy at first. I mean the major was so proud about how he was going to face the Americans and admit to his actions. He used to quote von Luck: 'Victory forgives all, defeat nothing.' The next day, he said he was getting out, that the Fatherland needed him. '*Kameraden,*' he said. 'One last race for Germany' and all that."

"He said that? 'One last race'?"

"Yes." Dietsch brightened. "He was very famous when I was a child, you know? Hitler himself nicknamed him the White Lion before his race against the Negro Americans in Berlin."

"He lost," Judge cut in. He wasn't interested in the glorification of his brother's murderer. "You were saying?"

"The major told us he needed the baize from a billiards table," said Dietsch. "Fischer and I work some days at the Post Hotel. He knew they had a game room. It was easy to remove, actually. Some of the men made a ruckus in the kitchen while we stripped the table."

Judge drew small satisfaction from the validation of his suspicions. "And you sewed it to the inside of his uniform so that when he turned it inside out he looked like a GI?"

"We had to work on the fabric a little. Darken it with oil, draw on the unit insignia."

"And the helmet? Where did you get the paint for that?"

Dietsch laughed, encouraged by Judge's knowing the tale. "The helmet was easier. We cut the camp ball in half and covered it with paint from the toolshed. Von Luck said 'Imitation is the bravest form of deception.'"

That was the second time he'd heard the name mentioned. "Who's von Luck?"

"General von Luck, of course. The major's trainer for the Olympic Games. A founder of the Brandenburg Regiment. Seyss spoke of him like a father."

Judge made a mental note to check if this von Luck character had made it through the war. "And Vlassov? How did Seyss know about him and Janks?"

Dietsch shrugged unconvincingly. "No idea."

Judge lurched forward and grabbed Dietsch by his jacket. "Now is not the time to start lying to me."

"I imagine Dr. Hansen told him. How else?"

How the hell did Hansen know? Judge wondered. According to Miller he left the camp at seven each night and didn't work at all on Sundays. Something still wasn't right. "And the knife?"

"Hansen. He could bring anything into the camp that would fit inside his medical bag. He brought the major extra rations to help build him up. Wurst, bread, even some fruit. The major often shared it with us."

Judge released the thin boy, giving him an easy shove toward the corner. "Where did Seyss go?"

Dietsch bent to pick up his cigarette. "He never told us. Just that he had to meet *kameraden*. Other SS men, people loyal to the Fatherland. I don't know who."

"Where was he meeting them?"

"I don't know."

"Munich?"

"I don't know." Dietsch insisted.

Discerning a deceitful glint in Dietsch's eyes, Judge rose from his chair and advanced on the soldier. "Dammit, tell me!"

Dietsch cowered, fighting back tears. "I don't know!"

Judge spun and kicked his chair to the ground. It was time for the strong-arm stuff. Time to call in Spanner Mullins. He imagined Mullins's voice, the Irish brogue whispering in his ear, "Either you get him to talk or I will." He thought of Seyss walking the streets of Munich a free man. He could still feel the bastard's hand on his back, giving him a shove that was meant to end his life. Judge circled the room, tensing the muscles in his arms and shoulders as he walked, clenching his fists. In the end, it always came to this. Knock out a man's front teeth and he'll confess like a drunk on the steps of St. Patrick's. As Mullins said, "Sorry, lad, there's just no other way to make sure he's telling the truth."

Looking over his shoulder, he caught sight of Honey peeking through the door. The young Texan was nodding his head, telling him it was okay to unleash a couple of good ones on this feckless kid.

Suddenly, Judge rushed at the prisoner, latching his hands on his shoulders and shaking him forcefully. The urge to hit Dietsch blossomed inside him like a physical desire. He didn't know if it was the frustrations of the day or just a return to his inglorious self, but God help him, he wanted to punch this kid in the face with everything he had. This schoolboy punk who'd leveled his machine guns at men his own age, American men, and pulled the trigger.

"Dammit, Dietsch!" he yelled. "Tell me the truth."

Dietsch flinched, raising both hands to protect his face. "He wasn't stupid, you know. He knew you'd come looking for him. He wouldn't tell us anything that might jeopardize his mission. I've told you what I know. I want to see my wife. You promised." And then he broke. Tears poured from his eyes and he sobbed, all the while sure to keep his arms about his head. "My wife. You promised."

Judge broke off, his anger ebbing as he backed away. Dietsch was scared witless and fright often made a person honest. Moreover, his words had the ring of truth. A man like Seyss would never reveal his destination to his accomplices. But Judge would never truly know if he'd gotten everything out of Dietsch until he braced him. And that he wouldn't do.

Colonel Miller followed him outside the supply shack. "You didn't mean what you said about a forty-eight-hour pass?"

Judge stopped in his tracks and faced the paunchy camp commander. "No, Colonel, I didn't. Keep Dietsch locked up for a month. He can leave as soon as he tells you where Seyss went. If he does, get on the horn to Sergeant Honey or myself at Bad Toelz. Are we clear on that?"

Miller saluted. "Absolutely, Major."

Honey drew Judge to one side. "Begging your pardon, sir, but we don't have a month. Today's Wednesday. We got till Sunday midnight. That's four days."

Judge bristled at the reminder. His fist clenched reflexively and he wanted to hit something, somebody, and he was thinking Honey's earnest mug would do just fine. Instead, he slapped his thigh and stalked off to the jeep.

Four days.

It wasn't enough time.

15

ERICH SEYSS WAS GROWING ANNOYED with the portly American sergeant.

"As you can see, I am from Heidelberg. I am only asking for what every discharged soldier has been promised: a one-way ticket home. If you please, just have a look . . ."

The sergeant waved away the document giving Seyss's identity as one Erwin Hasselbach. "This is the last time I tell you, Fritz. Your denazification papers aren't enough anymore. Too many of you boys are giving fake papers and using the trains like they were your own taxicabs. New system as of today. You need an actual ticket, and to get one of those you'll have to go back to the Center for Discharged Soldiers. Show them your papers and they'll issue you one pronto. You can be on this train tomorrow. *Verstehen Sie?*"

Seyss had too much experience traveling in areas newly liberated by German forces to be entirely surprised. The situation was dynamic, tacticians would say, though chaotic was, the more appropriate term. Either way, he had been taught to deal with this kind of thing. In battle and its aftermath, change—rapid change—was the only constant. He certainly couldn't blame Egon Bach for the development. He'd just have to find another way to board the train.

Seyss smiled obligingly as his mind worked the situation. The last thing he would do was present himself at a discharge center, especially now that Major Judge and his colleagues knew he was in Munich. Besides, not all soldiers received a train ticket home. Many were herded into outdoor holding pens to await transport by truck convoy. The wait often ran to days. Worse, if there was a problem with a false *persilschein*, as the American sergeant had mentioned, there were sure to be a host of intelligence officers checking those corralled at the discharge centers for false papers.

"Come on, Sarge," said Seyss, his smile stretched to the breaking point. "Let's be civil. Send me back to the center and I'll never make it to my sister's wedding tomorrow."

An anonymous hand shoved in the back.

"Beeilen Sie sich," growled a man in a torn mackintosh, teeth black as coal. "Hurry up. We all have our tickets. Do as the sergeant says. Get out of the way."

Seyss glanced over his shoulder. A restless line of men, women, and children snaked across the tracks and disappeared into the shadows of a warehouse. They were a slovenly lot: gaunt, ill shaven, all of them looking as if they were dressed in someone else's clothing. Like him, they'd been waiting hours in the morning sun for the right to board the daily train to Heidelberg. With the Munich *hauptbahnhof* little more than a mangled husk, the Americans had shifted civilian traffic to the freight railway station. The place was not well suited to the task. There were no elevated platforms from which to board the trains, no public water closets, and certainly no *bahnhof* buffets where one could enjoy a beer while ambling away the minutes. Hundreds of people swarmed over the tracks, their anxious steps raising a curtain of dust and grit. Like stones in a rushing stream, American soldiers stood among them, directing the forlorn travelers this way and that. What a mess!

The sergeant cleared his throat and when Seyss returned his gaze, he saw that two soldiers had come up on either side of him. The sergeant tilted his head and shrugged. One hand fluttered, a closing of the fingers that would normally signal "Come here."

Seyss looked from the beckoning hand to the weathered face and suddenly, he realized he'd been stupid hoping to persuade the bluff American. He'd scarcely have had better luck boarding the train with a valid ticket. With a single practiced motion, he unclasped Dr. Hansen's watch and placed it in the sergeant's palm. "It's Swiss. Universeal de Génève. Good for a round trip, I should think."

But the sergeant found no humor in the comment. Grunting, he thrust a thumb over his shoulder. "Private Rosen. Show Herr Fritz to his compartment."

Directly ahead, two trains sat side by side. The train on the left was reserved for Allied soldiers. Officers, first class. Enlisted, second class. Few men appeared to be boarding, and as he passed, Seyss saw that the compartments were deserted. Rosen nudged his shoulder, indicating he should advance toward the other train. *The train for Germans.*

Seyss threaded his way through the crowd boarding the endless string of cars. Twenty or thirty people waited at each entry. Most cars were already full. Compartments meant for six persons held twelve, not counting the children peering down from the luggage racks. Corridors running the length of each car were packed as tightly as sardine cans. Seyss hurried his pace. He'd be damned if he had gotten this far only to find the train full.

Killing Colonel Janks had, indeed, provoked a serious response. The occupational police hadn't stopped at sending Major Judge and his partner to Lindenstrasse 21. Signs of heightened security were everywhere. Checkpoints had been established at the Ludwigsbrücke and along the Maximillianstrasse. Teams of military police patrolled the streets, demanding the identity papers of men who matched his description—mostly those under forty with blond hair. Two MPs had boarded a tram Seyss was riding. He'd looked each squarely in the eye as they'd passed down the aisle but neither gave him a second look. Black hair was an excellent diversionary measure, but it did little to change a man's physiognomy—his eyes, his nose, his mouth. Emboldened, he'd offered his papers, but the policemen waved them away. A few more days and the uproar would die down. After that it wouldn't matter. Where he was going, the Americans couldn't follow.

Seyss finally spotted a passenger car with a few open places. He rushed toward it, only to be stopped by Private Rosen. "Keep moving,"

Rosen said. "You didn't think you're riding with the paying customers?"

SEYSS HAD NEVER SEEN SO many jerry cans. The entire freight car was full of them. Twelve high, twenty across, at least fifty rows deep. He didn't bother calculating. Thousands, at least.

"Go on, then," said Rosen. "Up you go."

A ladder had been laid against the wall of metal containers. A man hunched in the space between the green cans and the roof of the car, holding steady the ladder. *"Komm jetzt,"* he called down.

Seyss hesitated to join him. He'd had enough of tight spaces for a while and once the door was shut, he'd have no way out until it was opened in Heidelberg. To back out now, however, would appear suspicious. He'd traded a Swiss watch for this trip, a valuable commodity these days. The sergeant had outsmarted him. Seyss climbed a rung and ran a hand along the inside of the wooden door. An iron latch protruded from the rear of the locking mechanism. He leaned his weight on it and it gave way. Good. The door could be unlocked from within. It might take a while to clear a path through the jerry cans, but at least he wouldn't be left to starve on some forgotten siding.

He continued up the ladder, accepting a helping hand to pull him into the car.

"Welcome aboard the petrol express," said a heavyset man of thirty, give or take five years. The privations of war made it impossible to tell another's age with any accuracy. "Name's Lenz." He had cropped brown hair and a walrus mustache. A rumbling baritone matched the stern countenance. His accent placed him as a Berliner.

Seyss introduced himself as Erwin Hasselbach, and threw in a Wehrmacht unit and the name of a dead *Heer* colonel who'd commanded it. "I suppose we should count ourselves lucky we're not on the manure express," he said.

It was a longstanding tradition to award every route its own name, usually something to do with its cargo. The run from Berlin to Hamburg was known as the silk stocking express; Kiel to Cologne, the cod express; Munich to the Ruhr, the potato express. The fumes wafting from the mountain of empty five-gallon gasoline cans left no question as to how this particular train had earned its name.

"Ah, the manure express," said Lenz. "I know it well. That one steered a southerly course from Berlin to Berchtesgaden. But it wasn't manure they transported. It was bullshit."

Seyss wasn't sure if Lenz was baiting him or not, so he kept quiet. Too many of their countrymen were quick to declare themselves betrayed by their Führer. *We never wanted war,* they said. *Who dared speak against Hitler?* The same men and women had presented themselves in droves to cheer the invasion of Poland and France and Russia. Hitler had coined an expression for such good-weather supporters: March violets.

Seyss raised his head enough to find he could not bring himself to a sitting position. The space on top of the cans was tighter than he'd feared. He closed his eyes for a moment, ordering himself to be strong. Then leaning on an elbow, he made himself as comfortable as possible and tried to restrict his breathing. The trip to Heidelberg would take eight or nine hours, depending on the condition of the tracks. It was not going to be easy. His only consolation was that he'd arrive by midnight, twelve hours ahead of schedule.

A few minutes later, Rosen returned and took away the ladder. "Bon voyage," he called, then slammed the door closed.

THE TRAIN LUMBERED OUT OF the station, creaking, and moaning with every rotation of the locomotive's wheels. A cool breeze cleansed the car of the noxious fumes and Seyss pressed his face against the wooden slats, grateful for some fresh air. He was glad to be moving. The familiar pitch and roll of train travel eased his discomfort, both real and imagined.

"So, you're from Heidelberg?" he asked Lenz, when his light-headedness had faded.

Lenz crawled across the unsteady metal carpet. "Yes. And you?"

Seyss shared his deceit. "Born and raised."

Lenz broke out laughing. "You're a fucking liar, you Swabian bootlicker."

"Say that to all the boys you pick up on the Ku'damm?"

Lenz laughed louder, but all the while Seyss could feel his eyes sizing him up. No doubt he was wondering what this other fool had done to find himself stuck on top of a few thousand stinking cans of gas. Lenz clamored toward him and Seyss could see his eyes. They were dark and pouchy, dragged down by doleful black circles.

"*Sind Sie Kamerade?*" Lenz asked with a grunt.

Seyss obeyed his gut instinct. "First SS Panzer Division."

"Ah, one of Sepp Dietrich's boys. I served in the Leibstandarte under him before I transferred to Das Reich. Unterscharführer Hans-Christian Lenz at your service."

Seyss extended his arm to shake Lenz's hand. He wanted to say that he'd also served in the Leibstandarte Adolf Hitler, but he'd revealed too much as it was. He certainly could not tell Lenz his real name. "Why Heidelberg?"

"Darmstadt, actually. My brother has set up a little business for himself. He asked me if I might come and join him for a while. I said 'Why not.'"

"A business of his own? Is that right?" Seyss could smell larceny a mile away and Lenz's flashing eyes did little to rob him of the notion. Still, he played along as his part demanded. "A baker, is he? We had a baker named Lenz in our company. Matter of fact, he came from Berlin, too."

"Sorry, old man. My brother was in the Kriegsmarine. A submariner, if you can believe it. And still alive."

"He's a lucky one."

"And enterprising. Freddy keeps his fingers in a number of pies. A little of this, a little of that. It's not a bad time for a man who keeps his eyes open."

"Ah." Seyss thought Lenz a little too proud of his brother's role as a black marketeer. He'd never approved of the middlemen who made a living, and sometimes a fortune, trading on the miseries of others. As a rule, they were no different from carrion fowl, feeding off the bones of the sick and the dying. Still, Lenz seemed a decent enough sort. Maybe his brother was the exception.

"And you?" asked Lenz. "What takes you to Heidelberg? Friends? Family?"

"Friends," said Seyss. When he didn't elaborate, Lenz gave an unpleasant guffaw. "A woman, then?"

"No." Seyss looked away, despising the man's assumption of familiarity. It had been foolish to engage a complete stranger in conversation. Just because Lenz had served in the same branch did not mean they had something in common. Hundreds of thousands had worn the uniform of the SS. Those that he had counted as friends were long dead. From now on, he really must learn to keep his mouth shut.

Lenz asked what was wrong, but Seyss did not reply. After a while, the Berliner scooted to the far side of the car and was quiet.

The train rolled west, passing through Augsburg, then Ulm. The cities appeared relatively undamaged. The spire of the cathedral in Friedrich Square rose majestically in the afternoon sky. Twice the train stopped for an hour as cars behind him were shunted to a siding and others added in their place. The wait was interminable. The dizzying fumes and increasing temperature combined to make his cozy little spot a fulsome hell. Seyss figdeted constantly, one eye for the roof lest it decide to collapse, the other on the sky, the dirt, any passing object that assured him that the outside world was only a few inches away. He needed all his willpower to keep from carving a path through the cans to the door and leaping from the car. And each time, just when he thought he could stand it no longer, the engineer sounded his whistle, the car lurched forward, and slowly, mercifully, they were on their way.

STUTTGART WAS A WASTELAND, A pile of rubble ten kilometers long. Chimneys of brick and mortar still stood, but the homes they had warmed were gone. Factories were a total loss. Stuttgart was the ball-bearing capital of Germany and as such, a principal target of Allied bombing missions throughout the war. How many raids had it taken to flatten the city? Twenty? Fifty? And how many bombers? Ten thousand? As if in a dream, he saw them passing overhead. Swarms of dull green insects floating across the sky, their shadows combining into a gray cape that carpeted the entire countryside. And the drone. God, he'd almost forgotten the drone. A low-pitched buzz that reverberated in your bones and set a stream of acid pissing in your gut. Louder and louder, until your entire body shook and you could scream, "Stop, you sons of bitches. Kill me, but there are women and children down here, too," and the man standing a foot away from you would put a hand to his ear and shout back, "What?" They dropped the HEs first, high explosives to concuss the walls, bring the buildings down on themselves, then the incendiaries, fire bombs to melt the glass and steel and ruined machinery into one giant gob of unsalvageable nothing.

"Let them come," he whispered in a melancholy voice. "If this is all that is left, the Reds can have it."

THE SUN WAS SETTING AS they passed through Karlsruhe an hour later. Heidelberg lay eighty kilometers due north. Another two hours aboard the petrol express. The air had cooled considerably. A thick cushion of cloud hovered low on the horizon. Far away, lightning flickered, but Seyss couldn't hear the thunder. He lay his head on an arm and closed his eyes.

A sudden thud awakened him. The car was completely dark. He could barely make out his companion's shadow at the far side of the car. "Lenz," he yelled. "What was that?"

"A new engine?"

"Too close. It came from the car in front of us." Seyss hustled toward the sound, picking his way over the jerry cans as nimbly as a cat. Men's voices carried from somewhere down the track. He peered from the car, searching for a clue to his anxiety. Something felt wrong. For a soldier, that was enough.

The train shuddered, then began rolling forward. He tapped his leg in rhythm to the pulse of the engine. Faster, faster. He slid to his left and stared from the slats. Stars shone from the ground. He squinted his eyes and saw that he was looking at the night sky's reflection in a body of water. They were headed toward a broad river.

"It's the Rhine," he said, as if announcing its discovery.

"We don't want to get off on the other side," said Lenz, who was staring at the river from the opposite end of the car. "The French control the Saar. That must be Ludwigshafen, we're looking at."

"So?"

"So? The French aren't as forgiving as Uncle Sam or John Bull. Your *persilschein* means nothing to them. Haven't you heard? They're sending our men to labor camps in Biarritz and Avignon. I'm all for a holiday, but that's not exactly my style."

Seyss recalled Robert Weber telling him about the French government's policy of using captured German soldiers to man their factories and mine their ore. At the same moment, he remembered Rosen's words as he closed the wagon door. *Bon voyage.* And, suddenly it clicked. The Americans had put them into a car bound for the French zone. Two mouths fewer for the occupational army to feed. Who knew how many more men were in the cars behind them? As if to confirm his thoughts, the train veered left and he heard the hollow thump of the forward cars crossing onto the bridge.

"We're crossing the fucking Rhine!" shouted Lenz.

Seyss scuttled toward the door and began hoisting empty jerry cans and throwing them over his shoulder. Lenz joined him. When a small square had been cleared, Seyss jumped into the opening and began handing the cans up to his companion. He looked outside. The train was gathering speed, but their car had not yet come to the bridge. He lifted a can, then another. He jumped down a level. Empty gasoline cans fell onto his shoulders. The fumes were overpowering. The car jostled violently under him. They were on the bridge. Another few cans and he found the latch to the door. Wrapping his palms around the iron arm, he shoved it downward with all his strength. The lock disengaged and the door slid open. He swung from the car and looked ahead of him. Twenty yards farther on a platoon of soldiers waited, strung out along the wooden ramparts leading to the far side of the bridge. The silhouette of their helmets identified them as French. *Poilus.* Thirty feet below flowed the Rhine.

He smiled despite himself. The sergeant in Munich palming his watch. Private Rosen wishing him bon voyage. Brilliant! The men would have made the SS proud.

He looked up at Lenz, then back at the Frenchmen. Dammit. There was really no decision to be made. "Lenz, get your ass down here."

The stout man dangled over the edge of the shifting ledge. This was no time for hesitation. Seyss grabbed his feet and gave them a tremendous yank. Lenz tumbled down, all two hundred pounds of him and a dozen jerry cans, to boot. Seyss linked arms with him. "Ready?"

Seyss leaped from the train before Lenz could answer. The two men landed in a heap and rolled onto their backs. Fifteen feet away, a soldier raised his weapon. *"Arrêtez!"*

Seyss picked up Lenz and shoved him across the ramparts. "Jump!"

A shot was fired, then another. Lenz took a step forward and disappeared from view. Seyss followed a half second later. The water was cold; the current faster than he expected. He glanced up and saw a dozen rifles pointed at him. Then he was in darkness, safe under the bridge.

"Lenz!"

"Over here."

"Are you hit?"

"By a lousy frog? Never."

"Kick against the current. We must remain under the bridge."

"My brother was the sailor. Me, I'm infantry all the way." The gargling of water replaced his voice, then, "Shit. I can't keep this up."

Seyss swam toward the gravelly voice. A jagged piece of debris slammed into his cheek and he found himself sucking down a mouthful of water. Lenz was flailing now, arms slapping the water, head bobbing up and down, his motions growing more spasmodic, more hysterical. Seyss ducked under the water, surfacing behind the larger man. He positioned an arm around his shoulder, but Lenz knocked it off, spinning in the water, throwing both arms around Seyss as if hoping to climb up and over him. Christ, thought Seyss, it was like holding up a boulder. Frantic hands groped his shoulders, his shirt. He kicked violently, working to free Lenz, to turn him around so that he might drag him to a bridge support.

Suddenly, Lenz went under and a moment later, Seyss did too, dragged down by desperate fingers clawing at his waist and the frayed web belt that held his gold. Finally, he pried the fingers free, managing to wrap his forearm around Lenz's neck. Two firm kicks brought the men to the surface.

"*Ruhe!*" shouted Seyss through gasps for breath. Calm down! He laid an arm around Lenz's neck and began kicking toward the nearest pylon. Floodlights erupted from the western shore. Pale beams swept the water but did not penetrate beneath the bridge. He swam harder. After another minute, he pulled Lenz onto a rough concrete abutment, then joined him. Above them, footsteps pounded back and forth along the ramparts built to support the bridge. Voices called out in French and English, but he could not make out what they said.

Seyss lay still, gathering his breath. One hand checked his breast pocket for the Russian Colonel Truchin's identification. Good. Still there. The other fell to his trousers and the web belt that no longer circled his waist. He was standing in a snap, eyes combing the abutment, running over the flowing green water. It was hopeless. The gold was gone. And to his horror, so was his wallet, and with it two thousand dollars. He was penniless.

A new round of cries forced him to postpone his mourning. His first priority was to get to safety. They had one option and one option only. They must drift north a mile or two under cover of darkness, then swim to shore. It was doubtful the Americans would search for a couple of krauts trying to keep themselves out of French hands. He explained his idea to Lenz, who grunted his approval. One thing was certain: The man could not stay afloat long by himself. He would need assistance.

Seyss swam into the river and treaded water until he could find a piece of debris large enough to support Sergeant Hans-Christian Lenz. Part of him wanted to abandon the man right here. Lenz could drown for all he cared. He'd already brought enough bad luck. The idea never took root. A German officer's foremost duty was to his men.

Spotting a warped piece of wood large enough to have been a road sign or a section of flooring, he yanked it to his body and swam back to the pylon.

"Take this," he instructed Lenz. "Hold it above your chest and float under it. You must keep your head under the water for as long as possible until we are far from the bridge. Take a deep breath, then under you go. *Alles klar?*"

"*Ja. Alles klar.*" Lenz pulled at the tips of his mustache. "I should have guessed you were a filthy officer. What? A captain? Major? Or were you one of the ambitious pricks they promoted to colonel?"

"Major was as high as they saw fit."

"Maybe one day you'll tell me your real name."

"Maybe." Seyss offered a smile of good luck. "Off you go. I'll be right behind you."

Lenz held the piece of wood under his arm. With his free hand he grasped Seyss by the shoulder. "You saved me twice tonight. Once from a vacation on the Côte d'Azur, and then from a trip to a much hotter destination. Maybe one day, I can—"

"Shut up, Lenz. Time to swim."

CHAPTER
16

Upon his return to Flint Kaserne, Devlin Judge set out to track down General Oliver von Luck. It was six in the evening and outdoors the summer weather was inviting. A bold sun promised the local beer gardens a healthy crowd. Indoors, the *kaserne's* hallways were deserted. Gone were the legions of smartly attired soldiers making their daily rounds. Passing an open door, he'd hear a hushed voice or a muffled laugh. In the gloom of the endless corridors, a shadowy figure shuffled from one office to the next. A skeleton crew could put Germany to bed. Administering the peace was a less urgent pursuit than fighting a war.

Judge had been given a large office on the second floor. Four pine-top desks were spaced evenly around the room, scarred leftovers from the Academy's glory days. Among the initials and dates carved into their yellowed surface, he had found the inscriptions of several promising cadets. "1000 Jews equals 1 German." "*Lebensraum.*" Living space. And most haunting, the single word "*Vernichtung*" written ten times over in a perfect column. Annihilation. He had tried to repeat the word all ten times, but couldn't. It was physically impossible. After the fifth repetition, the word caught in his throat as a gush of nausea flooded his body. Above his head, an exposed pipe ran the length of the ceiling.

Droplets of water leaked from one end of it into a tin bucket set in the corner.

But nothing was as bad as the mural. Painted across the rear wall was a Teutonic knight in full chivalric armor, blue eyes focused on the sun-lit horizon, blond hair tousled by the wind. He rode a fiery black steed and brandished a gleaming sword. A scarlet Nazi armband was the artist's sole concession to modernity. Above the scene floating among puffy clouds was a silver ribbon bearing the words *Mein Ehre Heisst Treue*. Loyalty is my honor. Every time Judge looked at the picture he cringed.

Along with the office and the lovely artwork, he'd been given three aides. Two of them were on the road, visiting divisional offices of the military police. A third, one PFC George Merlin, an acned teenager from Iowa, had gone home for the day. As for Honey, he'd left for Munich to run down a lead. Someone from the local arm of Bob Storey's Document Collection Division had come across the personnel records of the First SS Panzer Division and Honey wanted to check if any of Seyss's comrades lived in the Munich area. Afterward he planned on finding himself a billet.

Judge slid back his chair and with a resigned sigh set to work. First, he sent queries to all CIC substations regarding last known whereabouts of General Oliver von Luck. Next, he transmitted wires to the seven regional chiefs of what remained of Germany's criminal police, known as the *Kripo*, asking for their cooperation in the search. The process was painstakingly slow, demanding the filling out of a mountain of forms, requests, and authorizations, each in triplicate. At ten past midnight, after a half hour of haggling with the night operator, he managed to get a direct line to Washington, D.C., and put in a call to Headquarters Military Intelligence at the War Department. Judge kept his request simple: Please forward all information regarding the last known posting of General Oliver von Luck, German Army. Urgent. To add a little zip, he said, "by order of General George S. Patton, Jr.," then hung up the phone.

"So you're looking for Ollie von Luck?"

Judge jumped in his chair, his eyes seeking the source of the words. A hunched figure lurked in the doorway, face cloaked in shadow. He had a high-pitched voice that delivered his English with a thick German accent.

"Who are you?"

"Altman is my name. Klaus Altman." The man stepped into Judge's office, the glare of the overhead light reflecting off his bald pate. He was young, no more than thirty, dressed in a pressed gray suit that despite its obvious quality looked as if it belonged to a taller man. A pronounced brow hid pale, anxious eyes. An aquiline nose and ruby lips curled in a salacious sneer completed the picture. He looked for all the world like a dirty-minded vulture. Advancing a step, he flashed a United States Army identification, holding it long enough for Judge to take a careful look.

"I am employed by the CIC substation in Augsburg," Altman went on. "Lieutenant Delvecchio is my commanding officer. I understand you're working with one of my colleagues, Sergeant Darren Honey?"

"That's correct." Judge motioned for Altman to take a seat, his heartbeat slowly returning to normal. The compact man shuffled forward, offering an ingratiating bow as he pulled the chair close to Judge's desk. Judge didn't know what scared him more: this little creep's midnight visit or that the counterintelligence branch of the U.S. Army was employing Germans, presumably former members of the military, presumably Nazis, as agents. "So you know von Luck?"

"Of course. He was a famous man, even well regarded . . . once."

Once. The ominous tone in Altman's voice warned of bad news to come. "What can you tell me about him?"

"You're familiar with the Abwehr? The intelligence wing within the Wehrmacht run by Wilhelm Canaris. The man for whom you are looking, General Oliver von Luck, served as Canaris's deputy chief from 1939 to 1944. Both men were active members of the Twentieth of July plotters, the cabal of officers who attempted to assassinate the Führer at his military headquarters in East Prussia."

"*Wolfschanze.*" Judge gave the German name of the headquarters. The wolf's lair.

"Ah, you speak German. Excellent." Altman grinned while cocking his eyebrows, as if the two shared an appetite for an exotic dish. When he spoke next, it was in his native tongue. "Von Luck is dead. He was arrested with Canaris and tried by the People's Court, Roland Freisler presiding. You're aware of Freisler's record?"

"Shit." Judge couldn't stop the word from escaping. "Yes, I am."

In the wake of the failed attempt on Hitler's life over five thousand men and women had been executed, many of them tried and convicted by said Roland Freisler, a strutting, raving sadist who derived overt and grotesque gratification from verbally lacerating the accused in his kangaroo court. The most prominent of the plotters were hung by piano wire and left to die a slow, excruciating death. Hitler had demanded that the executions be filmed.

"We know that Canaris was killed," said Judge, "but do you have confirmation that von Luck received the same punishment?"

"Someone so close to Canaris could not have survived."

Judge recognized an evasive answer when he heard one. "Do you have any proof he was executed?"

"Proof, no," replied Altman crisply, his integrity impugned. "I was stationed in France at the time, in Lyons. But believe me when I say von Luck could not have escaped the Gestapo's grasp." The pride in his voice left no doubt as to the German's wartime affiliation. "I'm sorry if you are disappointed."

"Thanks for the information, but I'll keep checking all the same."

"Suit yourself." Altman placed a hand on the desk and leaned close. "Might I ask if this is in connection with your search for Erich Seyss?"

"It is. Von Luck was Seyss's trainer for the Olympic Games. I assume Erich Seyss is what brings you here at this late hour."

The German answered a simple yes, mumbling an insincere apology for disturbing him, before delving on. "Excuse my curiosity, Major, but I had to speak with you in person. You see, I'm a little confused by what's been happening these last few days. It seems you're mounting an awfully large operation to bring in one man. Is there, perhaps, any information you are holding back that you might care to share with me? Any idea why Seyss is staying in the country?"

"We're not withholding any information, Mr. Altman. You have everything we have."

Altman waggled a finger, affecting a far-off glance. "If it were me, and I'd killed an American officer to get out of a camp, I'd turn south and keep going until I hit the Adriatic. Maybe I'd try for Naples. Either way, I'd get out of the country as soon as I possibly could. It must be something awfully important for Seyss to remain in Germany."

"There's nothing more I can tell you, Mr. Altman. It's as simple as that."

But even as the words left his lips, Judge was thinking of the dog tags Honey had retrieved from the basement of Lindenstrasse 21, hearing Corporal Dietsch recount Seyss's words. "One last race for Germany." He mulled his impressions over, mixing in the decidedly suspicious cast to Altman's voice. *It must be something awfully important for Seyss to remain in Germany.* Looking up, he found Altman's dull blue eyes boring into him, and suddenly, unaccountably, he grew breathless and a little dizzy. He remembered feeling the same way only once before, the first time he'd been to the top of the Empire State Building. Peering out over Manhattan, past Central Park into the Bronx, east to Brooklyn, and west up the Hudson River, he'd nearly fainted at the immensity of it all. He'd never imagined the world was so big. The revelation was as frightening as it was inspirational. A similar sensation swept over him now, a notion that he was tapping into something larger than he knew. And the thought dashed through his mind that he'd be smart to turn around this second and go home without asking any more questions. Francis could fend for himself.

"Too bad, then," said Altman. "I'm sorry for disturbing you so late in the evening, but my work demands I keep a rather odd schedule." His voice registered disappointment but his squirming lips never lost their lascivious posture. "I hope you didn't take fright."

"No," Judge lied, "not at all." He stood, still trying to shake off the discomfiting feeling as he accompanied his visitor to the door. "Mind if I ask what CIC has you doing these days?"

Altman shrugged helplessly in his too large suit. "I'm terribly sorry but most of our work is classified. I can only say that many of the men we're looking for here in the western zone are proving useful in the East."

Judge shook the man's hand, wishing him good-night. It was clear that Altman was referring to his former colleagues in the Gestapo. Gestapo stood for Geheimstaatspolizei. The secret state police. For the past ten years, they'd been spying on their fellow Germans. All they had to do was turn their snooping apparatus in the opposite direction and spy on the Russians. The work was the same. The only difference was to whom they reported. *Useful indeed.*

"At least we know Erich Seyss is in Munich," Altman said in parting. "If he stays in Germany, we'll find him. Let's hope you scared him underground. That's my territory. There's only so many places a man can hide."

Judge watched the man slip off down the corridor. His footsteps were exceptionally soft, little more than brushstrokes against the flagstone. Then they were gone, like a rain that had abruptly stopped. Judge strained his neck, squinting into the darkness to make out the man's crooked silhouette, but he saw nothing. Shivering, he crossed the hall to the rest room. He had an overwhelming desire to wash his hands and face. Suddenly, he felt very dirty.

CONTRARY TO WHAT HE TOLD Major Judge, Darren Honey did not proceed to the Munich arm of Colonel Robert Storey's Document Collection Division. The personnel records of the First SS Panzer Division had, in fact, turned up, but Storey had already received them in Paris. Nor did Honey, as he'd also told Judge, inquire about finding a billet for noncommissioned officers. Pointing the nose of his jeep north, he left Bad Toelz and made his way out of the foothills and into the lush plain that surrounded the city of Munich. As the roads worsened, and he began dodging shell holes, craters, and piles of rubble taller than the buildings they'd once comprised, he sat up straighter and his smile vanished. Soon his face took on a decidedly unpleasant cast.

Darren Honey was sick of war and sicker of being smack-dab in the middle of it. Most of all, he was sick of being someone else. His post in the 477th Counterintelligence Company of the United States Army was only the latest in a string of covers too long to enumerate. He hadn't landed at Morocco with Patton in '42, nor had he endured Anzio beach with Mark Clark. Everything he had told Devlin Judge about himself was false, including his name. The only honest thing about his appearance was the ribbon adorning his chest that denoted the Silver

Star. He'd been awarded the commendation in recognition for actions taken in Paris, France, on the fifth of June 1944, one day prior to the Allied landings in Normandy. He'd been sworn never to divulge what exactly he did, but it involved making sure that certain German generals visiting the French capital for a bit of Rest and Recreation were kept far away from their respective divisional headquarters in Normandy. It had cost quite a few lives.

Honey's work came under the heading SO, or special operations, known within the Organization of Strategic Services, or OSS, simply as Department II. His rank, not that it counted for much, was actually captain, which for a poor kid from Arlington, Virginia, who'd never even graduated high school, wasn't too shabby.

The OSS was America's secret intelligence service. Formed in 1941, just months before the Japanese attacked Pearl Harbor, it had already placed thousands of agents around the globe, from Burma to Bulgaria, Singapore to Stockholm. The man who commanded the OSS, who had built it from the very ground up, was named William J. Donovan. His heroics in the First World War as an officer in the Fighting Sixty-ninth had earned him the Congressional Medal of Honor, along with the nickname "Wild Bill." Contrary to his colorful moniker, Donovan was a mild-mannered, avuncular man, with thin gray hair and kind blue eyes. In the years between the wars, he'd made a small fortune as a Park Avenue attorney and consultant to many of America's largest corporations. He didn't speak loudly, but something about him made you pay close attention to his every word. People called him charismatic and magnetic. Honey called him sir, and did exactly as ordered.

Guiding the jeep across the Maximilliansbrücke and up Maximilianstrasse, Honey sighed with distress. Munich was an absolute wreck. Eight-five percent destroyed, according to the Allied bombing survey. All this destruction was getting to him, making it harder and harder to keep up his smiling persona as the ever-ebullient young sergeant from Texas. There came a point when enough was enough. He'd seen it in others: the constant irascibility, the inability to get a decent night's sleep, the need to keep moving, even if there wasn't a damned thing to do. And he was reaching that place himself. He didn't know what would happen if he ever got there. Some men started crying and didn't stop for a month. Others blew their brains out. Neither alternative sounded very appealing. He just hoped it didn't happen soon. He didn't want to disappoint Wild Bill.

Ten minutes' drive took him to an enormous redbrick building, formerly belonging to the Bavarian postal authority, that was more or less intact. Pulling over at the end of the block, he hopped from the jeep and entered the building. Today the boss was in town, down from Nuremberg where he was helping Justice Jackson check out the Palace of Justice as a possible site for the war crimes trial. Donovan was very concerned about Erich Seyss and anxious that everything possible was being done to track him down. He was also concerned about the men behind the investigation—especially Devlin Judge—though he wouldn't say how or why. He wanted to hear everything that had happened at Lindenstrasse this morning. Honey's job was to watch, listen, and report back.

Mounting the stairs to the third floor, Honey mulled over some of the things Donovan had told him three days ago. Apparently Seyss was guilty of a lot worse things than the Malmedy massacre. He had done unspeakable things on the Russian front. *Unspeakable.* That was Donovan's word and he didn't use it lightly. Seyss was dangerous all right. One of Hitler's best. Donovan had said something else, too— something that made Honey very nervous. This wasn't about a mere prison escape and the murder of an American officer. It was about something bigger.

As Darren Honey knocked on Donovan's door, he had the feeling he was about to learn what.

JUDGE ARRIVED IN HIS DRIPPING office the next morning at seven, prepared for a long wait. Altman's visit had unsettled him. If Oliver von Luck was dead, the investigation was, too. Unless the personnel records of the First SS Panzer Division listing the homes of Seyss's comrades panned out, Judge had nowhere else to turn. He'd be left chained to his desk, twiddling his thumbs for the next three days while praying for Seyss to show himself and trip an alarm. He shot the wall calendar an unfriendly glance. Thursday, July 12. Three days until his transfer expired.

Time. He needed more time.

Bracing himself for the fact von Luck was dead, he spent an hour drafting a comprehensive list of divisional headquarters whose military police he would contact to keep the heat on Erich Seyss. The Seventeenth in Stuttgart, the 101st in Munich, the Seventh Cavalry in Heidelberg—which if he wasn't mistaken was George Armstrong Custer's former unit.

He was glumly whistling the Garry Owen when his phone rang five minutes later. It was headquarters of military intelligence at the War Department in Washington, D.C. In three rushed sentences, a timid lieutenant named Patterson confirmed Altman's report, then abruptly hung up. Von Luck was, in fact, a Twentieth of July conspirator. He was arrested, tried by the People's Court, and convicted. Sentence presumably death, though no official word had ever been received as to his fate. Click.

Judge threw down the phone, cursing the world. He damned Altman for being right and Lieutenant Patterson for confirming it! Pushing himself away from his desk, he rose and paced the perimeter of his office. There had to be another way to gather information about Seyss. Shadow his friends, track down his lovers, locate members of his extended family, but Judge had no time to gather such information. Stymied by his lack of resources, he sought refuge in anger. What kind of cruel gift was it to give a man every means to track down his brother's killer while denying him the time to see the job through?

Fifteen minutes later, Judge's world righted itself.

A captain with the military police detachment of the Forty-fifth Infantry Division radioed in that he recalled there being a prisoner named von Luck confined to a bed at Dachau. Yes, that Dachau—the oldest and largest of Hitler's concentration camps situated fifteen miles northwest of Munich. A hospital had been set up on the premises to nurse the camp's ill back to health. Though infirm, von Luck was under arrest as a security suspect. How could anyone forget that name?

Judge immediately contacted the officer now commanding Dachau and confirmed that the von Luck in question was, in fact, General

Oliver von Luck, formerly deputy chief of the Abwehr, formerly trainer to German national champion Erich Siegfried Seyss, and that he was alive and in sufficient health to be questioned. An appointment to interview the prisoner was scheduled for two o'clock that afternoon.

Judge slammed his hand onto the desk and let go an enthusiastic, if abbreviated, rebel yell.

He was back in the game.

17

GEORGE PATTON WAS LIVID. The war had hardly been over sixty days and he'd been transformed from a general of the finest fighting men on God's green earth into a cockamamie combination of bureaucrat, politician, administrator, and nursemaid. If this was what victory wrought, to hell with it! He wanted war. It was a children's game compared to the tasks he'd been charged with as military governor of Bavaria.

Standing in his office on this warm, sunny morning, cigar in his mouth, he ran over the matters that needed his attention. He had to fix the roads, rebuild the bridges, repair the waterworks—including the whole damned sewer system. A toilet hadn't flushed in Munich since 1944. He had to demilitarize and denazify the civilian government, essentially meaning he had to fire every goddamned man and woman worth a damn. He had to look after the care and provisioning of a million American soldiers, a million German POWs, and a million ragtag displaced persons whom nobody, especially himself, wanted anything to do with. And all of this . . . *all of this* . . . he was supposed to accomplish without the help of any German who had ever been a member of the Nazi party! It was madness. Seventy-five percent of the country's 60 million citizens had had some tie or another to the National Socialists. Ike might as well ask him to juggle with one arm tied behind his back.

Worst of all, now he had to hold hands with the godforsaken Russians as if they were a couple of besotted newlyweds. Madness!

A crisp knock on the door to his office relieved him of his miserable thoughts. "What is it?"

The door opened and two men walked in, Hobart "Hap" Gay, his chief of staff, and a squat, bowlegged Russian supremo he didn't recognize. They all looked like apes anyway.

"Sir, I'd like to introduce Brigadier General Vassily Yevchenko," said Gay, a tall, plain-looking general who had served with Patton since 1942. "General Yevchenko insisted on seeing you this morning. It seems there's some problem with a few fishing boats we captured on the Danube River two days ago."

"Excuse me, General," Yevchenko cut in. "These boats on Danube. On *east side* of river and filled with German soldiers."

Patton advanced a step, his cheeks coloring at the sound of the barbarian's slur. All it took these days was the sight of a manure-brown uniform to set his blood racing. He'd had it up to his eyeballs with wining and dining the Russians. Since V-E Day, he'd eaten enough stuffed pig, borscht, and caviar, drunken enough vodka, and witnessed enough Cossack line dancing to last him the rest of this life and the next. It took every restraining muscle in his body to keep him from drawing his pistol and shooting this degenerate descendant of Genghis Khan right here and now.

"So?" barked Patton. "What the hell do you want me to do about it?"

"On behalf of Soviet government, we demand return of boats and prisoners immediately. All are property of Soviet armed forces."

"What did you say?" Patton asked. "Did I hear something about a demand?"

Earlier he was livid. Now he was plain furious. Patton shot a disbelieving glance at Hap Gay, who shrugged his shoulders, then returned his attention to this pathetic example of Russian manhood. Stepping closer to the Russian, he saw that Yevchenko was sweating like a stuck pig.

"We demand return of river craft. They are property of Soviet armed forces."

Hearing the Russian's demand for the boats turned Patton's mind to another subject that rankled him. Since occupying German territory, the Russian Army had been stealing every piece of machinery that wasn't nailed down—washing machines, typewriters, radios, you name it, they grabbed it—and sending it back home. As for the big stuff, factories, refineries, foundries, they had entire divisions trained to unscrew every last nut, bolt, and screw and ship the lot east to Moscow. Scavengers is what they were. Vultures. What was worse, loudmouthed New York Jews like Henry Morgenthau not only condoned Stalin's behavior, they insisted the Americans and Brits do the same. His crazed Morgenthau Plan—which Patton had figured for nothing more than some sort of ancient Talmudic revenge scheme—proposed robbing Germany of every last piece of industrial machinery it possessed. An eye for an eye, and all that. The crafty Semitic bastard even went so far as suggesting the Allies place members of the German military into indentured servitude for a period of ten years. Christ, but they were the same, the Jews and the Bolsheviks. Didn't anyone see that the only ones the Americans could count on were the goddamned Germans themselves? Madness!

"Two tugboats, one barge, one skiff . . ." Yevchenko was describing the boats he "demanded" that the Americans return. "Rowboat with oars and dinghy."

Suddenly Patton had had enough. Offering the Russian general his neatest smile, he strode to his desk, opened the top drawer, and drew out his pearl-handled revolver. With his smile firmly in place, he returned to Yevchenko—who by now had given up quivering for a posture of sheer frozen terror—cocked the pistol and placed it squarely against the man's beribboned chest.

"Gay, goddammit!" he shouted, "Get this son of a bitch out of here! Who in the hell let him in? Don't let any more Russian bastards into the headquarters." He turned to Paul Harkins, a senior member of his staff, who had joined Yevchenko's gripe session midstream. "Harkins! Alert the Fourth and Eleventh Armored and the Sixty-fifth Division for an attack to the east. Go! Now!"

Gay and Harkins dashed from the room to implement his orders.

Yevchenko, his pudgy countenance a squeamish yellow, remained face-to-face with Patton. After an eternity, neither man giving an inch, the Russian yelled "Devil!" then turned on his heels and ran after them.

When his office was once again empty, Patton let out a victorious belly laugh. In fact, he would have preferred to cry. This should be a day of rejoicing, he said to himself, without a worry about the future and the peace they'd fought for. But as no man would lie beside a diseased jackal, neither would he, George S. Patton, ever do business with the Russians.

He circled his desk, running a hand along its polished veneer, then collapsed into his chair. Churchill had had the right idea. Get into the Balkans, drive north into Central Europe, and take Prague and Berlin. Patton himself should have been in the German capital now. He'd pissed in the Rhine, why not on the Reichstag?

Restless with anger, frustration, and, despite the mountain of problems before him, boredom, he planted his hands onto the desk and stood, making a tour of his office. He stopped in front of a grand window overlooking the Isar River and the town of Bad Toelz. Past that lay a vast green plain, ideal territory for a rapidly advancing army of armored cavalry. And past that the East.

Patton picked up the telephone and rescinded the orders he'd given in Tevchenko's presence. He was already in enough trouble with Ike for taking his daily equitation in the company of SS Colonel von Wangenheim. At least those bastards in the Waffen-SS knew how to fight. Strike like lightning, take no prisoners, and attack, attack, attack! They were magnificent sons of bitches! And they weren't half wrong about what to do with the Jews, either. As for the Russians, they were scurvy bastards. The cooks in his Third Army could beat the living hell out of them.

Gay returned to the room with news that Patton had another visitor.

"Dammit, Hap, it better not be another red."

"No, sir. It's a delegation of city fathers. I believe, General, they wish to award you a commendation."

Patton checked his watch. "By God, send them in, Hap. About time somebody thanks us for the bullshit we're putting up with."

"Right away, sir," said Gay before retreating through the double doors.

Patton straightened his jacket and ran a hand along his collar, wanting to be sure that all of his stars were easily visible. The Boche loved pageantry almost as much as he did. Crossing to the window, he took up his position, hands clasped behind his back, eyes to the horizon. It was a decent pose, one that Napoleon used to greet his generals and lesser dignitaries. He fixed his gaze on a steeple in the distance, but his thoughts traveled far beyond.

To Prague. To Berlin. To Moscow.

East.

CHAPTER

18

INGRID GUIDED THE WHEELBARROW DOWN the center of the dusty road. Her hands were raw, her shoulders sore and swollen. *Five more steps*, she told herself. *Five more steps, then I can rest.* She steered the heavy load around ruts and rocks and bumps and furrows, squinting to drive the sweat from her eyes. And when she had taken five steps, she took five more, and then another five.

Normally the trip to Inzell took less than an hour on foot. The road cut across the far side of the valley, skirting the lake before plunging into the forest where it descended rapidly in a dizzying series of switchbacks. Five miles and fifteen hundred feet later, it reached the village. Today, however, the journey might as well have been fifty miles. She'd left Sonnenbrücke two hours ago and was barely at the far end of the meadow. At this rate, she wouldn't make Inzell until noon. She refused to think about the return trip up the mountain.

Gathering her breath, Ingrid struggled to adjust her grip on the slick handles. Her pace was deliberate, not only because of the weight of the load but because of its contents. Ninety-six bottles of wine lay in the iron bed, each wrapped in a damask hand towel borrowed from the linen closet. To be safe, she'd lined the wheelbarrow's rusted bed with the smallest of her mother's embroidered tablecloths. While the eight cases of Bordeaux wouldn't enjoy the bumpy trek to Inzell, at least they'd reach their destination intact—which was more than she could promise herself.

Breathing in with one step, out with the next, Ingrid maintained her sober pace. In an effort to redistribute the load from her hands to her shoulders, she had fashioned a makeshift harness from the coarse rope Papa kept to bind fallen game. The harness was attached to the center of the bed and passed over her shoulders and around her neck. A chamois cloth laid against the nape of her neck protected her exposed flesh from the splintery twine.

A half mile ahead, the road disappeared into the shadows spread by a curtain of Arolla pines. A soft breeze skittered past, then died, teasing her with the relief the distant shade would provide. She spotted a patch of grass at the foot of a pine and decided it would make an ideal resting place. *Five more steps*, she whispered to herself.

A quarter of an hour later, she was there.

Collapsing onto the grass, Ingrid closed her eyes. The forest buzzed and chirped and squawked with the frenetic joy of a warm summer's day but all she could hear was the throbbing of her own heart. After a moment, she sat up and took stock of herself. Her palms were an angry pink. Pale ovals surfaced across the underside of her fingers. Soon they would become blisters. Even seated, her legs trembled with fatigue. Pulling the cloth from her shoulders, she ran a hand along the back of her neck. The shallow groove left by the harness was hot to the touch. She checked her fingers for blood. Thankfully there was none.

Legs stretched before her, hands brushing the cool grass, Ingrid remained motionless until her heartbeat calmed and the sweat ceased pouring from her forehead. Her eyelids grew heavy. She wanted to sleep. A lazy voice told her not to worry about the return trip up the mountain. She could get a lift with an American serviceman. They were everywhere these days. Though forbidden to fraternize with Germans, none paid the rule much heed. Besides, she'd never had a problem convincing men to bend the rules—or even to break them.

Drifting off, she entertained a vision of herself stumbling into Inzell in her torn blue work dress and stained apron, the silk foulard tied around her head dark with sweat. Her face was blotchy; her lips crusted with spittle. She looked more like a haggard *hausfrau* than a damsel in distress. The horniest GI in Germany wouldn't give her a second look!

Shaking off her desire to sleep, she stood and walked to the wheelbarrow. Several bottles had shifted during the journey. She rewrapped each and positioned them carefully on top of the pile. How easy it would be to drop one, she imagined. To lighten her load by a single, heavenly pound. Angered by her lingering lethargy, she dismissed the thought. Then what would she bring home to Pauli?

Ingrid bent her knees and draped the harness around her neck. Taking firm hold of the wooden grips, she rose. For one excruciating moment, every muscle in her being screamed. Clenching her jaw, she allowed herself one deep breath, then began walking. The path was three miles, all downhill.

She had done it before. She could do it again.

THE VILLAGE OF INZELL BOASTED a grocer, a butcher, a clothing store, and a combination tobacconist and kiosk. The stores were evenly spaced along either side of a narrow road. All were identical two-story buildings of burnished wood and whitewashed cement topped with dark shingle roofs. Running up the mountainside behind them were a host of chalets, cabins, and huts. Window boxes blossoming with daisies and dandelions brightened every sill. To all appearances, the war had never ventured into this alpine valley. At the far side of the village, a tall stone fountain shaped like Napoleon's Obelisk shot water into a circular pool. Next to it stood a railway station, complete in every detail except one. No tracks passed before the passenger platform. Construction of the spur from Ruhpolding to Inzell had stopped in February 1943. After Stalingrad, every ingot of steel, every bar of iron, and every cord of wood was diverted to the protection of the Reich.

Setting down the wheelbarrow next to the fountain, Ingrid lifted the harness from her neck, then peeled the foulard from her hair and dunked her head into the cold water. A shiver of pride and relief swept her body. After rinsing her hands, she pulled her hair back into a ponytail and smoothed her dress. Her damp fingers made sure it clung in all the right places. Now she could do business.

"Good morning, Frau Gräfin Bach," chirped Ferdy Karlsberg as she entered his tiny store. "How are you this lovely day?"

Like every grocer she'd known, Karlsberg was short and fat and, if not a pincher, at least a leerer. He had ginger hair and bright blue eyes and cheeks so bloated she swore he must be caching a dozen acorns for the winter. As usual, he was having a great deal of trouble keeping his eyes from her dress. Today, though, she welcomed his interest.

"Good morning, Herr Karlsberg," she answered, determined to match his good cheer. "I'm wonderful, thank you." She didn't dare say it was much too hot for trudging down the mountain with a thousand-pound wheelbarrow. Instead, she chose her most vulnerable smile. "The usual, I'm afraid."

She removed a yellow card from her dress and passed it across the counter. Her ration card entitled her to three loaves of bread, two hundred grams of meat, one hundred grams of butter, one hundred grams of sugar, a pound of flour and a pound of wheat each week. Theoretically, it was enough to ensure a daily intake of twelve hundred calories for three adults and one child. But theory died a quick death in the real world. The meat—sausage, actually—was often rancid. The butter, sour. The bread always black and stale. There was nothing wrong with the sugar, flour, or wheat once one removed the rat droppings.

Karlsberg tore a square of brown paper from a dispenser on the wall and laid it on the counter. Turning his back to her, he ran a hand along his shelves collecting first the bread, then the sausage. Naturally he chose the smallest ones. He measured out the flour and wheat, weighing them on a scale she was sure ran a few ounces heavy, then placed each in a paper sack. When she asked about her sugar and butter, he shrugged. "The food authority failed to provide any in the latest delivery. I am sorry."

Ingrid offered Karlsberg her best smile. The food was hardly enough to feed a growing boy, let alone Papa, Herbert, and herself. She'd spent hours figuring how she might get her hands on a ration card entitling her to more food. Miners in the Ruhr were receiving double rations, as were farmers and skilled laborers. A widow and her child were hardly vital to the nation's reconstruction.

There was another way.

She recalled her visit from General Carswell, his kindly smile and flirtatious manner. *Would she be interested in answering some questions about her father's activities, say at the Casa Carioca in Garmisch?* Eyeing the meager provisions set on the counter, she decided she'd been naive to decline so quickly.

Karlsberg wrapped the bread and sausage, and using both of his stubby hands, slid them across the counter. "Is there something else I can help you with?" His eyes were fixed on the only thing he found more appealing than her wet dress—the wheelbarrow outside his front window.

Ingrid smiled coyly, baiting him. "Are you sure you don't have any sugar?"

Karlsberg blushed, then grew angry at his shame. "Come around back and don't make any trouble."

Ingrid guided the wheelbarrow to the rear of the building where the grocer was already waiting. She found the charade ridiculous. Everyone in the valley knew Ferdy Karlsberg was a black marketeer. She supposed Herr Schnell, the local constable, had insisted he run his operations from the back of his store. It was just like a Nazi to condone an illegal activity as long as it didn't soil the impression of legitimate business.

"What do you have to offer today?" Karlsberg asked, his smile back in place.

In the two months since the war had ended, Ingrid had become an expert in the workings of the black market. Reichsmarks were practically worthless, yet Germans were not permitted to own dollars. A new currency backed by a new government would not be introduced for a year or two. Still, people wanted something to eat, smoke, drink, and wear—in that order. The fiat of the new Germany was cigarettes, preferably American, preferably Lucky Strike. Want a pound of ham? Three cartons of Luckies. A bottle of White Horse scotch? Five cartons. A pair of hose? One carton. But most Germans did not have access to the American post exchange. For them—and Ingrid, who included herself in this number—any household item of value would do, provided you had someone to sell it to. Cameras and binoculars were in particularly hot demand. Wine, unfortunately, less so. For her, men like Ferdy Karlsberg existed.

Ingrid handed him a bottle, gauging his reaction as he removed the linen cloth.

Karlsberg's eyes glowed when he eyed the label—a 1921 Château Petrus. "Is it all this quality?"

She nodded. What did the fool expect Alfred Bach kept in his cellar? A few Rieslings and a Gewürztraminer?

For the next hour, Karlsberg examined the bottles one by one, making notations on a block of paper. Petrus, Latour, Lafite-Rothschild, Eschezeau. Wines fit for a king. When he had finished, he tallied up his figures, and pronounced, "Ten thousand Reichsmarks."

"That's all?" Ingrid was unable to conceal her disappointment. Ten thousand Reichsmarks sounded like a lot, but these days it was only equal to a hundred prewar marks.

"The market dictates the prices, not I, Frau Gräfin." He led her up the rear stairs into his back room. "How may I be of service?"

Ingrid handed Karlsberg a prepared list. His eyebrows rose and fell as he studied the paper. He gave her breasts a final ogle, then said, "Let us see."

Karlsberg drew a blue linen curtain to reveal a wall of cardboard cartons and wooden crates. Spam. Peaches. Pears. Corned beef. The bounty of the American army. He took several cans from each and set them on the counter. An ice box squatted in the corner. He opened it and took out a half dozen boxes of Danish butter and a dozen eggs. A burlap bag full of sugar slouched against the wall. He emptied two brimming scoops into a paper bag. Apples. Potatoes. Corn. Soon the counter was covered with enough food to keep her household fed for a month.

She sifted the goods. Something was missing. "I asked for steaks. Last week you assured me that you would have some good U.S. chops."

Karlsberg removed his spectacles and cleaned them with his apron. Several times he glanced up at her, only to look away when he met her gaze. Clearly he was mustering his courage. "I have the steaks," he said haltingly, "but I've given you all I can for the wine."

"You said ten thousand reichsmarks."

"And I've given you ten thousand reichsmarks' worth of groceries."

"Nonsense!" she exclaimed. "These bottles cost at least that much *before the war*, if you were fortunate enough to find them."

"Certainly, Fräu Gräfin is correct. However, customers are less discerning these days. A Latour may bring more than a simple *vin du table*, but not much."

Ingrid fought to hold her tongue. The prick might as well have both hands in her pockets stealing her money. She could feel her face flush with anger.

Karlsberg reached below the counter and brought out a carton of Chesterfields. "Take some cigarettes. You can *kompensieren*."

Kompensieren meant to trade or to barter. This is how it was supposed to work: Ingrid would take Karlsberg's cigarettes to a nearby farm and use them to purchase a hen or two, a dozen eggs, maybe even a gallon of fresh milk if she was so lucky. Bundling up her supplies, she'd find a train into the city—Munich, let's say—and trade half her eggs for lightbulbs, one of the hens for heating oil, a pint of milk for some medicine. If particularly canny, she might end up with a few cigarettes to spare, and at day's end, repurchase a bottle or two of wine from Karlsberg to toast her business acumen.

Good luck!

Ingrid had neither the time nor the opportunity to go from one vendor to the next trying to bargain for eggs or chickens or cigarettes. She lived in a secluded valley, fifty kilometers from the nearest town of any size. She had Ferdy Karlsberg and that was that. The only thing she could do with the Chesterfields was smoke them.

"It was steak I requested. It is for my boy."

Karlsberg stared at her long and hard, then went to the freezer and took out a white box that he placed on the counter. "Here are the steaks," he said, lowering his head as if ashamed by this show of weakness. "But you'll get nothing else out of me."

But Ingrid had seen something in the freezer that held far more appeal than the steaks. "Is that ice cream I saw in there?"

Karlsberg smiled. "Vanilla and strawberry."

Ingrid's first thought was of Pauli. He adored ice cream and hadn't had a spoonful of the stuff in over a year. He would be mad with joy. She could practically hear him giggling. Slow down, she cautioned herself. Even with an ice block or two in the wheelbarrow, the ice cream would melt long before she arrived home. Her only chance of getting the ice cream home in some kind of edible condition was to find someone to drive her there and on this of all days, she hadn't seen a single GI. It figured. Another possibility came to mind. Ferdy Karlsberg used to deliver their groceries in an old brown Citroën truck. If anyone had gasoline, it would be he. As a black marketeer, he had connections, and Lord knew, he was as frugal as a Swiss.

Suddenly Ingrid was acting, not thinking. Recalling his lascivious glances, she grabbed his apron and pulled him closer. Before she knew what she was doing, she had whispered the proposition in his ear. Karlsberg turned beet red. His eyes were wide with surprise and desire. "Well?" she asked. "Is it a deal?"

"*Jawohl, Gräfin.*" The disrespect had evaporated from his voice.

Ingrid stepped away from the counter and shook her hair loose. A streak of heat soured her body, momentarily promising nausea. Drawing a deep breath, she steeled herself to her task. She unbuttoned the front of her dress, pulling down the sleeves one at a time. And when she was sure she had his fullest attention, she unsnapped her brassiere and pulled it off her shoulders. There she stood, daughter of Germany's richest industrialist, object of adoration for field marshals, famous actors, champion drivers, and the like, breasts pale and exposed, nipples embarrassingly erect, in front of a fumbling *bunzli* whose face had grown so red, so feverish, that the mere whisper of a pinprick would make him explode. And all for a quart of vanilla ice cream. She'd take two quarts, goddammit. Let him stop her!

Karlsberg let slip a petulant whimper and the next thing she knew, he was over the counter, clammy hands groping her breasts, moist breath wet in her ear, moaning about love and desire and she didn't know what else. Ingrid wrestled free of his clumsy grasp, fighting off the inquisitive hands, then taking an abrupt step to the rear. The excited grocer tumbled headfirst onto the floor, landing in a pile at her feet. The entire incident had lasted no more than ten seconds.

Ingrid rushed to fasten her brassiere and button up the dress. But she held her ground. Neither shame nor fear nor acute humiliation—his or hers—would separate her from her groceries. She waited until Karslberg dusted himself off, then addressed him in her most formal voice. "Be sure to load everything into the truck *before* you get the ice cream. And bring an ice block or two along just in case."

Karlsberg remained frozen to the spot, his cheeks angry, his eyes accusing.

"*Sofort!*" she shouted. "Right away."

Karlsberg jumped to work.

CHAPTER

19

NUMBER 61 RUDOLF KREHLSTRASSE SAT at the end of a wooded lane high on a steep mountain near the outskirts of Heidelberg. It was an unremarkable house, leaves of faded yellow paint falling from its neglected woodwork, birch shingles curled with age. Set back from the street among a clutch of leafy oaks, it cowered like the shy girl at a party, the homely lass who went home with her dance card empty. Erich Seyss double-checked the number, then strolled up the walk and rapped on the door. Heavy feet sounded from the rear of the house. Waiting, he gazed at the city below.

Heidelberg had escaped the war unscathed. Declaring it a hospital city seven months earlier, the high command had transferred the local garrison—by then a Volksturm detachment peopled with elderly men and teenage boys—fifteen kilometers north to Mannheim. Red crosses painted on fields of white decorated dozens of city roofs, mute pleas to the Allied bombers, who by then held mastery of the sky. It was a quaint convention, and one, to his surprise, that the Allies had honored. Looking to his left, he made out the medieval redbrick ruins of the *schloss*, at once majestic and crestfallen, slumbering in the morning haze. And below them, the Neckar flowing lazily under a half dozen crumbling bridges, bisecting the city into old town and new. The view had looked the same in 1938, in 1838, and a hundred years before that. It was the Germany of Martin Luther, the Great Elector, and the Kaiser; the Germany of Hegel, Bismarck, and Hindenburg.

Twisting his head, he peered north. On the horizon, a plain of ash and rubble interrupted lush fields of green. Mannheim, an industrial city of half a million, had been razed from the map by Allied bombs. A cigarette burn on the fertile landscape. *And whose Germany was that?* he wondered. The answer came to him as the front door squeaked open. It was his.

"*Ja?*"

Peeking from behind the door was a husky man with accusing dark eyes, a slow wit's underbite, and short black hair glistening with tonic. He wore a white shirt buttoned to the neck and a black blazer riddled with moth holes.

Seyss pushed open the door and walked into the house. "Jesus, Bauer," he said. "You look like you're headed to a funeral. You must learn to relax. It's summertime. Birds are singing, the sun is shining."

Bauer bowed, his stubborn features finding no humor in the remark. "It is an honor to welcome you to my home, Herr Major."

Seyss patted him on the shoulder. "Call me Erich. We left our ranks behind with our uniforms and our pride. How have you been keeping yourself?"

"There is still work, at least for now. Rumor is the Americans will shut down our factories any day. You'd think with so few plants still working, the Allies would leave us with what we have. But no, they want to bring the entire country to its knees."

"Don't worry, Bauer. Egon won't let that happen. He's a fighter, isn't he?"

Bauer nodded, but his furrowed brow betrayed his doubts.

Heinz Bauer was a man whose life was defined by his work, the third generation of the Heidelberg Bauers to give his life to Bach Industries. As chief of factory police at Bach Munitions Work No. 4, his mandate was simple: Keep the imported labor or *ostarbeiter* working. Storming the floor in the black uniform of the civilian SS, truncheon in hand, he was a sight to behold. The smallest complaint, the slightest slowdown in work, was met with a blow from Bauer's truncheon or a kick from his gleaming jackboots. A single word always punctuated the warning. *Arbeit!* His nickname was Heinz the Terrible, and he treasured it more than a commendation from the Führer himself.

The interior of the house was as shabby as its facade, but fastidiously clean. Threadbare carpets beaten to within an inch of their lives covered cracked wooden floors. Faux Louis XV chairs lurked in dark corners. Somewhere there was an immaculate sterling tea set sitting atop a polished coffee table. Seyss was sure of it. He'd find the same sad paeans to respectability in every house along the block. The German working class was obedient if not original. A photograph of the Führer held prime place on a wooden dresser in the living room. Next to it lay his copy of *Mein Kampf.* And behind them, a photograph of his deceased wife. State first. Family second.

"I understand you've rounded up a few of my men?" Seyss asked, peeking his head round a corner.

"Just two, I'm afraid. Biedermann and Steiner. They're in back. Kuprecht and De l'Etraz didn't show."

"Just as well. We'll be better off as a squad of four. Let's go say our hellos. I'm anxious to see the boys." Seyss was moving faster now, a blur of decision, an officer of the Reich once again.

"Please, Herr Major, one moment," called Bauer. "Herr Bach phoned earlier. He demanded that you call at once. The phone is this way."

"Demanded, did he?" Seyss asked in amusement. The prospect was out of the question. He didn't want Egon to learn he'd lost the two thousand in cash he'd been given. *Terminal,* he would say, was your first and only responsibility. Egon could sod off. A civilian couldn't understand an officer's duties to his men. Seyss would get the money himself. It was a question of pride. "Later, Bauer. Right now, we have more pressing matters."

"*Jawohl,* Herr Major."

Bauer lowered a shoulder and led the way to a musty salon at the rear of the house. Two men sat smoking on a worn couch. The nearer one was blond and broad-shouldered with a fair complexion. His name was Richard Biedermann. He was a handsome man, if one could forgive the kidney red scar meandering from his chin to his right ear. Shrapnel posed difficulties for even the best battlefield surgeon. Hermann Steiner was less imposing, a paper pusher by the look of him. Short and thin, with greasy black hair, rimless spectacles, and a rat's inquisitive snout. Seyss knew better. Steiner was the battalion sniper. He'd never known a better shot.

"Good morning, boys," he said. "It's been a long time. Keeping yourselves out of trouble?"

Both men rose sharply from the couch, shaking Seyss's hand while wishing him a buoyant good-morning. Seyss patted each on the arm, asking how they had made out since the end of the war. Both had served under him during the Ardennes offensive and through the last months of fighting. Both were wanted in connection with the affair in Malmedy.

"Forget about us," said Richard Biedermann. "We're worried about you." Members of Seyss's unit had nicknamed Biedermann the Cub for his close physical resemblance to Seyss and his cloying habit of sticking near his commanding officer.

"Oh?"

Biedermann handed Seyss a newspaper. "This morning's edition."

Seyss gazed at the front page of the *Stars and Stripes* and found his own picture staring back at him. It was the photograph taken upon his incarceration in Garmisch, better even than the one in his *soldbuch*. He forced a smile even as his stomach dropped. Was this Judge's doing, too? He should have shot the man when he'd had a chance.

"Once a star, always a star," said Hermann Steiner. "It seems, Major, you are famous again."

Seyss tried to laugh but managed only to groan. "Be serious. Do I look anything like the man in that photograph?" He plucked the spectacles from Steiner's nose and put them on. "And now?" He lost his posture and shuffled from one side of the room to the other. "Just another poor German looking for something to eat. How many of us are there? A million? Two million? Ten? Do you think this photograph is enough to see me captured? Besides, where we are going, there are no Americans to look for us."

"It's not the Americans we are worried about," said Biedermann. "There is a reward, too. A hundred dollars at the American post exchange. Not bad, these days."

Seyss kept his smile glued to his face, but inside he acknowledged a swell of disappointment. Biedermann was right. These days a German would sell his mother for a hundred dollars, then ask how much he could get for his father. Access to the post exchange was an even better idea. With a hundred dollars, a man could purchase cigarettes enough to earn a fortune on the black market. This was, he had to admit, very bad news.

Casting an eye at Bauer, Biedermann and Steiner, he wondered just how quick one of them might be to turn him in to the authorities. None of them knew the true nature of their mission. They'd been asked to accompany Seyss to Berlin, no reason given save on a matter of importance to the Fatherland, and they'd accepted. Six years of war had conditioned them not to ask questions. For their services, they'd been promised a one-way ticket to South America via the port of Naples. A Croatian priest in the Vatican, the Reverend Dr. Krunoslav Draganovic, was providing travel visas to all those who could prove themselves good Catholics of blameless character and morals. It turned out members of the SS were a particularly religious lot. Along with a certificate attesting to their unblemished souls, an administrative fee was required. Fifteen hundred dollars was deemed adequate to cover the reverend doctor's travails. The proceeds to be earned on the black market from Seyss's reward would cover that fee twofold. The Americans were proving cleverer than he had expected.

"Even the *Kripo* is looking for you," added Steiner. "An inspector came round the bar asking too many questions. He was a real bumbler, but others might not be."

Seyss decided to confront any hesitation head-on. "If any of you men want out, you can go. I know plenty of Germans willing to take a risk for the benefit of our country. We have lost the war, true. But I, for one, am not willing to lose the peace."

Heinz Bauer stepped forward and clapped his hand on Biedermann's muscled shoulder. "We're not going anywhere."

Biedermann shook his head. "*Kein Angst, Herr Major.* Don't worry, Major. We wouldn't desert you."

Steiner sat down on the couch, nonchalant as ever. "Jesus, with all this talk we could be in Berlin already."

Seyss thanked the men, then pulled up a chair. "So what have you got for me?"

Bauer licked his lips and leaned forward. "What we're looking for is in Wiesbaden, fifty kilometers up the road. The Wehrmacht kept a lockup for Russian prisoners there until late last year. Everything taken from them is stored there: Guns, ammunition, uniforms."

"And the price is still a thousand U.S.?"

Bauer nodded.

"Including the truck?"

"Yes, of course. Everything exactly as I told Herr Bach." His eyes creased with worry and Seyss knew he'd have to tell Bauer soon about losing the money.

"Go on, now. You've got me excited."

"Our contact is an American officer," continued Bauer. "What with the military police in an uproar and half their army looking for the dreaded criminal, Erich Seyss, he won't go near the usual spots. I had a hard time convincing him not to cancel our agreement. He's agreed to meet at the Europäischer Hof. A group of music professors from the university plays for a thé dansant every afternoon at four."

"The Europäischer Hof is out of the question," Seyss scoffed, more irritably than he'd wanted. "The only ones there will be American troops."

"Actually, just officers. My contact decided a meeting would be more inconspicuous among his colleagues."

"And you agreed? Jesus Christ, Bauer, what about the nonfraternization rules? No Germans will be allowed inside."

"Oh, he wouldn't sell these guns to a German," retorted Bauer. "I told him I was representing a Britisher. A private collector. Your mother *is* English or something, right?"

"Or something."

Seyss sighed loudly while running a hand along the back of his neck. He imagined himself walking into a salon packed full of American officers, trading quips with a colonel from Milwaukee while slugging back a couple of drinks. He couldn't pass himself off as an Englishman. He didn't have the manners, the jargon, or the sickening self-effacement that came so easily to a Brit. An Irishman, though, was a different story.

With a decent blazer, a haircut, and a pair of new glasses, no one would recognize him. Besides, who would dare think he'd infiltrate their ranks? Seyss caught himself. He'd said the same thing about his returning to Lindenstrasse.

"Bring me your best suit," he said to Bauer. "Whatever you'd wear to your daughter's wedding. Hurry up, then."

"Already done, sir." Bauer shuffled from the room, returning a minute later with a navy suit folded over one arm, and a shirt and tie on the other. "Size forty long. Neck fifteen and a half. Shoes an eleven."

Seyss tried on the jacket. A little loose but more than passable. Bauer might look like a half-wit, but he was sharp as a tack. Something to keep in mind. "So tell me, what name does our man go by?"

CHAPTER
20

EVERY GERMAN CITY OF SIZE OR REPUTE boasts at least one five-star hotel. In Heidelberg it was the Europäischer Hof. Three wings of weathered dolomite granite dominated a cobblestone courtyard. Ceramic planters brimming with colorful flowers prettied the marble stairs that rose to the lobby. At either side of a revolving door, a military policeman replete with white helmet, white spats, khaki uniform, and Sam Browne belt, scrutinized the arriving guests. The afternoon thé dansant was an officers-only affair.

Seyss lent his step a spritely air as he climbed the stairs to the hotel. Passing the MPs, he threw in a tap of his shoe to show his delight at the cheery music drifting from the main salon. "Lovely day, eh, boys?" he ventured, sure not to slow his pace. Hesitation meant uncertainty, and uncertainty that for some reason he shouldn't be there.

"Have a nice time, sir," one MP replied. The other had already focused his attention on a brace of general officers at the foot of the stairs.

"Aye," said Seyss, and he was past them. So much for his picture in the paper. He felt strange, almost gay, masquerading as an Irishman. His new suit fit better than he had hoped. His shoes, were they to be inspected, supported his cover nicely. Brogues from Churches of London. His lack of identification might prove problematic, but he had a story up his sleeve just in case. Something about being rolled by a German whore. They were a tough lot, he was prepared to say, and angry . . . but who could blame them? As for his cover, he had decided upon a reporter. The country was lousy with them. Wearing a white cotton shirt and a maroon club tie, he was the embodiment of the victor arrived to claim the spoils.

Seyss strolled past the reception desk and up a few stairs, letting himself be guided by the music. The salon was packed with American officers, most in forest-green jackets and khaki-colored trousers, all with a stiff drink in hand. He passed through their ranks, offering a polite nod, a hushed hello, and once, a brief handshake, when a drunken lieutenant offered him a scotch on the rocks. He paused to take a pull of the scotch, and in a second polished the whole thing off. He slid across the floor keeping a beeline for the bar. On the stage, a quintet attired in dinner jackets was playing an unfamiliar song with an upbeat tempo. Suddenly a young officer hopped onto the stage and began belting out the lyrics.

"*Bei mir bist du schön . . .*"

Hearing the German lyrics, Seyss did a double take, then laughed loudly, hoping to cover his surprise. It was a sign, he told himself. A none-too-subtle reminder just how close Germany and America actually were.

"I'd take the Andrews Sisters over that lout any day," boomed an officer who had appeared at his side. "Maxine's the one for me." He was a homely man with a pencil-thin mustache, a shorter and fatter version of the jug-eared American who'd starred in *Gone With the Wind.* An oak-leaf cluster adorned his epaulets. "Everybody's crazy for Patty: the thick blond hair, those bedroom eyes. Not me, friend."

Seyss had no idea who the Andrews Sisters were, or who Maxine was, for that matter. Still, it was clear the officer expected some kind of answer. "Yes, indeed," he answered. "Maxine's a gorgeous lass."

"*Maxine?*" The officer eyed Seyss oddly. "What are you, kidding me? She's the homely one. But she's safe. You wouldn't have to worry about her running around on you when you're over here. And boy, does she have a set of pipes."

Seyss wasn't sure if he was referring to her tits or her tonsils, so he simply nodded his head, wanting to escape further conversation. "Indeed, Colonel. A fine set."

A hand on his arm prevented his departure. "What are you, a Brit?"

Seyss retreated a step, forcing a smile. "Irish, actually. Just over to do a story for the local paper."

"Sorry, guy. Didn't pick up the accent. A short round ruined the hearing in my left ear." He extended a hand. "Abe Jennings, nice to know you."

Behind his grin, Seyss gritted his teeth. "Jerry," he responded heartily. "Jerry Fitzpatrick." He'd chosen the name with a bent toward irony.

"Hello, Jerry. Where you from over there?"

Seyss sighed inwardly. He was due at the bar any minute now. "County Mayo. Have you been?"

"Me? Heck, no. But you have to say hello to a chum of mine, Billy McGuire. He's always going on about his aunt or uncle in County Antrim. Stay right here, I'll go get him."

"Certainly." But Seyss had no intention of doing any such thing. He waited till Jennings was across the room, then hurried to the bar. He checked his watch and saw that he was five minutes late. Taking a seat on a leather stool directly under an ornate cuckoo clock, he glanced to his right and left. He was looking for a Captain Jack Rizzo. Bauer's description of the man was less than perfect: tall, dark hair, loud—a typical American. Funny, Seyss thought. He would describe a typical American differently. Chatty, undisciplined, and lazy, with lousy posture to boot.

A steady stream of officers approached the bar, ordered drinks, then headed back to the main salon. Half fit Bauer's description. Not wanting to call attention to himself, Seyss asked for a whiskey, paying with a lone twenty he'd discovered floating in his pockets.

The crowd was growing by the minute. At least a hundred Americans milled about the dance floor: officers, civilians, and plenty of women. One or two couples had pushed their way to a corner of the parquet floor and were dancing. With all the talk it was becoming difficult to hear the band. Seyss gave himself ten more minutes, then he'd go. He didn't want to risk being caught up in conversation with Jennings or his buddy McGuire from County Antrim. Americans were so damned friendly. Five minutes', gabbing and they thought they were your best pal. The last thing he needed was to meet someone who'd actually been to Ireland.

A hand on his shoulder interrupted his thoughts.

" 'Pardon me, boy, is this the Chattanooga choo-choo?' "

Seyss inclined his head and spoke the insipid words that had been rattling inside his head all day long. " 'Track twenty-nine, boy, can you give me a shine?' "

"Jack Rizzo, how are ya?"

Seyss introduced himself as Jerry Fitzpatrick, and said he was fine, thank you.

Rizzo leaned on the bar, snapping his fingers to garner attention. "Bartender, give me a double scotch, easy on the ice." He pointed to Seyss's half-empty glass. "You okay or you need another?"

"I'm good, thanks."

As Bauer had said, Rizzo was tall and dark, but his doleful eyes and heavy beard gave him the appearance of a Mediterranean—what the SS Eugenics Office would label "skull type IV—not suitable for incorporation into the Reich."

"Your pal told me you wanted to have a look at some of my merchandise," Rizzo said.

"That would be lovely," Seyss answered equably. "I'm in the market for some rather specific items. I'm planning on opening a small museum back home in Dublin. I hope it doesn't inconvenience you too much."

"That's what I'm here for, friend. Not to worry." Rizzo tapped his hand in time to the music, looking this way and that. With a mighty swig, he drained his cocktail, then leaned closer, and whispered, "Wait till you see this place. Goddamn warehouse is loaded with enough of Ivan's crap to start another war."

"*Another war?*" Seyss knitted his brow in horror. "We wouldn't want that."

"Just joking, Jerry. Drink up and let's get out of here."

THE ARMORY IN WIESBADEN WAS the size of a soccer field and had been hastily built from cheap corrugated iron. Installations similar to it had sprung up all over Germany in the fall of 1941 when on a front two thousand miles long, the Führer's armies had advanced unchecked across the Russian countryside. What glorious days! One city after another had fallen: Kiev, Minsk, Smolensk. In their wake, the conquering troops had left behind a million prisoners of war and the weapons they had laid down. Captured soldiers were marched to the rear, or when expedient, shot. Their weapons—pistols, machine guns, tanks, and artillery—were destroyed or loaded onto flatbeds for shipment to Germany.

Seyss waited in the front seat of the Buick as Rizzo spoke to the lone sentry guarding the armory. It was clear by their easy banter that the two were well acquainted. A bill or two exchanged hands, and after a pat on the back, the sentry pulled open the gates and waved them through. Rizzo drove the Buick to the rear of the armory, braking beside a pair of tall barn doors. "Shall we see if we can find what you're looking for, Mr. Fitzpatrick?"

"Very kind of you indeed." Seyss swung open the door, glad for the chance to stretch his legs. Speaking English for the past three hours had left him with a terrible headache. Rizzo was the kind of man who viewed silence as a personal threat. He'd gabbed constantly, demanding Seyss's view on everything, from the best way to avoid the clap to the question of trans- versus consubstantiation. Everything two good Catholic boys needed to square between them.

Rizzo went round to the trunk and returned with two army-issue flashlights and a crowbar. He handed a flashlight to Seyss, and said, "Power only runs till seven around here. Even with the lights on, it's pretty dim. I know my way around this place, so follow me."

Seyss watched Rizzo unlock the doors, biting his tongue to keep from saying that he, too, knew his way around the place. Stepping inside the pitch-dark warehouse, he ran a hand along the door frame until he felt the rounded plastic form of a light switch. He flicked it and a few doddering bulbs came to life. A mountain of crates rose before him, a pine ziggurat of Soviet weaponry.

Rizzo turned on his flashlight and shone it into the gloom. "Your pistols, rifles, machine guns, and whatnot, are right in front of you— these six aisles to the left. Ammo is kept in a separate pen at the back of this dump. Uniforms are all the way to your right. Ivan's trucks are in the garage next door. Beauts, wait till you see."

Seyss tucked away the information. "Let's start with the firearms, shall we, Captain?"

"You're the boss, Jerry."

Seyss moved quickly from one aisle to the next until he found what he was looking for. He brought down a crate of Tokarev TT-33s and had Rizzo pry it open with his crowbar. He removed a pistol and examined it. Little effort had been taken to properly pack the guns. A stubble of rust grew from the barrel. He grasped the slide and drew it back. It didn't budge. He picked up another pistol, then another, until he'd found four in working condition. Laying them on top of the crate, he moved on. A little looking turned up a decent submachine gun, a Degtyarev PPSh-41, or *Pepshka*, still packed in cosmoline, and a Mosin-Nagant sniper's rifle with a scope attached and twenty-seven notches cut into its stock.

"If you don't mind, I'll need a few rounds as well." Seyss adopted a docent's earnest tone. "We would like to give our visitors the fullest idea of what our boys were up against."

Rizzo hesitated a moment, then shrugged, and told Seyss to follow him. Inside the ammo pen, Seyss gathered a few hundred rounds of various shells, no more than the four-man team could divide among themselves. If they needed more, they would find it en route.

Getting his hands on the proper uniforms took less time than he had expected. An hour of digging through heavy cardboard cartons turned up two dozen tunics of coarse pea-green wool whose sky-blue epaulets bore a slim golden stripe. The uniforms belonged to the NKVD—the Russian state security police that functioned as a combination of his own Gestapo and army field police. He picked out three he thought would fit his men, then spent a few extra minutes making sure he found a suitable uniform for himself. He knew firsthand that officers of the NKVD took particular pride in their appearance. On three separate occasions, he had masqueraded as one—the last time in Kiev for an entire month. Posing as Colonel Ivan Truchin, hero of Stalingrad, he had convinced the local artillery commander to place his guns at the city's southern flank in advance of a German counterattack he knew would be coming from the north. His experience had imparted to him one lesson above all others: Ordinary Russian troops feared the NKVD more than the enemy itself.

Seyss hefted the uniforms and carried them back to Rizzo. "And the truck?"

"Near the loading dock. Follow me." Rizzo led Seyss down a long aisle, then turned left. Five steps farther on, a heavy iron door blocked their path. Rizzo fiddled with his keys before selecting the proper one and shoving open the door. "We've got about a dozen GAZs, some Zhigulis, even a couple of Fords sent over during Lend-Lease."

Parked inside the garage were at least twenty trucks, a dozen tanks, and a slew of self-propelled artillery pieces. Seyss patted the hood of the nearest truck, smiling. Proximity to heavy weapons and transport never failed to boost a soldier's spirits. He had the guns, the ammo, the uniforms, and now, even the two-and-a-half-ton truck Egon had promised. The runt was to be commended. All Seyss needed was the money to pay for it and the plan might work—at least this phase of it.

The Soviets had established a permanent residence in the heart of Frankfurt, seat of the American military government, ostensibly to strengthen ties with the American command, but in fact to monitor and interfere with the work of Dwight Eisenhower and his deputy, Lucius Clay. Each day at 3:00 P.M. a truck bearing members of the diplomatic mission and packed with booty liberated from the western zones departed the residence for Berlin. Their route was always the same. Friedrichstrasse to Wilhelmstrasse, then a left turn onto the autobahn. What better cover could Seyss want than to pass his team off as members of the diplomatic mission? American military police would be reluctant to stop a truck carrying four Soviet soldiers. Once they crossed into the Russian zone, they could travel free of any worries.

"Nice," said Seyss, patting Rizzo on the back in a show of bonhomie. "A wonderful addition to my museum. I'm thinking a diorama. The valiant Russians breaking out from Leningrad, advancing across Lake Ladoga to encircle the Nazi foe."

But Rizzo was uninterested in his plans for the exhibit. "So listen, this stuff's yours for a thousand even. Payable on receipt. But I can't let you have the truck until Saturday night. Still a couple arrangements I've got to make."

Today was Thursday. Were he to pick up the truck Saturday night, he'd have only one day to drive to Berlin. Terminal was scheduled to begin Monday at 5:00 P.M. Tight, but he had no alternative. He reminded himself he still needed to raise a thousand dollars. He had his own arrangements to make.

"That shouldn't be a problem. Have it in good working condition and gassed up by midnight. We'll meet outside the hotel in Heidelberg at nine and drive here together. We'll settle up then."

Rizzo motioned to the crates at his feet. "What about this stuff?"

"I'll take it all Saturday. And I mean it about the truck being in good working condition. Check the oil, the brakes, and throw a few extra cans of fuel in the rear."

"What do you want to do? Drive the truck to Ireland?"

Seyss smiled, but didn't answer. *Wrong direction, Captain Rizzo.*

CHAPTER

21

JUDGE BARELY MADE IT TO the side of the road before vomiting.

"You all right, chief?" Sergeant Honey called from his customary position behind the wheel of the jeep.

Judge waved a defeated hand and raised his head to answer, but what remained of his lunch beat his words to the draw. Head bowed, he fell to one knee. Even close to the grass, the air was rank, cut with a piss-sour stench that made his skin itch and his stomach buckle. The odor of decay clawed his airways, suffocating him. He couldn't erase the smell, but he could block it. Closing his eyes, he pictured himself in his mother's kitchen, perched like a hawk above the stove waiting for her apple fritters to come out of the frying pan. Small rings of apple dipped in a honey batter, fried in cooking oil, then dusted with powdered sugar and cinnamon. As a child, he'd liked nothing better in the world, the scent most of all. The vividly rekindled memory subdued his olfactory nerves and after a few more breaths, he was able to get to his feet. *Apfelkuchen* was what she'd called the dessert, and like the fetid air he was breathing, it was a uniquely German creation. The reminder of his blood heritage caused him to flush with shame.

Wiping his mouth, Judge trained his eyes on the source of the foul stench. One hundred yards down the road, a wide steel gate striped with barbed wire stood open, beckoning. Three words were inscribed above the gate. *Arbeit Macht Frei.* He read them and shivered. Work shall set you free.

He had arrived at Dachau.

A village of low-slung barracks greeted the two Americans as they entered the camp, long gray buildings hewn of cheap lumber. Twenty, thirty, forty . . . he lost count quickly. Visible to the left was a windowless blockhouse from which four redbrick chimneys rose into a hazy sky. A sign next to the gate gave the camp's name. Under it was written, *Liberated April 29, 1945. Forty-fifth Infantry Division, United States Army.* Judge added his own postscript. Founded 1933 as a political reeducation center. Converted to a Konzentrationslager, or KZ, in 1936. He didn't know when it had begun gassing and cremating its inmates.

"Let's get this over with as quickly as possible."

Honey nodded. For once, he did not smile.

THE HOSPITAL WARD HAD WHITE walls and a warped wooden floor and stank of disinfectant and excrement. Screens had been nailed over each window but a squadron of flies buzzed in Judge's head as he walked down the aisle. A single fan hung from the ceiling, turning too slowly to do any good. Twenty iron beds lined each wall. Their occupants lay still under the sheets or sat with feet drawn under them. Shaved heads, sunken cheeks, emaciated chests that under their cotton pajamas resembled the keel of a sailing ship. And, of course, the eyes. Unblinking. Unfaltering. Eyes that knew death as an everyday companion. At first, it was hard to tell one man from the next. Starvation had provided the patients with a startling familial resemblance.

The man seated on the cot in front of Devlin Judge appeared no different from the rest. According to intelligence records, General Oliver von Luck was fifty-one years old. He looked seventy. Gray stubble covered his scalp and chin. Everything about him was shriveled and sunken except his eyes, which were alert and sparkling and, at two o'clock this Thursday afternoon, maybe even cheerful.

"If you think I look bad now, you should have seen me a month ago," said von Luck, by way of introduction. "Down to eighty pounds,

I was. It wasn't my own people who nearly killed me, it was your GIs. Hershey bars were the first real food I'd eaten in months. The sugar put me into shock. My heart, it stopped like that." He snapped a finger. "But, *mein Gott*, it tasted heavenly."

Judge mumbled something about being glad the general was still alive, and after giving his name and Honey's, provided von Luck with a brief explanation of the reason for their visit.

"So he came through alive?" von Luck asked. His English was impeccable.

"You're surprised?"

"One can only dodge so many bullets." Von Luck's voice was tainted by a survivor's fatalism.

"I understand you knew him well."

"I taught him. I coached him. I ordered him into battle. I knew him as well as one man can know another."

Judge reached into his briefcase and removed the slim file his team had put together on von Luck. Inside was a clipping from *The Black Corps*, the monthly magazine of the SS, dated June 1936. It contained a photograph of von Luck standing next to Erich Seyss on a running track. The caption read, "Like Father and Son. The new Germany's revered coach, Colonel Oliver von Luck, with national champion, SS cadet Erich Seyss. The Führer anticipates victory in Berlin!"

He handed von Luck the photograph and watched him study it. The general brought the picture close to his face, squinting his eyes, and for a long time didn't move. He appeared to be staring through the picture and into his own past. Finally, he laid the magazine on his lap and sighed.

"More than anything, Seyss had the desire to be great," he said. "An indomitable will. Unfortunately, there is only so much a man can will his body to do. What success he enjoyed was a tribute to his hard work."

"And yours," added Judge.

Von Luck's rebuke was immediate. "Do not try to flatter an old soldier, Major."

Judge lowered his gaze to the floor, embarrassed by his mawkish behavior. The sight of von Luck and so many ambulant corpses had compelled him to a kindness more appropriate for a victim than a suspect. Von Luck may well have plotted against Hitler, but for years he had willingly served him.

"And as an officer?" Judge asked.

"The most aggressive, certainly. The most clever?" Von Luck shook his head. "But he could bluff. He was a Brandenburger, after all."

Corporal Dietsch had mentioned that von Luck had founded something called the Brandenburg Regiment. All traces regarding such a unit had come back negative.

"Just what is a Brandenburger?" asked Honey.

"The Brandenburg Regiment was established in 1938," said von Luck. "Our goal was to train soldiers to fight behind enemy lines. Not as commandos, mind you, though of course they were versed in sabotage and killing, but to actually become the enemy, to insinuate themselves into their units and cause total chaos, a disintegration of the enemy's command structure. We required three skills of our recruits: That they be fit, that they possess another language as their own—Russian, Polish, French—you can imagine which ones we found vital, and that they be bold. Any man can muster the courage to run into a hail of machine-gun bullets. That is simply adrenaline. We needed men with the self-confidence requisite to pass themselves off as members of an enemy unit for weeks, even months, at a time. Professional impostors, if you will."

Honey raised an eyebrow. "And this worked?"

Von Luck laughed with surprise. "Ask the Poles, or better yet, the Russians. Several times we managed to land a man inside Stavka command in Moscow."

"Little good it did you," said Honey. "You should have left Stalin well enough alone."

But Judge had stopped listening. Part of his mind had stolen back to Lindenstrasse 21 and he found himself meeting Erich Seyss's emotionless gaze as if for the first time. Seyss had called himself Klaus Licht from Bureau Five, Section A of the Building Inspector's Office. Only afterward had Judge caught the twisted humor. Bureau Five, Section A of the Reich main security office or Sicherheitsdienst dealt with the transport of Jews from occupied territories to death camps in the East. And Seyss had traipsed through Camp 8 wearing a deflated soccer ball on his head painted to look like an American soldier's helmet. As von Luck said, a professional impostor.

"Where did Seyss fit in?"

"He was seconded from the Leibstandarte Adolf Hitler to the Brandenburg Regiment in early '39. He saw duty in Poland and Holland, and, of course, in Russia. He was transferred back to the Waffen-SS in late '41."

"And in all those places, he worked behind the lines?"

Von Luck shook his head insistently, as if Judge hadn't quite grasped the idea. "No, Major, he lived behind the lines. *He became the enemy.* He spoke a little Dutch, but his Russian was that of a Muscovite. As a child, he had a White Russian governess."

Judge looked away, digesting the information. His attention was drawn to a bed three down, where a swarthy man, smaller and even thinner than von Luck, had risen and now stood shaking a fist in his direction. The man—he looked for all the world like a skeleton—met Judge's eye and held it, then lifted his smock, squatted, and with great deliberation shat on the floor. When he was finished, he scurried back to his bed and pulled the sheets over his head.

"Ah, no," moaned Honey. "Oh, God."

Judge felt his eyes water as bile rose in his throat.

But von Luck was unfazed. "Pay Herr Volkmann no mind," he advised. "Many of the prisoners—excuse me, *the patients*—have temporarily mislaid their manners. He's afraid that if he uses the commode, you'll steal his bed from him. Actually, he's quite civilized. An intellectual, believe it or not. Until '43, he was a professor of theology in Hamburg. His conscience chose an unfortunate moment to unburden itself."

Judge bit his lower lip and stared for a moment at his polished shoes. He couldn't decide whether he wanted to scream, to cry, or to wrap his hands around von Luck's fragile neck and snap it. Von Luck was too arrogant by half. It was increasingly clear that he harbored no guilt whatsoever about his role in fostering the system that destroyed men like Herr Volkmann.

Strangely, Judge sought solace in his brother's memory. He wanted to bury his head in Francis's shoulder and ask him why, and how, and what for, and he wanted God to answer. This was the equal of murder. This was the degradation of the human condition, the theft of man's dignity, his transformation into an animal, or worse, a savage. Judge had never felt more the apostate, his heart stuck between beseeching God and cursing him. Better yet, why say anything at all? What was the point if no one was listening?

Honey's clear voice slapped him to attention. "When was the last time you spoke with Erich Seyss?"

Von Luck appraised his interrogators with hungry eyes. "I risked my life to kill Adolf Hitler. Once I'm better, I do not wish to spend what remains of it in your custody, however benevolent. If you want my help, at least tell me why I am being detained."

"You've been classified as a security suspect," said Judge, less patient now. "Just because you decided you didn't like Hitler doesn't absolve you of any crimes you might have committed earlier. Besides, you botched it. All you did was leave Hitler a little deaf in one ear and more crazy than ever. We're waiting to see if something turns up against you."

"Such as?"

"Don't know. But seeing that you served as Canaris's deputy for four years, I wouldn't be surprised if we found something. Torturing prisoners of war. Shipping off Jews to Treblinka. Shooting political prisoners. If you acted within the confines of the rules of land engagement as prescribed by the Geneva Convention, you've got nothing to worry about."

"And if I cooperate?"

Judge suppressed a self-satisfied smile. He had him. "Then we'll see, won't we? Please answer the question, General. When was the last time you saw Seyss?"

"A year ago in Berlin. We exchanged a few words, then parted, each of us on our own separate way. Him to the front, me to Dachau. Amazing we both made it through."

"I thought he was like a son to you," said Judge. "Why no celebration? A beer at the officers' mess? Dinner and a night on the town?"

"I saw him, Major, during my interrogation in the basement of Gestapo headquarters." Von Luck smiled so that the jagged stumps of his teeth were visible. "It was where I had my dental work performed. Charming, don't you find?"

Honey squinted in revulsion. "Seyss did that?"

"Actually, the butt of his pistol. I believe it was a Walther .38. An excellent way of proving his loyalty to the Führer, don't you think?"

It was indeed, thought Judge. Ask an acolyte to destroy his mentor. A son to kill his father. He should feel shocked by the tactic, but he wasn't. His time in Germany was working on him. He remembered a picture he'd come across in his researches, a photograph of an interrogation cell taken at one or another government ministry in Berlin. Naked concrete walls bleeding with damp, sturdy iron rings bolted to them at different heights. Schoolboy's chair standing in the corner. Drain set into the center of the floor, cement around it stained black. For all intents and purposes, it might have been in the basement of Gestapo headquarters.

Judge glanced at von Luck, and he was there, in the cell with him, staring down at the general as he was tied into his chair, hands bound behind him, watching him grimace as the coarse ropes were pulled tight, shaving the skin from his wrists. The cell smelled clean. Carbolic soap and lemon oil. A man entered and took up position in front of von Luck. It was Seyss. He wore his camouflage uniform, Iron Crosses neatly in place, and his muddy jackboots. His cheeks were smudged with battle-field grime. His hair was its natural blond and a lank forelock hung across his eyes. He held a pistol in his hand. A Walther .38. Von Luck pleaded his innocence but Seyss paid him no mind. The pistol rose, then descended in a blur. And as Judge followed its dull gray arc, he was no longer looking at Seyss but at himself ten years earlier as he whipped a blackjack against the neck of a suspected murderer inside the interrogation room of the mighty Twentieth Precinct.

Judge blinked and the picture vanished. A second had passed, no more.

"Do you have any idea where Seyss might have gone?" he asked.

Von Luck shrugged. "You said he'd been contacted by *kameraden.* That would indicate fellow SS officers or members of the Allgemeine SS."

"The Allgemeine SS?"

"The civilian wing. Reserved for businessmen, politicians, and industrialists eager to demonstrate their loyalty to the Führer. I have no idea what such men might have wanted with Seyss. I was an officer of the Wehrmacht, Major. I am a professional, not a fanatic."

Judge thought it amusing how defeat tempered a man. Von Luck, the promulgator of such profound military axioms as "Victory forgives all, defeat nothing," and "Imitation is the bravest form of deception." To the professional soldier, passing oneself off as the enemy was an act of cowardice. And shooting a defenseless prisoner, a crime punishable by death. How much more fanatical could a professional soldier become?

"Still, I don't envy you your task," von Luck continued. "Once Seyss is committed to something . . . anything, he is unstoppable. Erich was never so much a Nazi as a patriot. He was fond of Houston Chamberlain. 'The ideal politics is to have none; but this nonpolitics must be boldly recognized and forced upon the world.' Understand that and you will understand Seyss."

Judge got the drift, if not the nuances. Shoot first, ask questions later. Not much of a clue to a man's whereabouts in a country of 50 million people. "So you've got no idea?"

Under the hospital smock, the wasted shoulders rose and fell, but von Luck's eyes held their focus. "Are you familiar with the work of Wagner?"

Judge nodded, while Honey shifted restlessly on his stool.

"Think of Erich Seyss as Parsifal unmasked. At once a romantic and a realist. A man willing to destroy himself, as well as everything and everyone around him, to validate his principles."

"*Götterdämmerung*," said Judge. *The Ring of the Nibelungen.* The mention brought back memories of the family gathered round the wireless on Sunday nights, listening to Wagner broadcast live from the Met. It had been his mother's one lasting link to Germany. Music. And he'd grown to love it as much as she. Brahms, Beethoven, and, of course, Wagner. His mother claimed he was the greatest German to have ever lived. She'd never mentioned he was its greatest anti-Semite, too.

"Bravo, Major." Von Luck leaned forward, his bemused expression indicating that he was ready to part with the information he held dear. "Did you know that Seyss deserted his post as Heinrich Himmler's adjutant to be with the woman he loved? He knew his punishment would be severe, yet he chose to go all the same. In the event, he was sentenced to twelve months with a punishment battalion on the eastern front. Only a true German would destroy his career for a woman."

"Who was she?" Judge phrased the question nonchalantly, but already his heart was beating faster.

"The richest and prettiest woman in Germany. Her name was Ingrid Bach."

22

SONNENBRÜCKE GLITTERED LIKE A SEASHELL in the morning sun, a fairy-tale chateau with spiral towers and stone battlements. Surrounded on three sides by soaring granite peaks, it stood alone in a lush meadow at the head of a valley deep in the Bavarian Alps, ten kilometers from the Austrian border. A jewel, thought Devlin Judge, as he viewed the castle from a road high above the valley floor. Worthy of a prince, not a scoundrel.

Finding Ingrid Bach had proven easy. Her father, Alfred, stood high on the United Nations War Crimes Commission's list of war criminals—ranked sixteenth among the first twenty-two to be tried that fall in Nuremberg—and his capture in April had made front-page news. "Germany's Cannon King Corralled," read one rag. "Bach Busted!" screamed another. Too senile to be put in the dock, he was being held under house arrest at his hunting lodge in the mountains. His daughter, Ingrid, was there, too, though of her own volition, acting as his nurse-maid and caretaker.

Judge held his breath as the jeep squealed around yet another hairpin curve. The road was in miserable condition, hardly more than a rocky furrow carved from the mountainside. Two feet to his right, the track crumbled and fell away. He had only to extend his head over the jeep's chassis to stare down a thousand-foot precipice. This part of the country had been dubbed the "national redoubt." In these mountains, it was rumored Hitler had constructed an *alpenfestung*, a mountain fortress into which his loyal soldiers could withdraw to marshal their strength for one last stand against the Allied forces. If true, he had chosen well. The dense forest and rugged terrain made the area impenetrable.

Judge glanced at his driver, an eager corporal supplied by Seventh Army HQ. Despite the hazardous road conditions, he seemed perfectly at ease, humming "We'll Meet Again" as he shifted through the gear box in preparation for another one-hundred-eighty-degree turn. Honey had begged off the trip, wanting to meet with sources of his own that he claimed might have information about Seyss's whereabouts. No doubt men of Altman's ilk.

The nose of the jeep dipped as it came around the curve. A rear tire dug into a pothole. The vehicle bucked, then shot down the road. Gasping, Judge fell back into this seat. He would never complain about Manhattan's streets again.

Fifteen minutes later, he arrived at Sonnenbrücke.

A pink granite driveway wound for a mile through waist-high grass. They passed a gazebo overlooking a pond slick with algae and a fractured dock extending from the shores of a small lake. Two jeeps were parked a half mile from the lodge. Several GIs, all with mitts, stood in a square playing catch. Apparently Alfred Bach posed little threat of escaping the bonds of his house arrest. The driver slowed and gave Judge's name to the nearest soldier. The GI threw a fastball to his buddy in left field, then waved them on.

Judge waited until the jeep had come to a complete halt and the engine extinguished before getting out. He hadn't thought about his ribs or his tailbone for the last two hours. It was his legs that were killing him, rigid as pistons and still braced for the unexpected tumble off the cliff. A loud bang in the woods beyond the lake made him duck his head. The sharp crack was followed by another, and then another, until it sounded as if someone were blowing off a string of firecrackers.

An elderly manservant in a black frock coat and striped trousers opened the door before he could knock. "May I help you, sir?" His

English was impeccable—Oxford or Cambridge or wherever all the snobs in merry old England lived.

"Devlin Judge, here to see Frau Bach." As he spoke there was a commotion behind the door. The butler took a step back and whispered something about "being polite," and "it not being her place," then stalked off. In his place stood a slender blond woman wearing a sleeveless brown dress.

"We've really had quite enough of your chums coming onto our land and acting as if they can take as much game as they please," she began, in the same faultless English. "Morning, noon, and night, that's all one hears. *Pop. Pop. Pop.* It's absolutely dreadful. Father detests it. He jumps in his bed every time a rifle goes off. He's very ill and needs all the rest he can get. That means peace and quiet." She paused long enough to study the rank insignia on his shoulder. "Major. And as for the chamois they're butchering, I shouldn't be surprised if the forests will soon be empty of them. One doesn't use a bloody machine gun to kill a small antelope. Wouldn't you agree, Major . . ."

"Judge," he answered. "Devlin Judge. Judge Advocate General's Corps." He winced at his mistake. "Excuse me, Provost Marshal's office." In the course of her speech she had moved onto the landing, so that now she stood only a few inches from him. She wasn't beautiful, at least not by New York standards. Her hair showed dirty roots and fell in an uneven tide onto her shoulders. Her face was too angular and bore not a trace of makeup. A universe of tiny freckles dotted her nose and cheeks. Her lips were dry, and in places, cracked. Why, then, was he so insistently cataloguing her faults?

She had set a hand on her hip and was nibbling at a chewed fingernail. "So?"

Inclining his head, he asked slowly, "So what?"

"So what are you going to do about the ruckus? Just because we lost the war doesn't mean you can step all over us. The shooting is driving us mad. Forget about Papa. *I'm* going to kill myself if it doesn't stop soon."

Judge needed a moment to recover from her verbal barrage. Making a half turn, he stared out at the forest, and as if sensing his attention, the shooting stopped.

"Congratulations, they've taken another chamois." Her triumphant grin stank of sarcasm. She looked over his shoulder, but not before he noticed that she had a chipped front tooth. "I should bloody well charge for them. Twenty dollars a head. That would solve things."

"I assume you are Ingrid Bach," Judge said finally, his patience wearing thin.

"Go to the top of the class, Major. If you don't mind, though, I prefer my husband's name. Von Wilimovsky. Ingrid *von Wilimovsky*. These days Bach is about as bad as Hitler. Pity us, don't you?"

Pity wasn't the word he had in mind. Disdain and scorn were more like it, and if she continued rambling on like a broken phonograph, he'd add despise to the list, too. He hadn't expected her to be overtly contrite, but Christ, she could at least play at humility. Instead, she was just one more rich girl waiting for the favors she was owed.

She stepped into the entry and motioned for Judge to follow.

He was inside a medieval lair, a wood-paneled great room that could swallow his one-bedroom apartment whole. A minstrel's gallery circled the perimeter, and below it hung enough portraits to fill the Met. The paintings were spaced at three-foot intervals. Here and there, however, one was missing, leaving him with the impression of a decaying set of teeth. A great fireplace yawned at the far end of the room, dark, unlit, and tall enough for a man to step into.

Seyss, you here? Judge thought to himself. In a place this big, he could keep himself hidden for years. Maybe he should have taken Honey's advice and brought along a few men to search the premises.

"I expect you're here to see Father," she said. "He's no better than last week. The doctors call it *zweite kindheit*. Second childhood."

Judge saw no reason to disabuse her of the notion. "Keep 'em talking" was the interrogator's cardinal rule. She led him into a small parlor, with throw rugs and easy chairs and lace-curtained windows looking onto the lake. The horns of a dozen small mountain goats and, he guessed, chamois, decorated the paneled wall. Sitting down, she freed a cigarette from the folds of her dress.

Judge tucked his cap under an arm, drawing a Zippo from his pocket. He'd never been a smoker, but experience had taught him that good manners opened doors as well as loosened tongues. "Allow me."

"An officer *and* a gentleman," she said, guiding the lighter to the cigarette. "How pleasant."

Judge lowered himself into an armchair opposite her, gazing at the lake, then at the imposing mountains. Not a bad place to pass the war. On the table next to him was a petite green porcelain vase. A second glance revealed a glass cabinet against the wall filled with similar pieces.

"*Schönes Dresden,*" he said, speaking German to satisfy an unannounced urge to impress her.

Ingrid Bach brushed the vase with her fingertip. "Meissen is my one true love. Did you know that King Augustus thought it would prevent him from growing old 'An antidote to decay,' he called it. When he died, they counted forty thousand pieces of porcelain inside his palace."

"My mother was a collector, too," said Judge, looking to establish a common ground.

"Oh?"

"Well, not exactly. She had two pieces."

Ingrid laughed, then caught herself. "That's a start, anyway. Why didn't you say you were from Berlin?"

"My mother was from Berlin," he said. "I'm from New York." He never volunteered Brooklyn.

"My cousin is from New York, too. He's in the Foreign Service. I believe he's traveling to Potsdam as we speak. His name is Chip DeHaven. Do you happen to know him?"

Judge raised a disbelieving eyebrow. Most recently, Carroll "Chip" DeHaven had served as an aide to President Roosevelt at Yalta and Teheran, but he had made a name for himself as first secretary to the U.S. embassy in Moscow. During the first years of the war, he'd been a vocal supporter of Lend-Lease and one of the few to call for America's early entry into the war. Judge couldn't imagine that she was related to such an East Coast blue blood. "Your cousin is Chip DeHaven?"

"Father's sister's second son. Just don't call him Carroll. He positively hates that name." And when she saw his continued skepticism, she shot him a nasty glance. "Five eleven Fifth Avenue. Corner of Sixty-second. Just up from the Sherry. We used to visit when I was a little girl."

She meant the Sherry-Netherland Hotel, of course. Suddenly he found her smug delivery overbearing. He knew why, even if he didn't care to admit it. She was the rich girl lording it over her poor guest. Every bit as annoying as the Yalies who infested the U.S. attorney's office. *The Sherry.* As if she owned the place. No doubt she'd crossed on the *Hindenburg.*

"Actually, I'm not here to see your father," he said, sitting straighter to signal that the pleasantries were over. "I'm an investigator with the Third Army. That's General Patton's outfit. I came to speak with you."

Ingrid Bach's face lost its color. "Me? Whatever for? Shouldn't you be chasing down my brother? I mean, he's the shit of the family. I'm just a nurse and widow."

Judge had never seen a guiltier response. The shifting of focus off herself; the hands grappling at each other; the voice jumping half an octave. She was up to something. The only question was whether it was harboring a fugitive war criminal.

"We're looking for a man whom we have reason to believe may have visited you recently."

Her glib tongue had suddenly grown tired. "Oh?"

"His name is Erich Seyss."

"Erich Seyss?" For a moment longer she stared at him with wide eyes. Then her shoulders dropped and she loosed a relieved sigh. "Do you mean to tell me you've come all this way to ask me if I've seen Erich. Whatever for? I'm sorry to ruin your day, but I've neither seen nor heard from him in ages."

"When exactly did you see him last?"

"October twelfth, 1939, *exactly.* My twentieth birthday. He told me he couldn't marry me. A lovely gift, wouldn't you say? It beat the hell out of anything Papa gave me."

She stubbed out her cigarette and pulled back a curtain to look over the lake. He could see that her mind was moving on to matters of greater importance. He was no longer a problem to be dealt with, just one to be dismissed.

"Has your father had any contact with Seyss?"

"Papa?" She kept her gaze fixed on the lake. "The only person Papa has contact with is me."

It was evident to Judge that she was telling the truth—about Seyss and about her father—but something compelled him to force the issue, maybe her brusque dismissal of his visit, maybe her unquestioned confidence, or maybe because, after Ingrid, he didn't have any place left to turn. "I'd still like to ask him myself."

She jerked her head from the window, her attention once again where it should be. "Papa is very ill. He does things to himself. I'm afraid I cannot permit you to see him."

But Judge was already rising from his chair and moving past her into the great hall. Nothing conveyed authority better than motion, even if he didn't have any idea where old man Bach was laid up. "I'm sorry, but I can't return to HQ without having questioned him about Seyss. Can you please show me to his room." It was not a request.

She stood at his shoulder, glaring at him with undisguised contempt. "Follow me."

She led him across the hall and through a large kitchen. A basket of wood sat next to a cast-iron furnace. A half-plucked chicken lay splayed on a cutting board large enough to slaughter a buck—which he realized was what it had been intended for. A bolt of silver fabric was draped across a chair, a needle and thread placed on the table nearby. Behind a glass partition, a wine rack ran from floor to ceiling. Only a few bottles remained. For such a wealthy family, the kitchen looked downright barren.

Ingrid walked ahead with a watchman's deliberate pace, not saying a word. Her silence dug at him like a pickax. Part of him wished he hadn't asked to see her father. He could tell her right now he'd decided it wasn't necessary; he could apologize and go back to Bad Toelz. But each time he began to speak the words died stillborn on his tongue. A stronger voice reminded himself that he was just doing his duty as a police officer. He wasn't there to be her friend.

ALFRED BACH LAY ASLEEP IN a large bed in a sunlit room on the second floor of the lodge. A white comforter had been drawn up over his shoulders so that only his mottled face and wispy gray hair were visible.

Judge approached the bed, staring hard at the wrinkled countenance. Conducting his preliminary research into Goering's wartime activities, he'd come across the Bach name time and time again. It had been May in New York and while everyone's eyes and ears were tuned to the horror stories coming from Dachau and Auschwitz and Buchenwald, he'd been reading the testimonies of foreign laborers who had toiled in Alfred Bach's myriad factories. Sixteen-hour workdays on unheated factory floors with no breaks given for lunch or dinner. Failure to meet daily quotas punished with flagellation, pummeling, and withholding of meals. Questioning a command, the same. One Russian laborer who had failed to properly arm a bucket of fuses was made to hop the length of the concrete floor (over one hundred yards) on his knees. When a kneecap fractured and he could no longer move, he was beaten with a rifle butt, then removed to the infirmary, where he was given neither medical care, food, nor a bed. He died the next day. One Bach factory mandated a particularly creative form of torture to inspire their lethargic "employees." The offender was placed in a wooden box two feet wide and four feet high while cold water was dripped onto his head. The punishment lasted between two and twelve hours. Pregnant women were not excluded. Such barbarous treatment was the rule, not the exception.

Conditions outside the factories were no better. Workers were housed in dog kennels or public urinals or made to sleep in open trenches in camps with no running water and no medical attention. They received two meals daily, a thin soup with rancid vegetables in the morning and a chunk of bread with a slathering of jam at night. Five hundred calories maximum. The men who supervised the factories and camps, the brutes who carried out these punishments, were not generally members of the German military but employees of Bach Industries assigned to the company *werkschütze* or factory police. The average "work expectancy" of a newly arrived laborer was "three months until exhaustion." Three months, then death. For each slave, Alfred Bach paid the Reich Labor Ministry four marks per day. Naturally, the workers received nothing.

There he lay, the man himself, Alfred Bach, eyes sunken, skin waxy, looking as harmless as any old man preparing to die. Stories abounded about his predilection for patrolling the factory floors, overseeing the smallest matters of production. While he'd never struck a man himself, he had known what went on inside his factories. He had condoned it. If nothing else, it had been his responsibility to contract with the SS or the Labor Ministry for adequate numbers of impressed foreign workers— read slave labor—to maintain his factories at maximum output. How else could he interpret his factory managers' constant demand for additional workers? How else could anyone?

"Mr. Bach, can you wake up for a few minutes?" Judge asked. "I'd like to ask you some questions."

The cannon king stirred. His eyes opened and he gazed first at Ingrid, then at Judge. "Good morning," he said. His voice was strong.

"Good morning," said Judge, heartened. "I'm sorry to disturb you, but it shouldn't take very long. My name is Devlin Judge and I'd like to know if—"

"Good morning," Alfred Bach repeated. He was smiling now.

"Yes, good morning, Mr. Bach." Judge looked across the bed to Ingrid, who stood with arms folded over her chest, her face vacant of any expression. "Now, then, if I might ask you—"

"Good morning."

Judge patted the man's arm. *Be patient*, he told himself. *Give the old-timer a minute to wake up.* He smiled at Ingrid to show he was understanding of her father's condition, that he wasn't the brute she took him for. A second later, a gob of phlegm slapped him in the face.

"Thief!" cried the old man. "Think you can take my company from me, do you? I won't permit it. No son can rob his father. I am a holder of the Golden Party Badge. The Führer will not permit it!" Alfred Bach lunged forward, swinging a gnarled fist at Judge. He missed wildly and the motion carried him halfway out of his bed. He was naked, his chest crisscrossed with scratches and scabs. Judge leaped forward and grabbed hold of one arm, then the other, guiding him gently back onto the bed. Ingrid patted her father's head, whispering for him to calm down. Suddenly the old man wrestled free, swinging his arm in a wide arc that battered Ingrid's head. She paid the blow no attention, taking hold of the offending arm and fixing it to the bed with a pair of cloth restraints. Following her example, Judge fell to a knee and took hold of the straps extending from beneath the mattress. A minute later, Alfred Bach was restrained.

Judge cleaned his face and rushed from the room. After a minute,

Ingrid joined him. They stood in the half light of the hallway, eyeing each other. "I'm sorry," they said in unison.

"No," said Judge, "let me apologize. I should have taken your word."

"Papa is very old and very angry. Thank you for being gentle with him. It's easy to lose one's temper."

"A little too gentle." Judge ran a finger along the edge of his tooth. "Did he do that?"

Ingrid mimicked the motion, tracing a chipped incisor. "Yes. He's rather strong for an old man, isn't he?"

Just then, a little boy came running down the hallway, excited by the commotion. At the sight of an American uniform, he stopped short, dashing behind his mother's legs for cover.

"Pauli. Don't be shy. Say hello to the major."

The boy stepped around his mother and extended a hand. He had straight blond hair that fell to his eyebrows and pale blue eyes. It was obvious to Judge that he was ten pounds too thin. "Good morning, sir," he ventured in accented English.

"I always knew who would win the war," Ingrid Bach whispered to Judge, then in a louder voice, "May I introduce my son, Paul von Wilimovsky."

Judge gave the boy's hand a firm shake. "Are you taking good care of your mother?"

"Yes, sir. I gather the wood and clean Grandpapa's bedpan."

"Pauli!" Ingrid tousled the boy's hair. "He's the man of the house. And you? Children?"

Judge was taken aback by the encroachment on his private sphere. Usually he would say "none," and move on to another subject. No one liked to share a passing acquaintance's bad news, especially when it concerned a six-year-old boy who had died of poliomyelitis. Frankly, it was easier not to say anything. Still, something about the way that Ingrid looked, child hugged to her waist, her broken life on unapologetic display, made him feel that lying would be harder than telling the truth.

"A boy," he said. "His name was Ryan. He left us three years ago."

Ingrid reached out a hand to touch him even as she hugged her boy to her waist. "My dear major, I'm so sorry." He was unable to look at her as she spoke. The immediacy of her grief threatened to reawaken emotions over which he had no control. "Pauli came three weeks early. For the first few days he refused to nurse. He was so fragile, so . . ." She let the words drop off. "I don't know how I would've managed without him. He's everything to me."

Judge looked at the hand on his arm, acutely aware of its insistent pressure and its assumption of intimacy. He and his wife had never touched after Ryan's death.

"You haven't had another?" she asked. The question was spontaneous, a gesture of hope.

"I wanted to, but it didn't work out. Anyway, we're not married any—" He cut himself off midstream, realizing he'd said too much already. Her sincerity, however unquestioned, was an invasion and had no place in the day's conversation. Whatever empathy he felt toward Ingrid Bach, he had to remember whose blood flowed in her veins. "No," he said, curtly.

Ingrid dropped her hand from his arm, retreating to the opposite side of the corridor. She led him down the back stairs, through the kitchen to the great hall. Pauli took off down the driveway as soon as she opened the front door and in a moment was lost in the high grass leading toward the lake. Judge spotted his driver playing ball with the other GIs. He placed two fingers into the corner of his mouth and whistled loudly, signaling for him to bring the jeep around on the double. Waiting, he turned to look at Sonnenbrücke's imposing gray facade. Veins of crystal swarmed inside each cut stone. No wonder the place glittered like a diamond.

Ingrid stood beside him on the brick portico, gazing down the valley. "Why are you looking for Erich?"

"He killed two men escaping from a prisoner-of-war camp. One was an American officer."

Judge thought it funny how the deaths of two men didn't sound like anything too urgent, and wished he could add to it. He remembered Altman's words, the sly suspicion that Seyss owned some ulterior motive for escaping other than simply to gain his own freedom. "One last race," according to Corporal Dietsch. "*Kameraden.*" Would Judge ever find out what it was?

"I thought most of our soldiers had already been released from your holding pens," said Ingrid.

"Most have. But Seyss was a special case. He was being held as a war criminal."

She averted her eyes and Judge could see a shiver rustle her shoulders. It was a subject about which she knew too much already. "And how did you learn about us? I mean Erich and me—that we were engaged to be married."

Judge looked over her shoulder, willing the goddammed driver to get his ass over here. Seeing the jeep approach, he returned his eyes to her. Christ, she was a mess. Her knees were bruised. Her dress bore greasy stains near her waist, where she wiped her hands when cooking. And she could do with a little makeup. He forced himself to imagine her together with the man whose picture he carried in his pocket. Seyss, the Olympian; Seyss, the owner of two Iron Crosses; Seyss, the man who'd murdered Judge's only brother and seventy more defenseless Americans.

She's a Bach. Remember that.

"I'm sorry," he answered, "but I'm not at liberty to say." Behind him, the jeep arrived with a screech of the brakes. He climbed in, offering the slightest doff of his cap. "If you'll excuse me, I'll be getting back. It's a long ride to Bad Toelz. I thank you for your cooperation. Goodbye, Miss Bach."

Somehow von Wilimovsky didn't suit her—the Bach name and its colored history were marked indelibly upon her—and this time she didn't correct him. She bobbed her chin, then turned and walked back inside the lodge.

BEFORE THEY REACHED THE CREST of the mountain, Judge asked his driver to stop. He stepped from the jeep and walked to the edge of the road so that he could stare down at Sonnenbrücke. So far below, it looked like a model cut set against a field of green. For a moment he thought he saw her standing in front of the castle, as still as one of the porcelain figurines she collected, then a cloud passed and he realized it had only been a ray of light.

CHAPTER

23

HEADLIGHTS PIERCED THE FALLING RAIN. First one set, then another, until an entire column was winding through the darkness and Seyss knew it was the convoy they'd been waiting for. The trucks were still far away, at least three kilometers by his reckoning, too distant even to hear the grumble of their engines. The parade of lights passed through the village of Kronberg, then traversed the flat countryside. He counted seven trucks in all. His eyes left them, advancing along the ribbon of black a shade darker than everything surrounding it. The road wound through a hamlet of barns and farmhouses, crossed a brook, then began the climb into the mountains toward his position.

"Sit tight," whispered Hans-Christian Lenz. "They'll be here in ten minutes. All we have to do is wait. My brother will take care of the rest. Tonight, we're garbagemen. We pick up all the trash that falls from the trucks!"

"What's on the agenda for tomorrow night?" asked Seyss. "Cleaning the sewers?"

Lenz grinned wolfishly. "It would give me great pleasure to tell an esteemed officer of the Waffen-SS to fuck himself."

"Would it, now?"

"Yes. Immense, in fact." Lenz wiped the water dripping from his mustache. "Know where I can find one?"

Seyss laughed dryly, hunkering down in the waist-high brush. Thank Christ for Lenz, he thought to himself. He had found his traveling companion in a dingy two-room flat in Darmstadt, exactly where he'd said he'd be should Seyss ever pass through town. It had been harder to convince Bauer to lend a hand with the operation without spilling news of it to Egon Bach. Ingenuity and improvisation were not words in Bauer's everyday lexicon. Pride was, however, and once Seyss had shared his personal reasons for not wanting to approach the Circle of Fire for assistance so early in the mission, Bauer had agreed to go along.

The Americans appeared firm in their desire to bring Seyss to justice. Jeeps with loudspeakers mounted onto their hoods patrolled the streets of Heidelberg, and he assumed every other large city, blaring his name and description and the crimes for which he was wanted. Some enterprising Yanks had even posted Wanted: Dead or Alive flyers bearing his photo all over Darmstadt and Frankfurt. Had anyone recognized him, they would have happily broken a bottle over his head and dragged him to the authorities to claim their cash reward. As it was, few people gave him a second look. With his black hair, borrowed spectacles, and adopted slouch, he looked like any other bedraggled survivor. Germans were too concerned with their own plight to keep an eye on their neighbors.

Seyss pulled his jacket closer around, shivering in the foul weather. "Biedermann, Bauer," he said in a tight whisper, "spread out along this side of the road. Steiner, you go with Lenz across the road."

"Who the hell is running this operation?" protested Lenz. "Me or you?" He shook his head and after muttering something about officers not knowing their proper place, turned to Steiner and said, "Come on, then, didn't you hear what the Führer said?"

Seyss watched as the two men shuffled across the slick road and disappeared into the undergrowth fifteen feet away. Lenz was too sarcastic for his taste, but a true kamerad. When informed of Seyss's dilemma earlier that evening, the stout Berliner had tugged at his mustache and shaken his head.

"A thousand American? That's ten thousand reichsmarks these days. Certainly more than my lousy life is worth."

"I won't argue with you there," Seyss had said. "But can you help?"

"Yes, but on one condition. I have a right to know who I am working with. You've told me your rank, now tell me your name."

Without hesitating, Seyss spoke his true name and explained why the entire U.S. Army was looking for him. He told him about killing Janks and Vlassov and nearly being captured by Judge. He required a thousand dollars to escape the country. While not the entire truth, it was all Lenz needed to know.

"You're that Seyss—the White Lion?" Lenz had crowed in disbelief. "I was at Olympic Stadium the day you ran. My entire family had crowded onto the U-bahn for the trip. It seemed like all of Berlin was there. You were magnificent."

"I was fourth and no such thing."

But Lenz would not be deterred in expressing his admiration. "You ran in the Olympic Games. You were our national champion. Don't be modest." He shook Seyss by the shoulders. "The White Lion himself. It's an honor to know you."

Politely, Seyss had beaten him back. "What about the money?"

"I can't give you a thousand dollars I don't have. But with a little luck, I can help you get your hands on something just as good." And with that, Lenz had gone on to explain the neat "business" his brother, Rudy, had set up for himself.

Every few days, a convoy of trucks left the American airbase at Darmstadt for the German army hospital in Königstein, seventy miles away. The trucks carried medicine, canned food, and other hospital supplies—all of it packed into cartons weighing between fifty and one hundred pounds. Through an American pal, Rudy Lenz had wangled a job where he not only supervised the loading and unloading of the trucks but chose the five-man team that did the actual lifting. His instructions to his men were simple: Stow the choicest items in the last truck, where the loading crew would ride to the hospital atop the sea of swaying boxes. The rest, Lenz had explained, was easy. "A milk run," in the slang of the American flyers.

Or so he had said five hours ago.

Seyss kept his eyes glued to the straight expanse of road leading from the village of Hoechs, on the flats below them. The spill of beams rounded a corner, a kilometer away. The first truck emerged from behind a stone wall and began climbing the hill. Its engine's lusty growl turned to a whine, then a howl as the driver worked his way through the gears. Soon the air was abuzz with the angry attack of seven two-and-a-half-ton trucks struggling up a steep incline.

Seyss flattened his body in the sopping grass, keeping his head raised just high enough to see Lenz across from him. The night smelled of jasmine and pine and a hundred other scents he knew and loved. The ground began to tremble, and he was unable to keep his stomach from trembling along with it. How many times had he lain like this during the war, submachine gun cradled in his arms, a company of men awaiting his command to attack? Each time he'd been paralyzed with fright, sure that when he'd raise his arm and cry for his men to attack, his voice would fail him and he'd collapse bawling onto the ground. The same fragility accosted him now.

Running his hands through the damp grass, he forced his breath to come slowly, deeply. The mechanized roar of the approaching convoy cleared his mind of his old fears. Never once had he flinched from battle. Never once had he failed at the decisive moment. But since leaving Villa Ludwig in Munich, a discomfiting question had haunted his mind's periphery: Why was he taking this last and greatest risk? To whom did he owe this service? To the Fatherland? To the memory of Adolf Hitler? To the German people? At one time or another, he had told himself that it was for any one of them. Horseshit, all of it! He had served. He had wept. He had bled. He owed no one a thing. Sensing the ground shake under him, ears assailed by the scream of twenty-eight wheels lumbering up a slick hill in the dark of the night, Erich Seyss faced down the answer he knew had been lurking inside him. He was doing it for himself. To keep whatever was left of him alive.

Lenz raised a hand, his signal to be ready to move. Seyss nodded his head in response. The lead truck was twenty meters away. Suddenly it sounded its horn, a sharp, ear-splitting bleat. Seyss spun his head to check if any of his men were visible. Biedermann and Bauer lay flat on their bellies, head to the ground. He looked back toward the road as the horn blared again. A pair of deer—a buck and a doe—escaped the truck's beams, darting into the tree line.

The first truck thundered past, then the second. All Seyss could see of the drivers was a fleeting glimpse of a cigarette's ember glowing in the pitch-dark cabin. The fourth truck passed and the fifth. He brought himself to his knees. The last truck rumbled by. He rose and began running up the hill behind the truck. Around him, Biedermann and Bauer were doing the same. Lenz trotted up the incline, Steiner close behind.

As if on cue, the tarpaulin at the rear of the truck fell. Two men stood at either side of the bay. Seyss guessed the fat one waving was Rudy Lenz. Suddenly, a torrent of boxes tumbled onto the slick asphalt. Seyss picked up the closest to his feet and carried it into the brush. The word *oleomargarine* was stenciled on the cardboard. He dropped it, then went back for another. The five men scrambled back and forth, slipping on the pavement, hoisting boxes, throwing them into the undergrowth, then advancing up the hill and doing it again. It was back-breaking work and before the taillamps of the last truck were out of sight, Bauer and Lenz were doubled over, gulping down air as if they'd been punched in the gut. Seyss ran all the harder for them. Corned beef, tinned milk, Hershey bars, lard, sardines, something called peanut butter, chicken, pickled herring, more corned beef, peaches, cherries, and flour. Finally, even he had to stop for breath. He stood for a few seconds, hands resting on his knees, staring up the dark slope. In the pounding rain, the trail of boxes looked like stepping stones climbing a waterfall.

It is straw, Lenz had said earlier. *And we will spin it into gold.*

Seyss gathered his breath and went after another carton. He didn't need gold. Just a thousand dollars and a Russian GAZ.

24

HIS NAME WAS OTTO KIRCH, but everyone knew him as the Octopus, said Hans-Christian Lenz, and he controlled the upper levels of the black market in the Frankfurt–Heidelberg corridor. He was a fat man, three hundred pounds if an ounce, bald as an egg with a schoolboy's apple cheeks and a rattlesnake's glassy eyes. Dangerous, Herr Major. Very dangerous. No one knew where he'd been or what he'd done during the war. Most guessed he'd laid up somewhere safe—Vichy, France, Portugal, maybe Denmark—waiting for the fighting to end.

Waiting for *his time* to begin, Seyss added silently.

The two men were driving south toward Mannheim in Rudy Lenz's battered prewar Citroën truck. The previous night's haul was loaded in the back, concealed behind a pile of brick and masonry. The added weight slowed the truck to twenty miles an hour. It was good cover. The only Germans driving these days were those rebuilding their ravaged cities. Every few minutes an American jeep or truck sped by, horn blaring. The victors owned the road along with everything else.

Traffic thinned as they entered the outskirts of Mannheim. Allied bombing had so completely destroyed the city that there were simply no more people living there. Lenz turned right off the main road and for the next forty minutes guided the truck onto a series of unpaved tracks, each bumpier than the last.

The Octopus ran his operation from the ruins of a turbine-assembly plant in the center of town, a part of the city that looked to Seyss as if it had been hammered flat into a million tiny pieces. Where the plant had stood was a mystery, for nothing remained taller than five feet. Not a thing. It was a desert landscape, with miniature dunes of rubble and ash rising and falling as far as the eye could see. At eight o'clock on a clear and breezy morning, not a soul was visible.

In the midst of this wasteland, Lenz cut the engine and announced that they had arrived.

"Where the hell is everybody?" asked Seyss as he climbed from the cabin.

"Wait and see. Whoever says the German is not a resourceful animal is mistaken."

Seyss walked to the rear of the truck, flipped down the tail, and began hoisting boxes to the ground. He couldn't share his companion's jovial mood until the transaction was completed and a thousand dollars, or its equivalent in Reichsmarks, lined his pockets.

"Don't bother," said Lenz, motioning at the boxes. "There's plenty enough men for that. We're *gross chieber*, you and I. Big-timers. We don't do our own lifting."

Seyss shook his head and kept hauling boxes from the truck. If nothing else, the activity helped relieve his tension. He had not slept well the night before, despite the success of their midnight raid. He was exposing himself too often. Walking too freely through cities rife with Americans and their lackeys. Revealing his name to too many people. He had no right to such bravado. He wasn't worried about Bauer or Biedermann or Steiner, but now Lenz, too, knew his identity. Yes, Lenz was a *kamerad*. Yes, he was doing him a great service by turning over the profits from his half of the take. But what about his brother, Rudy? It went without saying that he knew Seyss's name, too. Could *he* be trusted? The chain was growing longer. Sooner or later there would be a weak link.

A loud thump interrupted Seyss from his work. He put down the box in his hands and turned to see a line of men emerging from what looked like the maw of a coal mine, just fifteen feet away. The men approached the truck, several doffing their caps, and wordlessly took over the job from Seyss. A few minutes later the truck was empty and they'd disappeared back into the ground.

"I told you," said Lenz. Standing with his arms crossed and his droopy mustache, he looked more than ever like an angry walrus. "It's all underground here. Like the route to Hades."

Seyss smiled as he followed Lenz into the tunnel, but he was growing anxious. He didn't like confined spaces, much less ones controlled by the enemy. For some reason, that's where he had cubbyholed Mr. Otto Kirch. Torches wired to shell-pocked walls lit the way. The place smelled of kerosene and tobacco, not cigarette smoke so much as the dusky scent of an old cigar. The ramp gave way to a large flat deck. Squinting in the half-light, Seyss saw that the area had once been an underground garage. The ceiling was awkwardly low, as if a bomb had landed on it dead center and not destroyed it, but by its sheer weight dropped it by five feet. Ahead, their boxes were visible, stacked neatly under a dim bulb. *Electricity*, mused Seyss. *Somewhere there is a generator and the oil to run it. What else is down here?*

Presently a short, immensely obese man stepped from behind the boxes. He wore dark pants and a white shirt dotted with perspiration. A maroon beret sat atop his head like an egg cozy. Seyss needed no introduction. It was Otto Kirch. The Octopus.

"Welcome, gentlemen," he called, his voice high-pitched and nasal. "I was just completing my final tally. I commend you, Herr Lenz. An excellent take. Excellent!" He tucked his clipboard under a meaty arm and walked over to where his two visitors stood. "Come to my office. I don't conduct business in the open." He hooked an arm with Lenz and guided him toward a steel door cut into the nearest wall.

Seyss followed at a polite distance, knowing Kirch was questioning Lenz as to his colleague's identity. As much as Seyss did not like being here, Kirch must dislike his visiting. Each was a risk to the other's security. Ducking his head, Seyss passed through the steel portal into a short tunnel, maybe five feet long. He emerged into an airy chamber, mercifully with a higher ceiling, something akin to the hold of an oceangoing freighter but three times the length. His first instinct was to search for exits. On both walls he found steel doors similar to the one he had just passed through. A dozen circular ducts holed the ceiling, providing a steady flow of fresh air. Kirch, it seemed, had created his own underground complex, blasting his way from garage to bomb shelter to storm drain. The route to Hades indeed. Who knew how big a maze he had created?

Advancing into the brighter recesses of the shelter, Seyss made out a grouping of long tables peopled by no fewer than two hundred men and women. Their bowed heads and precise motions spoke of feverish work. Looking closer, he noted a corroded trough filled with brown twine running through the center of each table. At one table, the workers would deliver the leafy substance into the trough. At others, the workers plucked it out again.

Lenz caught him staring. "Cigarettes, you idiot."

Seyss took a step toward the tables, putting a name to the bold scent he had noticed upon entering Kirch's world.

"Yes, cigarettes," said Kirch. "The currency of the new Germany. Every day our precious reichsmark loses more of its value. The Allies forbid us to hold dollars. Still, we must buy and sell. We must trade with one another. What are we left with? Cigarettes. Lucky Strike. Chesterfield. Craven A. They have all the qualities of paper money. There is constant demand, a regulated supply, the size is convenient, and they last a reasonable time. Best of all, if you are very hungry, you can smoke one and maybe you will forget about your stomach for a while."

Seyss smirked at Kirch's hollow benevolence. The grotesque pig looked as if he hadn't missed a single course of a single meal his entire life.

The Octopus took up position at the head of the first table, motioning for Seyss and Lenz to approach. "Every day, I have an army of two thousand men scouring the streets of Frankfurt, Darmstadt, and Heidelberg for the butts of cigarettes. Waiters, policemen, prostitutes, each with their own patch of ground. *Kippensammler*, they're called. Butt collectors. The Americans toss away their smokes so indiscriminately. And why not? They are rich, no? Seven butts yield enough tobacco to make up one cigarette, which I can sell for four reichsmarks. Tomorrow it may cost five. I set the price. It's my private treasury."

Kirch set off from his "treasury" with a new urgency, leading them across the shelter, through another steel door and down a gargantuan sewer pipe lined with burgundy carpeting. Like many fat men, he moved quickly, not ungracefully. Two guards stood at the far end of the pipe, framing a set of golden doors that had been salvaged from a luxury hotel. Seyss laughed when he read the name engraved on the door push. *Vier Jahreszeiten München.*

Kirch allowed his customers to catch up before nodding to one of his bodyguards to open the door. One glance at the Octopus's office was enough to answer anyone's questions about why such stringent security measures were necessary two stories below ground at the tail end of an urban catacomb. King Solomon's mines was Seyss's first thought. Then the tomb of Tutankhamen, the boy pharaoh, and finally, Carinhall, Hermann Goering's lavish estate near Berlin. The vast room was a cross of all three. Piles of women's furs occupied one corner. Stacks of floor-size tapestries, another. Glass cabinets displayed a dozen diamond tiaras, and below them, collections of lesser jewelry, every bit as spectacular in their own right. Gold bars loaded atop wooden pallets winked dully from inside a caged enclosure. A selection of masterpieces hung on stained maple walls. Rembrandt, Rubens, some decadent modernists.

"Take a seat," said Kirch as he laid the clipboard on his desk and installed himself in a port leather captain's chair. "Mr. Lenz. Sergeant Hasselbach, was it?"

"Erwin Hasselbach," clarified Seyss as he settled into his chair. Did Kirch sound suspicious or was it his imagination?

"Four boxes of margarine, two boxes of peaches, a box of Hershey bars . . ." Kirch read from his tally sheet, continuing until he had orally catalogued every box but one. "And finally, one thousand doses of penicillin. The women of Germany will be grateful."

Lenz gave Kirch the belly laugh he'd expected.

"You boys hit gold this time," said Kirch. "Eight hundred dollars or eight thousand reichsmarks. Take your pick." He waited a second, then chuckled. "Or I could pay you in cigarettes."

"*Nein, nein,*" rumbled Lenz, still in the throes of his merriment. "We'll take dollars. *Danke.*"

"*Eight hundred dollars?*" Seyss cut in, sliding to the edge of his chair and engaging Kirch one on one. "That's all you propose paying us for the entire lot?" He scoffed to underscore his view of such a paltry offer. As he had to split the sum with Lenz, he wanted to goad Kirch into offering two thousand U.S. Anything less left his problem unsolved. "Why, I can take the penicillin alone to my colleagues in Munich and receive twice that much. A thousand doses will bring ten thousand U.S. on the street. I don't suppose you handle the retail end of things, so let's say you unload the entire crate for four thousand dollars. Is twenty percent all you see fit to pay your suppliers? And what about the rest? The peaches, the margarine, the Spam . . . goodness, Herr Kirch, it is enough to stock a corner grocery for a month. Eight hundred dollars, you say? I'm afraid we cannot accept. Come, Hans-Christian, we have a little work in front of us, yet."

Seyss tapped Lenz on the arm, signaling for him to stand. Kirch followed them both through porcine eyes. He spoke as the two men reached the glass doors.

"That is enough, Herr Hasselbach," he called. "Herr Lenz, please instruct your impetuous colleague to retake his seat. You, too. If eight hundred is too little, perhaps you can tell me what is appropriate? And then you might wish to add why I shouldn't simply shoot you here and now? The cost of two bullets—even American ones—is significantly less than eight hundred dollars."

Seyss guided Lenz back to their chairs. When they were seated, he removed his glasses, polishing them with the tail of his shirt. "Let's be frank, Herr Kirch. Business is good. Prices are high. Demand even higher. It's hardly time for gentlemen to quibble. Shoot us if you like, but I imagine you'll have a harder time coming across medicinal stores of such undisputed quality. Otherwise, pay us three thousand U.S. and we'll see you next week."

"Three thousand?" Kirch laughed. "I should shoot you both to rid the world of such arrogant pricks. Fifteen hundred. That's double my first offer. You'd be smart to take it and run."

"Twenty-five hundred," countered Seyss, "and I'll guarantee the penicillin."

Kirch licked his lips, his abundant cheeks glowing. He was enjoying the negotiations. "Two thousand, and I won't hear another word."

"Twenty-two hundred and we'll be silent as the grave," said Seyss.

"Done."

Seyss could not help but loose a short laugh as a monumental weight lifted from his shoulders.

He would have his money.

He would have his truck.

He was as good as in Berlin.

AGAIN ALONE IN HIS SUBTERRANEAN treasure chest, Otto Kirch returned to his desk and withdrew a crudely printed flyer bearing the heading "Wanted: Dead or Alive." He studied the photograph of Sturmbannführer Erich Seyss and compared it to his mental image of the man who had been seated in his office five minutes earlier. Hasselbach was no sergeant, that was for certain. Only an officer had the balls to negotiate like that. But was he this man? The man on the flyer had light hair and wore no spectacles. Still, it was easy enough to change one's hair color and to put on a pair of glasses. Kirch traced Seyss's face with his finger, nodding his head as his certainty grew. Focusing on the eyes, he suddenly met Hasselbach's victorious gaze and jumped in his chair.

A minute later, he picked up his telephone and dialed a number. "*Ja?* Herr Altman. Good news. I think I've found the man who you've been looking for."

CHAPTER
25

THE MAN WHO CALLED HIMSELF Klaus Altman stood in a grove of pines, fifty feet from the end of the paved road. He was staring at the entry to a bland little house blessed with a lovely view over the rooftops of Heidelberg. The owner of the house was inside, as were two of his guests. But they did not interest him so much as the man who had not yet arrived . . . the man whose shadow he'd been tracking for over a day.

Altman removed his jacket, and folded it neatly before laying it on a patch of grass. Settling into a crouch, he pulled a hankie from his pocket and wiped his balding crown. The day was warming up quickly and the heat was making him uncomfortable, and if he was honest with himself, nervous. Since meeting with Major Devlin Judge, he'd been working hard to find a trace of Erich Seyss. The little voice every police officer possessed told him that Seyss would be his ticket to bigger things within the counterintelligence section of the United States Army, for which he now worked. Tracking down your former comrades was a surefire way to demonstrate your loyalty to your new masters. Altman was nothing if not adaptable.

During the past thirty-six hours, he'd made a tour through the nightspots favored by former members of the SS—the Haifisch Bar in Heidelberg, the Red Door in Darmstadt, Mitzi's in Frankfurt—keeping a not-so-casual eye peeled for men who had served with Seyss in the First SS Panzer division. He'd also peppered his contacts in the black market with questions about the White Lion's whereabouts. A man on the run left a trail. He needed new identity papers, a safe spot to stay, a woman, and a way out of the country. There were only so many places to obtain such goods and services in postwar Germany and Altman knew them all. When Otto Kirch telephoned reporting that he had seen Erich Seyss, Altman was pleased but not altogether surprised.

Kirch had proposed a trade of sorts. A guarantee that his operations run undisturbed for the next six months in exchange for information where Seyss could be found. (Naturally, Kirch had refused to reveal where or when he had seen the wanted man.) Altman agreed and Kirch gave him the name and address of one Hans-Christian Lenz, domiciled in Darmstadt.

A stream of sweat ran into Altman's eye, interrupting the recounting of his latest triumph. Damn this heat! One day he'd move someplace cooler. Somewhere in the mountains, maybe South America. He'd heard Peru and Bolivia were lovely. Many of his friends were there already. He dabbed an eye with his hankie and soon his good mood was restored.

This Lenz was a stubborn sort. At first he'd tried to deny even knowing Seyss, let alone where he could be found. Naturally, Altman had methods of persuading him otherwise. Seven years in the Gestapo had taught him all he needed to know about making a man talk.

And Lenz's information *was* invaluable. He'd revealed where Seyss was staying in Heidelberg, as well as the names of his associates. He'd admitted that he did not believe Seyss was leaving the country. A man with his skills could be in Tokyo by now. So why, Altman had asked, did Seyss need a thousand U.S. dollars if not to escape Germany? The answer had required a little cajoling and a very stubborn thumbnail. Lenz had overheard Bauer and Biedermann discussing a buy they were going to make from a crooked American officer. He did not know what exactly they were purchasing, except that it was located at an armory in Wiesbaden. Another nail and Lenz had revealed the mother lode. Saturday night, he'd croaked. Midnight.

Altman grimaced at the memory. It was distasteful extracting information from a *kamerad*. He counted himself fortunate to have been stationed abroad during the war, in France, where he'd been spared such unpleasantries. He'd had no qualms about questioning the French. In fact, he'd rather enjoyed it. None more than an agent of the Maquis, or underground, known as Max. Max was a tough nut to crack. First they'd worked on his hands. Then his feet. Then his teeth. Not a word. Altman had been forced to drastic measures. A fourteen-inch water hose inserted into the man's anus followed by twenty gallons of ice water had done the trick. *Désolé, mon pot.*

Max's real name was Jean Moulin. During the war, he had been chief of the resistance in Vichy, France.

Altman's real name was Klaus Barbie. As chief of the regional Gestapo, they'd called him the Butcher of Lyons.

Barbie settled down for a long wait. He fished in his jacket pocket and drew out a sandwich wrapped in wax paper. Liverwurst on white. Taking a bite, he mashed the soft bread in his mouth. Delightful! He was suddenly very happy with himself for having spared Lenz's life. Fingernails grew back. He'd done the man no real harm.

Smiling, Barbie balled up the wax paper and stuffed it in his pocket. He had not yet told his superiors at CIC Augsburg a thing about what he knew. They'd rush over, storm the house, and go home with an empty net. First, he wanted to see Seyss. He wanted to lay his eyes on the White Lion. Once he knew that the most wanted man in Germany was staying at Rudolf Krehlstrasse 61, he'd go to his superiors and present his plan. Not to Augsburg, he decided, but to Bad Toelz. To Major Devlin Judge. Clearly, Judge was a man of importance. Just as important, he was respectful. He would be sure to reward Herr Altman generously for his travails.

The Butcher of Lyons was sure of it.

CHAPTER

26

JAKE'S JOINT WAS A LIBERATED *gasthof*-turned-roadhouse situated in the rolling countryside thirty kilometers southeast of Munich. *Liberated* meant that American GIs had taken a liking to the modest restaurant and lodging place and promptly evicted the owners of forty years to claim it as their own. The only compensation given was a swift kick in the pants and the good fortune to have survived the war.

At nine o'clock on a Friday night, the airy establishment was packed to the gills with servicemen, civilians, and far too many women for them all to be American. A ten-piece band crowded onto a makeshift stage blasted swing tunes into a miasma of smoke, sweat, and booze. The walls were covered with souvenirs gathered by the victorious American Army, mementos transported from the boot of Italy to the beaches of Normandy for seemingly no other purpose than to decorate Jake's. A street sign posted above the entry read Paris 20 km. A poster behind the bar cheerily proclaimed, *Calvados de Bretagne—Il fait du bien pour madame quand monsieur le boît!* Roughly translated, "Brittany Calvados—Does wonders for a woman when her husband drinks it!" A café table complete with an umbrella advertising Cinzano sat in its own private corner.

And above it all—the buzz of drunken conversation, the roar of good-time music, the clank of plates and the clink of glasses—hung the well-lubricated hum of a victorious army. Jake's Joint was jumping.

"What are you drinking, sir?" asked Darren Honey as he and Devlin Judge settled down at a wobbly table on the second-floor landing that overlooked the dance floor.

"Give me a scotch." Judge heard the trumpeter launch into the first bars of "One O'Clock Jump," then added, "What the hell. Make it a double."

"That's more like it. We're off duty, Major. Time for some R and R."

Judge watched the Texan lope toward the bar. The kid was right. He needed to relax a little. He'd been pushing himself too hard and it was beginning to show. The trail from Garmisch to Sonnenbrücke hadn't yielded a thing. Dietsch, von Luck, Ingrid Bach, nothing they'd said was worth a damn. Four days of hitting one dead end after another. Like the kid said, time for some R and R.

Judge loosened his tie and kicked out his legs. A few couples began dancing and little by little a space cleared for them to do their stuff. He could tell right away they were the real thing. The couples were working on their rhythm, getting to know each other before slipping into the more serious moves. A husky corporal swung his gal out, then spun her onto his back, rolling her over till she landed on her feet. She shimmied for a couple bars, then to the delight of the crowd, slid smoothly through his legs.

Honey returned from the bar and set down four glasses of scotch. "Cheers, Major. Don't give up just yet. It's only a battle, not the war."

Judge picked up a glass and brought it to his lips. "I'm not giving up. Just figuring where we go from here."

"Half this damn country is checking their shorts for Seyss. Something will turn up."

Judge felt at once proud and embarrassed by the younger man's unbridled optimism. Once he'd had that same piss and vinegar. "Will it? And your rogues' gallery? Any word from Altman or one of his cronies?"

" 'Fraid not," said Honey, "but they're looking." And when Judge sought his eyes for further explanation he glanced away, his cloying grin appearing a moment later, along with the dime-store adage to just be patient.

Judge waved away the entreaty. Patience had never been his strong suit and with two days remaining to track down Seyss he had none to spare. He took a jolt of scotch, shivering as it coasted down his throat. "What's he up to, eh, Honey? You given that any thought? Can you tell me why a war criminal sure to draw the hangman's noose decides to stick around and tempt fate? He went to that house for a reason. Tell me why and I'll tell you what he's got planned."

Honey scooted his chair closer so as not to shout. "Don't get your imagination into high gear. A lot of these soldiers stick around because they don't have anywhere else to go. They've been in Russia, France, Greece, or God knows where, these past six years and the last thing they want to do is leave again. They want to stay close to whatever friends and family they've got."

"Are you calling Seyss a homebody?" Judge railed at the mention. "Didn't you hear von Luck? He doesn't live with the enemy. He *becomes* one of them. A Brandenburger, for chrissake! The man's been trained to pass himself off as the enemy. Bastard's probably sitting at the next table."

Honey shrugged, a sheepish look souring his face. "Looks like Seyss has gotten to you."

"Of course he's gotten to me. The sonofabitch killed my brother, stole the gun out of my hand, then damned near killed me. Hell, it's not just him. This whole upside-down country has gotten to me." He started on his second glass of liquor, relaxing as the alcohol warmed his belly. "Don't worry, Sergeant. I'm not giving up. I'm just hoping for a change of luck."

The band launched into "Air Mail Special," one of Goodman's classics. The clarinet soared over the throbbing drums, the saxes and trombone jumping in behind them. Judge tapped his foot to the up-tempo beat. Normally the song put him in a swell mood, the straight-ahead rhythm and brass attack making him forget his problems for a few minutes. Tonight, the music and the memories of home it called up only deepened his anxiety.

Two days remained until his orders were rescinded. Forty-eight lousy hours.

He wasn't concerned about what it would mean to Francis should he fail to bring in Seyss. Or that Seyss's capture was the only way he had to apologize to his brother for his hubris. Francis would forgive him on both counts. He'd say it was the effort that counted. But then, Frankie would forgive a rummy a lifetime of boozing if he said he was sorry on his deathbed. Nor was he fearful that he might let down his country—which he took in the form of George Patton and Spanner Mullins—though the relentless achiever in him desperately wanted to satisfy them, too.

Savoring the cheap booze's fiery drizzle, Devlin Judge cast a gimlet eye on his own ambitions, his own desires, wondering if getting his hands on Seyss wasn't just a way to put his own unsettled dilemmas to rest, if Seyss was the trophy he needed to prove he was as good as the rest of the men in this place, the notch in his belt signaling another opponent dispatched. Twenty-nine without a loss.

Going a step further, he wondered if Seyss was the answer to the contentious issue that had plagued him these last four years: That by choosing to continue his work for the U.S. attorney's office instead of seeking military service, he had neglected his obligations to his country. Or to put it more colloquially, that he was a yellow-bellied careerist.

December 7, 1941. A brittle, sunny afternoon in Brooklyn. Judge sitting in the living room of his third-floor walkup with his boy, Ryan, four years old. The two listening to the radio, counting the minutes until the *Chase and Sanborn Hour* begins. Edgar Bergen and Charlie McCarthy. Judge thinking they were the funniest damn thing ever to hit the airwaves. Suddenly the music stops, Gene Autry cut off as he warbles the refrain from "The Lonesome Cowboy." The announcer's stern voice, aquiver with righteous indignation, declaring, "This morning at eight A.M. local time, forces of the Imperial Japanese Army attacked the United States naval base at Pearl Harbor in the Hawaiian Islands." Ryan crying out in protest, "More music." Judge wrapping his arms around the boy, pulling him to his chest, asking him to hush, just for a minute. The announcer going on, "The battleship *Oklahoma* and two yet unidentified vessels are reported sunk with grievous loss of life." And then the words that delivered a chill down America's spine. "President Roosevelt will address a joint session of Congress tomorrow morning at ten A.M., it is said, to ask for a declaration of war."

War. It had finally come to America. Not from across the Atlantic as so many had feared, but from the Pacific. A surprise attack. War!

And Judge's first thoughts, the initial gut response of a thirty-one-year-old rookie lawyer: *A lot of guys are going to leave the office and join up for this thing. If I stay put and keep my nose to the grindstone, I can be at the top of the heap when this mess is over.* The army needed "bodies, not minds," Tom Dewey had said. Who was Judge to disagree?

There it was, then.

Erich Seyss was his confession and his penance, his expiation and absolution, all tucked into a black-and-silver uniform with a death's-head embroidered on its collar and his brother's blood on its cuff.

Happier now that he'd given a name to his frustration, Judge turned his ear away from himself and back to the music. The band really was very good.

"You a dancer, sir?" asked Honey.

"Me?" Coming from deep left field, the question made Judge grin. "Yeah, Sergeant, I know a step or two."

"Go on down. Plenty of dames waiting for you. Go on and *sprechen Sie* to them. After all, it's legal now."

Earlier in the day, Ike had called a press conference to relax the rules against nonfraternization. Servicemen were free to talk to children and widows, he'd said, but should do their best to steer clear of former Nazis and "good-time" girls.

"You go on," said Judge. "I'm going to stay here."

Honey stood from the table, upsetting his chair. "Don't be shy. You're divorced, remember? Won't be no one looking over your shoulder but me."

Judge read the urgency in Honey's eyes and was unable to keep a part of it from infecting him. "Go on. Maybe I'll be down in a few numbers."

Honey shook his head sorrowfully, probably thinking, *Old fart doesn't know what he's missing,* then hurried off.

Judge scanned the dance floor, more comfortable observing than participating. The American girls were easy to pick out. Busy smearing on lipstick or sharing secrets with a girlfriend, they huddled in circles of four or five, angora castles waiting to be stormed. Most were WACs or secretaries sent over by the War Department to help with the administration of the American zone of occupation. The fräuleins were a different story. Scattered through the crowd in ones and twos, they moved with an overtly sexual intent. Cats on the prowl. Their eyes were rimmed with black pencil, their lips painted fire-engine red. Coy was a word they'd never heard. They wore blouses cut low and dresses slit high. They showed more curves than his wife had on their wedding night. Meeting a Joe they liked, they'd offer a frank stare, then follow it with a lingering touch on the arm, a hand draped across an olive drab shoulder. It wasn't a dance floor so much as a bazaar. The thought that these women were readily available, that they were practically asking to be bedded, aroused him.

Deciding he needed another drink, Judge made his way down the stairs and into the middle of the fray. The music grew louder, the smoke thicker, and his head lighter. He was aware of every nudge, every glance, every whispered "Hi, Joe." Still, he kept his eyes lowered, ashamed to meet their direct glance. He reminded himself he was an observer, not a participant, but that tired voice got drowned out in a hurry. He tried *A gentleman doesn't act this way*, and got the same results. Lifting his chin, he cast an appraising look at the young fräuleins around him. He was shocked, and, if honest, titillated at their acceptance of his brazen scrutiny.

Judge found the bar and ordered a scotch, happy for a moment's respite from the melee. Yet no sooner had the drink been poured than a raven-haired girl of twenty bullied in beside him, took the glass full in her fist as if she were grabbing a can of Schlitz, and emptied it in one long draft. She stared at him long enough for him to notice that she was very pretty, then picked up his hand and laid it on her breast. *"Komm, Schatzi,"* she said huskily, then in some sort of pidgin English, "Take me your haus, Captin. You dutti Yanki bastid. Less go fickin."

A hungry hand kneaded his trousers. Judge yanked it away, scolding her in a Berliner's precise German. "That's enough, sweetheart. Go find a boy your own age. Run along, now."

Watching her disappear into the crowd, Judge's hungry eye was arrested by a flash of silver. A tall, languid blonde in a silver satin dress danced cheek to cheek with a slack-jawed man of fifty sporting three stars on either shoulder. Judge could not see her face, but he could see the general's and he recognized it immediately. Leslie Carswell, commander of the Seventh Army, whose headquarters Judge had spoken with the day before to arrange the meeting at Sonnenbrücke. The couple swayed to the music, and as the song came to an end, Carswell cocked a knee and gallantly dipped the woman in his arms.

It was then that Ingrid Bach threw back her head and looked directly at Devlin Judge.

JUDGE'S FIRST THOUGHT WAS THAT it couldn't be Ingrid Bach. He wouldn't classify the women at Jake's Joint as prostitutes, but they weren't paragons of virtue either. War had forced on them a terrible hardship and to survive they'd decided to partner with their occupiers. Their rewards were silk stockings, Hershey bars, cigarettes, maybe even a place to stay for a couple of weeks. It was a decision born of economic necessity, which was what made her appearance all the more startling. Ingrid Bach was hardly poor. The woman lived in a home the size of the Frick Museum.

Certain that he was mistaken, Judge returned his attention to her. She was applauding with the crowd, but still she stared at him. The sea-blue eyes, the sharp nose, the blond hair now immaculately dyed and coifed—all conspired in an instant to erase his doubt. He practically expected her to march over and begin lecturing him about the poor chamois being shot on her estate. And nothing could serve as more potent confirmation than the look of abject shame that spread like a shadow across her features, as she, too, recognized him.

Suddenly, everyone was in motion. The band eased into "Body and Soul," the crowd began dancing, and she was lost, a silver fan twirling slowly on the far side of the floor.

Judge abandoned his post at the bar and cut through the crowd. Ingrid's discernable humiliation stayed with him the entire way, lending his step an aggressive edge while resuscitating his earlier guilt. He had hardly earned the right to act as wildly irresponsible as the men around him. He hadn't slogged over the Alps or braved withering fire at Omaha Beach. He hadn't breached the Siegfried Line or fought his way across the Rhine. Hell, he hadn't even gone to boot camp. On the contrary. He'd spent the past three years dressed in gray flannel suits and Egyptian cotton shirts, eating at Toots Shor three days a week and at Schrafft's the other two.

Bodies, not minds, Judge told himself. He'd been serving his country, too.

Crossing the floor, he bumped into Honey cheek to cheek with a chesty fräulein, then forced his way between two couples practically glued together at the waist. Ingrid Bach saw him coming and dug her head into Carswell's shoulder. Judge didn't slow for an instant. Reaching Carswell, he tapped him boldly on the shoulder.

"Excuse me, sir, but may I respectfully cut in?"

Carswell dropped Ingrid's hand and stared at Judge's sweaty brow, loosened tie, and five o'clock shadow. Obviously, he thought the man a drunk. "You may respectfully go to hell, Major."

The snap inspection gave Judge the opening he needed. In a single fluid motion, he slid in front of the general, found Ingrid's hand, and let the crowd sweep them away.

Ingrid Bach lifted herself on a toe to glance at Carswell's outraged countenance. "Very cheeky, Major. Bravo."

"You know us New Yorkers. We're not always the best-mannered guys in the world, but we have heart."

"Heart? When you left this morning, you were positively frigid. All business. I'd thought we might at least be cordial."

Judge offered a conciliatory grin. He'd go cordial a step better if it might help squeeze some info out of her about Seyss. "I was a little overwhelmed by the house and meeting your father. It's hard to figure out who you can trust in this country."

"Maybe so, Major. But it's not fair to judge an entire nation by the actions of a few."

Judge nodded, wondering with which group she lumped herself. No doubt the former. Another innocent bystander.

The music swelled as it reached the first chorus. Judge was careful to hold Ingrid away from him so that their bodies did not touch. She stood a few inches shorter than he and he imagined that if she came a step closer, she'd fit nicely in his arms. This pleased him enormously. Guiltily, he wondered why.

"Known Carswell long?" he asked, curious as to their relationship.

"Me?" She smiled enthusiastically. "Yes, ages, actually. My cousin, Chip DeHaven, introduced us years ago. We're old friends."

"Chip DeHaven . . . from the State Department? I didn't realize Carswell was from New York? I'd always taken him for a southerner. Give him a beard and he'd look like Robert E. Lee."

"No, actually, he's . . ." Suddenly, Ingrid averted her eyes and her smile crumbled. "You've caught me in a fib. I don't know General Carswell. I haven't the foggiest where he's from. He's been asking me out for weeks. Finally, I gave in and said yes. I hope you don't think I'm . . ." Her words trailed off as her eyes fell to the ground. "I'm very embarrassed."

"Don't be."

"Look, if you want to know why I'm here, it's the same reason as the other girls. I don't take kindly to poverty."

"But you're a Bach."

She let go an ironic laugh. "Didn't you hear Papa this morning? We've nothing left. My brother Egon took control of the business two years ago. He convinced the Führer that if Bach Industries was to pass to the next generation intact, the business as a whole must be deeded to him. Egon gave us a few hundred thousand reichsmarks as compensation, and Sonnenbrücke, of course. He thought he was being generous but the money was spent before the war had even ended. I'm lucky not to have been expelled from Sonnenbrücke. Carswell hinted it would make an excellent retreat for officers."

"He must like chamois."

"That's not funny, Major," she replied sternly, but beneath her schoolmarm's tone, he detected an impish humor.

They swayed with the music for several bars, growing more comfortable with one another. When the musicians went to the bridge and the tempo quickened, Judge even dared a modest spin. Ingrid responded to his direction perfectly, releasing his hand, turning beneath his outstretched arm, then returning to him with the primest of smiles.

Judge quickly looked away, aware that he was enjoying himself more than circumstances allowed. But a second later, he put his lips to her ear, speaking softly. "I asked for this dance so that I might apologize for disturbing your father this morning. I should have taken your word about the severity of his illness. I'm sorry."

Ingrid bowed her head. "Apology accepted, but I'm still curious why you thought I'd know where Erich Seyss is."

"Even the smartest criminals head for their wives or girlfriends when they're being pursued. Most know we're keeping an eye on their loved ones, but they can't help it. I guess they realize that eventually they're going to be caught or killed, so they're willing to risk a final good-bye."

He didn't want to say he had no other place to look.

"I would have thought he'd left the country. Show up in a month or two on one those U-boats that keep surfacing in South America."

"Not a bad guess, except that we saw him Wednesday morning in Munich."

"You saw Erich?" It was impossible not to hear the distress in her voice.

"I ran into him at his home. If things had turned out differently, I wouldn't have had occasion to visit Sonnenbrücke." He shrugged to show it was his fault that Seyss had escaped. "You wouldn't have any idea why he'd go there?"

"To see his father?" Ingrid offered. "Why do any of us go home?"

"No, the house was a wreck. Abandoned. I was just thinking that if he'd risk going there, he might risk coming to see you."

"That I doubt, Major."

"Sure he's not cuddled up in one of your bedrooms? Admiring your collection of Dresden?" Ingrid was his last connection to Seyss; only reluctantly would he give up on her.

"No, Major. He is not." Her iron gaze ended all further inquiry.

Just then the crowd closed in around them, as if drawing a collective breath, and Judge found himself cheek to cheek with Ingrid Bach. He smiled awkwardly, trying to say this wasn't his idea, but the smile did little to slow his racing heart. To his surprise, she smiled, too, lifting her delicate chin to rest above his shoulder. The smell of her perfume, the nearness of her arctic-blond hair, the pressure of her lithe body—after two years without a woman, it was too much to bear. Desire flushed his body, a fever so overwhelming as to become almost palpable. It gripped him; it suffocated him; it sent a charge of electricity racing from the balls of his feet to the roots of his hair. Unconsciously, his hands tightened their grip around her firm waist. And that wasn't the only part of him constricting with desire. With a start, he realized he was fully aroused. In "a state of sin," Francis would have said with a chuckle. Dancing close to him, Ingrid had to have noticed. Delicately, he arched his back to ease the pressure of his body against hers, but it was impossible. The crush of dancers was simply too much.

The music slowed and the horns held the last note for several bars. Judge quickly dropped her hands and applauded. "Thank you for the turn around the floor. I enjoyed it."

Ingrid responded with graceful politesse. "The pleasure was mine. You're a fine dancer, Major."

Staring into her eyes, Judge had a desperate urge to wrap his arms around her and kiss her full on the lips. He felt his head moving toward hers, his body drawing near. Catching himself at the last moment, he averted his gaze and pulled up, instantly shamed and embarrassed by his unharnessed cupidity.

"Good n-night, then," he stammered, taking a plodding step backward.

"Good night," she said softly, then turned and vanished into the crowd.

Judge looked around him, expecting to see Carswell plowing toward them, steam spitting from his ears. But the general was nowhere in sight. Judge hit the bar and ordered another scotch. He felt panicked, as if he'd just avoided being hit by a car. Welcoming the drink, he knocked it back in a single motion. What a mess! Deny it or not, he, a United States attorney, an officer in his country's army, was very much attracted to the daughter of one of Germany's most notorious war criminals, the onetime fiancée of the man he was hunting. Part of him bowed to an onslaught of guilt, but part of him refused, and he knew it was the spell her physical presence had cast on him. *Wait till tomorrow*, he told himself. *This whole thing will have worn off.* Somehow he wasn't reassured.

Momentarily, he became aware of a commotion at the rear of the building. GIs and civilians were dashing up the stairs and forming a vibrant, boisterous throng. The crowd was congregated around the dormer windows that looked over the hardscrabble parking lot at the rear of the club. He heard shouts of "Put it down," "Go home, Fritz," and "Get out while you can."

Judge ran up the stairs and pushed his way through the crowd. He was surprised to find the mood jovial, GIs standing on their tiptoes asking each other "What do you see?" with undisguised prurience. Maybe a fellow had been caught with a fräulein in flagrante in his jeep, he wondered, and his buddies were giving him a little ribbing.

A gunshot exploded not twenty feet away, and someone said, "You missed, General. Try again."

Maybe not, thought Judge, smelling the powder even before the laughter erupted. Knifing ahead, he could see the pistol's silhouette, a ribbon of smoke drifting from its muzzle.

"What's going on?" he asked a wildly grinning GI.

"General's gonna bag him a kraut."

"What?" It was hard to hear over the raucous buzz.

"Dumb German sumbitch trying to steal a spare tire from the general's jeep," said the GI. "Won't stop even though we're yelling at him."

Judge pushed the man aside and looked out the nearest window. In the parking lot, a man was working valiantly to pry loose the spare tire from the rear of a jeep. He didn't seem to be taking any note of the catcalls and warnings directed his way. Or the gunfire.

Judge looked to his right. Separated by a cordon of soldiers, General Leslie Carswell steadied his arm on the windowpane and fired another shot.

"Stop!" yelled Judge, even as a cheer went up. Looking out the window, he saw that the would-be thief had fallen to the ground. He wasn't dead, just wounded. Raising himself to one knee, he dragged himself across the parking lot.

"Take another crack at him, General," urged a southern voice. "Some hot lead would do the boy good."

Smiling madly, Carswell braced his arm and took aim out the window. "Just you watch, son."

"Don't shoot," shouted Judge. "Can't you see the man is injured?"

Carswell turned toward Judge's voice, and recognizing him, said, "This is a frontier, dammit, and that kraut is gonna get himself a dose of frontier justice." He nodded at a heavyset sergeant in sweat-soaked khakis next to him, then pointed the gun at Judge. "Get that man out of here. He's a menace."

The brawny soldier rustled through the crowd, laying an arm on Judge's shoulder. "Get lost, Major."

Judge grabbed the man's tunic and delivered a solid uppercut to his chin, sending the sergeant to the floor. If this was a frontier, he'd make his own law. A corporal half his size jumped into his place and slugged Judge in the stomach, but Judge was too riled to feel anything. The kid from Brooklyn was alive and well and looking to bust anybody's mug who got in his way. He stutter-stepped, then brought his forehead down on the corporal's nose, breaking it and sending the man to the floor.

"Carswell," Judge shouted, peeling back the audience. "You don't kill a man for stealing your tire."

Carswell sneaked a peek at Judge. Hurriedly, he set his arm on the windowsill, raised the gun, and fired. The voice of the crowd died in time to the weapon's report. Judge spun his head and peered into the parking lot. The thief lay facedown ten yards from the jeep. He was no longer moving.

"I'll kill any fucking Nazi I like," said Carswell, holstering his pistol. "That boy was breaking curfew and stealing from a general officer. I got every right to protect the property of the United States of America. Remember, Major, this is our country now. Our laws. And our women."

Carswell pushed past him and ambled down the stairs.

Jesus, thought Judge, *that prick just killed a defenseless man and he looks like he's had a game of pool and a good piss.* Watching him strut to the bar, he felt a red tide flow inside him. It wasn't anger or rage, it was something beyond that, an impassioned and deeply felt desire to see justice done. To acknowledge with his fists his resolve for a better world.

Carswell didn't see the punch coming. Judge simply grabbed his shoulder, swung him around, and gave him as solid a right hook as he'd ever delivered in a lifetime of barroom brawls, street spats, and gutter fights. Carswell spit out a tooth, then dropped like a rock.

Honey materialized from the crowd, latching on to Judge's arm and dragging him toward the front door. "We have to leave immediately, Major."

"I'll take my punishment," said Judge, shaking loose Honey's arm. With a man shot in the parking lot and a three-star general roughed up, the military police would be there any minute. Turning toward the bar, he spotted Ingrid Bach helping Carswell to his feet. Against his will, a flash of jealousy fired his cheeks. How could she even look at that son of a bitch? He felt as if she had rammed a knife into his gut and was slowly twisting it. He'd never learn.

"Major, the military police are already here," Honey was saying, his rubbery face even more animated than usual. "They're waiting for us out front."

"What are they waiting for? If they want to arrest me, they can come in."

"Dammit, Major, this isn't about your hitting the general—you'll have to deal with that later." Honey took him physically by the shoulders and shook him. "We got him. I told you to be patient. He's in Heidelberg."

Judge felt the booze and the adrenaline and the welt of his attraction to Ingrid abruptly dissipate. In their place came a nervous energy, a clear burning excitement.

"Seyss. You're talking about Seyss? He's in Heidelberg?"

"Yessir!" shouted Honey, smiling now, nodding his head vigorously. "Altman tracked him down. The White Lion is ours."

28

EARLY THE NEXT AFTERNOON, INSIDE a torpid Quonset hut at Airfield Y31 on the outskirts of Frankfurt, five men gathered round a conference table to review for a third and final time their plan to capture Erich Seyss. Each betrayed the anxiety gnawing at his gut in his own particular fashion. Spanner Mullins ripped at the cuff of his splendidly pressed uniform, eyes darting from one man to the next as if trying to guess who held the ace of spades. Darren Honey slouched in his chair, hands drumming the table, his shit-eating grin stowed in a safe place. Next to him sat the German informant, Klaus Altman, ramrod straight in his too-large suit, forehead awash in sweat, cracking one knuckle, then the next. An outsider and wanting everyone to know it.

Nearest to Judge stood Major General Hadley Everett, Patton's dapper chief of intelligence, caressing his gambler's mustache as he droned on about the necessity to arrest Seyss before the Big Three arrived in Berlin.

"Georgie tells me Ike is counting on some good news to pass on to President Truman when the three meet in Berlin tomorrow," Everett said. "Our efforts to bring in Seyss coincide with the kicking off of the operational phase of Tallyho. I can't imagine a better way to get things started than to capture Seyss. It would send Fritz just the right message." He shot Judge a bullying glance, walleye holding him for a second before caroming to a far corner. "Not to mention free up some precious resources *and* please everyone concerned."

Great, thought Judge, he should have figured someone would turn the hunt for Seyss into a political football. Stealing a glance at his watch, he saw that it was only two-fifteen. The temperature was ninety and climbing. Above the table, a fan turned too slowly to do anything except push the clouds of cigarette smoke from one side of the hut to the other. He felt miserable. His head pounded in time to his heart. His tongue had grown a coat of fur. And no wonder . . . he'd polished off a half bottle of booze last night. If that wasn't enough, the knuckles of his right hand ached as badly as his bruised ribs. All morning he'd been waiting for word that General Carswell was pressing charges. Laughing, Mullins had told him not to worry. Ike would be none too pleased to learn that a lieutenant general under his command considered plinking unarmed, if larcenous, Germans part of a Friday evening's entertainment.

With Everett finished speaking, Mullins lumbered to his feet and walked to the south end of the table where he addressed himself to a chalkboard set on rollers. A schema of the Wiesbaden armory decorated the black slate.

"Once more for those of you in the bleachers," he began, and Judge saw Everett flash a grin. One point for Spanner. "Dusk falls at ten thirty. Immediately afterward, we'll move our lads into position around the armory. Troops from Military Police Company Seventy-three will be divided into four platoons and positioned here, here, here, and here." He banged his chalk at the four corners of the outpost. "Sergeant Honey will take the platoon opposite the entry. Two platoons with yours truly will be opposite the garage, so that when we get the signal from Major Judge, we can illuminate the poor bastards and make sure no one shoots one of our own, namely the villainous Captain Jack Rizzo. You may stand and take a bow."

Rizzo was seated in a far corner of the Quonset hut, along with a pair of brutish MPs to keep him company at *ten*. Hearing his name he smiled glumly and wisely chose not to respond. He'd been pulled in at ten that morning as Judge, Mullins, and Honey were en route to

Frankfurt in an army transport. According to Altman's unnamed source, Seyss was doing business with the American officer who controlled the keys to an armory in Wiesbaden. As there was only one armory in town, the path quickly led to Rizzo, who as it turned out was already under suspicion of selling Russian weapons to his fellow GIs. Given the choice between fifteen years at Leavenworth or a dishonorable discharge, Rizzo not only confessed to his crimes but promised his full and complete cooperation.

"As for you, Captain," Mullins continued, pointing a finger at the swarthy black marketeer, "you're to play it very cool indeed, which I imagine should pose no problem at all to a man of your criminal bent. You're to lead your chum Fitzpatrick, as Mr. Seyss calls himself, and whoever accompanies him, into the armory and take them directly to the spot where we've gathered the weapons." Mullins indicated a bay deep inside the armory adjacent to the doors leading to the garage. "Understand?"

Rizzo said yes.

"Good lad. And there you'll wait, making small talk, twiddling your thumbs, picking your I-talian nose for all we care, until you hear my signal." Here Mullins produced a silver whistle from the folds of his uniform and gave it a good long blow. Everyone rushed to plug their ears and Judge was pleased to note a look of discomfort on Everett's face. "And when you do, you'll be smart to hit the ground double-quick. Got that, boy-o? Remember, you'll have a friend close by. Won't he, Dev?"

Spotting his cue, Judge walked to the blackboard. He accepted the chalk from Mullins and drew an X next to the small box that indicated where Rizzo had placed the weapons Seyss wanted to purchase. "I'll be lying on top of the stack of crates, just above and behind you, Captain. You don't have to worry about a thing. I'll be keeping an eye on you the entire time you are inside the armory. Just be sure to maneuver Seyss into the open so that a direct line of fire exists from the garage to the weapons. We don't want him playing hide-and-seek inside the armory. Too many guns and too much ammunition."

Indicating to Rizzo where Mullins would be positioned, Judge asked himself again what Seyss wanted with Russian weapons and uniforms.

How had he been able to locate his former comrades so rapidly? And how, according to Altman's informant, had he gotten his hands on a couple thousand dollars even before selling supplies pirated from an army convoy? Maybe he'd been digging up cash back at Lindenstrasse along with the dog tags. Or maybe somebody else had given the money to him.

Disturbingly, Judge seemed the only man at the table concerned about Seyss's motives. Everyone else was focused simply on getting the arrest. After all, Everett had pointed out, once they had Seyss it didn't matter a good goddamn what he wanted to do with the weapons. Even Honey had agreed. Four rifles, four pistols, and four uniforms were hardly something to worry about, he'd said. As for the truck, no one had the faintest idea what Seyss wanted with it and no one cared. End of discussion.

But Judge had never been satisfied to close a case with a bundle of questions left unanswered. Simple curiosity demanded that he know what the White Lion was up to, what "last race for Germany" he'd been planning to run. After all, if Seyss failed, there might easily be someone ready to take his place. Replaying the questions, Judge came to the same conclusion over and over again. Seyss was not acting alone but as part of a larger preconceived plan. The word *conspiracy* came to mind, then flitted away. Only by capturing him could Judge learn the scope of his endeavor.

"When I see that you're in a safe spot, I'll signal Colonel Mullins to order his men into the armory," he continued. "Three clicks on the walkie-talkie, right, Colonel? We'll hit the sirens, throw open the garage doors, and turn on the kliegs. The sound and light should be enough to make everyone freeze in their tracks."

"You mean piss their pants, don't you, Dev?" Mullins cracked, and everyone laughed, even Judge.

"I guess I do."

The plan was his creation, a variation on the standard "bait and wait." It had been Honey's idea, however, to put a man inside the warehouse, and to his dismay, Judge had heard his own voice volunteering for the role. He would have preferred taking Seyss and his cronies at their hideout in Heidelberg. Seyss was a cagey one, though. According to Altman, he and his comrades had left the house early this morning, all going separate ways. It was the armory or nothing.

Replacing the chalk in its tray, Judge walked over to Rizzo and laid a hand on his shoulder. "If all goes according to plan, everyone will walk out of there in one piece. *Capische?*"

Rizzo grinned morosely. "*Capisco.*"

"All right, then. We adjourn until twenty hundred hours."

KLAUS ALTMAN GRABBED JUDGE'S ARM as they crossed the runway and headed toward the jeeps that would drive them to Heidelberg.

"So, Herr Major, it appears you will have your White Lion."

"As long as he shows, I don't see what can go wrong."

"I'm sure nothing will go wrong. Still, I can see you are still curious. Inside you asked what Seyss is doing with Ivan's uniforms, his guns. Do you really have no notion?"

Judge shrugged his shoulders, interested in Altman's views but not wanting to encourage him. The man was set to receive a promotion and a pay raise if Seyss was caught. That was already too much. "Didn't you hear the others? It doesn't matter what he's doing, so long as we catch him."

"I have my own ideas. Uniforms, guns, a truck with a full tank of gasoline and extra jerry cans. It seems he is planning a trip."

"That much I gathered."

Altman tugged on his cuff. "He is going east, Herr Major. East."

"East," Judge repeated. The word made him shiver.

Altman nodded, smiling his lascivious grin. "The question is why."

CHAPTER

29

WHERE WERE THEY?

Egon Bach held the receiver to his ear, damning the endless ringing. *Pick up*, he grunted. *Pick up!* Impatiently, he thumbed his spectacles to the bridge of his nose, oblivious to the perspiration fogging each lens. For two hours he'd been calling, dialing the number every five minutes, allowing the phone to ring twelve, fifteen, twenty times before hanging up. The Americans had tracked down Seyss. They had discovered his intention to purchase the Russian arms and transport. An ambush was planned this very evening to capture him. *Pick up!*

Egon stood in the factory foreman's office on the production floor of Bach Steelworks facility number seven in Stuttgart. Hovering beyond the glass partition were two MPs, his constant escorts when venturing outside of Villa Ludwig. With the Amis' blessing, he had come to supervise the initial retooling of the plant. The machinery used for years to turn out armor plate, military tractors, and 88s was being reconfigured to manufacture products destined for a civilian, rather than military, economy. The large gun lathes and milling machines in machine shops twenty and twenty-one that had been used to produce heavy gun tubes would be reset to manufacture steel girders and sewer pipes. Railroad tire shop three, housing twenty-three lathes, a dozen grinders, and two shell banders, would henceforth labor to turn out streetcar wheels instead of high-caliber artillery shells.

The businessman in Egon should have been ecstatic. Customers were customers no matter the cut or color of their garment. And the Americans paid cash. But today Egon was less the *konzernschef* than the son of his country, and the commotion taking place just then in the southeastern corner of the plant horrified him. An entire company of American engineers were gathered around the behemoth fifteen-thousand-ton press, swarming on it like bees to a hive. The press was monumental. The base plate was fifty feet long and forty feet wide. The four stainless-steel driving columns were sixty feet high and capable of guiding the stamping plate with a force of some 30 million pounds. The fifteen-thousand-ton press was the jewel in the family's crown, so to speak, responsible five years earlier for the creation of the Alfried Geschütz, the largest mobile artillery piece built in the history of mankind.

Egon saw the gun in his mind, as clearly as if examining its blueprints. A polished steel cannon one hundred feet in length weighing 250 tons. Nearly three stories high when set atop its own railcar, it looked like a monstrous tank, but in place of a turret was a breech block the size of a locomotive. The majestic gun fired armor-capped artillery shells twelve feet long (without the propellant casing!) each weighing sixteen thousand pounds. Everyone knows the crack of a rifle. Imagine, then, the bang when a seven-ton shell is fired with enough high explosives to lob it twenty-five miles behind enemy lines! Despite his funk, Egon grinned malevolently at the memory. Apocalypse! It was the sound of the apocalypse!

Egon looked on as a mobile crane rolled in, a steel mesh workman's basket dangling from its hook. Two soldiers inside the basket swung an iron cable around the uppermost pinion. A whistle blew and the basket was lowered to the floor. There followed a controlled explosion christened by a puff of gray smoke. The crane rumbled forward, lifting the engineers to the appointed spot where, with a thumb's-up, they signaled that the pinion had been successfully blown.

Step one in the dismantling of the massive press.

The first act in the emasculation of the Reich.

Running a hand over his close-cropped hair, Egon raised himself up on his toes, shaking his head. Below in the crowd—among, yet distinctly apart from, the American engineers—stood four representatives of the Soviet government, recognizable by their coarse woolen jackets and coarser Slavic features. All were grinning like schoolboys.

Untermenschen, Egon cursed.

Though American engineers were responsible for dismantling the press, the great machine was not destined for Pittsburgh, Detroit, or even Long Beach. Once disassembled, it would be placed on a train carrying it eastward to its new home, somewhere in the Union of Soviet Socialist Republics. The press that had made the Alfried Geschütz would soon be in the employ of Stalin and his greasy comrades.

Unable to bear watching, Egon ripped the glasses from his face and began vigorously cleaning the lenses. Only a year ago, Bach Industries had controlled major industrial facilities in twelve countries. Tungsten mines in France. Ore in Greece. Shipbuilding in Holland. Steelworks in Ukraine. All listed on the books for their acquisition price: one reichsmark. The rewards of a grateful nation. They were gone now, returned to their former owners. It was a pity, but he could not hold himself to blame for their loss. The rape of Bach Industries under his very eyes, well, that was another matter altogether.

Sliding on his spectacles, Egon dialed the Heidelberg exchange for the final time. As the phone rang two hundred kilometers to the north, he ran a manicured finger over the buttons of his vest. *Pick up*, he muttered. *Pick up*. This was Seyss's doing, he decided. The man was impossible to control. What could he have been thinking, venturing onto the black market when his picture was plastered over every square inch of the American zone of occupation? Did the man think himself immortal? It had been a mistake using him after he'd killed Janks and Vlassov. Seyss was too much the loose cannon Ruthlessly efficient, yes, but also completely unreliable—Egon's best and worst bets rolled into one.

Ten. Eleven. Egon's worry grew with each unanswered ring. God forbid the Amis succeed in arresting Seyss and his men. Seyss wouldn't say a word, but what about the others? One of them was bound to talk. The Americans would put two and two together: Seyss, the decorated Brandenburger, headed to Berlin dressed as a Russian on the eve of Terminal. An idiot could deduce what he had planned. *Pick up!*

After twenty rings, Egon slammed the receiver into its cradle. One of the MPs shot him a concerned glance through the glass partition but Egon waved him off with a broad smile. The smile was a ruse. He was damn near apoplectic with worry. Where were the fools? He had fall-backs set up. Another armory in Bremen. One in Hamburg. Friends to spirit Seyss to safety. He must warn them off the mission.

A second muffled explosion drew his attention back to the press. Another bolt had been blown. The crowd of engineers threw out a boastful hoorah. In a day, all that would remain of the press would be a few loose screws and a pool of grease.

Returning to his desk, Egon picked up the phone. To hell with Seyss and Bauer. There was no longer any time to waste. There existed only one man he might still call to avert a disaster. Egon dialed the number and placed the phone gingerly to his ear, preparing himself for the raw and untethered force on the far end of the line. When the party answered, he spoke rapidly, careful to temper his frustration with the proper respect. He could not reach his men, he said. He had no way to warn them. Other measures must be taken. If, that is, the listening party still desired to see the mission to its conclusion.

The man laughed, a resonant chuckle full of enough confidence and bravado to make even Egon relax for a moment. "*Natürlich*," he said. "I'll do what I can."

And when Egon hung up, he breathed that much easier. His care-fully conceived operation might still come off. Yet he could not deceive himself any longer. Seyss could not be trusted. He'd already put the mis-sion in jeopardy once. If, by some miracle, he were to escape tonight, he would do it again. It was his nature. Egon decided then and there to keep an eye on Seyss himself. There remained one meeting that Seyss could not miss. One chance for Egon to intervene.

Just then, a shrill whistle ripped the air. Rushing to the window, Egon grimaced as a steam locomotive was shunted onto the loading track and lumbered across the factory floor, whining to a stop adjacent to the fifteen-thousand-ton press. Two flags drooped from atop the engineer's cabin, both red with golden accents.

Egon saw them and shuddered.

The Hammer and Sickle.

INGRID BACH STOOD NAKED BEFORE the full-length mirror, carefully studying her body for clues to her ruinous behavior. Her eyes were clear, if pouchy from lack of sleep; her shoulders sunburned from her excursion to Inzell several days before. Her breasts were full and if no longer as firm as she would have liked, still round and high on her chest. Her legs were taut and slender, and except for a patchwork of bruises— medals from her campaign to keep Sonnenbrücke in working order— those of a woman in her prime.

But she saw none of this.

Staring at her reflection, she recognized only a succession of her failed selves. The teacher, the actress, the doctor, the painter she'd sworn to become and hadn't. The jilted lover, the ungrateful daughter, the false wife, the inadequate mother . . . the possibilities stretched before her like an endless tapestry of her own weaving. She was an embarrassment. To herself, to her family, and, harking to the faraway cry present in every German's soul, to her country.

Behind her, the sun continued its evening descent, its last rays burning the sky a fiery orange. In its wake, the shadows of Furka and Brunni, the hooded peaks that held Sonnenbrücke in their eternal purview,

lengthened and grew obscure, menacing her in a way her own conscience never could.

Turning from the mirror, Ingrid crossed the bedroom. An antique
oil lamp rested on her dresser and next to it a box of matches. The basement was full of the lamps, leftovers from the days before electricity
ventured so deep into the mountains. Sonnenbrücke had belonged to
the Hapsburgs then. Franz Josef himself had built the lodge in 1880, his
idea of a cozy family retreat. Foreseeing the need to gild his family's
flight into exile, he'd sold the property to her father sometime during
the Great War. An aphorism about one man's misfortune being another's luck came to Ingrid's mind. She wondered whether Papa was a scavenger or a savior. She decided both, which, given her current unchari-
table mood, was worse than being either.

Removing the lamp's glass veil, she struck a match, then fired the
tattered wick. She waited for the flame to catch, then lamp in hand,
padded to her dressing room. Seated at her vanity, she was confronted
once again by her own damning stare. How could she account for her
recent behavior? Exposing herself to Ferdy Karlsberg in exchange for a
few quarts of ice cream; dating the scoundrel Carswell as a prelude to
requesting increased rations. And if he'd balked, she asked herself, if
he'd whispered that he could only give these things to his mistress, then
what? Would she have slept with him? Would she have compromised
her body as she already had her spirit? Never, she resolved vehemently.
But part of her remained unconvinced.

After washing her face, Ingrid returned to the bedroom. Off came
the decorative pillows, off came the bedspread. The window was open
and a cool breeze swept her body, leaving her skin prickled with goose
bumps. Walking to the sill, she thrust her head into the night. Ten minutes after the sun had dipped below the mountains, the valley lay hidden
beneath an impenetrable shroud. She dropped her eyes to the brick portico twenty feet below. One push and she would be free. Free of her
guilt, her worry, her shame. Free of the cursed name that haunted her
from morning till night. The Bachs—bankrupt whores of a broken
Germany. They'd whored for the Kaiser, for Weimar, for the Führer.
Who was next? Why, the Americans, of course. Ingrid, with her plat-

inum hair and ruby-red nail polish, was only continuing the family tradition, if on a smaller scale.

Which brought her face-to-face with Devlin Judge. He hadn't asked
her to dance solely to apologize for having disturbed her father. He'd
wanted information about Erich, she was sure of it. Another American
seeking to exploit her company for his own interest. Still, she couldn't
scold the man, not after what he'd done to Carswell. She had little doubt
that he was under military arrest. She couldn't imagine what would happen to a German officer should he strike a field marshal. A firing squad?
Twenty years' hard labor? She shuddered at the prospect. Her Erich
would never do such a thing. Any objection he harbored toward
Carswell's behavior, he'd deliver during a private moment, if at all. He
was a soldier to the core. But Judge was an attorney, likewise acquainted
with the consequences of disregarding regulation. Why did one obey his
superiors and the other his conscience?

The unexpected entry of Erich Seyss into her intimate thoughts
thrust Ingrid back in time. She saw herself standing in the window of
her apartment on Eichstrasse, her secret lovers' nest in the heart of
Berlin. She felt Erich steal in behind her, his fingers waltzing up her
legs, over her belly, caressing her breasts. "So, *Schatz*," he'd said in his
dead-on imitation of Adolf Hitler, "only ten more children until you
receive the gold medal of German womanhood. This is no time to rest.
We must work, work, work!"

That was the Erich she had fallen in love with: the unannounced visitor, the wild and tireless lover, the trustworthy confidant who had
encouraged her to take an apartment unbeknownst to her family, the
adroit mimic ready to lampoon even the most sacrosanct of subjects.
Her best friend.

But even as they had fallen to the bed, giggling mischievously as
they raced to undress each other, part of her mind had remained on
guard. There was another side of him, too, one she'd begun to see with
disconcerting frequency: the hidebound soldier, the slogan-hurling
party man—"*Kinder, Kirche, und Küche*," "*Ein Volk, ein Reich, ein Führer*,"
"*Deutschland Erwache, Jude Verrecke!*"—the vitriolic anti-Semite. In
short, the ideal Nazi every Aryan aspired to become.

And in the heat of their lovemaking, when he was deep inside of her, arms pulling her to his body, when they were as close as man and woman could be, she looked into his eyes and asked herself which of these men he truly was?

And the absence of an answer frightened her.

A sudden breeze cooled the room. Catching a chill, Ingrid rushed to her bedside and wrapped a hand-knit afghan around her bare shoulders. She returned to the window, eager for the scent of cooling pine and night-blooming jasmine. Her thoughts of Erich faded and she found herself, instead, thinking of Devlin Judge. If she'd learned anything from Erich, it was to distrust her instinct.

She wondered if she'd been hasty in ascribing ulterior motives to Judge's actions. With a guilty smile, she acknowledged that he hadn't only been thinking about his investigation. Pressed so close to him, it had been impossible to ignore his desire. Any stirrings she'd experienced in return were purely reflexive. Still, she couldn't help but remember the feel of his body, his confident hands, the scent of his neck. He'd smelled of scotch and sweat and temper and decision. How long had it been, anyway? One year? Two? No, it had been longer. She hadn't slept with a man since April of '42 when Bobby went east. Three years, she mused, both aghast and amused. She'd never have guessed she could go so long without companionship. It couldn't continue like this forever.

But she would never consider someone like Judge. He was just another victorious soldier eager for his foreign fling.

In the distance, a kingfisher let go his mournful call, a scratchy bellow that accentuated her melancholy and forced her lacerating eye back upon herself. If she was to question Judge, why not herself? What made her think he would consider her, even for a moment? Whatever longing he felt was no doubt as reflexive, as instinctive, as her own. He was a lawyer and an investigator. He knew full well the crimes of which her father had been accused. He would never want a woman who carried the tainted blood of a war criminal.

The question of her own guilt in the matter arose daily.

Upon her demand, her father's lawyer, Otto Kranzbuehler, had slipped her a copy of the indictment. The stories were difficult to comprehend, let alone believe. Twenty-five thousand workers had perished in the Essen facilities alone. Beatings, starvation, murder—the charges described a litany of brutalities beyond her imagining. Yet how was she in any way responsible? She hadn't set foot in any of her father's plants for ten years. Business was never discussed at home and the Bach women were not encouraged in their interest in the family's affairs. Still, part of her refused to relinquish her guilt. She was a German. As a citizen, was it not her duty to know what was happening in the country of her birth?

Ingrid searched the ink-black night for an answer and found none. For the second time that night she found herself examining the portico below for a solution to her problems.

One push.

The driveway was miles away, the cut brick hard and unforgiving. She imagined her fall—the sudden drop, the rush of air, the terrible thud. But her problems would not perish with her. How would Pauli eat tomorrow? Who would look after Papa? How would Herbert manage?

Frightened by her mere consideration of the idea, Ingrid spun from the window and rushed to her bed.

One more day, she promised herself.

One more day and things will be better.

CHAPTER

31

THE ARMORY WAS AS STILL AS a mausoleum. The place smelled of cosmoline and petrol and the dank rot of ten thousand wooden crates. It smelled of defeat, thought Erich Seyss as he stepped inside and a towel of moist air settled around his neck. The last time he'd come, a string of dying bulbs had provided some light. Tonight, the building lay shrouded in darkness. Electricity had been cut six hours ago. Looking into the maw of the building was like staring into the abyss, a black so complete it was without dimension.

Seyss helped Rizzo close the barn-sized doors, then switched on his flashlight and whispered for his men to form up. A pool of beams grew at his feet as Bauer, Biedermann, and Steiner formed a circle around him. The three had made their own way to Wiesbaden, uniting at a friendly bar a short distance from the armory where he and Rizzo had picked them up. "My associates," Seyss had explained succinctly, and in a tone that begged no elaboration. He'd ordered them not to speak in Rizzo's presence and so far they'd obeyed. He had no idea how the American would react if he knew he was arming four SS troopers. Seyss suspected Rizzo already had a hint. Two days ago, the American hadn't stopped talking the entire drive up from Heidelberg. The south side of Philly, the delicious German fräuleins, Artie Shaw versus Harry James,

Stalin versus Churchill—Rizzo had an opinion about everything and everybody. Tonight, he hadn't spoken two words.

"I take it our merchandise is where we left it?" Seyss asked.

"Sure," said Rizzo. "I mean, why shouldn't it be? Nobody's been here since the other day."

There it was again . . . the edginess.

"Simply asking, Captain. No need for worry."

Rizzo laughed apologetically. "I don't have too many museum curators looking for Russian machine guns."

"Pity. You'd be a rich man."

"Give me some time," cracked Rizzo, his voice steadier. "We just opened for business."

Seyss relaxed a notch. That was more like the Rizzo he knew. "Lead the way. Once we gather up everything, we'll take a look at the truck. You have it ready?"

"Yep. Gassed up and rarin' to go. She's a beaut. A Ford deuce and a half with Ivan's red star painted big as life on the hood and the doors. Must've been shipped over during Lend-Lease. Whatever you do, promise me you'll get it the hell out of town in a hurry. Anybody stops you, just speak a little Russkie and pretend you don't understand what they're saying."

Seyss smiled inwardly. That was precisely his plan. "Come the dawn, we'll be far from these gates. Don't be worrying yourself, Captain."

"That's what I wanted to hear, Mr. Fitzpatrick. Follow me."

Rizzo set off as if on a forced march. From the entry, he turned left, counting off the stacks of crates as he passed them. Reaching six, he made an abrupt right turn and vanished into one of the narrow corridors that ran the length of the armory. Seyss followed close behind, then Bauer and the others. Their flashlights cut a shallow path, barely illuminating the concrete floor five feet in front of them. Above their shoulders, the crates brooded like crumbling statues to a pagan deity.

Seyss felt at home in the darkness, his incipient fear of tight spaces lost amid the trudging of rubber-soled feet and the hushed intake of breath. A frisson of excitement warmed his stomach, the same self-congratulatory sensation he experienced before a race when he sized up the competition and determined he would win. He reminded himself that this was only a preliminary heat. The main event would engender a return to Berlin, a return to the city of his greatest triumphs and his greatest defeats.

Arriving at a crossroads of sorts, Rizzo thrust his flashlight in front of him and made a sweep of the area. "There you are, Mr. Fitzpatrick. Your next exhibit."

Seyss handed his flashlight to Bauer, then stepped past Rizzo. The guns and uniforms he had picked out sat on top of a pile of splintered palates: the Mosin-Nagant sniper's rifle with twenty-seven notches cut into the stock, the Pepshkas with their drum barrels, the Tokarev pistols, the pea-green tunics with sky-blue epaulets. Everything exactly as it had been left. A metal trunk rested on the ground next to the pallets. He flipped open the locks to find the ammunition he'd requested. But all that was no longer enough. Proximity to his goal made him the greedier.

"Grenades," Seyss called. "For true authenticity, our exhibit will require a few dozen grenades."

Rizzo hesitated, looking lost. "They're in the ammo pen."

"Go get them."

Rizzo checked over his shoulder, looking toward the entrance to the garage as if expecting someone to answer for him. "They'll cost you more."

Seyss pulled an envelope from his jacket and handed it to Rizzo. "Surely you'll toss them in gratis. It would be the gentlemanly thing to do."

Rizzo opened the envelope, running a thumb over ten hundred-dollar bills. Again he glanced over his shoulder toward the garage. "I don't know. Guns, a little ammunition, that's one thing. Grenades, they're a whole 'nother ball game. And if you don't mind my saying, your friends don't look too much like gentlemen."

Behind them, Bauer, Biedermann and Steiner were sorting through the uniforms. Though they spoke in hushed tones, one could not mistake the clipped cadence of their language.

"The war has made rogues of us all, I'm afraid," said Seyss, his patience at an end. Something was wrong. He could feel it. Rizzo was too nervous, too much changed from their last visit. Removing Bauer's work-issue Luger from the lee of his back, he pointed it at Rizzo's chest, and said "The grenades, Captain. It's not a point for discussion."

"Give me a break, will you?" Rizzo's hands shuttled from one pocket to another searching for his key ring.

"Front left," said Seyss. "Don't pretend you don't know where they are."

Rizzo muttered something about "fuckin' Nazis" and how "he never wanted to do this in the first place," then in a fit of frustration, threw the keys at Seyss. "Get 'em yourselves. They're free. All you want. Where do you think you're going, anyway?"

"Where am I going?" Seyss cringed at the remonstrative twang to Rizzo's voice. Staring hard at the American, he caught the man's gaze dart high above his shoulder, the brown eyes open wide in expectation. He knew the look. Hope, impatience, desperation rolled into one. Spinning his head, he followed Rizzo's eyes, but saw only the fuzzy outline of crates receding into the darkness. Someone was there, though. He knew it. He yanked Rizzo by the collar and jabbed the pistol's snout under his jaw. "What's happening here, Captain?"

"Nothin's happening. What do ya mean?"

Seyss levered the barrel up, so that the gun sight punctured his skin. "Say again?"

Rizzo moved his mouth, but no words came out. Or if they did Seyss did not hear them. For at that moment, a siren wailed, a door flew open, and the midnight sun burst into the armory.

*W*HICH DUMB SON OF A BITCH *turned on the kliegs?*

Devlin Judge buried his face in his arm, squeezing his eyelids shut to block out the brilliant light. Who turned on the lights? Who ordered the siren? No one was supposed to have moved until he gave the signal.

Lifting his head, Judge pried open an eye. Spears of shimmering white punctured his dilated pupils. The light immobilized him, nailing him to his splintery perch on top of a stack of Sokoloy machine guns. One hand slid to the walkie-talkie by his waist. It stood upright, its antenna poking through a draft vent cut in the roof. No, he had not keyed in the signal by mistake.

For two hours, he'd been waiting for Seyss. Waiting for the White Lion to show his prized skin. From his vantage point high above the armory floor, he'd followed Seyss's progress through the armory. Everything had been going according to plan—Seyss and his men arriving at twelve midnight on the nose, Rizzo leading them to the guns and uniforms, keeping the conversation light. Then Seyss had asked for the grenades and Rizzo had broken. *A few more feet*, Judge wanted to yell at him. *A few more feet and we would have cast the net!*

An entire company of military police surrounded the armory, 175 men in all. Armored personnel carriers stood at all four corners of the compound. Two jeep-mounted klieg lights had been set up inside the garage to ensure proper visibility. But no one was to have budged, no one was to have moved a muscle, until Judge keyed in the signal and Mullins blew his goddammed whistle.

Forcing open his eyes, Judge saw the armory floor awash in a spectral light. Seyss stood directly below, a gun in his outstretched hand. He looked no different than he had a few days ago, hair dyed black, dressed in a navy jacket and trousers. His plan withering around him, he appeared cool and relaxed. Rizzo cowered a few feet away, raising his hands to his face as if to defend himself against a blow. It struck Judge how they looked like actors on a stage, their every feature defined, their movements dramatized by the kliegs' merciless vigil. Then, as if a casual afterthought, Seyss raised the pistol and fired it point-blank into Rizzo's face. Rizzo dropped like a sack of manure. No thespian could replicate the ocean of blood advancing across the concrete floor from the back of his head.

For one long second, all was static; a beautifully lit diorama scored by a bullet's earsplitting report and a siren's undulating wail. Seyss stood poised above Rizzo's body, while his comrades were captured in various positions of distress. Bauer, the stockiest and oldest of them, stared blindly into the blaze of the kliegs; Steiner, the spindly clerk, checked the chamber of the sniper's rifle with a marksman's competence. And Biedermann, blond and cagey, crouched behind the steamer trunk packed with ammunition. Then came the bone-crunching staccato of a heavy machine gun and all was motion.

Chunks of wood and tin and concrete erupted from the walls, the floor, the mountains of rotting crates, arcing through the air like exploding rock. Seyss ducked his head and dashed for protection behind the nearest box. With his pistol, he motioned for Steiner to fire at the light. His exhortations came too late. The lanky dark-haired man managed only to lift the rifle to his shoulder when he was caught in the chest with a string of bullets. He had no time even to scream. Lifted off his feet, his thorax burst in an ejaculation of torn flesh and viscera. As his body hit the floor, Judge saw that he had been cut in two. Seyss was yelling for Bauer to get down and for Biedermann to come to him. But Bauer was already down, digging his nails into the concrete floor as if he were hanging from a cliff. And Biedermann, hiding behind the ammunition box, looked as if he wasn't going anywhere either. A thirty-cal bullet penetrated the trunk, setting off a chain reaction of small-arms fire. A split second later, rounds began to explode inside the box. Biedermann looked this way and that, indecision creasing his features. Just as he began to move toward Seyss, a bullet exited the trunk, finding his jaw, and a microsecond later, his brain and skull. A cap of gore sprayed from his head and he collapsed.

Judge yanked his pistol from its holster and took aim at Seyss. *Safety off, hammer back.* All evening long, he'd been wondering how he'd react when he saw him, whether, as Seyss himself had advised, he'd shoot first and ask questions later, or if he'd heed his commitment to an orderly arrest. But the turbulent events of the moment, the cacophonous sound and fury erupting all around him, freed him from the choice. Tightening his finger on the trigger, he acknowledged his darkest wish and swore to bring it to fruition.

The Colt bucked in his hand, the first shot going high and to the right, tearing a gaping hole in the crate above Seyss. He fired twice more, but the bullets went astray.

Seyss spun, bringing his pistol in line with his eye, trying at once to aim and to glimpse the man who wanted to kill him. For a split second, their eyes locked, the hunter and the hunted, the prosecutor and the pursued. The light cast Seyss's face with a crystalline clarity—the cut of the jaw, the flared nostrils, the determined set of his milky blue eyes.

Nowhere could Judge read fear. The world was exploding around him, his comrades lay dead and dying, yet Seyss maintained an expression of absolute assurance.

Judge pulled the trigger again, missing, as Seyss let off four rounds in rapid succession. Flame spit from the pistol and Judge slammed his head onto the crate, raising an arm to protect his face from the shards of wood slicing through the air like broken glass. Two inches from his head yawned a jagged hole as large as a pumpkin. He rolled away from it and brought his gun to bear on Seyss.

But Seyss was gone, running across the open floor toward Bauer, his last unwounded comrade. His excursion was short-lived. Three MPs brandishing Thompson submachine guns darted through the door leading from the garage, their entry presaged by ragged bursts of fire. Seyss skidded on a heel as he fought to return to the relative safety of his previous position. He fired twice, felling two of the policemen, and a third time shattering one of the kliegs.

Still the siren wailed.

Judge felt a reckless tide swelling inside him. Everything was going wrong. Rizzo was dead. So were Seyss's comrades, and now, two American MPs. The army had a term for this: FUBAR—fucked up beyond all recognition. All because some stupid sonuvabitch had turned on the kliegs before he'd been given the order. Overcome with anger, remorse, and most of all frustration, he jumped to his feet and yelled as loudly as he could, "Seyss! Stop, you yellow bastard!"

Seyss turned as if slapped. Never compromising his stride, he raised his gun and pulled the trigger. Nothing happened. He was out of ammunition. Judge took dead aim at the moving figure and fired. The first bullet was high, showering Seyss with a barrage of splinters. The second appeared to pass right through him. A jagged chunk of wood spun from the crates behind his shoulder and struck him in the head. Seyss stumbled, bringing a hand to his face as he collapsed to the ground. Judge stepped close to the edge, craning his neck for the sight of blood, even as he contained a triumphant whoop. Had he shot him? With Seyss halfway to the unlit recesses of the armory, it was difficult to tell.

Yet even as Judge strained to make out the prostrate form, a bullet tore into the box at his feet and another passed so close to his head as to make his ear stop up. Two more bullets sliced the air above him and Judge flung himself to the rough surface. Suddenly, he was shaking with fear. A lightning peek around the armory revealed no errant marksmen. He focused once more on Seyss. The German lay still.

But then something else caught Judge's eye. From the far side of the building, down the row from where Seyss lay, the weakest of lights blinked once, twice, three times. A firefly in the nocturnal gloom. The pattern repeated itself. Short. Long. Short. Dot. Dash. Dot.

Only then did Judge notice that the siren had stopped.

His heartbeat pounded furiously as an urgent voice shouted into the vaulted space. "Grenade!"

Two silver pineapple-shaped canisters sailed into the armory, bouncing once, twice, three times across the floor. Judge's immediate response was to look toward the ammunition pen. There, behind a chain mesh fence, stacked to within inches of the armory ceiling, were crates of bullets, mortars, artillery shells, and every other god-awful explosive device the gods of war had seen fit to deliver unto man in the twentieth century. He imagined a sliver of white-hot shrapnel cutting through a crate and piercing the sheath of metal that enclosed the gun-powder. First one crate would blow, then another and another. The whole armory would go up in a conflagration of Wagnerian propor-tions. The explosion would make *Götterdämmerung* look like a scout's bonfire!

With a speed and finesse he did not know he possessed, Judge pulled himself through the draft vent and onto the corrugated roof. Lying on the cold surface, his breath coming in halting gasps, he dared a final glance into the armory. His last sight even as the first grenade exploded was of a bare slab of concrete decorated by a few specks of blood and a black Luger. Where a second before a man had lain, there was nothing.

Erich Seyss was gone.

CHAPTER

32

JUDGE'S ROOM AT THE American Military Hospital in Heidelberg was small and sterile, a ten-by-ten cubicle with an iron bed, a freestanding armoire, and a night table decorated by an electric fan and a pitcher of water. A brittle light filtered through rain-streaked windows, casting a jaundiced pall across the peeling linoleum floor. A single set of footsteps drifted from the hallway, then faded, leaving only the rattle and whoosh of the persnickety fan and the patter of raindrops pelting the window. Judge's vigilant ear seized upon the noises and mistook them for a familiar and terrible sound. In his half sleep, he was transported to another hospital room, this one in Brooklyn, not Heidelberg, and he saw a younger version of himself standing next to a monstrous metal box someone had cheerfully decided to call an iron lung. His son was inside the box, lying on his back so that only his head protruded beyond a plastic collar. The rushed intake of breath, the labored wheezing that had brought father to son's side, belonged to him, or rather to the machine that breathed for him, its constantly regulated air pressure taking the place of paralyzed muscles, forcing the four-year-old's lungs to expand and contract.

Judge reached out to touch his boy. He could see him so clearly—

the frightened eyes, the sallow cheeks, the indomitable smile. He just wanted to hold his hand.

Ryan turned his head, and as their eyes met, Judge trembled, for he knew his son was alive.

"Daddy."

Judge woke, bolting upright as the memory of his boy slipped away from him like sand through his fingers. He remained still for a few seconds, caught in the never-never land between dream and reality. A few more breaths and he wasn't sure he'd seen him at all.

Judge rested for another minute, then took inventory of his injuries. His cheekbone was swollen, tender as a ripe tomato. One tooth was lost. His shoulder was bruised and his hands scraped and raw. But nothing compared to the knot on the back of his head and the jackhammer it powered, drilling deep inside his skull.

Hoping for a moment's respite, Judge closed his eyes. But instead of darkness and calm, he saw the explosion all over again—the white-hot flash that slapped his eyes, the rolling ball of fire, the instantaneous thunderclap. Somewhere in there, he'd been tossed off the armory roof like a rag doll and fallen twenty feet to the ground below. What happened after that, to him and to those inside the armory, he didn't know.

In the hallway, a new pair of footsteps approached, steady as a drumbeat, then stopped abruptly. A firm hand rapped on his door.

"Come in," called Judge in a bluff voice that made his head throb.

The door opened and a patch of salt-and-pepper hair peeked around it. Next came the watery blue eyes and the sharp nose. "The lad awakes," chimed Spanner Mullins as he walked into the room. "You've been asleep since they brought you in here. Sixteen hours by my count. Let me have a look at you, then."

Judge offered a weak smile. Not counting his ex-wife, Mullins was the closest thing to a relative he had. How was that for a sad thought? "I'm okay," he said. "Just cuts and bruises."

Mullins looked him up and down as if eyeing Friday's piece of fish. "Not bad considering the plunge you took onto an asphalt deck."

Judge didn't want a shoulder to cry on. Only one issue concerned him. "Did we get him?"

Mullins ignored the question, pointing to Judge's cheek and grimacing. "Are you in much pain?"

Judge sat up straighter. For a second, his head swelled and the pounding trebled. Just as quickly it died off. He could move, but only slowly. *Did we get him?*

Mullins laid a meaty hand on his shoulder and gave a kindly squeeze. "We did, lad. Gone to his Maker has Mr. Seyss, along with two of his closest friends. May they dance in hell with the devil himself."

Judge asked Mullins for a glass of water and took a short drink. As the water trickled down his throat and into his stomach, he waited for it to ignite some flame of jubilation, some rush of relief and joy coupled with an adrenaline-fueled arrogance that once again he'd succeeded. But those emotions were nowhere present. Seyss's death was a hollow victory, late in coming and paid for dearly.

"He had *three* men with him last night. Which one made it through?"

"Bauer, the fat one," said Mullins. "He managed to drag himself out before the grenades went off."

Bauer was the factory worker in whose home Seyss had shacked up. Judge could still hear Seyss yelling Bauer's name, and a moment later, exposing himself to a withering fire in an effort to save him. There had to be some bond between the two men. What might link a factory worker and a field grade officer, though, he didn't know. "How bad is he?"

"Ruptured eardrums and soiled nappies. He's in the prisoners' ward downstairs."

"Anyone talk to him yet?"

"About what?" Mullins sounded genuinely surprised, but then his practiced ignorance had always been a source of pride. Judge set down the glass of water, too tired to push him on it. "Just tell me one thing: Who turned on the kliegs? I never gave the command."

"It was an accident. One of our boys heard the voices. He thought Rizzo was in trouble. Got excited. You know how these things happen."

Yeah, Judge said, he knew, but in fact he wasn't so sure. Flipping on those lights wasn't like pulling a trigger. A nervous finger wouldn't do it. No, by God, you had to take hold of that switch in your fist and tug it from ten o'clock to two o'clock. And what idiot tossed in the grenades? Everyone knew that the armory was chock-full of ammuni-tion. Rizzo had made a point of it before agreeing to go in, joking that no one had better toss a lit cigarette his way. Judge didn't want to think about who had taken a couple shots at him. Something about three strikes.

"Whoever it was, I hope you court-martial the dumb son of a bitch."

Mullins dropped his head. "That won't be necessary. Only the Lord can punish him now. The same explosion that knocked you off the roof killed four of our MPs. Six more were badly hurt. And that's not count-ing the two Seyss took care of."

"What?" Judge felt a stone tumble onto his chest. He opened his mouth, but could only gasp in disbelief. Six men killed, six injured, just to bring in one man. Counting Seyss and his ill-fated crew, it was a reg-ular massacre.

"And Honey? Where did he get to?"

"Docs didn't know when you'd come round so he headed back to Toelz this morning. He told me to give you his congratulations." Mullins' voice cracked. "Blessed be Mary, but the whole place went up like a keg of powder."

"Dammit, Spanner, it *was* a keg of powder!"

Judge let his head fall to the pillow. He had only himself to blame for the debacle. He should have killed Seyss when he had the chance. Suddenly, his beliefs in the sanctity of the law and a prescribed moral order were an embarrassment—somewhere between thinking the earth flat and man come from Adam and Eve. Closing his eyes, he offered a brief prayer to his brother, asking for forgiveness. Yet even as his thoughts left him, something caught in his mind, not a word but an image—a picture of a bare slab of concrete, vacant and unremarkable, except for a smudge of blood and a black Luger. And off in the distance, blinking like a miner's helmet in an abandoned shaft, a single point of light. Short. Long. Short. *Dot. Dash. Dot.* SOS. A crude signal for Seyss to get the hell out of there.

"Did you recover Seyss's body?" he asked Mullins.

"What's left of it."

"What do you mean, 'what's left of it'?"

Mullins drew himself to attention, mindful of the suspicious note in

Judge's voice. "I mean the whole place went up. Mr. Seyss left behind a nasty corpse."

"You're sure it's him?"

"Bauer identified the body. Altman confirmed it, too."

"What the hell does Altman know?"

Mullins' cheeks flushed scarlet at Judge's contemptuous tone. Moving to the foot of the bed, he directed an angry finger in his former detective's direction. "Now, you listen to me, Devlin Judge. No one else came out of that armory alive. We had that building surrounded. I was at one exit, Honey the other. *You* positioned us there. So don't go getting any crazy ideas."

"Fine," Judge replied calmly. You didn't argue with Mullins. "But I'd like to see the body."

"I spent all morning in that bloody morgue identifying those kids. I've seen worse, but not much, and not often, thank the good Lord." Mullins ran a hand across his mouth and Judge could see that he was very upset. "If it'll make you sleep better, you can go check the body, yourself. Altman will give you the tour. He's down there now."

THE MORGUE WAS LOCATED IN the basement of the hospital. It was a large antiseptic room with green linoleum flooring and white tile walls. Like morgues everywhere, it smelled strongly of formaldehyde and disinfectant. A row of gurneys bearing the remains of the men killed the previous night in Wiesbaden was parked against one wall. One, two, three . . . Judge stopped counting the crisp white sheets. A dull ache took the place of his heart.

Altman burst through the swinging doors at the far side of the room, a satisfied smile plastered to his lips. "Congratulations, Major. I'm delighted to see you in one piece."

"Thank you, Mr. Altman." Judge could see that the Gestapo man expected a pat on the back for having tracked down the White Lion. With Seyss dead, he'd have his promotion. That was enough. "I understand you've identified Erich Seyss."

"Actually, it was Herr Bauer who identified the body. I simply confirmed his opinion." Altman scurried to the third gurney in line against the wall. "I trust you have a strong stomach."

Judge was dressed in a hospital bathrobe and pajamas. If he got sick, at least he wouldn't be puking on his own clothes. "Strong enough. Let me see it."

Altman pulled back the sheet.

Judge glanced at the disfigured body, clenching his jaw to arrest a flight of bile. Seyss's face resembled a crushed pomegranate. "Excuse me, Mr. Altman, but half of this man's skull is missing. How do you know with any certainty that it is Erich Seyss?"

Altman responded eagerly, pointing out the butchered physiognomy as he went. "We can still see the lips, some of the nose and the jaw. I suppose we could request the dental records but I'm afraid they would be a long time in coming. Besides, this is clearly the body of a man who served in the SS." Lifting the corpse's right arm, he pointed to a star-shaped scar the size of a beverage coaster on its underside. "Sturmbannführer Seyss's last command was on the southeastern front against Malinovsky's Ninth Army. It was common for SS men fearing imprisonment at the hands of the Russians to eliminate their blood group tattoo." He turned the arm over and pointed to a smaller scar the size of a cigarette burn, just below the shoulder. "A bullet here removes all trace of the marking."

"You're saying Seyss shot himself through the arm to remove the tattoo."

"More likely he had his sergeant shoot him. It was a common practice. One of his comrades, Herr Steiner, who served under him in the last months of the war, bears a similar scar. Would you care to see it?" Altman sounded like a headwaiter asking if he'd like to try the daily special.

"No, thank you." Judge turned from the gurney. The body appeared to match Seyss's height and weight and it was wearing the same gray flannel trousers. Still, he was troubled by the profound injury to the face. And he didn't remember reading anything in Seyss's medical record about a distinguishing scar under his right arm. Maybe he was being overly suspicious. With armed soldiers posted at every exit, escape from the armory would have been impossible.

And the flashlight? Judge asked himself. Had it been one of his own men showing Seyss the way out?

Thanking Altman, he spun on his heel and crossed to the exit. But reaching the door, he pulled up suddenly. "Tell me, Altman, how many bodies did we recover from the armory?"

"Nine."

Judge turned and strode past the row of gurneys, figuring the casualties in his head. He'd seen five men killed with his own eyes: Rizzo, Biedermann, Steiner, and the two MPs shot by Seyss. Mullins said four more soldiers had been killed when the ammunition dump exploded. Arriving at the ninth gurney, he said, "We're one short."

"Excuse me?"

"We're missing a body."

"No, no. You're thinking of Biedermann. As you recall, he was killed taking refuge behind a foot locker filled with ammunition. When the locker exploded, he simply disintegrated."

"And his boots?" challenged Judge. "Did they disintegrate, too?"

Altman parried the thrust with ease, ever guarding his solicitous tone. "Certainly not. But as the armory held over five thousand uniforms, *including boots*, it would be difficult to identify which pair was his." He bowed ever so slightly. "Anything else, Major?"

JUDGE FOUND MULLINS PACING THE hallway outside the morgue.

"There are only nine bodies, Spanner."

"What of it?"

"You bought Altman's line about Biedermann disintegrating? I can see how a shell from a Howitzer would obliterate every trace of a man, but a hand grenade, even a few dozen bullets . . ." Judge shrugged. "They'd just make a big mess."

"You yourself saw Biedermann hit," said Mullins. "He fell right next to the ammo box. Whatever was inside it exploded like a Chinese firecracker. And that was before the rest of the place went up."

Judge nodded, weighing his own suspicions against the facts of record. "Has anyone checked the body's blood type against Seyss? Can we get a copy of his dental charts?"

Mullins ran a hand across the back of his neck, his brow assuming its earlier scarlet coloration. "Seven Americans died nabbing this Nazi bastard. I'm damned well not going to tell Georgie Patton that Seyss is still on the loose, because you alone refuse to believe it. This is no time for a doubting Thomas."

"Especially since by now he's told Ike and Ike's told the president. After all, Operation Tallyho wouldn't be a success without Seyss being rounded up."

"It's got nothing to do with Tallyho!" shouted Mullins, moving closer and clamping both hands on Judge's shoulders. "Make no mistake, Mr. Seyss died inside that armory. That is his body on that gurney. Bauer said so and Altman confirmed it. Understand?"

Judge broke from his grip and began walking to the elevator.

"Ike cut you seven days to bring in Seyss and you did it in six," called Mullins, rushing to catch up. "You should be proud, boy-o. Who knows? There might even be a promotion in here somewhere for you. It's time to think of the future again. There's a flight out tomorrow at noon for Munich. We'll gather your gear at Bad Toelz and have you back in Paris by nightfall. Play your cards right, and come the trials, you'll be in every newspaper round the world."

Judge slowed, regarding Mullins earnestly. A week ago, a position on the International Military Tribunal meant everything to him. Another rung up the ladder. The chance to serve his country. The opportunity to gild his professional name. Today it left him uninspired. It was another man's dream.

What had he been after? Justice or merely glory?

"Tell me, Colonel Mullins, has anyone asked Bauer what Seyss was planning to do with the Russian guns and the Red Army uniforms? Didn't Altman say they belonged to the NKVD? Why do you think Seyss wanted to pass himself off as a member of the Russian secret police?"

Corporal Dietsch's words echoed in his mind. *It's some kind of mission. A final race for Germany.*

Mullins winced at the questions. "I make it my business *not* to make it my business. Seyss is dead. Case closed. Bauer will be tried in a German court for black marketeering and as an accomplice to murder."

Judge sighed and pressed the call button. He was tempted to lower his head and call it a day. Good men had died. They had a body and an identification. He should count himself lucky to be alive. Better yet, he could return to the IMT with an even heart and put his energies back into his career.

But what is it you want? Justice or glory?

He wanted Seyss.

He refused to go on building his career atop a compromised conscience.

"Okay, Seyss is dead," Judge heard himself agreeing. "But would you mind if I had a few words with Bauer? Technically, he is my prisoner."

Mullins eyed him warily. "You believe that, do you? Or are you just trying to get back on your uncle Spanner's good side?"

"So we're on first-name terms again?"

"All you had to do was nab Seyss." Mullins held open the elevator door. "You can talk to Bauer first thing in the morning before we pack up for Bad Toelz. What we all need now is a good night's rest."

"Amen," said Judge, yawning. But he had no intention of going to sleep.

CHAPTER

33

THE CLOCK ON THE WALL READ ten past nine as Judge entered the prisoners' ward later that night. A lone MP sat outside the door, dozing. Judge tapped him on the shoulder and flashed his identification. "I need some time alone with my prisoner. Why don't you grab a cup of coffee?"

The guard checked the face on the ID against the banged-up man in uniform standing in front of him. Raising a hand to his mouth, he masked a deep yawn. "Sure thing, Major. His ankle's cuffed to the bed. Need the keys?"

"Why not?" Judge winked. "Maybe we'll take a walk."

The MP knew what that meant. With hooded eyes, he handed over a small pair of keys, then bustled down the hallway.

Judge pushed open the swinging doors and entered the ward. Beds ran up and down either wall. All were empty but one, mattresses rolled up to expose rusting iron lattices. The room had the melancholy air of a summer camp boarded up for the winter. In the farthest corner, a heavyset man with cropped dark hair and no discernable neck slouched on his bed, reading a newspaper. Printed in large boldface print, the headlines read, "Big Three to Meet at Potsdam Tomorrow."

The first postwar conference was set to open tomorrow at 5:00 P.M. Truman, Churchill, and Stalin would meet near Berlin to decide the political future of Germany and the European continent. Reparations would be set, borders drawn, elections scheduled in countries returned to their native habitants. Mostly, though, the Allied leaders would discuss which measures to take to prevent Germany from ever waging war again. They'd failed at Versailles in 1919. From the harsh measures being bandied about in the press, Judge did not think they'd fail again.

"So, you've come to get me out of here?" said Bauer, lowering the paper and offering a dingy smile. "You're late."

"Sorry," answered Judge, dismissing the jest. "Wrong man. I'm the guy who was looking for your friend, Major Seyss. I understand you identified his body this morning."

Bauer shrugged noncommittally as if to say that was his business, now leave him alone. Judge knew better than to press him. Under no circumstance could he suggest that he harbored doubts whether Seyss was, in fact, dead. "You're a lucky man. Seyss, Biedermann, Steiner, all dead. You're the sole survivor."

Bauer leaned closer, squinting his eyes. "Now I recognize you. I saw you in the armory, standing up on top of the crates yelling like John Wayne. By the way, you're a lousy shot."

"I don't have much practice. Even as a cop, I wasn't very good. A guy had to be very close for me to hit him. About as close to me as you are."

"Is that a threat?"

Judge returned the same noncommittal shrug. Normally, he'd spend some time asking Bauer a string of easy questions, getting him accustomed to saying yes, building a rapport between them, but tonight he didn't have time for any games. He unlocked the German's cuffs, then took out a pack of Lucky Strikes and offered him a cigarette. He hadn't met a German yet who didn't smoke. "Mind telling me what Seyss planned to do with all that Russian equipment? Why the guns and uniforms? Where you boys were headed in that truck?"

Bauer kept his gaze on his feet, not saying a word. He smoked like a survivor, keeping the cigarette burning until the embers singed his callused fingertips.

"Look," said Judge, "the game is over. Whatever you fellows had planned is not going to happen. I'd appreciate your cooperation. It'll go easier on you if you tell me the truth."

Bauer grunted, clearly contemptuous of Judge's supplication, but he said nothing.

"Let's go back a step, shall we? How did Seyss find you? You're a factory worker, not a soldier. Did you know him before the war? Are you related somehow? I saw how he tried to save you. I'd be hard-pressed to do the same for my own brother. Or what, did he just show up on your doorstep and suggest you hop on down to the armory and buy some machine guns, maybe pick up a couple of bratwurst on the way?"

At that, Bauer's eyes rose to his, but still he didn't speak.

Judge let a minute pass, the German's silence goading him, provoking a swell of anger. He wasn't mad at Bauer so much as disgusted with everything he'd witnessed since coming to Germany. The bombed-out cities, the deplorable living conditions, the pauper-thin population, the madness of Dachau, the degradation not only of the German people but of the Americans, as well. Janks starving his prisoners to line his own pockets, Carswell plugging krauts to satisfy his bloodlust, and somewhere tied up in it all, Ingrid Bach, fallen princess of Sonnenbrücke, selling herself to look after her family. Somehow, he managed to keep the growing rage from his voice.

"Only three questions concern me: Where were you going? What were you planning on doing when you got there? And who put you up to it? Rather, who put Seyss up to it?"

Bauer smirked. "That's four questions."

Judge punched him hard in the eye, toppling Bauer over the side of the bed. His fist stung and he saw that he'd split a knuckle. Though upset, he hadn't considered hitting Bauer until that moment. It had just seemed like the necessary thing to do, and for once, no antiquated notions of propriety braked the impulse. Strangely, guilt figured nowhere in his emotions. Instead, he felt both happy and clever, as if he had just discovered an easier way to complete a tiresome job and it came. It came to him that he'd been foolish not to have sweated Fischer and Dietsch. And that Germany was no place for the Marquess of Queensbury.

Picking up Bauer by the scruff of his collar, he settled him on the mattress. "One: where were you going? Two: what were you planning on doing when you arrived? Three: who put Seyss up to it?"

Bauer's lips moved, maybe a word escaped. For a moment, he looked as if he were truly lost, unable to tell up from down, but just as quickly his jaw set and his face took on the same combative look.

Judge delivered a backhand to the cheek and Bauer cried out. He was surprised at how quickly it was all coming back—the jab to the brow, the uppercut to the jaw—everything Mullins had taught him and he'd sworn to forget. "It's silly for us to be acting this way," he went on in his sincerest voice. "I want you to take a second. Relax. Decide if we have to go on like this."

Bauer slumped a little, pondering the question. "I'm confused about who's the boss around here. Why don't you guys make up your—"

Judge slugged him in the stomach, at a spot two inches below the sternum. Bauer doubled over and fell to the floor. He lay there for a minute, looking for all the world like a fish out of water, squirming and kicking, and finally, sucking in great swaths of air. Judge kneeled beside him, one hand on his throat. "Herr Bauer, I asked you a simple question. Either you will answer me or we will go on as before. I can assure you I have no other appointments this evening."

"Enough," croaked Bauer, pushing away Judge's hand. "I give up. I wish you Amis would make up your minds. First you tell me to keep my mouth shut and everything will go easy. Now you want to hear the whole story again."

Judge extended a hand and helped Bauer to his feet. "What's that?"

"I already told you everything. Didn't you believe me?"

"No, no, before that. Who told you to keep your mouth shut?"

"One of you. Same uniform. He didn't give me his name, either," said Bauer. "Speaks German like you."

"Was he the man who told you he'd get you out of here tonight?"

"He said nine o'clock. Is punctuality only a German trait?"

Judge let the information pass, certain it was Hadley Everett or one of his men. Right now, he was only interested in what Bauer could tell him about Seyss. "Just repeat everything you said earlier and we're square."

"*Stimmt das?*" Bauer wiped at his lip. "You're sure? Our deal still stands? Six months in the cooler, then I'm free to go?"

Judge wondered what had happened to standing trial as a black marketeer and accomplice to murder. "It stands."

Bauer stood, brushing off his pajama and trying hard to regain his dignity. "Babelsberg," he said.

"Babelsberg what?" demanded Judge. The word meant nothing to him.

"That's where we were going. Babelsberg. Our Hollywood. Fritz Lang, Emil Jannings, Marlene Dietrich—they all made movies there. That's why we needed the truck. The guns and uniforms were to help us fit in. It's just a business matter. No concern for you."

"A business matter?" This was rich.

Bauer struggled onto the bed. "*Ja*. We were to drive to Babelsberg, go directly to the *herr direktor*'s villa and take possession of the engineering drawings. That was all. Then we come back home."

"Two hundred miles into Russian territory for some engineering drawings?" Judge was unable to hide his skepticism. "What the hell were they for?"

"I have no idea."

"But you were willing to risk your life for them?"

"Of course," said Bauer. "Herr Bach paid me generously. Two months' salary. Five hundred reichsmarks. Besides, he said it was of utmost importance to Germany."

"Did he?" Judge betrayed no excitement at the mention of the Bach name, but his joy was that of a man granted a last-minute reprieve. "And which Herr Bach are you referring to? Alfred or Egon?"

Bauer shot him an incredulous look. "Why, Herr Egon, of course. He has been running the concern for two years now."

Judge recalled Ingrid's mention of the *Lex Bach*, Hitler's edict granting Egon Bach complete control of Bach Industries. If Egon had been running the company for two years, why the hell hadn't the War Crimes Commission issued a warrant for his arrest? It wasn't only the factory chiefs who were being hauled before the docket. Sure, Alfried Krupp was in jail, but so were ten of his top lieutenants. The same went for the big shots at I. G. Farben, Siemens, Volkswagen, and so on.

Confused, he sat back on the iron springs and ran a hand through his hair. Wheels within wheels, Mullins would say.

"Herr Major, may I offer *you* a cigarette?" Bauer reached beneath his bunk and took out a crushed pack of Chesterfields. "I don't care for Lucky Strikes. Have one of mine."

"No, thanks," said Judge, eyeing the wrinkled pack. "I don't smoke." Chesterfield was Honey's brand. Obeying a hunch, he said, "I see my colleague left you some of his cigarettes. Young man, a sergeant?"

"Three stripes," said Bauer, drawing parallel lines on the sleeve of his pajama. "Yes, he was young. A fine Aryan."

"And he spoke German?"

"Perfekt!"

It was Judge's turn to feel as if he'd been sucker punched. What the hell had Honey been doing talking to Bauer? Honey, who couldn't even get out a comprehensible *wie geht's?* Honey, who according to Mullins had returned to Bad Toelz early that morning?

Staring at the floor, Judge worked to regain his bearings. Bauer's copy of the *Stars and Stripes* lay at his feet. On the front page was a photograph of President Truman onboard the U.S.S. *Augusta* mooring in Brussels the day before, and below it, another showing the burnt wreckage of the Reichstag. The place was a mess, a jungle of twisted steel and crushed concrete. Three thousand Germans had died defending the place and five thousand Russians taking it. One lousy building. And for what? The city was already lost, ringed by a million Russian soldiers. He flipped the paper over and read the headline once again. "Big Three to Meet at Potsdam Tomorrow."

A final mission for Germany.

And then he had it. Why Seyss wanted the weapons, the sniper's rifle, the pistols, why he needed the uniforms and the truck. And it had nothing to do with engineering drawings.

A final mission for Germany.

He whispered the words and the hairs on the back of his neck stood at attention.

"Just one more question: Babelsberg, that's near Berlin, right?"

Bauer rubbed his chin, nodding. "About twenty kilometers outside of the city. Actually, it's closer to Potsdam. Just next door, in fact."

CHAPTER
34

JUDGE GRIPPED THE STEERING WHEEL with both hands, ten o'clock and two o'clock, like Mullins had showed him in the hospital parking lot. One foot held the accelerator to the floor, the other rested above the brake, just in case. He'd been driving for six hours, a midnight run on the famed German autobahn. The four-lane highway was nearly deserted, the world's straightest river with a surface you could skate across. He'd passed Karlsruhe, Stuttgart, and Augsburg, seeing only unlit exit signs and stunted silhouettes, and now he was nearing his destination.

"Pick up von Luck. Bring him straight back and the secret's between us," Mullins had said, in response to Judge's entreaty that Seyss's body be positively identified. Bauer's statement had raised enough questions to trouble even Mullins's rule-bound conscience. "I'll get Georgie Patton to extend your transfer by twenty-four hours. Then it's straight back to Paris with you and we'll pick up any loose straws."

Judge knew of two people who could look at what remained of the body on gurney number three and say with any certainty whether or not it was Erich Seyss. Of them, only von Luck could provide insight into Seyss's actual intentions, and in doing so, validate Judge's suspicions. Neither Mullins nor Judge believed Seyss would venture into Soviet-held territory for something so pedestrian as engineering drawings. The first thing a police officer learns is that there is no such thing as coincidence.

As for Honey and his reasons for interrogating Heinz Bauer, Judge could only guess. Maybe he'd received orders from CIC to grill Bauer. Maybe he'd done it on his own, hoping to prove his mettle and wangle himself a promotion. Whatever the reason, Judge was puzzled why he'd given Bauer the order to keep quiet. Certainly, Honey knew that Judge wouldn't leave without questioning him. Either he hadn't expected him to use his fists to get the information or there was someone else he didn't want Bauer to speak with.

Eyeing the speedometer, Judge kept the jeep traveling at a constant sixty-five miles per hour. Driving wasn't as difficult as he had imagined. A few turns around the hospital courtyard with Mullins in the passenger seat screaming "brake, clutch, shift, gas," and he'd been ready to go.

A sliver of daylight appeared directly ahead, cutting the horizon in two. The sliver widened into a band, then lost its borders as the cloudless sky was suffused with a warm orange glow. Heralding the dawn's arrival, a prickly crosswind picked up from the north, freighting the air with the rich smells of land under cultivation. He breathed deeply, his eyes watering at the loamy scent and its promise of rebirth and renewal. And slowly, a new sense of confidence took root inside him and grew.

The jeep sped past a large sign reading München—Nord, letters of white offset against a deep blue background. Judge followed it off the tree-lined autobahn and into the city's torn-up streets. Maneuvering the jeep was more difficult now, a clumsy ballet of gas and clutch, one hand welded to the wheel, the other to the stick shift. Piles of splintered wood and serrated masonry twenty feet high choked the roads. He steered crazily around them. On the sidewalks, clutches of women huddled around smaller mountains of redbrick, chipping away mortar and lattice so that they could be used to rebuild their city. *Trümmerfrauen*, they were called. Rubble women.

Judge searched for signs leading to Dachau. Despite the abject destruction, no important intersection was naked of arrows pointing the direction to towns in the vicinity. He turned left, then right, entering the village that gave the notorious camp its name. It was market day. Vendors bustled across the town square, erecting stalls for their corn and beets and potatoes. He stayed on the main road another ten minutes and found himself traveling a familiar country lane. More familiar still was the rank scent souring the air. He did not slow the jeep as he passed through Dachau's gates.

A sentry stood guard at the base of the stairs leading to the camp headquarters. Judge announced his business and was immediately ushered into the camp commander's office. A short, stiff-backed officer dressed in fatigues shook his hand, giving his name as Captain Timothy Vandermel. "Follow me, Major. The CO is waiting for you in the emergency ward."

Vandermel led Judge across the camp. Behind fifteen-foot fences topped with razor-sharp concertina stood row upon row of low-slung barracks. Hundreds of slack figures wandered the dirt infield between them. Many still wore the blue-and-white striped uniform issued them at Auschwitz, Belsen, Sachsenhausen. Men sat around open fires, smoking, talking in agitated voices. Women tended laundry over salvaged oil drums. Children let loose high-pitched screams as they chased one another here and there.

"DPs," said Vandermel. "More and more are pouring in every day. The Jews want the hell out of Germany and who can blame them? Most want to go to Eretz Israel, their homeland in Palestine, but the Brits won't have them. The Ukrainians *can* go home, but they don't want to because they're afraid Uncle Joe will shoot them. Anyone who surrendered is a coward in his book. As for the Poles, they can't go back to Poland even if they wanted to. Don't ask about the Hungarians, Romanians, Bulgarians, Latvians, or Estonians. Give you one guess where they'd all like to go, the lot of them."

"America."

"Bingo."

And we don't want them, either, Judge added silently.

Vandermel unlatched a wooden gate cut into the fence and motioned him into the hospital compound. Judge was surprised to see two MPs standing at the entrance to the ward. Before he could ask what they were doing there, a pair of officers shunted out the screen door and onto the landing. One was tall, with a martinet's ramrod posture and a steam shovel's iron jaw. Judge recognized him from his previous visit as

Colonel Sawyer, the camp commander. He was old army, a former stable mate of George Patton's when the two were stationed at Fort Myer, Virginia. The other was chubby and balding, a sad sack of a guy with the caduceus pinned to his lapel. A doctor.

"Your timing is impeccable, Major," shouted Sawyer, waving him over.

Judge mounted the stairs and saluted. "How so?"

Sawyer coughed, averting his eyes, and Judge knew bad news was coming. "Your man von Luck is dead."

"What?" Judge grew immediately suspicious. "The guy was doing fine last night. What happened between then and now?"

"One of our orderlies found him this morning," said the doctor, who gave his name as Wilfred Martindale.

"I'd ordered von Luck to get cleaned up for his excursion," added Sawyer. "The old general was lying there stiff as a board. Went in his sleep." He said it grudgingly, as if von Luck had welched on a debt.

"Was he ill?" asked Judge.

"No, no," said Martindale, approaching Judge as if he were the bereaved. "That's what surprised us. His health was improving daily. He'd gained five pounds in the last week alone. Still, considering how the body had been so weakened by malnutrition, illness, and, of course, the psychological burdens of simply trying to keep oneself alive, it's amazing Mr. von Luck survived as long as he did."

They were inside the ward, walking slowly between the beds, a funeral procession clad in olive and khaki. Harrowed faces peered at them from the refuge of their iron beds. The same squadron of flies that had attacked during his last visit dove from the ceiling again, marauding Judge and his escorts. He recognized Volkmann, the poor bastard who wouldn't leave his bed to go to the bathroom, and tried to muster a smile. Volkmann nodded gravely, his hunted eyes saying he'd tolerate Judge's presence for a short while, but he'd better not push it.

Von Luck's body had not yet been removed. Covered by his bedsheet, it lay meek and rigid, leaving only the shallowest outline. Judge grasped the sheet with both hands and slowly peeled it back. Death had not robbed von Luck of his patrician bearing. Chin raised, mouth ajar, he seemed to be barking out one final order.

"What's the verdict?" Judge asked, frustration getting the better of him. "Heart attack, stroke, lumbago . . ."

"The death certificate will list natural causes," said Dr. Martindale in a tone that made clear he did not find the remark humorous.

"Natural causes." Judge mulled over the diagnosis, while a suspicious voice whispered in his ear, *There is no such thing as a coincidence.* "Mind if I take a closer look?"

Sawyer ruffled his brow. "A closer look? At what?" he chortled. "Haven't you seen a dead Nazi before?"

Judge took that as a green light. Stepping closer to the bed, he bent at the waist and placed his nose near von Luck's mouth. He sniffed for the scent of almonds but smelled nothing. He could rule out cyanide. Probing von Luck's neck with his fingers, he checked for signs of strangulation—a crushed larynx or a damaged windpipe. Both were intact. He unbuttoned von Luck's pajama, examining his thorax for injuries. A professionally wielded stiletto could be inserted between the ribs to pierce a man's heart, leaving a small entry wound and almost no bleeding. But von Luck's chest was clean and so was his back.

"Was von Luck taking any medication? Penicillin, maybe?"

Martindale shook his head. "He was given a tetanus vaccination three weeks ago. He took a few aspirin each day for his headaches. Other than that he was healthy. We kept him here to eat, sleep, and regain his strength."

Judge rolled up von Luck's sleeves and checked for a pinprick or light bruising, indications that an injection had recently been administered. Ten cc's of potassium chloride could kill a man in less than a minute, leaving him looking as peaceful as if he'd died in his sleep. Both arms were pale and without blemish. He scanned the neck for similar marks. Nothing.

Sawyer cleared his throat theatrically. "If you're finished, Major, we'd like to get the corpse out of the ward as soon as possible."

But Judge wouldn't be hurried. Lowering himself to one knee, he leaned over the bed and brought his face to within inches of von Luck's. Placing a thumb on the corpse's right eye, he slid back the eyelid. The eye stared at the ceiling, its fully dilated pupil partially obscuring the pale blue iris. Next he studied the vitreous humor. Barely visible were clusters of what appeared to be minuscule starfish, but were, in fact, ruptured capillaries lying just beneath the eye's surface. Conjunctival hemorrhage was the medical term. It was a phenomenon that occurred when the body was unable to take in air and the brain was robbed of the oxygen it needed to function. Four years with homicide had provided Judge with a specialized medical education.

Slowly, he cautioned himself.

He checked the other eye and found a similar discoloration.

There is no such thing as coincidence.

Standing, Judge returned his gaze to the row of beds running along both walls. As if cued, all heads were turned toward him. He noticed then that every patient had the same growth of hair, about an inch, and realized that they must have all had their heads shaved for lice at the same time. Whatever had happened in here last night, they'd seen it.

"Well, goddammit," bellowed Sawyer, sending a wad of saliva arcing through the air. "Don't stand there looking like the cat that swallowed the canary. Spit it out."

Judge remained silent for a few moments longer, asking himself if it was prudent to tell Sawyer what he'd discovered. If it might assist in the investigation. He answered no to both questions. "You can take von Luck away. He's no use to me now."

Sawyer patted Judge on the back and told him to cheer up. The world was a better place with one less Nazi in it. Judge smiled as required, but as the implications of his discovery sank in, he found himself gripped by a new and insidious anxiety.

Who knew that he had harbored doubts about Seyss's death and that he had believed von Luck could confirm or deny them? Who knew he was coming to Dachau? It came to him that if someone believed Oliver von Luck could prove the corpse on gurney three did not belong to Erich Seyss, he might also believe that Ingrid Bach could do the same.

Judge decided he must reach Ingrid Bach as quickly as possible. Only by conscious effort could he slow the pace of his footsteps.

Upon reaching the threshold of the ward, Judge felt a weak hand tug at the hem of his jacket. Somewhat annoyed, he reined in his step. It was Volkmann and he was extending his arm toward Judge in a gesture that indicated he wished to shake his hand. Judge hesitated, then gave him his grip.

"Never trust the police," Volkmann whispered, his English nearly without accent.

Judge felt a small hard-edged object being pressed into his palm. He didn't know how to respond so he said "Thank you," and wished him a speedy recovery.

"Jesus," called Sawyer from the door. "He's worse than you, Doc. Talking to every one of these savages as if he were their best friend."

"I'll be right there," said Judge. Opening his hand, he ventured a quick glance downward and saw a small rectangular red-and-white ribbon with a burnished star in its center—the chest decoration given to winners of the Silver Star. He looked back at Volkmann hoping for further explanation, but Volkmann had turned away, his duty fulfilled.

"Headed back to Heidelberg?" Sawyer asked when the two had reached the jeep parked in front of the camp headquarters.

"No, I'll be heading to . . ." Judge paused, finding Sawyer's gaze a shade too inquisitive. "I'll be heading back to Third Army HQ at Bad Toelz. If I get my things packed in a hurry, I can catch a six o'clock plane to Paris. This investigation is finished."

Sawyer leaned against the jeep, tapping the vertical angle iron rising from the front bumper with the palm of his hand. "You tell old Georgie that the next time we're on the polo field I'm gonna whip his rich behind, will ya?"

"It might be wise to phrase that a little nicer, but I'll pass along the message."

Climbing into the jeep, Judge fired off a last salute, then gunned the engine. He had no intention of returning to Bad Toelz. He was headed due south, to a glittering seashell of a castle named Sonnenbrücke in the heart of the Bavarian Alps.

General Oliver von Luck had not died of natural causes.

He had been suffocated.

35

IT WAS NEARLY NOON WHEN Devlin Judge arrived in the town of Inzell. If the drive from Heidelberg to Dachau had proven easy, the same could not be said for the trek to Sonnenbrücke. Once outside Munich, the road had begun a steady climb uphill, narrowing to the width of a Brooklyn sidewalk, then assuming an unfriendly series of twists and turns that left his stomach queasy and his arms cramped. The soaring pine vistas and plunging granite gorges were only feet away, but miles beyond his internal horizon. Since leaving Dachau, he'd been pre-occupied by a single matter: the betrayal of his visit to the camp and the murder of General Oliver von Luck.

At first glance, it seemed an open-and-shut case. Who but Mullins knew he harbored doubts about Seyss's death? Or that he wanted to use von Luck to identify Seyss's body? Honey could only intuit such things and he could hardly have known that Judge would act so quickly. Knowledge and opportunity seemed to point to Mullins.

What then was Judge to make of the military ribbon Volkmann had gifted him? The Silver Star was one of the nation's highest military dec-orations, awarded to recognize conspicuous heroism and gallantry in combat. Fifty percent of the men who received it did so posthumously.

It was hardly an everyday trinket. Physical evidence so rare was a prosecutor's dream, to be ignored at great peril.

Your chauffeur's got himself a Silver Star, Mullins had said. *He's a hero.*

Opening his hand, Judge stole a glance at the ribbon of red, white, and blue, and his doubts about Sergeant Darren Honey multiplied. Why had Honey secretly interrogated Bauer? Why had he instructed him to keep their conversation a secret? And to whom had he divulged the explosive content of Bauer's statement? Honey was bright, ambitious, and, Judge was beginning to realize, very, very sly.

Yet the consideration of motive prevented Judge from closing his case. Why would someone want to disguise Seyss's escape from the armory? To ensure that Tallyho was graded a success? To keep George Patton smiling? No, sir, answered Judge. Killing von Luck went far beyond currying favor with a superior. In the wake of Bauer's revelation that Seyss had planned to lead his men to the outskirts of Berlin, accomplices to von Luck's death were not only accessories to murder, but quite possibly treason. Seyss was not going to Babelsberg. He was going to Potsdam. And Judge had a good idea what he planned to do once there.

More than ever, then, he needed to prove that Seyss was alive. He required a witness who could point at the butchered remains lying on a gurney in the basement of the American Military Hospital in Heidelberg and state with irrefutable certainty, "That is not Erich Seyss." Only then could he return to his superiors, present Bauer's confession, and demand that the search for the White Lion be reinstated.

Steering the jeep past an ornate fountain, Judge braked in front of the village grocer. However detailed his road map, it did not show the route to Sonnenbrücke. When he'd come before, it was via a different and even more mountainous path. The store was small, half again as large as a Coney Island hot dog stand. Inside, a single counter was surrounded by sparse shelves that sagged with the memory of better times. The grocer's cheery disposition belied his dim commercial prospects. When asked for instructions how to reach the Bach family's hunting lodge, he escorted Judge to the front stoop and pointed to a steep dirt-and-gravel road peeling off from the east side of the fountain. "Take that trail two kilometers until you come to a fork. Stay left, always going up, up, up. After another kilometer you come to a beautiful old oak at least twenty meters tall . . . don't turn there. Continue past it until . . ."

His words were stepped on by the shrill rev of approaching engines.

Two jeeps barreled into Inzell, careering round the fountain, then shooting up the road to Sonnenbrücke. Each carried four soldiers. A raiding party, thought Judge, images of rampaging Injuns flooding his mind.

Dashing from the store, he threw himself behind the wheel of the jeep and turned over the engine. It coughed and sputtered, then caught, firing fitfully. He grasped the gearshift and thrust it into first gear. Executing a U-turn, he slammed his foot on the accelerator and peeled out of Inzell like a rider for the Pony Express.

The road was steep and straight, graded from the dirt of the hillside. An army of enormous pine trees blocked out the sun, lining both sides of the path like an honor guard of Frederick the Great's giant bodyguards. He downshifted into second gear, then plunged the gas to the floorboard. Through a curtain of dust, he could see the tails of the jeeps far in front of him. One after the other, they disappeared. Judge slowed. A moment later, he heard the growl of their engines approaching. Raising his head, he caught sight of the first jeep traversing a switchback twenty feet above his head. A shower of dirt and gravel sprayed his vehicle. Instinctively, he lifted a hand from the wheel to shield himself from the debris, and in that moment he lost his chance to navigate the hairpin curve ahead. Bringing the jeep to a halt, he ripped the gearshift into reverse and backed up ten feet.

His troubles had just begun. Starting the jeep on flat ground was one thing; starting it on an incline quite another. Time after time, he muscled the gearshift into first, applying the gas with his right foot while gently releasing the clutch with his left. Time after time, the jeep bucked, stalled, and slid farther down the hill. *To hell with this*, he thought, frustration heating to molten anger. Finding reverse, he cocked his head over a shoulder and guided the jeep back down the road into Inzell. Once on flat ground, he started over.

Hurry! he urged himself, images of von Luck's rigid body coming to mind.

Fifteen minutes later, he reached the top of the hill. The jeeps were nowhere in sight. He had no trouble, though, finding Sonnenbrücke. It stood at the far end of a grassy valley, protected by towering stone sentinels.

Judge powered the jeep toward the fairy-tale castle, hurtling down the bumpy lane at seventy miles per hour, faster even than he'd dared on the autobahn. Nearing the entry to Sonnenbrücke, he spotted the twin jeeps advancing on him from far down the limestone drive. He slammed on the brakes and spun the wheel so that his jeep diagonally blocked the road. He wondered what ruse they'd used to lure Ingrid Bach from her home, or if they'd said to hell with it and killed her right there. His hand dropped to his side in a vain quest for his pistol. It had gone up with the rest of the armory. All the while he searched for a flash of platinum hair.

Climbing onto his seat, he waved his arms, gesturing for the jeeps to stop. When the lead jeep had closed to within thirty yards, he saw that Ingrid was not in either vehicle. Puzzled, he stopped his frantic signaling and jumped to the ground.

"You okay?" yelled the driver of the lead jeep, slowing to a halt. His rank and insignia gave him as a master sergeant assigned to the 101st Airborne, part of Carswell's Seventh Army. "The little green beast give out on you?"

Judge ignored the question, rushing to his side. "Where is Ingrid Bach?"

"I'm sure she's inside, sir," answered the sergeant, crewcut, fat, and fifty.

"What business did you have with her?"

The sergeant looked dumbfounded. "Why, none. My men and I form part of the detachment guarding Alfred Bach. What his daughter does or doesn't do is her own affair."

"Or the general's," cracked a wiseacre from the bleachers.

So the word had spread, thought Judge. There was no more efficient conduit for passing along rumors than the United States fighting man. "Who were the soldiers who just arrived?"

"Them?" The sergeant peered over his shoulder. "Changing of the guard. Ten minutes late, I might add. Don't tell me they were racing again?"

"No," said Judge, dragging his foot in the dirt. "Just a misunder-standing on my part. Sorry to bother you."

"No problem at all, Major."

Judge offered a sheepish wave as the jeeps set off down the drive. He wasn't angry at making a fool of himself so much as at drawing attention to his presence. Von Luck's murder had left him edgy, feeling as if his stomach were lined with broken glass. It came to him that his worries for Ingrid Bach might have as much to do with his interest in her as any immediate danger she was in. In his agitated mood, he dismissed the notion as an insult to his professionalism. He was simply doing his duty.

A few hundred yards farther on he came to the group who'd flown by him in Inzell. The sentry asked his name, unit, and the purpose of his visit before waving him on. Judge craned his neck to get a view of the guard's clipboard. There it was: his name scribbled in black ink, the time of arrival given as 12:22, and under the column headed "purpose," the words "personal business." A record of his visit for anyone who cared to check.

Ingrid Bach answered the door herself. She wore a simple calico dress, a stained apron tied around it. Her hair was bundled into a scarf, albeit a silk one. Her face was pale, without a trace of makeup. *Sit her on a street corner, give her a brick to clean, and she'd still look like queen of the ball,* thought Judge as he entered Sonnenbrücke's foyer.

"They're still shooting my precious chamois, Major, if you've come to see about that." She said it reticently, leaving it open for him to take up where they'd left off Friday night.

"Police business, I'm afraid."

"Oh?" Her body stiffened reflexively at his tone of voice.

Moving into the great hall, Judge removed his cap and tucked it under an arm. "I need you to accompany me on an errand. You'll need a change of clothes, a toothbrush, whatever items you usually require for an overnight visit."

"I beg your pardon?" she said.

"I'll have you back by tomorrow afternoon at this time." He checked his watch. "Maybe earlier."

She placed a hand on her hip and he could see she was readying one of her patented barrages. This was her territory, she was going to say, and she wasn't going to be pushed around. "You don't really expect me to—"

"Now!" Judge said louder than he'd intended. "This is not a request. Go upstairs and get your things together. Hurry it up."

Ingrid Bach took a tentative step closer, her hand raised in mute protest.

"Please," said Judge, softly this time. "We need to leave quickly. We have a long drive in front of us."

Herbert, the butler, approached from the recesses of the hallway, Ingrid's blond son at his side. The old man asked if everything was all right. She nodded curtly and smiled, asking him to take Pauli upstairs. She'd come in a minute.

"We will be back tomorrow?" Ingrid eyed him doubtfully.

"By noon. I promise." Judge watched the boy disappear upstairs. "Can Herbert manage with your son?"

"He's practically his father. My sister, Hilda, is with us now, too. She arrived yesterday to help care for Papa."

Hilda—the daughter being held in a pen outside Essen pending review of her role in the daily affairs of Bach Industries. They're war criminals, all of them, Judge warned himself. *Off-limits.*

Ingrid paused before retreating up the stairs. "May I at least ask what this is about?"

Judge met her inquisitive gaze. "It's about him," he answered. "It's about Erich Seyss."

NEITHER OF THEM SPOKE UNTIL the jeep was down the mountain and traveling at a comfortable speed along the autobahn. Ingrid kept her face turned away from Judge, playing the part of unwilling prisoner with the same aplomb she brought to her roles as hausfrau, estate owner, and belle of the ball. Judge was amazed at her ability to corral her curiosity. Feeling intimidated by her self-control, and maybe angered by it, too, he guarded his silence. It was difficult. Part of him wanted to explain why he had kidnapped her so brusquely and what would be required of her once they reached Heidelberg. Another part of him wanted to grill her mercilessly about Egon's ties to Erich Seyss. Instead, he used the quiet to consider what exactly he could tell her about Seyss and how much he could reveal about Bauer's plans. He did not want to burden her with information that would only serve to endanger her life.

Finally, he could stand it no longer. "Aren't you interested in where I'm taking you?"

She granted him a victorious glance. "I imagine I'll find out soon enough."

"Heidelberg," he said. "To the military hospital."

Her head snapped toward him. "Is he hurt?"

"Not exactly."

Ingrid looked away, her eyes trained on the horizon. She understood that tone, too.

"We'd like you to identify his body," he said. "He was gravely wounded. It won't be pleasant." It was imperative that she believe Seyss was dead. Only that way could he gauge the veracity of her reaction if, as he hoped, she claimed the corpse wasn't his.

"I'm the only one you have?"

Judge nodded, wanting to add, "You're the only one I can trust." He watched as she took a cigarette from her purse, cupped it between her hands, and lit it with a Zippo similar to his own. Given the open cockpit and the roaring wind, it was no small feat. After taking a long drag, she lifted a knee onto her seat and shot him a scornful look. "So you found him, then you killed him."

Judge scoffed. "He got himself killed. He was an escaped war criminal wanted for the murder of an American officer. We caught him operating on the black market."

"Funny to think of a man surviving the war only to be killed during the peace."

"He was hardly an angel. He had it coming."

" 'He had it coming,' " she said, mocking his deep voice. "You sound like Gary Cooper. So American. So sure of what's right and what's wrong."

Judge gripped the wheel harder, knuckles flaring white. "Not always. But this time, yes, I'm sure."

"Erich was sure, too. Sure that Germany had been wronged by the *diktat* of Versailles. Sure that all ethnic Germans wanted to be united under a single Germany. Sure that England would never enter the war against us. He used to say Poland had been dealt and shuffled more than a deck of cards."

"I thought he wasn't political."

"That's not politics, my dear Major. It is destiny."

Judge thought it was hogwash, but kept to his line of questioning. "Would Egon agree?"

"Egon?" If she was surprised at the turn of conversation, she did not show it. "Well, yes. As long as destiny increased the *konzern's* order book. If we were in the business of school wares, I can assure you he would have fought tooth and nail against Herr Hitler. But, alas, our family is in the business of selling armaments. War increases our fortunes."

"So he and Seyss had something in common?"

"They both wanted a strong Germany. But six years ago, you could have said that about all fifty million of us."

"They weren't friends?"

"Friends?" Ingrid's sardonic laugh infuriated him. "Egon hated Erich. He was everything Egon wasn't. Tall, handsome, a soldier. You don't know Egon. He's short. His eyesight is terrible. He's like a wolverine, an ugly little creature with sharp fangs and claws. He's absolutely vicious. Erich, of course, was our White Lion."

"Of course," said Judge, not bothering to hide his disdain. But the provenance of his next words mystified him. "And he had you."

Ingrid dropped her eyes, and when she answered her voice had gone flat. "Yes. For as long they allowed him."

36

THE AMERICAN MILITARY HOSPITAL STOOD on a broad hilltop at the southern edge of Heidelberg. Formerly known as the Universitätspital, the building was squat and rectangular, a beige three-story brick plopped down in the midst of a verdant forest. As dusk surrendered to night, the sky flushed a deep azure. Few lights burned in the windows. A shortfall of coal was forecast for the coming winter. Even hospitals had been ordered to cut their use of electricity.

Judge brought the jeep to a halt under the porte cochere extending from the hospital's main entrance. A steady stream of nurses, doctors, soldiers, and visitors trickled in and out the door. He checked over his shoulder for the trail car that had never materialized, then scanned the parking lot to the far side of the building. A dozen army vehicles were scattered haphazardly across the wide space, suggesting that they'd arrived at different hours during the day. Thus comforted, he climbed from the jeep.

"We'll make this quick," he said, offering Ingrid his hand to help her from the jeep.

Inside, he presented himself to the information desk and asked if Colonel Stanley Mullins was anywhere in the hospital. The reply came that Mullins had returned to the provost marshal's office in Bad Toelz.

Judge was relieved at the news. He didn't relish confronting his former precinct commander with his suspicions of impropriety. Who had arranged for Judge to pick up von Luck? Mullins would ask. Who had seen to it that his transfer to the Third Army was extended by twenty-four hours? Who was it that just last night spent an hour teaching his former charge the rudiments of driving an automobile? Judge could hear the insulted voice, decrying his complicity. "Are you completely daft, lad? D'ya think I'd lift you up with one hand, only to knock you down with the other?"

And in truth, Judge was disposed to believe him. With every passing hour, the Silver Star assumed a greater role in his deliberations. Not only was the award uncommon but most of the men who'd received it had already shipped out of Europe. Decorated combat vets had first dibs on spots back to the U.S.A. The fact was that Darren Honey was one of the few soldiers so decorated still in Germany. In court, Judge would have considered the ribbon a strong piece of evidence.

After stating his business, Judge was told to wait until an orderly arrived to show him to the morgue. He'd barely taken a seat next to Ingrid Bach when a thin young man dressed in a white lab coat limped out of the elevator and waved at them as if they were long-lost buddies. "Good evening, sir," he announced in passable English. "I am Dieter. Please come with."

Dieter was nineteen with shaggy brown hair and a survivor's all-weather smile. The Americans had taken his leg at Omaha Beach, he explained, and given him a new one in Frankfurt, just three weeks ago. No hard feelings, okay? Even Ingrid Bach smiled at his unsinkable good cheer.

"You want to see what body?" he asked, as the three descended in a cramped elevator.

Speaking German Judge said, "Seyss, he was brought in Sunday morning with the Americans who were killed in Wiesbaden."

Dieter grimaced. "Bad business, eh? Like the war all over again." He showed Ingrid and Judge into the same tiled viewing room where yesterday nine gurneys had been lined against the wall. "Wait here. I'll be right back."

The room was empty except for some metal tables placed in each corner and the large operating light that hung from the ceiling. One sniff made Judge's sinuses burn. He'd forgotten how overpowering the odor was. Placing a hand under Ingrid's elbow, he said, "It will be very quick. All I need is a nod yes." *Or no*, he hoped desperately.

"I understand," she said.

Dieter returned five minutes later, a confused look on his face. "Seyss was here, sure. But it says he was sent for cremation today."

"Today?" Judge robbed Dieter's hands of a sheaf of papers. The top page held an order transferring body 9358, Sturmbannführer Erich Seyss, to the crematorium. The order was signed by Colonel Joseph Gregorio, chief of hospital administration, and countersigned by General Hadley Everett. "Has the body already been disposed of?"

Dieter snatched the papers back from Judge. Smiling, he peeled off the top sheet and read from the page below it. " 'Pursuant to order number six nine one issued by the United States Army of Occupation, military government of Bad Würtemberg, Mandatory Conservation of Coal, effective July 15, 1945, all nonurgent uses of coal are to be hereby discontinued"—he thumbed to the next page, taking up in midsentence—"therefore all bodies sent for cremation shall be transferred to Section D, Graves Registration, for immediate burial."

Judge was growing impatient. "Do you still have the body?" he demanded.

Dieter shrank an inch. "Sure, just in a different place. I only came to tell you it would be a while." He shot a glance at Ingrid. "Americans . . . always in such a hurry."

He returned five minutes later, his entrance presaged by a stubborn caster in need of oil. Having rolled the gurney to the center of the room, he took hold of the white sheet with both hands. "Tell me when you are ready."

Judge stepped forward, stopping a foot from the gurney. Ingrid Bach took her place at his shoulder. She clutched his hand and said yes. Dieter removed the sheet. In preparation for cremation, the body had been stripped of clothing. It lay naked, its skin a translucent blue. The wound to the head was crusted and black, a malignant crater.

"It's not him," said Ingrid Bach, after hardly a second had passed.

Judge stammered, "H-how could you—"

"It's not him, dammit! Put back the bloody sheet!"

Dieter hastened to comply.

"But you didn't even look at his face," Judge protested when they'd left the morgue.

She spun to face him, addressing him with her most venomous glare. "I didn't have to, Major. He was my lover. Don't you think I'd know?"

And turning, she rushed down the hall.

THE JEEP WAS WHERE THEY had left it, parked directly across from the main entrance. Dusk had turned to evening. The air had grown cool. Judge grabbed his travel bag from the backseat and took out a khaki windbreaker bare of rank or insignia. Ingrid slipped a white cardigan from her bag and placed it over her shoulders. One glance told him it was cashmere. If she needed money so badly, first thing she should do was sell her wardrobe.

Settling into the driver's seat, he turned over the ignition. For once, the engine fired smoothly, starting on the first try. Illuminating the headlights, he slid the gearshift into first and guided the jeep off the hospital grounds. He shifted to second. Usually it was a tricky affair, but this time the gearshift advanced easily. Like a hot knife through butter. He was finally getting the hang of it.

"I suppose you're disappointed?" Ingrid asked as they pulled out of the parking lot. She had folded her arms across her stomach and he could see she was shivering slightly. The body had shaken her more than she wanted him to know.

"On the contrary. I never believed it was Seyss to begin with."

"No?"

He shook his head, offering an apologetic smile. "I can't tell you anything more. I can only say that you've been a tremendous help."

"I suppose I should be grateful," she replied, her tone caustic and insincere. "Finally, a chance to help the victors. Or would *collaborate* be the more appropriate term?"

Judge ignored her sarcasm, granting her the right to be upset. "It's more important than you think."

"Is it, now? To what? The army or your career?" Not expecting an answer—or, Judge suspected, not wanting one—she plied on. "That was a dirty trick to play. I'm still trying to figure out your reasoning. Help me, would you? Did you think if I knew you had doubts it was Erich, I'd try to convince you otherwise?"

"I just wanted to gauge your reaction. That's all."

"You thought I might lie to protect him. Just like at that squalid little roadhouse the other night, quietly asking me more questions about Erich, as if we were sharing confidences. You were trying to catch me out on something. After all, I'm a Bach. I can't be trusted. No, no, don't say anything, Major. I remember the look of disgust on your face when you met my father."

"I had to be sure," he retorted. "I didn't have any other choice."

Ingrid looked away, laughing dryly. "Another one just following orders."

"That's enough!" Judge slammed the base of his palm against the steering wheel, causing Ingrid to jump in her seat. He let go an exasperated sigh, feeling his neck flush hot; even as he was robbed of further words. It was impossible to pick the truth from the residue of her anger. Not knowing where to begin, he concentrated on the road and kept quiet.

Approaching a sharp turn, he downshifted the vehicle into second, suppressing his desire to keep a foot on the brake just in case. His growing confidence behind the wheel, however, did little to allay the pool of anxiety welling in his stomach. Anyone keeping tabs on his movements would by now have learned that he had visited Dachau, and upon being apprised of von Luck's death, proclaimed his intention to return to HQ military government in Bavaria. How long would it take until they grew worried about his failure to show up at Bad Toelz? This evening? Tomorrow? *Or had they already?* Once they made the discovery, he had little doubt their first call would be to the guard detachment at Sonnenbrücke to inquire if one Major Devlin Judge had come to visit Ingrid Bach.

The implications of Ingrid's confirmation that the body did not belong to Seyss were only now beginning to take root. So far, only one thing was clear: Until his superior officers could be made to believe that

Seyss was still on the loose and take proper action, Ingrid Bach's life was in danger.

Rounding a curve, Judge braked hard, confronted by a string of flares sizzling in the center of the road. At their head, a jeep was parked horizontally across the road. A lone soldier waved a flashlight, signaling for him to stop.

"Excuse me, sir, but we've got a bad accident down the hill a ways. Had to close the road until we get it cleared up." The soldier shined the flashlight down an asphalt lane veering from the main street. "If you'll follow that route, you'll come into town at Wilhelmplatz. Take you an extra five minutes."

Judge stared at the sparkling flares, the short-lived arc of the red-and-gold embers setting off an internal alarm. "What happened?"

"A six-by-six flipped onto its side and collided with an ambulance coming up the hill. The driver said he was trying to dodge some DPs coming out of the forest. This part of the country's crawling with 'em."

"Was anyone hurt?" Ingrid asked, concern etched on her face.

"I'm not sure, ma'am. Let's hope nothing more than a few bruises and some jangled nerves."

Judge returned the man's salute. "Thanks for the information."

"No problem, Major. Have a good night."

Judge eyed the soldier warily, but the GI was already walking past him, giving the same news to the nurses in the jeep behind them. A moment later, the four women pulled up to Judge's bumper. The two in the back were throwing sweaters over their white uniforms, madly freeing bobby pins from their hair; the gal driving rushing to apply a fresh coat of lipstick. Four girls headed out for a night on the town. None looked over twenty.

Hearing their infectious giggles, Judge dismissed his worry and accelerated down the hill. The road curved gradually to the right, then descended steeply into a ravine. The forest encroached on the road, forming a canopy over their heads that blocked out the night sky. He glanced to his right, catching only Ingrid Bach's mute profile and the evanescent sheen of her platinum hair.

"Okay, I apologize for not sharing my doubts with you. What do you expect? I'm a lawyer. I'm trained not to trust people."

"Especially the family of war criminals, right?"

Now it was Judge's turn to get angry. "Look, you wanted an apology, you got it. I can't change whose blood runs in your veins. Or that you almost married the guy I'm looking for. If you're curious whether it makes me a little uncertain, you're right, it does. You're a smart woman. How would *you* react?"

To her credit, Ingrid pondered the question, vitriol replaced by deliberation. Tucking a strand of hair behind her ear, she said, "I'm quite aware what you think of us. I've read the counts against my father. I've seen some of the testimony against him. You can't know what it is like to learn that the man you've adored and admired your entire life is some kind of monster. Frankly, I still can't quite comprehend it."

"You didn't know what went on in his factories? No idea at all?"

Ingrid shook her head slowly and he could see she was still answering her own charges. "I'm afraid armor plate and proximity fuses aren't a particular interest of mine. I've hardly been out of the mountains for the past three years. But to answer your question, Major, no, I wouldn't have told you either. That doesn't make your actions right, though. If I sound at all contrite, it's because I wasn't completely honest with you earlier when you asked if I'd had any contact with Erich. What do you expect? I'm a German. I'm trained not to trust Americans."

Judge laughed and the tension between them was broken. He was careful not to push her to talk. If she had something to say, he'd give her her own good time to say it.

"The day we met you told me Erich had escaped from a camp for war criminals. What had he done?"

Judge looked her up and down, admiring her willingness to stare truth in the face. "For one, he ordered the murder of a hundred unarmed American soldiers. They were prisoners. They'd given up their weapons. He herded them into a field and ordered his machine gunners to open up on them. When they were done, he walked the field himself. Anyone he found alive, he finished with his pistol. December the seventeenth, 1944. Malmedy, Belgium."

Ingrid's face remained passive, her sole response to the news a sudden twitching of the eyes that vanished as quickly as it had come. "So, then, it's not because he killed an American officer escaping that you want him so badly?"

"No," said Judge, adding silently, "it's for a lot more than that."

Ingrid bowed her head and it sounded as if she was laughing at herself. Judge wondered how she must feel to learn that those closest to her, the men she'd hugged and kissed, and in Seyss's case, made love to, were devoid of conscience, that their every positive quality was stained by a hideous darkness.

"What will happen now?"

"Nothing's changed," he said, though, of course, everything had. "We'll keep looking until we find him."

Suddenly, Ingrid looked up, her eyes once again inquiring, full of fight. "And there's no chance you might be mistaken?"

"I'm afraid not."

Ingrid sighed. "No, I suppose not." She composed herself for a moment, gathering in her knees and sitting straighter in her seat. When she talked, it was in a casual, unhurried manner. They might have been discussing a long-lost mutual friend. "I kept track of Erich for a couple of years through Egon. The two had some dealings with each other during the early part of the war, and every now and then I'd hear a word about him. Erich was Himmler's adjutant, helping the larger industrial *konzern*s procure foreign contract labor."

"You mean slave labor."

"Yes. Slave labor." The words were barely a whisper and she swallowed hard after saying them. "Erich worked with the Military Production Board, parceling out workers to the plants deemed most vital. I never really thought about what he was doing. It sounded so official, so routine. He was just a soldier carrying out his government's instructions. Now I realize he was sending men and women from the camps in the East to our factories."

"Yes, he was."

"Earlier today when you asked if Erich and Egon had something in common, there was something I didn't tell you. Actually, I only thought of it later, but by then I'd decided I didn't like you, and you could go to hell. They were both SS men, our Egon and Erich."

"But I thought Egon wasn't a soldier."

"He wasn't, but he was a member of the Allgemeine SS. They were businessmen and politicians, bureaucrats, too, close to Himmler, all very much involved in the SS's various campaigns."

The Allgemeine SS. Judge shivered. Von Luck had mentioned the organization himself. *Kameraden.*

"He never came and visited me, though," Ingrid went on. "I wasn't lying when I told you I hadn't seen him for six years. The last I heard, Egon said he'd been transferred to the East. That was in 1943, right after Stalingrad."

Judge kept his eyes focused on the road while his mind bore in on Seyss. Where had he gone after escaping from the armory? Had he been injured? Might he have given up his plan to go to Berlin? Finding no answers, Judge hashed out his own quandary, figuring how to proceed if he wanted to catch Seyss.

He considered contacting Mullins, but discounted the idea. It wasn't Mullins he couldn't trust but the men around him. He'd have to go higher. He considered approaching Hadley Everett, Patton's dapper G-2, head of intelligence for the Third Army, and, in principle, Sergeant Darren Honey's commanding officer. He saw Everett's signature ordering Seyss's body to be cremated and decided against speaking to him. There was only one man whose military record placed him beyond reproach.

George Patton.

He would go to "Blood and Guts" himself.

In the passenger seat, Ingrid Bach was working to light a cigarette. Cupping the lighter in her hand, she flicked the flywheel again and again. She wasn't having such an easy go of it this time. Catching his gaze, she said, "Too windy."

Judge wondered how it could be windier driving twenty-five miles an hour on a country road than sixty miles an hour on the autobahn. Instinctively, he extended a hand to check for the windscreen, but it was down. Someone had lowered it while they were inside the hospital. Having driven all day in the open air, wind buffeting him from right and left, he hadn't noticed the light breeze tickling his face.

The discovery that someone had tampered with his vehicle rekindled the suspicious buzz that had soured his gut since leaving Dachau that morning. Darting a glance over his shoulder, he spotted the jeep full of nurses rounding a bend. Everything okay back there. But why wasn't there any traffic approaching from the opposite direction? He should have checked the accident itself. And if traffic was officially diverted, why hadn't an MP been directing traffic instead of a regular GI? Something else struck Judge as odd; something the soldier had said. *No problem, Major. Have a good night.* Judge's rank insignia were covered by his windbreaker. There were no oak leaves pinned to the epaulets of his jacket. How could the man have known he was a major?

Judge leaned forward in his seat, squinting his eyes to make out the contours of the road beyond the headlights' wash. The route had narrowed considerably. The canopy of leaves and branches hovered close above their heads, an impenetrable dark mass. He felt like Ichabod Crane galloping pell-mell down Sleepy Hollow. The nose of the jeep disappeared as the vehicle sped down a rolling dip. Judge's stomach rose to his gullet. Ingrid let loose a yelp of surprise. The road flattened and in the instant before the jeep passed between two massive oaks, he saw it. A sparkle of silver at eye level. The word *werewolf* bulleted through his mind. At the same instant he saw that no angle iron rose from the bumper, and it came to him that this was not his jeep. He grabbed Ingrid's head and shoved it into his lap, then fell on top of her. The whisper of razor-sharp metal stung his ear. The jeep veered right, its tires digging into the hardscrabble shoulder. Forcing himself upright, he grasped the wheel and returned the jeep to the center of the road.

The jeep behind him. The nurses!

Judge pressed both of his feet onto the brake and rammed his fist onto the horn.

"What is it?" Ingrid shouted, hands clutching the dashboard.

But Judge had no time to answer. Even before the jeep skidded to a halt, he jumped from his seat and ran back along the road, thrashing his arms in the air, yelling for the nurses to stop. Down came the jeep, barreling over the dip, its headlights bobbing, then diving as the road steepened. Over the engine's whine, he could hear the nurses yelp with surprise, their young voices a giddy mixture of fear and excitement.

"Get down," he yelled, knowing they could not hear him, sensing the jeep accelerate even as it should be slowing. He prayed that an angle iron was welded to their front bumper, though usually only those vehicles used by military personnel carried such protection. The beams hit him in the eye and he heard the engine rev.

"Stop!"

Then he heard a stifled cry, two heavy thuds, and the jeep careered dangerously left, crashing head-on into the intractable trunk of a hundred-year-old oak.

He walked now, his step sobered by what he knew he would discover. Ingrid Bach arrived at his side, breathing heavily, eyes wide with fright. Two of the nurses had been expelled from the jeep and lay in the road, their bodies twisted unnaturally. The wire had hit both below the eyes, snapping their necks even as it slashed through their noses deep into the skull and lifted them forcibly out of the jeep. Judge guessed they had been sitting in the backseat. The two in the front had suffered a quicker death. Both were slumped against the dashboard, headless, blood pumping from their necks like water from a hydrant.

Ingrid fell to a knee, her scream dying stillborn in her throat, then buried her face in the lee of her arm.

Judge tore his eyes from the grotesque panorama, helping Ingrid to her feet and rushing her to the jeep. Whoever had strung the wire might well be waiting nearby to ensure that their job was carried to fruition. He implored Ingrid to hurry, but she was half frozen with shock. With every step, he expected to hear the whiplash crack of a bullet fired in their direction.

"What is it?" Ingrid asked him when they were back in the jeep. "What's going on?"

But Judge was not ready to give an answer. Either to himself or Ingrid Bach.

Slamming the gearshift into first, he stepped on the accelerator and drove the jeep up the hill.

CHAPTER

37

"Rum," Sergeant Den Savage whispered to himself. "Very rum indeed."

Savage, a licensed civil engineer who had enlisted with the King's Own Hussars in September of 1939, liked to think he'd had a decent war. Tobruk, Sicily, Normandy. Just the whisper of such storied names earned him an appreciative glance from the most hardened warrior. If he was lucky, it even got him a pint gratis at the local NAAFI pub.

But Savage was no soldier. There'd been no storming of enemy parapets for him. No jumping from a plane behind enemy lines or braving a foreign beach under a hail of fire. Beau Geste, that was the next man. At five feet two inches tall and one hundred three pounds dripping wet, Savage was well aware of his physical limitations. "A bloke should know his place," he liked to say, "and mine is to the rear, thank you very much."

The entire world knew about the Desert Rats. Well, Den and his team called themselves the Pack Rats. It was the job of this particular engineer of the King's Own Hussars to collect, label, and store all weapons confiscated from the enemy. He'd taken potato mashers from the Afrika Korps and Schmeissers from the SS, rocket launchers from the Hitler Youth and pocketknives from the Volksturm. He knew every gun, rifle, and grenade used by the German Army and the ordnance to go with it. Still, for everything he'd seen and done, today's job bothered him.

"Rum," he whispered to himself again. "Very rum indeed."

Savage strode down the center aisle of warehouse B392 in Dortmund, Germany, whistling for his men to gather round. The warehouse was packed to its gills with small arms and ammunition confiscated from Hitler's baddies. Most had been taken by Monty himself, Field Marshal Bernard Law Montgomery, that is, England's highest-ranking soldier (who, Den liked to point out, was no heavyweight himself). And Savage made sure the weapons were stored in kind. Pistols with pistols, rifles and rifles, machine guns, rocket launchers, mines, grenades . . . well, he could go on forever, couldn't he?

"All right, lads, listen up," he shouted when his thirty-five-man platoon had drawn close. "We've a bit of work ahead of us and I don't want to hear any complaining from the pews. Church mice, lads. Follow?"

"Ah, shut up, Sarge, and let us hear the bad news," shouted Jimmy McGregor, a mealymouthed little bugger from County Antrim. You could always count on the Irish for a bit of lip.

"Right, then, McGregor. If you're so keen, I'll let you have it right off, won't I?"

And for the next fifteen minutes, Savage outlined in excruciating detail the work order that he had received earlier that morning—the order that had his stomach growling with uncertainty. Savage's men were to remove every weapon in the warehouse—all of which they had previously catalogued, cleaned, greased, and packed—strip them of their protective cosmoline coating, reinsert the firing pins, and return them to their wooden crates. Worst, though, was the final instruction. The crates were *not* to be nailed shut.

"But Den," asked McGregor, in his sheepish Antrim brogue, "without grease the guns will rust quicker than tin in a rainstorm."

"Don't you go worrying about rust and the natural order of things, Jimmy McGregor," said Savage. "The order's from Monty himself. You have any questions, you're to take it up with him. Now get to work."

Savage dismissed his men and returned to his office. He knew he'd been short with McGregor, but damn it all if he could help it.

Something about the order just didn't sit right with him. You see, for once, Jimmy McGregor was right.

You only stripped guns of their grease and reinserted their firing pins if you expected to use them. And very soon at that.

Rum, thought Savage, *very rum indeed.*

CHAPTER

38

"I NEED TO SPEAK WITH General Patton now!" Judge said for the second time, his frustration bound and balled into a tight fist. "It cannot wait. I repeat, it's a matter of grave importance."

It was eleven o'clock at night and he was standing inside the headquarters of the 705th Field Artillery Battalion in what used to be the *rathaus*, or city hall of Griesheim, a quaint hamlet twenty miles south of Frankfurt. Three hours he'd been driving, anxious to put as much distance as possible between himself and his "last known whereabouts." Satisfied that he and Ingrid were for the time being safe, he'd stopped at the first spot where he could contact the one man who might put an end to this nightmarish situation.

"Major, I don't doubt you for a minute," came the reply. "But the general is in Berlin visiting Ike and the president. All communications to him are routed through Third Army HQ. Anything you want him to hear, you'll have to tell me. I'll pass along the news first thing in the morning."

Judge held the phone away from his ear, biting his lower lip to keep from shouting. It hurt trying to be polite. It actually *hurt*! "Excuse me, but may I ask with whom I'm speaking?"

"Colonel Paul Harkins," came the gruff voice, the emphasis very definitely on "Colonel."

"Excuse me, Colonel, I should have told you that this is a matter pertaining to the ongoing search for Erich Seyss. General Patton asked me to contact him no matter what the time if I had any news. Once he hears what I have to tell him, I am certain he will applaud your initiative in allowing me to give him the news personally."

It hurt!

Harkins's laugh felt like a slap in the face. "Nice try, Major. Listen, if it's about that brouhaha in Wiesbaden a couple nights back, let me put you through to General Everett's staff. That's his bailiwick. What's the big deal, anyway? I thought Seyss was dead."

Suddenly, Judge found his patience had abandoned him and his powers of persuasion, as well. "I . . . must . . . speak . . . to . . . Patton."

A tired sigh smothered the line. "Okay, Major, that's it for tonight. You're wearing me out."

"You're wearing me out, too, mac!"

Judge hung up before Harkins could have the satisfaction. For a second he stood still, staring at the dead receiver as if it were the mitt that had dropped the game-winning ball. A pimply clerk sat at a table marked Reception a few feet away. At every mention of Patton's name, he'd twitched as if given a couple hundred volts. Now he was staring at Judge with wide eyes, as if Judge were the general himself. So much for keeping a low profile.

"Everything all right, Private?"

"Yes, sir," replied the clerk, buttoning up his jaw. "Everything's fine."

"Carry on, then." *Jesus*, thought Judge, *I sound like a goddamn soldier.*

Fatigue slumping his shoulders, he walked from the foyer. It was still too soon for a widespread search to have been initiated on any kind of official basis. But his presence had been noted, and come tomorrow, should someone ask—as he knew someone would—it would be reported.

He'd spent most of the drive explaining the happenings of the past week to Ingrid—Seyss's escape from Camp 8, the blown arrest at

Lindenstrasse, meeting von Luck, Bauer, the debacle at the armory. Everything. Yet even as he'd recounted the events, he'd sifted through them, scrutinizing each carefully before positioning them like pieces of a jigsaw puzzle.

It was clear that members of the American military were intent on concealing evidence that Erich Seyss had not been killed at the armory in Wiesbaden, hence, that he was very much alive. Someone had suffocated Oliver von Luck. If he were to believe the unfortunate Herr Volkmann, someone who had been awarded the Silver Star. Someone had tried to kill Ingrid and himself, and was clever enough to disguise the murder as the work of the German partisans known as werewolves. Working his way backward, Judge could therefore assume that this same group—this *clique*—had purposely kicked on the klieg lights in an effort to aid Seyss's escape. No doubt the flashlights blinking out Morse code belonged to them, too.

And if Judge had retained any of his skills as a detective, he could take Bauer's confession to indicate that Seyss was not going to Babelsberg but to Potsdam, and that his trip had nothing to do with rescuing Egon Bach's mislaid engineering drawings.

But here he came to a halt. He had marshaled his evidence. He had presented his facts in a logical manner. He could envisage the crime itself. Yet the most crucial component of any prosecution was missing: motive.

Why were members of the American military assisting a fugitive SS officer and the scion of Germany's most powerful industrial family to carry out a heinous scheme whose success would ensure only personal heartbreak, national mourning, and political instability?

Outside, the night air was warm and humid, smelling of honeysuckle and cut grass. A cluster of clouds scudded past a swollen moon while a transport plane buzzed overhead. The jeep was parked in the forecourt of the *rathaus*. Ingrid sat in the passenger seat smoking, her hair mussed like a bramble by the steady wind.

"No one talks to Patton except his aide-de-camp," said Judge, his heels crunching in the gravel drive.

"Call someone else," she ordered. "Bradley, he's one of your heroes, isn't he? Why not try Eisenhower himself?"

"There is no one else. At least, no one I know."

"Find someone!" Ingrid looked away, as if wanting no more uttered on the subject.

"Didn't you hear me?" he fired back. "I don't know anyone else. I'm an attorney, not a soldier. I'm supposed to be in Luxembourg questioning Hermann Goering, not rushing across the German countryside with my tail between my legs."

"Well, go, then," said Ingrid, waving him off with a brush of her hand. "Go to the great Herr Reichsmarschall. And be sure to tell him that Papa's standing invitation to visit us at Sonnenbrücke is canceled. I'll be fine on my own."

"No, you won't," said Judge, rushing to the jeep. "You will not be fine on your own. Close your eyes and look at those nurses. That was supposed to be us."

Ingrid stared into his eyes, her features frozen into a mask of fear and hate and resentment. In her gaze, Judge saw his own fear, his own hate, his own resentment, not only of the mounting desperation of their plight but of her, of Ingrid Bach, blond doyenne of Berlin and New York, frequenter of the Sherry-Netherland Hotel, platinum princess born to a world that he'd always disdained. How dare she address him as if he were one of her servants? What would she ask for next? Her mink stole and lace gloves? Judge shuddered with frustration, but said nothing. He recognized the enmity she'd aroused for what it was: the flip side of his growing attraction to her. Guilty desire's ugly twin.

Judge stalked up the drive, the shifting gravel denying his anger a sufficiently dramatic exit. *No one talks to Patton except his aide-de-camp*, he'd told Ingrid. What about Patton's wife? What about when gracious Miss Bea gave Georgie a jingle? Did he tell her to get lost, too? Judge frowned. Crusty old bastard probably did, if the scuttlebutt going around Bad Toelz had anything to it. Word was Patton had himself a little number on the side, some distant family relation thirty years his junior he'd been screwing since he was stationed in Hawaii in the thirties. Her name was Jean Gordon, and apparently, just last May, he'd spent a few days closeted with her in London. V-E Day indeed! Judge bet the randy old goat wouldn't let a call from her slip by.

"Come here," he called to Ingrid. "I need your help."

"What now?"

"Come here!" He offered a hand to help her from the jeep. "You want to talk to Patton?"

"Me?" She eyed his hand, not moving a muscle. "Do I look like his aide-de-camp?"

"For your sake, I hope not, but do as I say and you might get to say a few words to the great man himself."

Ingrid might have been glued to the seat. "I have no interest in speaking to Patton, Eisenhower, Truman, or any other American for that matter."

Judge supposed he should be flattered to be included in such august company. "I'm not asking you, I'm telling you. Get over here, now!"

Ingrid shot him a dark glance, but responded to the edge in his voice. Lifting her slender legs, she jumped from the jeep. Judge explained his plan as he escorted her inside battalion headquarters. Ordering the adolescent clerk to get him an open line, he dialed the number for Flint Kaserne. When the operator answered, he asked to be put through to Patton's staff.

"Office of the military governor."

Recognizing Harkins's sandpaper baritone, he thrust the phone at Ingrid. "Go on," he whispered.

"Hello?" she said tentatively. Her English accent had crossed the Atlantic, docking at Oyster Bay. "I'd like to speak with General Patton."

"I'm sorry, ma'am. I'm afraid he's not in right now."

"Yes, yes, I know. He's in Berlin. I wouldn't dare bother him, but it's quite important that we speak. My name is Jean Gordon. Perhaps the general has mentioned me?" Ingrid shot Judge a frightened glance. He smiled tightly and gave her a thumb's-up.

"Yes, Miss Gordon. Colonel Paul Harkins here. How are you tonight?"

"I'd be better Colonel, if I could talk to George . . ." Ingrid paused before correcting herself. "I mean General Patton. I'm in a bit of a state, actually."

Harkins responded with requisite aplomb. "I'm terribly sorry, Miss Gordon, but the general left me express orders that he's not to be disturbed. He's dining with President Truman and General Eisenhower this evening. That's quite an event, even for him."

"I'm sure it is, Colonel Harkins, but . . ." Ingrid sighed, adding a note of desperation to her voice. "But not as big as the news I have for him."

"Oh?" Harkins's voice dropped a notch.

"News about a delivery we're *both* expecting. Something due seven months from now." Judge cringed as Ingrid delivered the coup de grace. "February twenty-second to be exact."

To his credit, Harkins answered in a flash, surprise nowhere in his amiable tone. "Well, Miss Gordon, in that case I'm sure the general wouldn't mind if I passed you along to him. He's at the Bristol Hotel on the Kurfürstendamm. The Kaiser's suite." Harkins rattled off a number and a second later Ingrid said good-night and hung up the phone.

"Well?" she asked, her cocksure grin answering her own question.

Judge wasn't sure whether to be elated or aghast. All he knew was that by noon tomorrow every Tom, Dick, and Harry at Flint Kaserne would be gossiping that come February, Georgie Patton was going to have himself an eight-pound, diaper-wetting bundle of joy. "My compliments. You were meant for the stage."

"That's me, the next Zarah Leander."

"Who?"

Ingrid rolled her eyes. "Irene Dunne."

"Naw," said Judge, "you've got her beat by a mile." *And Hayworth and Grable, too*, he added silently. He clicked the receiver and dialed the number Harkins had given. To be safe, he returned the phone to Ingrid and had her ask the hotel operator for Patton's room. The phone picked up before a single ring had been completed.

"General Patton's suite." The voice was smooth and cultured.

Judge put his hand to Ingrid's ear, and whispered, "That's Meeks, Patton's valet."

"Good evening, Meeks," said Ingrid, not missing a beat. "It's me, Jean. Dare I ask if my favorite general is about?"

"One moment, Miss Gordon."

Patton came on the line a second later. "Jean, darling. You don't know how nice it is to hear your voice."

Judge accepted the phone from Ingrid. "Excuse me, sir, but this is Devlin Judge, not Miss Gordon."

"*What the hell?*" barked Patton. There was a pause and he yelled something at Meeks, then came back on the line. "*Listen here, you son of a syphilitic whore, you think you can—*"

Judge interrupted the invective midstream. "General, it is imperative we speak. Erich Seyss is still alive."

"I don't give a good goddamn if Hitler himself is still alive," yelled Patton, "and selling pencils in Times Square. I will not tolerate a pipsqueak intruding on my private affairs. It's nearly midnight, you arrogant—"

"General, again I apologize, but Seyss is alive and he's heading for Potsdam."

Patton calmed long enough for Judge to imagine him clad in his black-and-gold army bathrobe, a cigar tucked in the corner of his mouth, then said, "Good Christ, man, what are you going on about? Everett informed me yesterday morning that Seyss was dead. I told Ike myself."

"He's mistaken, sir. Seyss's former fiancée herself confirmed that his body was not among the corpses." Judge continued speaking, eagerly recounting what he'd learned from Heinz Bauer.

"Potsdam," spat Patton. "What the hell's he want in Potsdam?"

Judge hesitated a moment, fearing to give voice to his suspicions. "The Big Three are there," he said finally.

"And?"

"Sir, I believe Seyss has gone there as an assassin."

"An assassin? Explain yourself."

Judge didn't answer for a few seconds. His first thought had been that Seyss was going after Stalin. After all, he'd been shot by Russians at the end of the war and the Soviets had occupied a great chunk of German territory. Why else the uniforms, the sniper's rifle, and the Russian six-by-six, if not to get close to Uncle Joe? But somehow Judge didn't figure revenge as Seyss's modus operandi. What good would it do his country to kill Stalin? Would it get the Red Army out of Berlin, or out of what had once been the greater German Reich for that matter?

Just the opposite. Kill Stalin and the Red Army would exact a terrible price. Hundreds of thousands of Germans were being held prisoner in Russian camps. Kill Stalin and Seyss would be signing his comrades' death warrant.

But if it made little sense to kill Stalin, what could be said for killing Truman or Churchill? Their deaths would only make the terms of the occupation more onerous. Von Luck's words still haunted him. *He's a Brandenburger . . . He's trained to become one of the enemy. Which one, dammit?* Judge asked himself. *The British or the Americans?* And so he answered both.

"Sir, I believe he intends to kill Prime Minister Churchill and President Truman."

"Truman, you say?" asked Patton. "Tonight at dinner, Mr. President graciously informed me that my uniform had more stars than the Missouri night. I won the war for him and all he cares about is how I dress."

Judge was astonished by Patton's flippant reply. "General, it's not just Seyss I'm talking about. Members of the American military are involved as well. They killed von Luck this morning before I could question him. And they had a go at me earlier this evening. Four nurses in a jeep behind me were killed."

"Slow down, Judge. I'm not up-to-date on the details. That's what I have Everett and Mullins for. Four nurses, you say, dead? Sounds to me like you've got yourself in a regular shit storm."

Finally Patton seemed to be taking his words to heart. "Yes, sir. I certainly seem to." And uttering the words, Judge stood a little straighter, a little prouder. It was the military working its way into his system, his brush with danger a laurel to be worn and applauded. The insight turned his pride to nausea.

"Call Everett and have him get you up here," ordered Patton. "I'm not prepared to accept your line of reasoning until I hear it face-to-face."

Everett, again. Suddenly, he was popping up everywhere. "That's out of the question, sir. I have reason to believe he may be involved."

"Jesus Christ, Judge. You're not making this easy. Just tell me where the hell you are. I'll send my driver, Mims, to pick you up. I've trusted him with my life every goddamn day for the last three years. If what you say is true, I'll need you in Berlin pronto. You can brief Ike yourself."

Judge hesitated, but realized he had no choice. Sooner or later he was going to have to trust someone. He gave Patton his location and listened as the general read it back to him.

"Who the hell was that cooing to Meeks? That Bach woman you carted off this afternoon?"

"Yes, sir," said Judge.

Patton laughed. "Christ, you've had quite some day—picking up a looker in Bavaria and getting some nurses killed in Heidelberg. I'll grant you one thing, Major, you've got initiative. I like that in a man. Stay put and Mims will be with you by dawn. Everything goes as planned, you'll be up here tomorrow at noon."

"Yes, sir," Judge repeated. But even as he hung up the phone, he felt a knot twist in his gut. He'd never mentioned Ingrid by name, nor had he said anything about Heidelberg. If Patton didn't keep abreast of the details, how did he know that he'd picked up Ingrid Bach or where the nurses had been murdered? Staring at the receiver, Judge felt paralyzed by the weight of his suspicions. It was a big leap to tie Patton to von Luck's death, to the murder of four young nurses, and ultimately to Erich Seyss himself. There might be a dozen reasons why Patton wouldn't care to admit to being acquainted with the details of the search for Seyss. Judge just couldn't think of any.

"And so? Will he help?" Ingrid stood with her hands cupped at her throat, rocking on her toes.

Judge stared into her pleading eyes, wishing he could give her the answer she deserved. "I'm not sure," he said. "We'll have to wait and see."

THEY STOOD ON A GRASSY escarpment at the outskirts of Griesheim, their arms brushing lightly against each other, an insistent breeze at their backs. The jeep was parked twenty yards behind them, nose pointed north on a rutted farm road. Their vantage point offered an unimpeded view of the village, and with help from the half moon's shallow light, they were able to make out the *rathaus*, the Reform church next door, and most important, either end of the two-lane road that provided the village's sole entry and exit. Abruptly, the wind dropped, leaving silence and apprehension in its wake.

"How long?" asked Ingrid.

"I'm not sure," said Judge. "Maybe a few minutes. Maybe until morn—" He raised a hand for quiet and turned his ear to hone in on a distant sound, much as a man might squint to sharpen his focus. A growl, the faintest of coughs, then silence. He advanced a step or two, his eyes scanning the dark. There it was again, the growl, and this time Ingrid heard it too.

"A car," she said.

"No," he corrected her. "A bunch of them. Probably jeeps."

The sound grew steadily, crawling over the rolling terrain, alternately screaming and sighing like a sawmill's stutter. A minute passed and the stutter was replaced by a throaty hum, hungry and ominous. The jeeps traveled the countryside with their lights doused, wolves advancing on an abandoned prey. Judge counted eight of them and knew it was no rogue operation. The vehicles sped past a hundred feet below, close enough for him to see the white stars emblazoned on their hoods; close enough to know it was the same military police of which he had so recently been a member.

Ingrid laid her hand on his arm, and for a moment they watched the unholy caravan close on the *rathaus* a mile away. "And now?" she asked.

But by then Judge was moving, grasping her hand and hustling to the jeep.

"Now?" His voice was tight, a rigid self-control holding back his fear. "Now we're on our own."

CHAPTER

39

ERICH SEYSS WAS COLLECTING cigarette butts. So far this morning, he'd scraped six off the pavement, and it was still early, just a few minutes before eight. Yesterday, he'd gathered 123, enough to make twenty fresh cigarettes and earn him a little more than fifty marks. Twenty hours scouring a thirty-meter stretch of concrete for the equivalent of half a dollar. The prospect of such an existence quelled any desire he harbored to rejoin the civilian world.

Tucking his hands into his pockets, Seyss took up position against a shrapnel-scarred column inside the portico of the Frankfurt Grand, a once opulent hotel now consigned to boarding American officers. French doors stood open granting him full view of the hotel lobby. At this time of day, the place was a sea of khaki and green. Officers crowded the reception baying like a pack of dogs for their room keys. They camped on every chaise and divan, drinking coffee, smoking cigarettes, and flagging down waiters with a shrill whistle and a shout. They flooded from the stairs, the elevators, the men's room, and the kiosk.

Locusts! thought Seyss. Worse than any plague.

Two of the offenders sauntered from the hotel, flicking their cigarettes at his feet.

"Merry Christmas, Fritz," muttered one.

"Yeah, happy birthday," added the other.

Seyss bowed and scraped as befitted his beggar's status, knocking the embers from the saliva-soaked butts before dropping them into his jacket pocket. Eyes scanning the lobby, he caught sight of a slim officer emerging from the elevator, scuffed pigskin briefcase in hand. He checked the man's epaulets for a pair of silver captain's bars and his lapels for the twin castles that denoted the corps of engineers, then studied his features. Yes, it was his man. One last time, he compared the breadth of the shoulders, the size of the waist, the man's height to his own. He smiled inwardly. A perfect match.

When the captain's key had been placed in the box below the number 421, Seyss left the shade of the portico. A short stroll took him to a newspaper kiosk at the corner, and there, he waited for his man to exit the hotel.

Frankfurt was abustle with grim prosperity. A turn-of-the-century steam engine dragged a lone streetcar up Mainzstrasse. Trümmerfrauen crowded every corner chiseling mortar from an ever-growing stack of bricks. Newspaper boys shouted the day's headlines while a gang of laborers trudged down the side of the road escorted by GIs front and rear. Watching it all through a sun-scratched haze, Seyss acknowledged a long-absent warmth blossom in his chest. Hope. And he knew that Germany would survive.

The realization sharpened his urgency to reach Berlin.

Two days had passed since the nightmare at the armory. Two days he'd earmarked for travel to the German capital and establishing local cover. Sunday was spent walking the forty kilometers to Frankfurt. Arriving, he phoned the contact Egon had given him, but the party did not answer. A check of the neighborhood showed it to have been resettled by American officers. Exhausted, he passed the night huddled in a vacant boxcar.

Venturing into the *stadtzentrum* the next morning at dawn, he expected to find the city crawling with military police, his face plastered on the front page of every paper. After Wiesbaden, he was certain the Americans would have pulled out all the stops. Curiously, there were no signs of heightened security. Neither his name nor face graced the daily papers. No more than the regular complement of MPs patrolled the streets and not a single jeep blared his name, description, or the details of his reward. It was as if the Americans believed him dead, alongside Biedermann, Bauer, and Steiner. The conceit was difficult to swallow. At least one man knew he was alive.

Seyss called to mind the taciturn figure who'd guided him from the armory. He was neither short nor tall, his features hidden beneath the brim of a sweat-stained fedora. Even his nationality was a mystery. Providing Seyss an olive field jacket and a peaked campaign cap, he'd rushed him to an unlocked gate in the perimeter fence and told him of a safe route to Frankfurt. Seyss knew better than to ask who he was. *Ein kamerad.* That was enough.

Just then, his captain appeared in front of the hotel, hand raised to ward off the morning sun. Bounding down the stairs, he turned right and passed Seyss at an officious clip. Seyss fell in behind him, sure to guard a distance of at least five paces. Unconsciously, he found himself matching the American's step, his arms swinging in a parody of a march. He could hear the steady click of the officer's spit-shined shoes stamping the pavement, their brisk *tap-tap* smacking of duty, honor, and to his German ear, the will to conquer. But Seyss didn't envy him his smart uniform and rakish cap. He no longer gave a damn about the trappings of glory. He envied the captain only one thing: his victor's élan. He had known it once. He swore he would know it again.

Seyss followed the American two blocks to the tram stop at the corner of Mittelweg and Humboldstrasse. Ducking into a shadowy corner, he waited until the number thirteen tram appeared and the captain climbed aboard. Seyss knew his destination without having to follow him: I. G. Farben, Germany's largest chemicals manufacturer. Dwight Eisenhower had declared the sprawling complex of modern buildings set within an idyllic parklike setting headquarters of the American occupational government. As for Farben, well, they were out of business. Demand for Zyklon-B wasn't what it used to be.

Seyss watched the tram trundle off, then retraced his steps to the hotel. He circled to the employee entrance and passed unnoticed into the employee locker room. One hour after the morning shift had begun, the place was deserted. He made his way through the maze of dented metal lockers, stopping at the farthest corner. He drew his knife and one by one began prying open lockers. He found what he needed on the third try: a clean white shirt, a matching waiter's jacket and a black bow tie. Removing the clothes, he caught a glimpse of himself in a nearby mirror. His hair was matted and greasy, the blond beginning to show in desultory patches, his clothing stained with sweat, soot and blood. Three days' growth of beard dirtied his face and, Lord knew, he smelled like a Jew in a cattle car. He offered his slovenly reflection a wink and a nod. Just your average German male.

"ROOM SERVICE."

Seyss knocked on the door to room 421, then stepped back into the center of the hallway and waited. Chin raised just so, white towel draped over an arm, he looked like any other waiter in the hotel. He raised his hand to knock again, but thought twice. Silence bred suspicion, but best not to take it too far. He looked over both shoulders, then dropped to one knee and examined the lock. It was an old brass affair with a keyhole capacious enough to see into the room. Undoing his belt, he threaded its metal tongue into the lock, feeling the smooth mass of the tumbler. Raising the tongue, he wedged the tip of his knife into the keyhole, so that it acted as a fulcrum upon which he could exert greater pressure on the tumbler. With a jerk, he flicked the knife downward, forcing the tongue against the tumbler and freeing the lock. He depressed the handle and swept inside.

The room was dark, curtains drawn against the morning light. Back pressed to the door, Seyss trained his ear for the sound of another man's breathing. Only colonels and above claimed a room for themselves. Everyone else doubled up. He heard nothing. Turning on the light, he walked to the center of the room, taking in the furnishings with a sweep of his head. Twin beds were pressed against either wall, a night table separating them. Only one had been slept in. A desk and chair decorated another wall. He walked back to the alcove and opened the closet. Several freshly laundered uniforms hung from one side of the rack. He removed one, then took a pressed shirt, a tie, socks, and underwear from the shelf above it. He threw all of it onto the bed and began to undress. Catching another glimpse of himself in the mirror, he realized he couldn't don the uniform without at least shaving. The sight of his scraggly hair and beard begged explanation. The Americans were a well-groomed lot, he'd grant them that.

If the bedroom was cramped, the bathroom was fit for a king. Marble floors and counters, gold-plated fixtures, a tub large enough to swim in, and directly above it a showerhead the size of a pie tin. Seyss stripped to the waist, then filled a mug with hot water. He added a dollop of shaving cream and using a lovely badger-hair brush, brought the soapy mix to a lather. Raising the brush to his face, he heard a sound at the front door, the unmistakable tinkle of metal against metal. *Move!* he ordered himself. He turned off the water, dumping the foam into the sink even as he bent and scooped up his shirt and jacket. The noise came again and he imagined a drunken hand fumbling for the lock. *Mach schnell!* Sweeping a hand across the light switch, he bolted into the bedroom, eyes darting to every corner for a place to hide. Again he noted the untouched bedspread and he cursed his carelessness.

Only a colonel draws a single room!

Behind him, the tumblers fell and the door opened a notch, froze, then closed again. A clumsy voice echoed in the hallway, "And next time, Stupak, the pot will be mine."

Seyss tiptoed to the alcove, knife drawn and resting at his side. He darted a glance to his left. The closet. He imagined the dark, the confinement, the close company of his own breathing. His skin bristled. What choice did he have? Finally free of the American military police, he could risk nothing to alert them to his survival. Two feet away, the door handle began to turn. Seyss drew a breath, opened the closet, and climbed inside.

Seconds later, the door to room 421 burst open, banging against the wall, then slamming shut. Inside the closet, the sounds were amplified tenfold and hit Seyss's ears with the raucous clap of a shellburst. He stood hunched over, head brushing the shelf above him, half wrapped in the uniform he'd come to steal. The American walked into the bedroom and collapsed onto the bed. (He weighed a hundred kilos easy if the chorus of screaming bedsprings were to be believed.) He had a woman with him and soon the two were laughing and giggling like a couple of horny teenagers. Their shoes came off, each thrown to a different corner of the room.

"*Musik? Ja. Ist gut?*" the lady asked.

Seyss heard a soft brushing noise that could only be the drawing of curtains, then the fuzz and static of a radio warming up. A female singer's voice drifted across the room.

"*Underneath the lantern by the barrack gate, darling, I remember the way you used to wait.*"

It was Dietrich herself singing "Lilli Marlene" in English for the Americans. *Christ*, thought Seyss, *they've even taken our music.*

Locusts!

Despite the absolute dark, he stood with his eyes open, arguing to himself that his sentence inside the closet would be of short duration. Five minutes, ten at the most. The two would make love, then drift off. He could slip out unnoticed, maybe even with a uniform draped over his arm. But as the minutes crawled by, and the sounds of the two pigs' love-making grew more fevered, he realized that was not to be. He might be trapped inside this god-awful prison for hours, maybe the entire day. He breathed deeply, repeating the same word over and over. *Ruhe. Ruhe.* Calm. Calm. He was sweating, yet his skin was cool to the touch, bordering on clammy. Every moment the air was growing warmer, his heart beating faster. He felt a box descending over his head, stopping up his ears and smothering his mouth. Cold hands closed around his neck. Pressure. Everywhere pressure.

He blinked, and once more he was in Camp 8, trapped beneath the kitchen while Janks bartered away the prisoners' supplies. He was at the Villa Ludwig walking down a sterile, white-tiled corridor with Egon Bach, descending deeper and deeper into the earth. He closed his eyes, hoping for a measure of peace, but was confronted instead with a kaleidoscope of his own memories, the confines of the closet allowing him no escape.

Just one bullet!

His own voice screamed at him as if he were a bald recruit.

Did you hear me, Gruber? One bullet per person. We must conserve ammunition.

Seyss was standing on a muddy ridge overlooking a dense forest in the rolling hills outside of Kiev. A ravine called Babi Yar. It was October of 1941, the height of autumn's magnificent pageant. The leaves burned red, yellow, orange, and every shade in between. A cool wind brushed his face, the acrid smell of spent powder making his eyes water. He heard another volley of shots and he blinked involuntarily. Then came the sniping that enraged him, single shots, here and there.

He turned and strode down the hill into the ravine, past the line of women. They were all ages: children, teenagers, mothers, the very old and the very young. They were naked, white as ghosts. One grabbed his cuff, pleading, "I am twenty-three. Please." Seyss did not look at her. He pulled free and walked to Sergeant Gruber, slapping him hard on the shoulder.

"Gruber, one bullet per person. Have your men take better aim, goddammit. We must conserve ammunition." He was saying the same things over and over. He knew it but could not stop himself. What else was there to say? He had orders. From the Reichsführer SS himself. One bullet per Jew. No more. He must enforce them. "Gruber, do you understand?"

"Jawohl, Herr Major."

Below Seyss was the pit, a strip of excavated land one hundred meters long, thirty meters wide, and five meters deep. He didn't know what idiot imagined they could place all the bodies here. The pile was already ten deep the length of it, and the women were still arriving, truck after truck. Two days now. How many were there? Ten thousand? Fifteen? A few of his men were walking over the corpses as if they were stones, skipping here and there, then bending over and placing their pistols to the back of a neck and pulling the trigger.

"You see, Gruber," Seyss was saying, pointing at the offender. "One bullet, only. Get that man. Bring him here. Now!"

"But, Herr Major, the woman was still alive."

"Get him!" Seyss could not allow logic to interfere with his orders. He heard a whistle blow and another twenty women were jogged into the pit. Two carried infants. *Funny*, he thought, *why don't they make more fuss?* A squad of soldiers lined up behind them. They raised their rifles and fired. The women collapsed. A baby cried and one of the soldiers ran into the pit and fired off a few shots.

"There," shouted Seyss, gesturing madly at the extermination squad, "Look, Gruber, that man is firing indiscriminately. One bullet. What is so hard to understand? Replace him at once."

Gruber averted his gaze. "With who?"

"Someone from Erhardt's company."

"They've been dismissed. Some of the men are upset. They are no longer fit."

No longer fit. Seyss knew what that meant. A little killing and they'd broken like children.

"Upset?" he yelled. "What about me? I am upset, too. What am I to say to Himmler when I return to Berlin? 'The men refuse your order.'?"

He remembered his last meeting with the Reichsführer SS. A leisurely perusal of the statistics just in from Einsatz Kommando A in Riga, his pal Otto Ohlendorf's command. There were 138,500 Jews killed, 55 Communists, 6 Gypsies. That meant 400,000 rounds of ammunition expended at a cost of two reichsmarks per bullet. Himmler inquiring in his unhurried professorial voice, "Unacceptable. Wouldn't you agree, Herr Sturmbannführer?" He flicked a paper or two, his finger coming to rest at a particularly bothersome figure. "Fifty thousand children. That's fine. But can you explain to me why our men require two bullets to eliminate a child? Solve the problem, Seyss. One bullet. See to it. The waste makes me sick."

Seyss strode to the endless line of women and pushed another twenty into the pit. "Take proper aim and use a single round," he shouted to the *Einsatz* squad. "Reichsführer Himmler is giving you a direct order. Do you understand?" He drew his pistol and passed behind the line of women, brushing the nose of his pistol against the bare nape of their necks. He stopped at the last woman. She had fine blond hair and a fair complexion. Hardly the Semite to look at, but he'd been fooled before. And placing the gun to the base of her skull, he pulled the trigger.

"You see. It's not so hard. One bullet!"

Inside the closet, Seyss cringed as the words reverberated inside his skull. Yet even as the tattered vestiges of his conscience hung in the dark beside him, he twirled the knife in his hand, turning the blade up to deliver a slashing blow, willing the officer to open the closet door.

Inches away, the American stood in the alcove, asking if the woman wanted a glass of water. She said sure, and he walked into the bathroom, humming along with the radio. Something about sitting under an apple tree. Seyss couldn't make out the lyrics. His mind was fuzzy. He was hot and his muscles ached. The soldier returned to the bedroom. Seyss heard a bottle being set down on the desk and a glass to go with it. Then the bedsprings again. The woman made a terrible braying noise as she was being fucked.

"*Sächliclikeit*," he whispered through gritted teeth. *Objectivity. Control. Discipline. You are a man standing inside a wooden box. The darkness is temporary. Consider it a test of your stamina, a measure of your physical abilities.*

But reason was no cure for his untethered anxiety.

Suddenly, the closet was unbearable. The jacket scuffing the back of his neck, the shelf collapsing upon his head, the musty odor scratching his nostrils, invading his throat. Worst, though, was the smell of his own body. He could no longer remain so close to himself. Still, for one more agonizing second, he managed to choke down his fears. He ignored the clothing crawling all over him and his olfactory distress. Squeezing his eyelids tightly, he even dredged up a moment of calm, if calm is what you call it when your skin is covered with goose bumps and your heart beating hard enough to crack a rib.

And then like a frayed cord, his discipline snapped.

"To hell with it," he said, and quietly hauled himself out of the closet.

The two were splayed across the bed, the American on top of his German whore, copulating vigorously. Seyss crossed the room in two strides, planting his knee in the crook of the soldier's back before he could turn his head. Dropping his knife to the bed, Seyss threw his left arm around the American's neck and took firm hold of the jaw. He braced his right arm across the rim of the man's shoulders, pulled the body taut against his knee, and gave a single ferocious twist to the left. The vertebrae snapped instantly and the body fell limp.

It was over in three seconds.

If the whore was screaming, Seyss couldn't tell. Her labored gasps sounded no different from her annoying bray. Shoving the American's corpse off her, he sat down on the bed, sure to retrieve his knife.

"Shh," he said, covering her mouth with a hand. "Relax. I'm not going to hurt you."

She was very pretty, no more than eighteen beneath all that cheap makeup. She had blond hair and deep blue eyes and for a moment she reminded him of one of the maidens he'd slept with in the Lebensborn hostel, some busty zealot from the Bund Deutscher Mädchen eager to provide the Reich with a passel of racially superior children. He looked at her again and realized he'd been mistaken. She looked like Ingrid Bach.

And as she ventured a smile, nervously nodding her cooperation, he kissed her on the forehead and plunged the knife into her chest.

THE UNIFORM FIT BETTER THAN he had expected. The trousers fell to his heel and not a millimeter below it. The waist was a few sizes too large, but a belt cinched it nicely. And the jacket fit as if tailor-made. He had shaved and showered, taking pains to doctor the raw groove where Judge's bullet had nicked his scalp. He had shampooed his hair thoroughly, so that no longer was it the same ink-bottle black but a dark, lustrous brown. Using a pair of nail scissors, he had cut it very short, then doused it with tonic and parted it directly above his left eye.

After giving his tie a final going over, Seyss buttoned up his jacket. In one pocket, he carried a little more than two hundred dollars and a picture of his sweetheart back home. In another, the few dog tags and identification card he'd picked up in Munich. He looked damned sharp clad in khaki. What a wonder it did for his soul to be in uniform once again. The wrong uniform, to be sure, but who was he to argue? These days everything was upside down.

Adjusting the cap squarely on his head, he brought himself to attention. Something was wrong. He checked the uniform, the tie. Everything was in order. What was it, then? He looked himself up and down until he found the problem. His posture. He looked as if he were waiting for the Führer to pass in review. *Relax, old man.* He dropped a shoulder and forced his stomach to droop. And in a moment he'd achieved the indolent attitude, at once cocksure and uncertain, of the citizen soldier.

Better, but not perfect.

Then he saw it.

It was his face. It was too closed. Too private. Too German. Americans were so trusting, so wide-eyed, so eager. Every feeling they'd had—every heartbreak, every crush, every promotion, every setback—was there to see, smack in the middle of their face.

Smile, he told himself, and taking a deep breath, stretched his cheeks from ear to ear. Raise your eyebrows. Open your eyes a shade wider. He thought of his childhood, a day at the carnival, the prospect of the Ferris wheel. He pictured himself at the top gazing over all Munich, then gave himself a fat sausage for good measure. Bliss!

He looked in the mirror and saw an American officer staring back.

Bringing himself to attention, he raised his right arm and laid his rigidly aligned fingers to the tip of his brow.

"Good morning," he said aloud, "Captain Erich Seyss reporting for duty."

DARREN HONEY HAD NEVER SEEN General Donovan in such a state. Normally a man of unshakable calm and storied reserve, Donovan was pacing back and forth across his office like a caged tiger, first shouting, then whispering, and yes, even growling. It was readily apparent how he'd earned the nickname Wild Bill.

"This Patton thing has become a mess," railed Donovan. "If you'd asked me a month ago, I'd have said all his talk about going after the Russians was just bluster. Something that riding partner of his, von Wangenheim, put into his head. Now I'm not so sure."

"The general still has that damned Nazi on the payroll?" Honey scratched his head in bewilderment. Since arriving in Bad Toelz in late May, Patton had taken his daily equitation in the company of his groom, one Baron von Wagenheim. Like Patton, von Wagenheim was an Olympian, winner of a gold medal in dressage at the 1936 games in Berlin. He was also an unrepentant Nazi who had spent the war as an SS colonel of cavalry. "I thought Ike would have put an end to that by now."

"Just one of Georgie's 'eccentricities,' says dear old Ike. He doesn't have any idea of the anti-Bolshevik, anti-Semitic bilge the old kraut is spewing."

"And Patton's falling for it?"

"Falling for it?" Donovan chortled disgustedly. "Why, he eats up every word like it's his Thanksgiving turkey. Georgie's convinced that Henry Morgenthau is a lunatic and that Stalin has his sights on the Eiffel Tower. He's put former Wehrmacht troops in charge of guarding a camp of DPs and he wants to commandeer a village in the mountains and turn it into a concentration camp for Jews. Instead of denazifying the place, he's hiring every goddammed one of them he can find. He's gone over the top, I tell you. Over the top!"

Donovan stomped to his desk and fiddled with a tape recorder. "I asked the Signal Corps to put a bug on Georgie's phone a week back. I want you to listen to this. You won't believe your ears."

Honey grimaced involuntarily. *A bug on Patton!* Weren't they supposed to be spying on the enemy?

Donovan switched on the recorder and a moment later a scratchy voice hollered across the room. There was no mistaking its owner. George Patton at his irascible best.

"Hell," shouted Patton, "we are going to have to fight them sooner or later. Why not do it now while our armies are still intact and we can have their hind end kicked back into Russia in three months? We can do it easily with the help of the German troops we have, if we just arm them and take them with us. They hate the bastards."

"You're preaching to the choir, George," chuckled a British voice on the other end of the line.

Donovan whispered "Monty" and Honey's stomach fell to the floor.

Patton went on. "You don't have to get mixed up in it at all if you are so damn soft about it and scared of your rank. Just let me handle it down here. In ten days, I can have enough incidents happen to have us at war with those sons of bitches and make it look like *they* started it!"

"We've already stacked the weapons," said Field Marshal Sir Bernard Law Montgomery. "One whisper of war and I'll have the bloody Wehrmacht rearmed within twenty-four hours. But that's all I'm prepared to do at this point. By the bye, your little Jerry still on the move?"

"Hell, yes," roared Patton. "The man's indomitable. If the entire

German Army were made up of sons of bitches like him, you'd still be trying to take Caen."

"That I very much doubt," retorted Monty, bristling at the insult. "Still, I don't know how you've managed to keep your boys off him. There's a photo of him in every constabulary in the British zone. Chap sets foot here, he's done for."

"It hasn't been easy. Ike stuck me with a real pain in the ass to head up the investigation. Probably the only man in Europe who could actually find 'my little Jerry.'" Patton managed a fair imitation of Monty's languid brogue. "But don't worry your aristocratic behind. Everything's well in hand."

"Right, then," said Monty. "I'll catch up with you in Berlin next week. Cheerio."

Donovan switched off the recorder, then fell into a worn leather chair next to his desk. "We taped it Friday afternoon. Patton's in Berlin now. How d'ya like it?"

Honey crossed to the window and looked down on Maximillianstrasse. Panes of glass rattled as a tram passed below, ringing its bell in advance of its next stop. The fact was, he didn't like it at all. He was tired of the subterfuge, tired of peeking into other men's lives—even if it was for the good of the country. He didn't like knowing that Ike was impotent and had been for the entire war (his girlfriend, the Brit Kay Summersby, was an agent, too) or that Patton was as mad as a heated-up bull rhino. Sometimes he couldn't believe that just three years had passed since he'd put on his country's uniform; three years since he'd been working as an assistant greens keeper at the Congressional Country Club just outside of Washington, D.C.

In March 1942, Donovan had taken over the club and turned it into a top-secret training center for agents of the OSS. Hearing Honey speaking German with one of the landscapers, he'd pulled him aside and begun questioning him about his background. The OSS needed native German speakers, he'd said, and Honey, the son of German-Czech immigrants, whose real name was Darius Honnecker, qualified as one. A month later, Honey was back at Congressional, not as a gardener but as an agent in training.

"Maybe the rumors are true, sir. You know, that General Patton took too many spills playing polo, one too many bumps to the noggin."

"You think George is crazy?" Donovan laughed off the suggestion. "People have been saying the same thing since he graduated from West Point. That wasn't one lunatic talking to another we heard. It was two old war horses plotting their final campaign. Besides, does it really matter?"

"No, sir, I guess it doesn't."

"I'm every bit as keen as Patton to stop the Russians where they are," said Donovan, "but another war is hardly the answer. Right now, our attention has to stay focused on the Pacific. We've got to finish off those damned Japs before we do another goddammed thing. You hear what Patton said about 'them starting it'? What does that rascal have in mind?"

Honey recounted Seyss's desire for Russian uniforms, weapons, and transportation, his mention of "a last mission for Germany," and Bauer's statement that Seyss was leading his men to Babelsberg. "If Seyss is going to Potsdam, it can only be one thing, can't it?"

Instead of being shocked at the news, though, Donovan appeared pleasantly surprised. "He's a clever goose, I'll grant him that. Patton always did want to take Berlin."

Honey shook his head, his disbelief mixed with contempt and horror. "Will you warn the president's security detail?"

"Right away, but unfortunately, security in Potsdam proper is being handled by Stalin's boys. He's got five thousand thugs in the woods surrounding the area. I doubt he'll let our men lend a hand."

Honey envisioned the countryside swarming with uniformed Russian soldiers. To someone accustomed to passing himself off as the enemy, their presence would be a godsend. "I don't think they'll stop Seyss," he said. "The man is very resourceful. He spent two years on and behind the Russian front. If Stalin's got five thousand of his men up there, he'll take that as an invitation to join them."

Donovan took to pacing again. "Problem is, Georgie's got his cards mixed up. It's Stalin who's holding all the aces. He has over three million men within fifty miles of the Elbe. Over a million pieces of artillery, too. Meanwhile, we've been hightailing our boys out of the European theater of operations as quickly as we can. We pick a fight with Uncle Joe, we could end up back at Dunkirk in sixty days."

Honey didn't like Donovan's brooding. "Even if we couldn't defeat the Russians, we could hold them in check."

"Could we? They outnumber us three to one. Their tanks are superior to ours and they have an unlimited supply of manpower."

"But you're forgetting something, General."

"Am I?"

"Our scientists, sir. I mean, they've been working on a device for a few years now. You can't help but pay attention to the scuttlebutt."

"You don't miss much, I'll grant you that." Donovan pulled a crumpled yellow paper from his jacket pocket that Honey recognized as an intercept of a top-secret diplomatic wire traffic. "Secretary of War Stimson received this yesterday."

Honey read the intercept.

"'Operated on this morning. Diagnosis not complete but results seem satisfactory and already exceed expectations.'" And skipping ahead, "'Dr. Groves pleased.'"

"I'm not sure I understand."

"One of those devices you've heard about is 'operational.' A single bomb the equivalent of twenty thousand tons of TNT. The damned thing works!"

Honey tried to figure out what twenty thousand tons of TNT could do. The biggest raids on Berlin and Dresden and Stuttgart, the ones involving two or three hundred bombers, had dropped no more than a hundred fifty tons of high explosives on a target. Donovan was talking about a single bomb capable of delivering more than a hundred times that amount. "Jesus Christ," he whispered.

"The Savior indeed," said Donovan. "This time I think we can safely say God is on our side. Problem is we only have two of them and they're both headed to Japan. Anything comes up with Stalin in the next ninety days, we're out of pocket." Sighing, he rose from his desk and joined Honey at the window. "Which brings us to our last complication, your friend Major Judge. Last we've heard, he's gone under.

Disappeared with Ingrid Bach twenty-four hours ago, after calling Third Army Headquarters and asking Paul Harkins for Patton. What do you think he's up to?"

"That's easy," responded Honey. "The same thing we are."

"Is he capable?"

Honey imagined the determined brow, the quick temper. "Of what? Getting to Berlin? I'd say yes. Of finding Seyss once he's there? Maybe."

Donovan mulled over his answer. "Judge certainly discovered that Seyss was still alive quickly enough. You were right guessing he'd try and use von Luck to identify the body, but you didn't foresee that he'd bring Ingrid Bach into this. You said he wouldn't expose the girl to anything dangerous. Why do you suppose he didn't come to us instead?"

It was an annoying habit of Donovan's to dissect his men's thinking, expose their faults, then go right back and ask them for another opinion. "I don't know," answered Honey. "Seems he doesn't trust us."

"'Us'? Who's 'us'? 'Us' doesn't exist. 'You,' I think, would be more accurate." Donovan stared at the afternoon sky, wagging a finger at an invisible adversary. "What I really need to know, then, is if Devlin Judge is capable of killing Seyss?"

Honey paused before answering, knowing he was treading on very thin ice. "I'm not sure. Either he's not as strong as he believes himself to be or he's holding part of himself in check."

"So, he might be, but it wouldn't come easily. He'd hesitate."

"Yessir. That's correct."

Donovan's eyes had taken on a dreamy cast. Once he'd told Honey that his job was not to see the world as it was but to see it as it would be in an hour's time. "Hmm," he whispered. "Maybe that's good."

"Sir?"

"Just thinking. Patton wasn't *all* wrong, you know."

And then the reverie was broken. Donovan wrapped an arm around Honey's shoulder and guided him to the door. "We've got a plane standing by to fly you to Berlin. There's no train running that way, so maybe you'll gain some time on Seyss. Al Dulles will pick you up and show you around town, introduce you to some of our contacts. You're cleared to attend the conference, but don't expect to get into the actual negotiating sessions. You know where Seyss needs to go to do his job. Keep an eye peeled and it shouldn't be too hard to spot him. And if you run into Judge, you might want to enlist his help in this thing."

Honey halted in midstride. "You sure? I thought we didn't want him involved in this any further."

"We didn't." Donovan smiled mischievously and Honey knew he was busy weaving some intricate plot. "But things are different now. Remember, Captain Honnecker, the only constant in our business is change."

Honey frowned inwardly, wondering when their work had become a business. "And what do I tell him?"

"Why, the truth. It's nothing he doesn't know already. Just make sure he keeps his mouth shut afterward."

Honey cocked his head, not sure he'd heard correctly. "Sir?"

Donovan responded to the pained expression on Honey's face. "Don't look so upset. We can't have anyone besmirching Georgie Patton's reputation. America does love its heroes."

CHAPTER

41

SOMETIME TOWARD DAWN, INGRID and Judge left the main road and navigated a series of dirt lanes, ending up in a small wood where they parked the jeep in a copse of birch trees. The night was silent, the air warm and misted with a fragrant dew. Ingrid was happy for the rest. Her bottom was sore from three hours of hard driving over untended farm roads. They'd stopped twice already, laying up for a quarter of an hour in torn-up barns, watching for any sight of Patton's thugs. An hour ago, they'd crossed a paved thoroughfare and they'd been on it ever since, passing through the towns of Hochheim and Walldorf.

Shifting in her seat, Ingrid faced her self-appointed savior. She was ready to inform him that she was leaving here and now, that whatever wild intentions he harbored, he could no longer count on her participation, that she missed her son very much, and finally, that she was tired, hungry, and in a most unpleasant mood altogether. But before she could manage a word, he was leaning toward her, one arm beckoning her to come close, his commanding brown eyes imploring her to solve some unspoken misunderstanding.

"Major," she said, crushing her back against the seat. "I beg your pardon."

Judge eyed her queerly. "The map," he said. "I'm sorry, but I can't reach it. Do you mind?"

Ingrid averted her gaze, embarrassed at her misperception, though not as relieved as she'd expected. Reaching beneath her seat, she found a well-creased map. Judge unfolded it, using her lap as well as his own as a table. *Damn him for not asking*, she cursed silently. There were numbers scribbled everywhere: this army, that corps, compass headings, phone numbers, she couldn't tell what. The only legible marks on the whole bloody thing were the fat black lines dividing her country into four pieces.

"We've got to get to Berlin as quickly as possible," he said, finger already tracing some imaginary course. "That's where he's headed."

"Go," she said. "But don't expect me to come with you. I have a family. Pauli must be worried sick about me."

"Pauli has Herbert and your sister. He'll manage fine until you get back."

"It's not a question of managing," Ingrid responded tartly. "Everyone in our country has been 'managing' for the last three years. Managing without enough sleep, without enough food. Managing without a husband or a brother or a sister. I am his mother. I will not allow him to *manage* without me."

"If you go home, that's exactly what he'll be doing. And not for a day or a week but for the rest of his life."

Frightened by his strident tone, Ingrid chose for her own one of a measured reserve. The clear-minded skeptic. Reason before emotion. Kant over Nietzsche. "You're being a bit dramatic, aren't you?"

"Am I?" Judge shrugged his shoulders, but his voice guarded its urgency. "You're my only proof that Seyss is alive. Whoever strung that concertina wire across the road knows it. It wasn't me they were after. It was you."

She'd been privy to facts and suppositions. She'd borne terrified witness as his suspicions were proven correct, first in Heidelberg, then Griesheim. Still, she was unwilling to accept his conclusions, even if deep down she knew they were true.

"Are you saying they'll be watching Sonnenbrücke? Don't forget we already have our own bodyguard, Father's personal jailers."

Judge fixed her with his gaze, his brow knit in earnest disbelief. "You just don't get it, do you?"

"How can you be sure he's going to Berlin? Maybe he's up and left the country?"

Judge shook his head as if he'd delivered the coming rejoinder a hundred times. "If he wanted to leave the country, he never would have gone to Munich, or to Heidelberg, or to Wiesbaden. Whatever his plan is, he's stuck to it despite knowing we're looking for him. Why should he quit now?"

"Guessing. Guessing. Guessing."

"Then why are we hiding here? If Erich Seyss had left the country, no one would give a damn if you were alive or dead. No one would have killed von Luck. Those poor nurses would still be alive right now."

"Erich has caused me enough pain," she said. "I won't allow him to interfere with my life any further."

"Then why do you still care about him?"

"I don't," she parried reflexively. "Not a wink."

"I see how you light up every time you talk about him," Judge said. "How you sit a little straighter, how your voice jumps a notch."

"Nonsense!" she said, and catching the accusatory cast to his eyes, saw she'd struck a jealous chord. She recalled his words on the drive up to Heidelberg. That he could believe for a moment that she still had feelings for Seyss enraged her. "Do you know why we never married? Do you?"

"No." It was a whisper. He had offended. He was sorry.

"When an SS man wishes to marry, he must submit his intended spouse's name to the SS Office of Race and Resettlement. There the woman's genealogy is laid out on a family tree going back five generations. In my case, three was enough. My great-grandmother was a Jew. That makes my blood one-eighth Semitic—enough for the SS to classify me as a Jew. They refused to grant Erich's request to marry me on the grounds that our offspring would tarnish the racial purity of the Thousand-Year Reich and he obeyed. Rather than transfer to a regular army unit where an officer is permitted to marry anyone he chooses, he obeyed. That's what he does, Major. He obeys."

Somewhere along the way she'd lost her reserve. Emotion had won out over reason. She'd been foolish to believe her heart could harness her head. And when Judge spoke next his voice had assumed the calm she'd abandoned. *This is what he does*, she thought. *He's a lawyer. He persuades people.*

"Tell you the truth, I don't want to go to Berlin either," he said. "Five hours ago, I went officially absent without leave. Patton doesn't have to make up a reason to have me arrested anymore. I've done it myself. Any chance I have for returning to the IMT is shot, and so is my job back home. Attorneys with an arrest record aren't generally welcomed before the bar. You don't like Seyss. Fine. I hate him. But it's beyond that now."

Ingrid railed at his self-control, feeling her own slip another notch. "You can't hate him. He's done you no harm. To you, he's just a shadow."

"No," said Judge, all emotion drained from his voice. "He's hardly a shadow. Erich Seyss killed my brother."

Ingrid stared at him, a floodtide of hate and disbelief and terror burning her cheeks. "I don't believe you."

"When I told you about the crimes Seyss was wanted for, I left out one detail: My brother was among the men he had killed. My brother was a priest, Ingrid."

Eyes locked on Judge, Ingrid felt her stomach climb inside her chest, her breath leave her. The world shrank around her until she heard only the panoply of arguments desperately jockeying for position inside her mind. She needed to believe that the man she had loved was a soldier, not a murderer. Things happened in war. Terrible things. He was only following orders. There had to be an explanation. Hurriedly, she tried to scrape some words together on his behalf. The jilted lover would not be made a fool of a second time. But any defense she hoped to offer died stillborn in her throat, slain by the ice in Judge's voice. Her chin trembled, then fell. "I'm sorry."

Judge raised his face to the night sky and blew out an exaggerated sigh. "Don't be. He ruined your life, too. Hell, he's still doing it."

"I'm not apologizing for Erich. I'm apologizing for myself. For my country."

He looked at her, puzzled. "But you didn't do anything."

The words stung more than she'd expected. "That's the point, isn't it?"

Judge's silence granted her the sense of guilt she'd been longing for. "Is that why you're going to Berlin?" she asked. "For your brother?"

"No," said Judge. "It's not about Francis. Not anymore, at least. I'm going because I don't have any other choice. Hell, even if I wanted to stop, I'd be arrested as soon as I showed by face at my billet. But it's not a question of that either. Offer me the chance to go back to Paris, no questions asked, I'd turn you down flat." He laughed a little, the moonlight casting a melancholy pall across his attractive features. "What I always liked best about the law was the black and white of it. You either did something wrong or you didn't. You broke the law or you didn't. Same thing now. If I don't do anything, it would be like committing a crime." He raised his head and Ingrid felt the power of his gaze. "Seyss is going to Berlin. I know it. Don't you see? I can't *not* do anything."

"I suppose not."

"But I need you to come, too. I don't have time to learn my way around Berlin. You know Seyss, where he might go, where he might hide. You have a house there, don't you?"

"Two. One in the city, one on the lake in Babelsberg."

"And I imagine you spent some time there with him?"

"Yes." The admission left her feeling dirty, the more so because of the respect with which Judge treated her. God, how he was different from Erich and Bobby. Neither of them would have asked her to go to Berlin, they would have bloody well ordered her. The comparison to her former lovers coupled with his close physical proximity made Ingrid see Judge in a new light, and she found herself wondering what a future with someone like him might be like. All she'd had to look forward to with Bobby was a role as loving wife and doting mother, a life no different from the one her mother had lived, and *her* mother before that. It was an existence built on her family's wealth, standing, and service to the country—none of which counted for a damn any longer.

Feeling a desire to touch him, Ingrid leaned over and kissed his unshaven cheek. "I haven't thanked you for saving my life."

Judge brushed the spot, the hint of a smile lightening his anxious mien. "Does that mean you'll go to Berlin?"

Ingrid bit her lip, wanting to say yes but hesitating and hating herself for it. Here was the chance her wounded conscience had dreamed of, the opportunity to act not as a German but as a woman true only to herself, and she was afraid to say yes. Staring into Judge's eyes, she drew from him the courage she didn't have herself.

"I can't *not* do anything," she said. And as the words escaped her mouth, she understood that responsibility was something one took even when one didn't want to.

"So, I convinced you?" he said.

Ingrid laughed softly. "Yes. But I've no idea how we'll get there."

NINE RAILWAY CARS TETHERED TO one another sat on a weed-strewn siding bordering a meadow on the eastern outskirts of Frankfurt. The cars were very old, all sleepers whose chalky green paint and immaculate yellow script had been eaten away by rust and neglect. A few letters were still visible: A flowery *D*; a faded *B*; the word *bahn*.

At first glance, the cars looked abandoned, their place on the rails sacrificed years ago to troop transports, flatbeds, and the unsparing commitment to "total war." But a closer look testified to their resilience. Wooden stairs and handrails descended from each doorway. An American flag drooped from a makeshift flagpole and a brace of military policemen bustled from one car to the next, climbing the stairs and pulling open the doors.

The railroad cars constituted one of seven "separation centers" in Frankfurt where members of the German armed forces could turn themselves in to be processed out of the military and returned to civilian life. Each man was promised ten marks, a half loaf of bread, some lard, cigarettes, and a one-way ticket home. Seventy-odd days after the end of hostilities, the flow of soldiers had slowed to a trickle.

Judge held Ingrid's hand as they walked across the clearing. If anyone asked, they were husband and wife. A day and a night together and already they wore the easy familiarity of a longtime couple. In dribs and drabs, men approached from all corners of the field, gathering in front of the first car in line. Ingrid tugged his hand and pulled him close. "Stop, Major," she said. "Look at these men, how they're walking, how they are carrying themselves. You have to walk like that, too. Slow down a little. Drop your head. Pretend you don't want to be here."

"I don't," he said. "Believe me."

Ingrid crossed him with a stern look. "You are humiliated."

Humiliated. The word sent a jolt of revulsion right down his spine. Judge stopped in midstride, newly aware of his prideful gait. He watched the Germans filing across the field. He wouldn't have said they looked beaten, just tired, their step hesitant rather than directed. Posture all but forgotten. *Humiliated.* And he realized he was seeing the physical manifestation of their survivor's penance.

Judge let go of Ingrid's hand and moved off toward the railway cars. Tucking in his chin, he viewed the world from the beneath the protection of a wary brow. He let his back slump and his chest sag, not overdoing it. He kept his stride even but unhurried. After a minute, they reached the sparse assembly gathered near the lead car.

He was dressed like the men around him, which was to say as a civilian, and poorly. He wore black trousers and a gray plaid workshirt. The garments were threadbare and filthy, and he was beginning to suspect the pants were ridden with lice. He'd bought the outfit from a man living at the *guterbahnhof* for a dollar and a pack of Lucky's. Another dollar had convinced the man to throw in his shoes. As for socks and underwear, Judge would keep his own. To hell with the risk!

A shrill whistle pierced the air. "I want one line starting here," shouted a private from his perch at the head of the stairs. "Single file, if you please, ladies. We are now open for business."

The shabby gathering fell into place reluctantly, like children heading back to school after summer break. A few of the hardier types hustled back and forth among them, barking out commands to straighten the line as if addressing a platoon standing for inspection. Military tradition died hard.

Judge drew Ingrid aside. "I don't know how long this will take. Find some shade and get some sleep."

"Still remember what unit you served in?"

He touched a finger to his forehead. "Don't worry, it's all up here."

Ingrid gave his arm a confident pat. "Then, Feldwebel Dietrich, I suggest you get moving."

Judge joined the line and in a matter of minutes was swallowed up in its ranks. No one looked at him oddly. No one questioned his presence. Why should they? Hair unkempt and greasy, beard working past a stubble, he was just another German who wanted to get home.

He was the enemy.

"Name!"

"Karl Dietrich."

"Pay book?"

"I'm sorry, I haven't got it. It's lost."

The sergeant looked up at Judge from behind a broad walnut desk, his lantern jaw and low brow twisted into a frustrated knot. Shaking his head, he plucked a form from an overstuffed tray, wrote the name Karl Dietrich upon it, then stamped it twice. "Another one ain't got his papers. Jesus H. Christ. Betcha he doesn't know who Hitler was either. *Der Führer,* huh? Ring a bell?"

Judge was standing inside the cabin of the first railroad car. The original furnishings had been ripped out—compartments, banquettes, the works—and replaced with a line of identical desks, cabinets, and unsmiling clerks. The place had all the charm of an induction center on Staten Island.

"*Hemd auf,*" ordered the sergeant. Shirt off.

Judge unbuttoned the plaid shirt and placed it on the table, only to have it flung back in his face a second later. "Get that piece of garbage off my desk!" the sergeant screamed. "Friggin' kraut. Just 'cause he's got fleas, wants to give 'em to everybody else. All right, Fritz, raise that left arm up high, let Uncle Sam see if you've been a naughty boy."

Raising his arm, Judge followed the sergeant's gaze to the flank of his bicep. He was being checked for the blood-group tattoo given to members of the SS. All down the cabin, Germans stood in similar poses, an unintentional parody of the Hitler *gruss.*

He was the enemy.

"You're clear." The sergeant stamped the form again, then handed it to Judge. "Take this to the next car. Give it to the doc. *Schnell! Schnell!*"

Judge picked up his shirt and made his way to the second railway car. A sign above the transom read Medical Examinations. Please Remove Your Clothing. Some wiseacre had drawn a line through the word *Examination* and written *Experiments* below it. Judge scooted down the passageway, taking his place at the end of a line ten deep. He removed his trousers, shirt, and undergarments, rolled them into a tight bundle, and tucked them under his arm. A quarter of an hour passed and the line didn't budge. More and more men filled the passageway. The space grew cramped, the smell rank and overwhelming. Momentarily, there was a commotion at the rear of the car. A voice yelled from behind him, "Move it! Coming through! Doc's here." A paunchy corporal snapping a leather riding quirt to his thigh passed by. He walked slowly, prodding the naked men in their genitals with the tip of the quirt, gifting each with a rude remark. "I seen bigger balls on a Chihuahua. That bratwurst or a knockwurst? Can't tell the difference myself. Would you look at that cannon cleaner? Heil Hitler indeed!" Spotting the disgust darkening Judge's face, he flicked the quirt at his rear, raising a florid welt. "Probably like that, don't you?"

Judge felt his every muscle tense as a prelude to snatching the quirt and shoving it down the obnoxious corporal's throat. Yet even as his neck flushed and he rolled forward on the balls of his feet, another emotion queered his rage—tempering it as a dash of bitters softens gin—and he realized he wasn't angry at all, but ashamed.

A firm hand squeezed his shoulder. "Calm down," whispered the soldier behind him. "Your *persilschein* will do you a lot more good than beating up that prick."

Judge turned, saying only "*Ja. Danke.*"

He was the enemy.

Just then, the doctor arrived. He was a German, like Hansen from Camp 8. A local recruited to do the Americans' work. Soon after, the line began to move.

The examination took less than two minutes. A peek at his throat and ears. A stethoscope to his chest. "Breathe deeply. Again." And a few questions. "History of tuberculosis? Gonorrhea? Syphilis?"

Judge answered no to all of the above.

"Fine, then," the doctor said, giving him a wink to go along with the red stamp on his papers. "Off to the front with you."

"SIT DOWN, DIETRICH. MY NAME is Schumacher. You look surprised to see a countryman in an American uniform. Don't be, there are a lot of us."

Judge was in car number three. An interview, he'd been told. Nothing more. Schumacher carried the easy authority of an officer born to the caste. Forty with black eyes, black hair, and a face that looked as if it had been stamped from pig iron. A colonel in the Signal Corps, if you believed his rank and insignia. Judge knew better. Counterintelligence was more like it. A Nazi hunter.

"You state here that you served in the Wehrmacht for six years, first with the Third Panzer Corps, General von Seydlitz commanding, then the Sixth Army under von Paulus."

"Seventy-sixth Infantry Division." Judge shifted in his seat, a witness giving false testimony. His war record mirrored that of Ingrid's oldest brother, Heinz, killed at Kharkov in '43. She'd told him all she knew, then grilled him on the facts for an hour. If any questions arose about what he'd done after Kharkov, he was prepared to say he had deserted.

"I take it then you spent some time in Stalingrad."

Judge said yes, and explained that he'd been wounded and airlifted to the rear before the encirclement. It was a safe enough lie. Few men had made it out of Stalingrad alive.

Schumacher looked impressed. "Lucky sod."

Judge nodded, then asked, "May I be so bold, Colonel, to inquire where you served?" He wanted Schumacher to do the talking.

"With Rommel in Africa. I was picked up at El Alamein. It was a short war, I'm afraid. I've been in the States for the last three years. Kansas. A marvelous place. Wide open spaces."

"Ah, America," Judge replied. "The Yankees. Mickey Mouse. Perhaps one day I shall go."

"Perhaps." Schumacher picked up Judge's personnel sheet and stud-ied it. "We've checked your name, Dietrich, against our books for those wanted for automatic arrest or intelligence interest. A lot of Karl Dietrichs on the list, but none listed with the Sixth Army. We're look-ing for SS primarily. Frankly, you look the type. Sly. Too smart for your own good. Sure you weren't one of Himmler's bootlickers?"

"No, sir."

"Sind Sie Kamerade?"

"No, sir."

Schumacher sighed and gave a begrudging smile. "I've been told to accept you at your word. Prisons too full as it is, you understand." He picked up a rubber stamp and held it poised above the sheet. A B stamp meant automatic discharge and a *persilschein*. Anything else meant trans-fer to a detention facility until more evidence could be dug up, either for or against. It was the risk Judge had to take to procure a ticket to Berlin. Suddenly, Schumacher dropped the stamp on the desk. "One question, Dietrich: your accent. I can't quite place it."

Judge had his answer ready. "Berlin, sir."

"Ah, Berlin." Schumacher said it with satisfaction, as if his dilemma were solved. But then he inquired further, "Where exactly?"

"Weissensee." The district where Judge's mother had grown up.

"Wannsee?"

Maybe Schumacher had lost part of his hearing. Or maybe he knew better. Judge sat up straighter, speaking louder to drive the anxiety from his voice. "No, sir. Weissensee. In the northern part of town."

Schumacher leaned across the desk, his black eyes boring down on Judge. "You mean eastern, Dietrich."

"I beg your pardon, sir?"

"These days Weissensee is in the *eastern* sector of Berlin. Naturally, you're aware that residents returning to the Soviet zone are subject to internment and interview before being granted a return visa? I hear it's a long wait. Two months or so."

"Wannsee," Judge blurted. "Near the lake. It's very beautiful."

"Ah, Wannsee. I thought that's what you said."

Schumacher picked up the stamp and with a mighty fist, pummeled the sheet. Judge dared a glance. A red B graced the bottom of the page.

HE HAD FILLED OUT HIS P-4 form, listing his name, his relatives, and his home address—all wonderfully fictitious. He had sat through a lecture on the proper manner for Germans to address American soldiers— it could be summarized in one word, "don't"—and a film narrated by Jimmy Stewart extolling the virtues of democracy. He'd sworn that he had never been a member of the Nazi party. He'd been handed a freshly typed document proclaiming him free of all ties to the German Army and the National Socialist Workers' party and eligible for any and all types of employment. His very own *persilschein*. He could use the same document to apply for a passport, a birth certificate, even a driver's license. He'd been given ten marks, a new pair of shoes (Florsheims!), and a paper bag crammed with tinned meats, bread, chocolate, and cigarettes. Most important, though, he'd received a ticket authorizing him to travel to Berlin on the next available transport.

Three hours after stepping inside the first railway car of Voluntary Separation Center 3, Frankfurt, Karl Dietrich was free to go.

Judge found Ingrid lying in the grass drinking a pint of orange juice given her by a smitten GI. He helped her to her feet and explained that a bus was leaving for Berlin in an hour from a transit center a kilometer away. The two jogged the entire distance, presenting themselves to a buck private manning the gate.

"I have a ticket for Berlin," Judge said, coating his English with a viscous German accent.

"Bus is full. We'll put you down for day after tomorrow. Name?"

Judge looked to his right and left. Seeing no troops nearby, he reached into his pocket and took out a twenty-dollar bill. "I need two seats on the bus. *Today.*"

The private clipped the bill from his hand, took his ticket, and returned his eyes to his clipboard. "Well? What're you waiting for? Bus leaves in thirty minutes."

CHAPTER

43

"WELCOME TO ANDREWS BARRACKS," shouted a bulky figure moving along the column of idling trucks. "Officers gather to the right and stay put. We'll get you inside, assign you a billet pronto, so you can get to bed before midnight. You Bettys who work for a living, grab your gear and come with me. We've got a few of our finest tents set up and awaiting your inspection."

Seyss slung his duffel bag over a shoulder and jumped from the rear of the transport. He followed the officer in front of him, moving to the right as instructed, crossing the pavement to a fringe of grass and waiting there. He was curious to discover exactly where in Berlin Andrews Barracks was located. A canopy covered the truck's rear bay, and as night fell, he'd been robbed of the chance to spot familiar landmarks. About thirty minutes ago, he thought he'd glimpsed some water, but that was no help. Lakes and canals crisscrossed the entire city. All he knew was that he was somewhere in the American sector, that is, in the southwest part of town. The lack of large buildings and the few clusters of trees still standing made him guess a residential district, either Steglitz or Zehlendorf.

Dropping his duffel, Seyss walked in a small circle. The corroded silhouettes of bomb-fractured buildings and burnt homes hovered in the distance like ghosts beyond the pale. The air stank of smoke and sewage and rang with the frenetic rattle of soldiers on the move. Behind him a mountain of rubble shimmered in the moonlight like a medieval cairn. To the south, he caught the flicker of an open fire, then another. He felt as if he were in Carthage after it had been sacked. But instead of sadness, he felt pride.

"We lost," he whispered, "but dammit, we gave them a fight."

Up and down the road, men continued to pour from the transports, a khaki stream disappearing into the darkening sapphire sky. The convoy of thirty-odd trucks, jeeps, and armored personnel carriers had left Frankfurt at eleven that morning, their cargo an E detachment of soldiers-cum-administrators sent to implement the rudiments of civic government in the crushed German capital. Seyss had bullied his way into their ranks, posing as an errant public affairs officer attached to Secretary of War Henry Stimson's party who'd missed his ride to Berlin two days earlier. The secretary promised leniency so long as he arrived before the commencement of the second plenary session, set for 10:00 A.M. tomorrow at the Cecilienhof in Potsdam. No one questioned his story. Nor did they ask for his papers. If he wanted to go to Berlin, they were glad to have him. There were too few Americans there as it was.

A few minutes later, the same loudmouthed soldier reemerged from the dusk, requesting the officers to pick up their campaign bags and follow him. Seyss complied, happy to be on the move. His legs were stiff from the long ride. Twelve hours to cover three hundred miles. The small group walked down a dirt path lined with whitewashed stones, then cut through the range of rubble mountains. A large placard set to the right of the path proclaimed Andrews Barracks. Gross Lichterfelde, Berlin. Established July 6, 1945. Second Armored Division. First Airborne Army. Beyond it loomed a campus of imperious gray buildings arrayed on three sides of a parade ground. He recognized them as surely as he would his home. Fifty meters ahead rose the proud halls of the Lichterfelde Kaserne, home to the SS Leibstandardte Adolf Hitler. Sight of his first posting as an officer nine years before.

A squad of military policemen stood in a semicircle next to the sign, and as Seyss passed, one shone his flashlight directly in his face. Seyss squinted his eyes, waving away the light. "Watch that, will you?"

"Mind taking off your cap, sir?"

Seyss took another step before stopping. "Excuse me?"

"Your cap, sir," the voice barked again. "Take it off."

Seyss paused, and turned slowly. The six military policemen had assumed a distinctly menacing posture. One stepped forward from their ranks, a short barrel-chested man with a Slav's heavy brow and the same truncated speech. "You. You're the man hitched a ride from Frankfurt? That right?"

"Yes," Seyss answered, smiling now. "That's right. Is there a problem?"

"Over here, sir. Now." The squat MP unsnapped his holster, withdrew his pistol and held it at port arms.

This is it, thought Seyss. *It was a trap all along. They opened up the bag and I walked right on in.* Retracing his steps, he brought himself to a halt in front of the Slav. Surprisingly, he felt no dread at the prospect of being captured, just a resigned fatigue. He brushed the cap from his head and stood there, arms thrust out in a gesture of bemused ignorance. *Go ahead*, he dared them. *Cuff me or shoot me. Just make up your mind quickly because in a second I'm going to draw my own gun and then none of us will have any choices.*

"Name?"

"Captain Daniel Gavin. Public Affairs." It was the name of a man he'd killed in the Ardennes on Christmas Day and he wore his dog tags around his neck to prove it.

"Let me see a copy of your G-3, sir."

What a G-3 was, Seyss had no idea. Shaking his head, he said the usual crap about this being some kind of mix-up. His voice sounded far away. He wished he had something clever to add, some joke or aside that would lighten the air and show that this whole thing was a mistake. For the first time in his life, his mind was a blank. He'd exhausted his store of bullshit.

"Your G-3, Captain Gavin. *Your personnel records.* And a copy of your orders. Please, sir. Now."

"Yeah, yeah. I've got it right here." Seyss dropped to a knee, unzipped his duffel and ventured a hand inside. His fingers traveled over his SS-issue buck knife—a souvenir, should anyone ask—then perused the folds of the clothing he'd stolen from Frankfurt. The MPs had formed a tight circle around him. Six beams lit his every move, and in their hollow light he found his fighting voice.

Erich Seyss was dead, he told himself. Killed in Wiesbaden three nights ago. The search for him had been called off. There was no reason for the Americans to suspect that Gavin's killer was headed to Berlin. This was all some sort of cock-up. Had to be. He took a deep breath, trying hard to decide if he wanted to die. He hadn't expected to be given the choice.

Just then, an officer broke through the circle. He was panting, out of breath. "This the man, Pavlovich?"

"Yes, sir," answered the short policeman. "This is him. Name's Gavin."

"But . . . but . . ." The officer pointed at Seyss and took a labored breath. "But, Sergeant Pavlovich, this man is a captain," he said reprovingly. "Our suspect is a major with the MPs, not the engineers. Jesus!"

The squat policeman said, "You sure, Lieutenant Jameson?"

"Didn't you take a look at the bulletin? They included a picture for numbnuts like you. Ah, shit, just forget it." Jameson extended a hand to Seyss and helped him to his feet. "Excuse me, Captain. Things are a little crazy right now. Everyone is in a tizzy about the flag raising tomorrow. President coming and all. Hope it was no inconvenience to you."

But Seyss only half heard him. His ear was still tuned to the internal chorus singing his certain doom. "I beg your pardon?"

"Barracks are down the path a ways," continued Jameson. "Sorry 'bout the mistake. Good night, sir."

"Yes, uh, good night, then." Seyss swallowed hard, finding his mouth parched and his feet bolted to the ground. A second passed and he retook possession of his faculties. A flag raising, Jameson had mentioned. The president was coming. He'd been too shell-shocked to ask where and when. He would make it a point to check first thing in the morning. Bending to zip up his duffel bag, Seyss replaced his cap, then hurried off to catch the others.

HE LAY ON A COT, staring at the ceiling of his old room. Directly above him was a door—*a door!*—nailed to the ceiling by some hapless recruit in a hasty bid to patch a shell hole. The room no longer smelled of camphor and linseed but mildew and rot. The same shells that had ruined the ceiling had rent tremendous chunks of cement from the walls. Given the barracks' location, it was a wonder it was standing at all. Five hundred meters to the south ran the Teltow Canal, the city's outermost ring of defense. There, in the first days of April, Marshal Chuikov had lined up all his tanks and artillery, thousands of guns in all, and for three days rained shell upon shell into the city. A quick walk through the dormitory revealed that the Russians had stripped the place bare. Nothing of use remained. Not a toilet. Not a sink. Not a faucet or a doorknob. Not a chair. Not a lamp. Not a desk or a dresser. Nothing! Even the paint appeared to have been chipped from the walls.

Locusts!

Seyss turned onto his side and tucked an arm under his head. Someone had scratched the number 88 into the wall. The numeral eight stood for the eighth letter of the alphabet, *H*, and repeated, it meant *Heil Hitler.* Alone in the dark, he whispered the words, needing to hear them spoken aloud once more.

"Heil Hitler."

And in that moment, the past rushed forward and grabbed him, a relentless assault of sound and vision that stirred his soul and quickened his heartbeat.

"Heil Hitler."

A thousand jackboots slapped the concrete in perfect cadence, their immaculate thud resonating deep in his gut.

"Heil Hitler."

The clipped tenor of the drill sergeant's command set him at attention, while the crisp attack of the drummer's tattoo promised him a share of his country's imminent glory.

Seyss closed his eyes, but sleep refused to come. The certainty of his capture and the shock of his reprieve had left him unbalanced. He needed to focus his thoughts on the future, not the past. It was difficult. As far back as he could recall, there had been only war or the prospect of it. Even in his heyday as his nation's greatest sprinter, he'd looked forward to a career as a soldier. Now the war was lost and he was forced to consider what lay ahead, what lay beyond Potsdam. Beyond Terminal.

First thing tomorrow, he would inquire about the president's visit. If Truman was coming into Berlin, he wanted to know where and when. The opportunity might be too good to pass up.

More important was the meeting scheduled for ten o'clock in the morning at 24 Grosse Wannsee. The residence of Herr Joseph Schmundt, executive vice president of Siemens and devoted member of the Circle of Fire. Seyss wished he'd arrived a day earlier so that he'd have had adequate time to reconnoiter the site. The ambush in Wiesbaden had left him cautious. The prospect of walking into an unknown building made him antsy. Maybe it was just a runner's aversion to relying on others.

Regardless of his worries, he would have to go. He couldn't expect to make his way to Potsdam and do his job without proper information about the security measures implemented to protect the Big Three. At a minimum, he needed to know the layout of the Cecilienhof, a floor plan of the homes where each leader was staying, their daily schedules, and if possible, a rota of the guards stating when they changed shifts. Most of all, he needed a fail-safe route across the Russian lines and into the conference area. Egon Bach had promised him all that and more.

Drawing solace from his lack of choice, Seyss finally let himself relax. There was a certain comfort to be found in the absence of alternatives. Resignation, some might call it. Duty, others. Seyss preferred fate. It had the added allure of predestination.

"Heil Hitler," he said again, this time silently. And falling into a deep sleep, he once more returned to the past, to an eternal moment when his life stretched promisingly before him, when his happiness lay in the wicked grin of an eighteen-year-old girl, when the Fatherland teetered on the precipice of destiny.

CHAPTER

44

THE GRÜNEWALD WAS A PICTURE OF controlled chaos.

A dozen trucks had arrived before them, a restless, belching column of iron and steel parked beside a grass berm deep in Berlin's largest park. Engines growling, they disgorged their human cargo. The passengers, most of whom like Judge—or rather, Karl Dietrich—were former German soldiers in transit to their homes, fled from the trucks and milled about a dirt clearing, huddled gray figures drifting in and out of the thickening dusk. Judge estimated their number to be three hundred, maybe more. It was too dark to tell. He wondered why everyone was hanging around, why they weren't legging their way through the surrounding woods back to home and family. A second glance supplied him the answer. A cordon of soldiers ringed the clearing, every man carrying a rifle at port arms.

Concerned, Judge looked closer. A dozen GIs walked among the Germans. They carried flashlights and billy clubs, the batons to lift suspicious chins and the lights to rake unshaven faces. They were singling out the bigger men; not the tall ones so much as the ones with some meat on their bones. Most had dark hair and a certain wideness of beam, and for a terrifying moment, Judge thought they were looking for him. Word had spread that he'd passed himself off as a kraut, he told himself.

He'd been an idiot to think he could get by unnoticed. The GIs prodded the larger men toward a fenced-in pen that Judge only then saw a hundred meters down the road. A few Germans resisted and the prodding turned nasty in a hurry. Shouts of pain and anger erupted from every corner of the clearing. The word *"arbeitspartei"* was uttered and Judge relaxed a notch.

It wasn't a manhunt. It was an impress gang.

Ducking inside the truck, he kept a tight hold on Ingrid's hand as the other passengers jostled past and jumped from the tailgate. A mild panic overtook him, a dreary mix of self-pity and anger. He didn't have to worry about being captured, just being stuck in a work gang.

The shouting grew louder as scuffles began to break out all over. A whistle shrieked and many of the GIs abandoned the cordon to join the fray. Ten seconds later, the clearing had devolved into a tangled braid of khaki, green, and gray. Judge figured that if he and Ingrid could slip along the side of their truck, then slide in front of its hood, they could make it across the road and into the impenetrable dark of the woods beyond. He explained the situation to Ingrid, then whispered, "Stay close. No matter what you do, don't leave me."

Judge threw a leg over the tailgate and jumped to the ground. Lifting a hand, he helped Ingrid down. Five feet away, a guard remained as immobile as a statue. Judge stepped toward him, asking in clumsy English, "What's going on?"

"We need some men to build us a decent HQ," answered the guard, his jaw moving under the helmet's lip and nothing else. "You krauts are stupid not to cooperate. Where else you gonna get three squares a day? Move along, now."

But Judge had no intention of "moving along," at least not to any work camp. He turned to his right and advanced along the side of the truck. He kept his eyes on the ground, his step purposeful but not hurried. *If I don't see them, they won't see me:* motto of a delinquent's youth. He shot a glance over the hood. It was less than twenty yards to the woods, closer than he'd thought. He slunk past the cab, then the wheel well, clutching Ingrid's hand as he cut between the trucks.

Just then, a billy club landed hard on his shoulder and he knew he didn't have a chance. *"Halten Sie sofort!"*

Judge turned to face a jug-eared sergeant backed by two privates. For another second, he considered fleeing. He told himself to drop Ingrid's hand and run like hell. A dash into the inky anonymity of the trees. One look at the grin animating the privates' eager faces robbed him of the notion. *Try it,* they were daring him. *We need the exercise.*

"Name?" the sergeant asked. He was a pudgy kid with a dimpled chin, red hair, and, of course, the jug ears. He spoke decent German.

"Dietrich," responded Judge.

"And her?"

"My wife."

"Where do you live?"

"Schopenhauerstrasse eighty-three," said Ingrid. "It's not far from here."

The sergeant chewed on the answer, his eyes taking a long walk up and down Ingrid's physique. Judge looked at her, too: a momentary glance that confirmed just how mismatched the two of them were. She was dressed in her navy cashmere cardigan, a white shirt and flannel slacks; he, in the torn and stinking garments of a railway-dwelling mendicant. Even after a twelve-hour journey her hair was in the finest order, her cheeks clean, her smile freshly pressed. As for him, he didn't need a mirror to confirm the worst. His hair was two days greasy and curling like an untamed vine. His beard, all nettles and bramble. His fingernails were black with grime, but when he rubbed them along his pant leg, they came away white with a coating of fine dust. DDT sprayed to kill head and body lice. What a pair they made: The princess and the pauper.

"Come with me," said the sergeant. He led them up the road a hundred yards to a series of blowsy command tents pitched in a line on the woods' edge. He pulled back a flap and showed the two of them to a trestle table set in the far corner, then addressed himself to a corporal who stood consulting a city map of Berlin that hung on the wall. "Anything happening in Wannsee tonight?"

The corporal ran his hand along the multicolored street map, as if gleaning information from its waxed surface. "No, Sarge. All quiet."

The sergeant motioned them to sit. "My name's Mahoney," he said, switching back to German. "Military police. I don't know when you left

Berlin but it isn't the same place it used to be. I'm not talking about combat damage. Wannsee got through pretty much intact, so you caught a good piece of luck, there. What I mean to say is that this town is a scary place at night. You do not want to be out after dark." He poked a finger at Ingrid. "Especially you, ma'am."

Ingrid shot Judge a glance and he shook his head imperceptibly. "You're very kind to warn us, Sergeant," she said, "but we really must be going. My mother is quite ill. I'm afraid it's a question of hours rather than days."

Mahoney continued as if she hadn't said a word. "It's the Russians I'm talking about. They're not much for respecting our zonal boundaries. At night, they take to the streets in packs. Trophy brigades, they call themselves. You'd think that after two months alone in this town they'd have taken everything they wanted. Unfortunately, they're after more than just loot." He offered Judge a respectful nod. "Begging your pardon, Mr. Dietrich, but your wife is what they're after."

Judge began to answer, but just then a tall captain strode into the tent calling for Mahoney. The sergeant shot to his feet and faced him. "Sir?"

"Any servicemen on that transport just in? Officers?" His crackling voice was redolent of hominy grits and black-eyed peas. A son of the South.

"No, sir. Strictly krauts and a few dozen DPs. Czechs this time."

The captain walked to a bulletin board next to the map of Berlin and posted a circular bearing the photograph of a dark-haired American officer with a solid jaw and a bull neck. It was a photograph of Devlin Judge taken on Staten Island the day he'd received his commission. "Take a gander when you get a chance," he drawled. "Patton himself wants this sumbitch's balls on his plate for breakfast. Sending us some of his men to help find him. Oh, and by the way, he may be traveling in the company of a lady friend."

Mahoney saluted as the captain departed the tent, then took a long look at the picture—ten seconds, by Judge's count. "As I was saying, Herr Dietrich, you don't want to be out on the streets alone with your wife." He was looking straight at Judge, eyes wandering from his jaw to his nose to his hair. "We spend most of our days dealing with rape and murder. What I'd like you to do is to stay with us tonight. Don't worry, we won't throw you on a work team. I can offer you a few blankets, a Spam sandwich, and some coffee. That should do until morning. Once the sun's up, the city's a different place."

Judge sat motionless in his chair, stiller than he'd ever been before. The absurdity of his situation was too much for him to comprehend, so he decided to understand none of it. An American disguised as a German sitting within plain sight of his own wanted poster while the noncom in charge was practically singing *"On the Good Ship Lollipop"* instead of arresting him.

Keeping his eyes to the floor—if only to avoid his own accusing gaze—he replied, "I'm sorry, but we'll have to take the risk."

Mahoney looked at Ingrid for support. Receiving none, he spun in his chair and asked his corporal, "Watkins, can you get these people back to Wannsee safe and sound?"

"What? Now?"

"Lickety-split, Watkins. How 'bout it?"

Judge stared hard at Mahoney, feeling a sudden fondness for the earnest soldier. He recalled a time when helping a man facing tough times was the normal thing to do. *The only thing to do.*

"Sorry, Sarge," said Watkins. "Everything that's not tied down has been requisitioned for the parade tomorrow."

"President's coming into town for a visit," said Mahoney by way of explanation. Standing, he shrugged his shoulders. "You're on your own, then."

He placed a supportive hand under Ingrid's arm and guided her outside. But as they approached the dirt road that separated the parade of tents from the forest, he slowed, shaking his head as if thinking twice about the matter. "Ah, what the hell? I'll drive you myself. Be my good deed for the day. Where did you say you lived?"

Ingrid cleared her throat before answering, glancing toward Judge for advice. The address she'd given Mahoney belonged to Rosenheim, the Bach family home in Wannsee, so named for its well-tended rose gardens. Rosenheim sat atop the list of spots Judge planned to reconnoiter in the morning, including residences of Bach family friends where he believed Erich Seyss might be hiding.

"Schopenhauerstrasse," Judge volunteered reluctantly. "In Wannsee."

"You can show me the way," said Mahoney. "Jump in."

Judge gave Ingrid his hand and helped her into the rear of the jeep, then took his seat. Listening to the engine turn over, Mahoney goosing the accelerator, he had the disconcerting notion that events were spiraling out of control, that he'd committed himself to a course that could only end in disaster, and he shivered. The jeep slowed as it approached the main road, waiting for a fleet of trucks to pass. The same convoy that had brought Judge to Berlin was headed back to Frankurt to pick up the next batch tomorrow.

Mahoney eased the jeep a foot closer to the road, anxious for the trucks to pass.

"Sergeant," a familiar voice shouted from somewhere behind them. "Stop right now! Do not go any farther."

Recognizing the syrupy drawl, Judge spun to find Darren Honey fifty yards away, running toward the jeep. Mahoney patted him on the leg. *"Nur ein Moment."* Just a second.

But Judge didn't have a second. The recollection of von Luck's stiff corpse left no doubt about Honey's intentions. Balling his fingers into a tight fist, he hit Mahoney in the jaw with a pistonlike jab, then shouldered him out of the jeep. The engine sputtered as the jeep lost its gear. Judge slid behind the wheel before it stalled altogether, finding first gear and gunning the vehicle between the last two trucks. Ingrid yelled in time to the blaring horn, but by then they were over the grass berm and into the woods.

"What are you doing?" Ingrid shouted.

Judge couldn't waste time explaining his actions. "You know your way through here?"

"Maybe. I'm not sure," she answered, flustered.

"I need a yes or a no. Now!"

"Y-yes," she stammered.

"Then get us into the city. I don't care where. We've got to disappear."

Ingrid pulled herself into the front seat. Leaning forward against the dash, she extended an arm toward manicured walkways that lay in the headlights' crescent. "Follow these paths. They'll lead to us out of the woods."

"How far?"

"Five minutes. Maybe ten."

Judge shifted his vision between the grassy landscape in front and the darkness that pursued. Just then, the first headlights appeared behind them and he knew they didn't have that long.

CHAPTER

45

A HALF MILE FROM THE American command post, they had disappeared into a dense wood with a cover so thick as to block out every sign of the sparkling night sky and the late-rising moon. It was the forest his mother had described sitting on his bedside reading the Brothers Grimm. A deep, dark, living thing, scented of pine and oak, and teeming with hobgoblins and fairies and, yes, even werewolves—though they looked more like the half-starved DPs crowding every road in Germany than any fanciful creature. It was the forest where Hansel and Gretel had gotten lost, but instead of a gingerbread house there was a ruined flak tower, a crippled ten-story superstructure where Hitler had positioned his antiaircraft batteries to discourage the marauding hoards from raining destruction upon the capital of his Thousand-Year Reich. It was the forest where Tristan wed Isolde, but all traces of its magical incarnations had disappeared, probably hauled off by the Russians, along with everything else.

The pair of headlights had expanded to a second, then a third, and Judge felt as if the entire army were after them. Two minutes into his fool's run, his headstart had been whittled down to three hundred yards and with every passing second was growing shorter. Rounding a sharp corner, he shot a glance over his shoulder. A bank of Eugenias momentarily blocked his view of the pursuing jeeps. Spotting his chance, he steered the jeep away from the security of the gravel walk and doused the headlights. He was driving among the trees now, weaving in and out like a skier negotiating a slalom course, careful to keep a ninety-degree angle away from the walkway. Beneath branches sagging with a summer's bounty of nuts and cones, the ground was feathered with a crop of knee-high grass, and with every unseen rut and gully, he grunted, all the while accelerating madly. Abruptly, he cut the engine and coasted to a halt a hundred yards on.

Ingrid raised herself in the seat, staring into the dark wood. "Who are they?"

"*Shh,*" Judge cautioned, ear attuned to the highly revving engines. Their insistent whine grew, and suddenly he could make out the trace of their headlights. Wheels skidding on the clay and gravel, the jeeps rounded the Eugenias. He held his breath, expecting the lights to bob as they, too, left the path, and a moment later to be illuminated in their beams. But the jeeps roared on, advancing on a phantom prey.

"*Who are they?*" Ingrid demanded again.

Judge answered as he restarted the engine, irritated by her obstinacy. "The same folks who arranged for the detour in Heidelberg. The fellas who want us to think Erich Seyss is dead. Is that good enough?"

Ingrid tucked in her chin, taken aback by his sharp response. "I suppose it has to be."

Judge pushed the jeep pell-mell through the trees, the howling engine a pitch-perfect echo of his own anxieties. Every few seconds, he turned his head to scout the encroaching dark. He saw nothing, but still his neck bristled. Overnight, he'd become the hunted, not the hunter, and the new role fit him as poorly as the lice-ridden clothing he'd picked up that morning. But there was more. At some point during the last twenty-four hours, he'd crossed over an interior meridian into unknown waters. He'd abandoned the rigid structure of his previous life, renounced his worship of authority, and forsworn his devotion to rules and regulation. He'd tossed Hoyle to the wind and he didn't care.

Yet it was this very betrayal of his past that confirmed his most closely held beliefs. That the rules man made were subordinate to those made for him. And when it came to choosing, a man had to use his heart, not his head.

Fine summation, Counselor, he added, mockingly. *Tell me one thing, then. If you're so damned sure of yourself, why are you shaking in your boots?*

Five minutes later, the curtain of foliage parted and they came to a large clearing. A café was visible to their right, and next to it, a large manmade pond, the kind where he would have launched a sailboat with Ryan. Judge swung toward the squat building, dodging a line of birch trees, as Ingrid read the sign above the entry.

"Rumplemeyer's," she announced. "If we follow the path leading to the café, it's only a few hundred meters to Zehlendorf."

"You mean the city?"

"Yes, a residential quarter in the southwest corner of town."

"We need a place to stay, somewhere reasonably safe. We can't risk sleeping outside again tonight. It's your city. Got any ideas?"

"Just our house in town and some of Papa's friends."

"Not good enough." The presence of Honey in Berlin made it impossible for Ingrid and Judge to seek refuge in any of her old haunts. If Honey was working with Patton and Patton was close to Egon Bach, then Judge had to consider all those addresses blown. "Isn't there some-place only you know about? At one of your old girlfriends', maybe? At a boyfriend's, even?"

"There is a place I know," Ingrid said haltingly, "an apartment not far from the university where I lived while a student."

He could read what was coming next. "But Seyss knows about it?"

"He was the reason I took it. It was our hideaway."

"That was six years ago," Judge said sternly. "Don't you think they've found a new tenant by now?"

It was her turn to offer a rebuke. "No, Major, you don't understand. I didn't rent the place. I bought it."

"And Egon? Does he know about it, too?"

"No," Ingrid replied adamantly. "It was our secret. Erich's and mine."

Judge mulled over their options. Even if Seyss was in Berlin, the odds were against his hiding out at his and Ingrid's old love nest. The U.N. war crimes dossier stated that he'd been stationed at Lichterfelde

Kaserne before the war. If Egon hadn't already fixed him up with a place, he'd have a dozen of his own in mind. While Judge desperately wanted to find Seyss, the idea of getting the drop on him in the middle of the night without a weapon wasn't exactly what he'd had in mind. Still, it might be an unexpected opportunity. Catch Scyss on the sly. Have him wrapped up and in custody by morning. To his realist's eye, it sounded too pat. Either way, they didn't have much choice.

"How far to this place?"

"Eichstrasse is in Mitte. I'd say eight kilometers."

About five miles. Fifty city blocks in Manhattan. A breeze if they could stay clear of the trophy brigades Mahoney had warned them about. Cocking his head, he listened for the retaliatory growl of his frustrated pursuers. The night was silent.

"Can you walk it?" he asked Ingrid. "Once in the city, we'll stand out like a sore thumb in this jeep. The first American patrol we see will either shoot us or have us arrested."

Ingrid smiled with the knowledge of a secret strength. "Yes, Major, I believe I can."

Judge slowed the jeep and when she'd stepped out, drove it a little ways into the woods. He found a dense grove of bushes and nosed the vehicle slowly into its embrace. Sliding from the wheel, he freed the crushed branches until the jeep was partially hidden from view. Hardly a masterful job of camouflage, but it would do until morning.

Rubbing sap from his palms, he jogged back to Ingrid.

"All right, Pocahontas," he said. "Lead the way."

THE BUILDING ON EICHSTRASSE WAS standing, and except for a fractured chimney and a corps of broken windows, undamaged. They'd circled the block twice before approaching, checking alleys and doorways for signs of surveillance. The neighborhood wasn't deserted; it was dead. Not a lamp burned from a single paneless window. Not a soul walked the streets. Neither a German, nor an American, nor for that matter a Russian was in sight. The feared trophy brigades had taken the night off.

Ingrid's apartment was on the third floor. "Just a studio," she had warned him, forgetting for a moment that they had more important concerns than the size of her apartment. They climbed the stairs quietly and when they neared her door, Judge signaled for her to remain behind. He approached as stealthily as he knew how, rolling his shoe from heel to toe, easing his weight onto the distressed floorboards. In his hand he carried a bent crowbar he'd picked up on the street; fine if he wanted to brain someone, but it wouldn't hold up long against a loaded pistol. Reaching the entry to her apartment he checked for signs of recent intrusion. A sheen of dust coated the brass doorknob. Cobwebs hugged the door frame. Laying an ear to the door, he listened. Nothing. If Seyss had been by, he'd kept his presence well hidden. Cautiously, Judge turned the knob to the right. Locked. Finding a rusted nail, he played with the keyhole until he'd picked the lock.

The apartment was empty. Even more surprising, it was untouched and as she'd left it six years before. Sitting squarely in the Soviet zone, maybe the Reds figured they'd get to it in their own time.

"Just a studio" meant just that: a large corner room with an armoire and chest of drawers set against one wall, a large bed against the other, with a couch and a coffee table in between. A mantle of dust an inch thick covered the furniture. Ingrid immediately tore off the bedspread and threw it into the corner. A few steps took her to the closet where she opened a Vuitton steamer trunk and removed a set of clean sheets.

"Don't just stand there," she said. "Get on the other side of the bed and give me a hand. It must be after two. I'm exhausted."

Judge did as he was told and in a few minutes the bed was made. He asked for another sheet and laid it atop the sofa, taking a few lap cushions into the hallway and pounding them until they were rid of dust. A quick check confirmed the absence of running water. Making use of a cleaning bucket, he went downstairs and found a spigot in the interior court of the building next door. A sign had been posted above it reading For Washing Only.

"Thank God, a little water," said Ingrid, seeing the full bucket.

Judge set in on the john. "You can't drink it until it's boiled."

"I wouldn't dare, but I do need to clean up a tad. Would you excuse me?"

"Sure." Judge walked around the apartment, yawning, stretching his arms, trying hard not to think of what had gone on here six years ago. The duvet Ingrid had laid on the bed was embroidered with the Bach family crest. Sitting, he struggled with the Latin motto: *Pax fortis, omnia.*

" 'In pcacc, strong. In battle strongest,' " Ingrid recited, sitting down next to him. "Charming, isn't it? Now you know why I kept it hidden."

"Better than mine."

"Oh? You have a crest as well?"

Judge dropped his head and laughed, but only for an instant. That was his Ingrid. The lady to her manservant. By now, he knew her well enough to know that her remark carried no condescension, just surprise and a genuine interest. Even without a penny in her purse, she would always be an aristocrat.

"Not a crest, no, but at least a motto. *'Nunc est bibendum.'* It means 'Now is the time to drink.' The old man was Irish. What do you expect?"

Ingrid grinned halfheartedly and when Judge looked closer he saw she was shivering. "You're cold?"

She shook her head. "I'm scared."

Judge put his arm around her. He tried to muster his most confident smile, but only managed to press his lips tightly together. Any rousing words would prove hollow encouragement. "Me, too."

"I wouldn't know it. You look like you were cut out for this type of thing."

"Me?" The thought of himself as a hardened soldier made him laugh. He looked at the crusts of dirt blackening his fingernails and cringed. "The only battles I fight are in the courtroom. It's a pretty placid affair, a few guys arguing with each other. Sometimes we even raise our voices. When it's over we go out and have lunch together."

"I saw how you struck General Carswell. You liked it."

"No," Judge retorted, picking out the sliver of derision in her voice. "I didn't." But even as he made his denial, his anger faded. She was right. He had liked it.

"I'm sorry," she said, laying her head on his shoulder. "I'm upset. I miss my son."

For once, Judge couldn't think of anything to say, so he remained quiet. Stirred by her presence, he drew her closer. It was a reflex, an instinct. No, he admitted to himself. It was desire, something he'd wanted to do since he'd first seen her; something his predetermined prejudices against the German *volk*, in general, and the Bachs, in particular, had prevented.

He brushed his nose against her vanilla-scented hair, smelling her, wanting her feminine scent to flush the omnipresent stink of charred wood and raw sewage from his nostrils. A delicate hand inside his shirt caused his breath to catch. Fingers skipped over his ribs, caressing his chest.

Judge tilted his head toward hers. He saw in her eyes the same desire that had gripped him at Jake's Joint and, that he now knew, had consumed him ever since. He kissed her softly, tasting her lips. She moaned, and pressed herself against him, and for the swiftest of moments, he thought, *I'm kissing a German*, and *I am kissing the enemy*, then he felt her mouth open to his and he knew she was simply a young woman who needed to be loved, a soul not so different from his own.

He kissed her long and deep, and she responded, searching hungrily for his tongue, her hands exploring his body, grasping, massaging him. Pent up for so long, his desire throbbed and grew hot inside him. Abruptly, he raised his head from hers, and for a moment they both stared at each other, a look of bemused surprise brightening their faces.

With a finger he traced the curve of her neck and her shoulders. He'd forgotten the silky feel of a woman's skin and his fingertips sent small currents of electricity dancing along his arm. "We're like a couple of teenagers."

She brushed his hair back from his forehead, drawing her hand gently across his cheek. Suddenly, she laughed huskily and pushed him flat onto the bed. "I never did this when I was a teenager."

"Did what?"

"Patience, Major Judge, and you'll find out."

Drawing up her skirt a notch or two, Ingrid guided a perfectly formed leg over him and straddled his chest. Slowly, she unbuttoned her blouse, freeing one arm, then another from her sleeves. Slipping a hand behind her back, she unclasped her brassiere and dropped it onto his belly. Posture erect, breasts bathed in the waning moonlight, she placed an ivory hand in his lap and began kneading him, moving her palm in slow circles as he lifted his hips to meet her. He touched his finger to her nipple and brushed it gently back and forth until it was erect, and Ingrid was quivering with anticipation. His body was suffused with a liquid warmth, an encompassing heat that pulsed in time to his heart. When he ran a finger over her lips, she shuddered noticeably.

"Now," she said.

Judge lifted her with his hands and guided her onto the bed next to him. For a few seconds, they stared at each other, intimate beyond their time together, each inviting the other into their soul. Eyes open wide, lips trembling with anticipation, Ingrid looked vulnerable yet supreme, eager yet frightened.

He moved slowly at first, tenderly. He kissed her shoulders and her neck, seeking diversion from the heat building in his loins. It was she who quickened their rhythm, she who rose to meet his thrusts. She was passionate and uncontrolled, and the volatile combination eclipsed anything he'd ever experienced. Her face grew flushed, her breath low and vibrant. She bit into his lip, fighting to stifle her moans.

"Devlin," she whispered, *"halte nicht. Halte nie."*

Judge tucked his face into her neck, aware that his movements were no longer his own. All of himself—his hopes and dreams, his fears and worries—was concentrated into a white-hot core at the center of her being. He closed his eyes and as he let himself go, he realized that his ardor for her extended beyond a physical craving and that Ingrid had rekindled in him the desire to love.

"What will you do?" she asked afterward.

"I'm going to find him," Judge said evenly. It didn't matter that he'd never been to Berlin before, he added for his own benefit, or that he didn't have so much as a scooter to get around, or that his own police were looking for him.

"Berlin is a big city," she said. "We walked for three hours to get here and we didn't even cross a quarter of it. He might be anywhere."

"If he were hiding, I'd give up. I'd say it was impossible. But he's not.

He's out and about. He's got a job to do and he's figuring out how to do it. Actually, I'm optimistic."

Smiling, Ingrid sat up on an elbow and ran a finger over his lips. "Optimistic, even?"

"Didn't you hear Sergeant Mahoney? President Truman is visiting Berlin today. All we've got to do is find out where and when and I'm betting Seyss will be there."

"I hope you'll let me go with you."

"The police'll be looking for the pair of us traveling together. We used up our ration of luck last night. Besides, there's something else I need you to do. I want you to get in touch with Chip DeHaven. You told me he'd written you that he'd be in Potsdam for the conference. Did he ask you to come up for a visit?"

"Well, yes, but I'm sure he was just being polite."

"Then let him show you his manners. He's your cousin. He'll have no choice but to see you when he learns you're in town. As a counselor to the president, I imagine he's quartered in Potsdam. Probably with Truman himself."

"I can't just go to Potsdam and tell Chip I'm here," Ingrid protested. "It belongs to the Russians now."

"That's true. We have to find someone to let DeHaven know you're in town."

"I'm afraid we're a little short of friends at the moment. Who do you propose?"

Judge asked himself who in Berlin might share his distrust of authority. The answer came in an instant.

Leaning closer to Ingrid, he ran a hand through her hair and whispered it in her ear.

46

Seyss rose at dawn, showered, and dressed in one of the fresh uniforms he'd taken from room 421 of the Frankfurt Grand. The walk to the mess hall was like a stroll down memory lane. Images of morning formation flooded his mind. He dismissed them outright. Nostalgia had no claim on his time today. Instead of herring, sausage, and hard rolls, he took eggs, bacon, and toast. The talk at the breakfast table was confined to one subject: Truman's visit to Berlin. The flag raising was set for twelve o'clock at the former Air Defense headquarters. On his way to the ceremony, the president would pass the length of the East–West Axis in review of the Second Armored Division. From the excited talk, Seyss gathered that practically every American soldier in Berlin would participate either in the parade or the ceremony, as would the cream of the American high command. Patton, Bradley, even Eisenhower, himself, were slated to attend.

It was, Seyss decided, the rarest of opportunities.

Newly confident, he crossed the parade ground and walked into the motor pool. A broad smile and a stiff bribe got him an MP's Harley-Davidson WLA, complete with windscreen, siren, saddlebags, and a rifle bucket (unfortunately empty). The mechanic was sorry he didn't have anything speedier. Everything else had been dragged out for the parade.

With a few hours before his meeting with Herr Doctor Schmundt in Wannsee, Seyss decided to make a tour of the capital. He was anxious to see how Berlin had fared, and more important, to discover the disposition of occupying troops in the different parts of the city. At Yalta, Stalin, Roosevelt, and Churchill had divided Berlin into three sectors. The Russians took the East, the British the Northwest, and the Americans the South and Southwest. After the war ended, the French crowed about wanting a piece for themselves, so the Brits carved a chunk from their sector and handed it over. Germany had become a cake, with all the victors claiming a piece.

Leaving Lichterfelde, he motored north toward Charlottenberg, patrolling the East–West Axis from the Victory Column to the Brandenburg Gate to view the preparations for the parade. Armored vehicles of every sort lined both sides of the eight lane road. Tanks, half-tracks, self-propelled guns. He stopped long enough to gape at the carcass of the Reichstag—still smoldering two months after its destruction—and the remains of the Adlon Hotel. Beneath the Quadriga, a crew of GIs was busily erecting a large wooden placard.

"You Are Now Leaving the American Sector," read the sign, with the message repeated in French, Russian, and lastly German.

From the Brandenburg Gate, he motored west following the contours of the river Spree. More than half of Germany's electrical industry had been located within Berlin's city limits and the waterway was a vital commercial artery. A few barges cut through calm green waters. Those heading east flew Russian flags and were loaded with machinery: boilers, presses, an endless assortment of steel plate. He wondered where reparations ended and theft began.

He sped past the giant Siemens factory—so big it was called Siemens City—and had a look at the AEG works in Hennigsdorf. He checked out others, too: Telefunken, Lorenz, Bosch. Their premises had been stripped. A few pieces of scrap lay scattered across the barren factory floors. Nothing more. He sped by Rheinmetall-Borsig, Maybach, and Auto-Union, the firms responsible for manufacturing the Reich's tanks and heavy artillery. Empty. Henschel, Dornier, Focke-

Wulf—the mainstays of the aircraft industry: Concrete husks all; nary a screw rolling on the floor.

Locusts!

The sight of the naked factories validated Egon Bach's and the Circle of Fire's every worry concerning the Allies' intentions for Germany. They were hell-bent on stripping the Reich of every last vestige of her industrial might. An agrarian state wasn't far away.

Nearing the edge of town, Seyss found himself gripping the handlebars more tightly, sitting higher in the seat. A candy-striped pole blocked the street ahead. One hundred yards farther on stood the Glienickes Bridge, the only one of three crossings open from which Russian-controlled Potsdam could be reached from Berlin. An American transport—a deuce and a half, in their streetwise vernacular— had just pulled up to the border. Eager to observe the relations between these reluctant partners, Seyss cut his speed and shunted the bike onto the sidewalk. Russian sentries in pea-green smocks swarmed over the truck like ants to their queen. One yelled for the tailgate to be opened. The American driver shouted an order and his troops poured out. Immediately, they formed a line and began unloading large cardboard cartons. Seyss was close enough to read the lettering on the boxes. *Evian. Eau Minérale.* Drinking water. Probably provisions for the presidential party.

The Russian officer spent a long time counting and recounting the boxes, tallying the total against a sheet on his clipboard. Finished, he blew a whistle and the American soldiers formed a single-file line. Each held out his dog tag as the Russian officer passed by. It was clear they'd been through the whole routine before, equally clear they didn't enjoy it.

As he turned the motorcycle around and headed north to Wannsee, Seyss remembered something Egon Bach had said during their meeting at Villa Ludwig. *How long before the flame of democracy ignites the cradle of communism?*

Soon, Seyss thought. *Very soon.*

GROSSEN WANNSEE 42 WAS A stern Tudor-style mansion set far back from the street on a heavily wooded lot in the southwestern corner of

Berlin. Tall iron gates circled the estate. A sprawling lawn cradled the house, sloping in the rear to the Wannsee itself, a calm expanse of water formed by an outcropping of the river Havel. Beds of pansies lined the redbrick drive and strands of bougainvillea enveloped the trellis. It was every inch the province of one of Germany's industrial titans. And that included the spit-polished black Horsch roadster parked before the front entry.

Seyss gave the house a last glance, then goosed the motorcycle down the shadowy lane. It had turned into a fine day. The air was cool, dampened by a morning shower. The sun hung at forty degrees, blanching the eastern sky. Breathing deeply, he enjoyed a surge of vitality, an invigorating shiver that made him see everything that much clearer. *Die Berliner Luft*, he thought sarcastically. The Berlin air. Citizens of the capital never missed a chance to boast about the restorative qualities of their city's air. It was a crock of horseshit, really.

Turning into a grassy lot, he brought the bike to a halt and climbed from the saddle. A few steps brought him to the crest of a gentle knoll. He ducked through a clump of bushes and was rewarded with an unobstructed view of the house. He checked his watch. Nine-thirty. Half an hour remained until his meeting with Schmundt. Enough time to scout the neighborhood and make sure no welcoming party had convened without his knowing.

The neighborhood was quiet. No traffic essayed the winding road. An elderly couple ambled from their home and Seyss waved a modest hello, the humble victor. The couple were less reserved. Shouting "Good morning!" in their best English, they greeted him with smiles meant for their richest relations. Two more innocents who'd abhorred Hitler and welcomed the Americans as liberators. Seyss smiled back, wanting to shoot them. Instead, he offered the woman his arm, and speaking to her in exquisitely fractured German, escorted her down the lane until they were well past his destination. A few nimble glances over her shoulder revealed nothing untoward. Schmundt's house was quiet as the grave.

At five minutes past ten, Seyss hopped the fence at the rear corner of the property and dashed toward the faux English monstrosity.

Shimmying a drainpipe to a second-floor balcony, he pried open a window and slid into a partially furnished bedroom that stank of urine. The Russians had been here, too. Yet no sooner had he opened the bedroom door and ventured a neck into the hallway than a voice called from below.

"I'm in the salon, Erich. Do come down."

Seyss grimaced at the familiar nasal voice. Egon Bach.

THE TWO MEN FACED EACH other across an empty room, separated only by their mutual dislike. The furniture had been carted away and the carpets torn out, leaving the floorboards exposed. Traces of blood smeared the eggshell walls.

"Finally, I see the real you," said Egon. "The adept at masquerade. The star of the costume ball. You always did look wonderful in a uniform. I'm jealous."

Every time he saw Egon Bach, Seyss needed a second or two to get used to the puny fellow. The narrow shoulders, the bottle-thick glasses, the inquisitive head two sizes too large for his body. He was a tortoise without his shell.

"Where's Schmundt?"

"Gone. Taken away with the furniture. I don't know where and you shouldn't worry." Egon approached Seyss and clapped his hands on the taller man's shoulders. "What's wrong, Erich? You don't trust me anymore? No calls from Heidelberg. Not a word from Frankfurt. I would have thought a thank-you was in order."

The touch of Egon's hands reminded him all over how much he despised the Jew: the presumptuous manner, the cocksure voice coupled with that sickening little swagger.

"For what? Pulling me from the frying pan or throwing me into the fire? Your address in Frankfurt wasn't worth a damn. The Amis had rolled up the entire neighborhood. Your friends were nowhere to be found. Or were they with Schmundt? Your Circle of Fire seems to be shrinking daily. I doubt your father had the same problems."

At the mention of his father, Egon colored a fierce red and dropped his arms to his sides. "If you'd called from Bauer's as agreed, we'd have had none of these worries. You have no idea the effort we expended to pull you out of that armory."

Seyss bowed theatrically. "Forgive my ingratitude. Next time, if you're going to send a man to help me out in a pinch, at least have him give me a lift. It was a day's walk to Frankfurt."

"We may have friends, but we have to move carefully. Others are watching." Egon stalked across the barren room and glanced out the window. "By the way, I've seen to it that the families of Steiner and Biedermann will be taken care of. I thought you'd be glad to know. Officer looking after his men and all that."

"So it was Bauer who ratted us out?" Seyss roared at the irony. "I knew it! Another of your recruits."

"Bauer?" smirked Egon. "You believe Heinz Bauer sold you out to the Amis? Oh, you are the arrogant one, Erich. I will grant you that. Bravo!" He clapped his hands with unbridled insolence, chuckling softly. "No, I'm afraid you have only yourself to blame for what happened in Wiesbaden. Whatever possessed you to deal with a man like Otto Kirch? You might as well have gone straight to Eisenhower."

"It was Kirch?"

"How else did you think the Octopus stayed in business?"

"I imagined the same way as you."

Egon ignored the jab and Seyss knew it was only so he could inflict one of his own. "Kirch was on the phone to the Americans five minutes after you left him. They found a Herr Lenz in Mannheim who was only too eager to reveal your whereabouts. Unfortunately, Bauer made it out of Wiesbaden alive. It would have been better for all of us if there were no survivors."

Egon paused long enough for Seyss to wonder if he was meant to be included. "So Bauer talked?"

"Against his will. I understand he had a long conversation with the American investigator who planned that charming soiree."

"Judge?" Seyss spat out the name like a dose of poison.

Egon shook his head reprovingly, while clucking his tongue. "Tell me, have you spoken to Ingrid, lately? I understand she's gone missing. Last seen with the same Major Judge at the American hospital in

Heidelberg. She was happy to confirm that your body wasn't among those in the morgue. He's been screaming about it to his superiors, but so far we've managed to keep things quiet. He's disappeared, as well. Officially absent without leave as of Monday evening."

Seyss wasn't sure what was being implied. "And?"

"'And?'" Egon threw his hands in the air. "What do you think, 'and,' you beautiful idiot? He knows. He was a fucking detective in New York City. Two nights back, he called Patton ranting about how you were still alive and on your way here to rid the world of Truman and Churchill. Patton's issued a warrant for his arrest on some trumped-up charge, but sooner than later Judge is going to find someone who believes him."

"You said he'd disappeared. Is there any reason to think he's headed to Berlin?"

"We don't know, and that's the only reason we're having this conversation."

Seyss caught the veiled threat and added it to his store of hate for the odious runt. "Nonsense," he said. "No way he could get here."

"You're here," said Egon. "I'm here. Frankly, I'm a bit surprised Major Judge hasn't joined the two of us for our little chat." Plucking his glasses from his nose, he began cleaning the lenses with a handkerchief. "Aren't you the least bit curious why this man is sticking to you like shit to a bootheel? You've nearly killed him twice. Any other policeman would have considered his duty fulfilled long ago."

Seyss was pacing the room. "If you've something to say, spit it out."

"You killed his older brother at Malmedy—the war crimes the Americans had you in the cooler for. When Judge learned you'd escaped, he had himself transferred to Patton's Third Army so that he could personally find you."

Seyss took in the information without emotion. If Egon expected him to be frightened he was sorely mistaken. Judge was an amateur. He had only to recall their encounter at Lindenstrasse to confirm his opinion. Brave, perhaps, but nevertheless an amateur. "Is that what you came up here to tell me?"

"I've come," Egon said, "because we no longer have the luxury of time. Originally we'd thought you'd have a week, eight days, to do the magic that made you such a hero. Unfortunately, that's no longer the case."

"Oh? Tell me then, Egon, what is the case?"

Egon marched over to the fireplace and picked up a blue folder resting on the mantel. "Read this. Everything you need to know is inside."

Seyss raised a skeptical brow and accepted the folder. An American eagle was emblazoned on its cover, the words "Top Secret" and "Terminal" stamped above it. He lifted the cover. The first memo was addressed to General George S. Patton, Jr.

"Patton gave you this?"

Egon grinned triumphantly. "A true friend of Germany."

Of course, thought Seyss. Who else could have ordered the Olympicstrasse cleared of traffic for a few hours? What better source to procure an authentic *persilschein*?

The first dossier contained information about the conference and its participants. Included were a detailed schedule of the daily plenary sessions, names of the Americans attending and their British and Soviet counterparts, a map of Babelsberg marked with the locations of the homes where Truman, Churchill, and Stalin would be residing, and a second map marked with the route Truman would take from the Little White House at Kaiserstrasse 2 to the Cecilienhof in Potsdam some ten kilometers away.

The second dossier concerned security measures. Names of the secret service officers assigned to the presidential detail. Military policemen seconded to the presidential security detachment. A proposed duty roster.

The third dossier contained similar information for Winston Churchill and, more interesting to Seyss, for Stalin, himself. Seyss recognized the name of the Russian general commanding the NKVD regulars dispatched to guard the town of Potsdam. Mikhail Kissin, nicknamed the Tiger.

The last held mostly mundane information—menus for each day's meals, a list of radio frequencies for daily transmissions to Washington, and finally, an urgent note stating that due to a lack of potable water in Babelsberg one hundred cases of French drinking water would be flown in each morning to Gatow Airport.

Seyss reread the final notice, seeing in his mind's eye a stack of cartons piled high beside an American supply truck and the words *Evian. Eau Minérale* stenciled on them. Egon Bach had struck gold.

"This is good, Egon. Very good. But it will only be of use once I'm in Potsdam. Have you been by the border? Stalin has it zipped up tight."

Egon reached into his jacket and handed Seyss a visitor's pass to the Cecilienhof issued in the name of Aaron Sommerfeld. "Mr. Sommerfeld is a member of the U.S. State Department's delegation to the conference. Currently, he finds himself in a hospital in Frankfurt laid up with a bad case of dysentery."

Seyss examined the pass. "It's for tomorrow."

Egon shrugged uninterestedly. He might have given him lousy seats to the symphony instead of a warrant for his death. "As I said, time is a luxury we no longer possess. You have yourself to thank."

Seyss slid the pass into his pocket. "There might be another way. Truman is visiting Berlin today to raise the flag over the headquarters of the American command. Naturally there will a speech, a tour of the building. Eisenhower will be with him. So will your good friend, General Patton. Get me a decent rifle and I'll take all three."

Egon was shaking his head before Seyss had finished speaking. "Truman isn't enough. We must have Churchill, too. Otherwise, the Brits will talk the Americans down. As for Eisenhower, no one will care. Soldiers are supposed to die. Besides, it must be in Potsdam. It must occur under the Russians' nose if it's to mean a thing. It must appear as if Stalin had sanctioned the entire affair. The cauldron must be made to boil, understand?"

But Seyss was in no mood for understanding. "Tomorrow, Egon? Are you out of your mind? You're giving me no time to plan, no time to have a look around. It's a *himmelfahrtskommando*. A one-way ticket to heaven! Suicide!"

Egon kept his eyes locked on Seyss, speaking as if the words hadn't registered. "Your name will be on the list of visitors arriving from Berlin. The others are press, a few VIPs. A bus leaves from the Bristol Hotel at nine in the morning."

"And a way out?" Seyss demanded. "Have you planned that for me too?" Suddenly, he was angry. Furious. Not only at Egon but at himself.

Of course Egon hadn't planned a way out. Why should he have, when Seyss himself hadn't expected to come out alive? But something had changed over the last days. He'd seen that Germany would survive and the thought of his country battling back from the brink instilled in him a new desire to fight with it.

"Come, come," said Egon. "You're being dramatic. I have every faith in your ability to wangle your way out. You couldn't expect me to think of everything."

Seyss laughed dryly. He felt as if he were stepping outside himself and looking back at a man he didn't know. A stupid man. Why *should* Egon Bach want him to escape? Seyss was the only man who could attach him to the murder of two world leaders. Egon couldn't afford to have a loose cannon careering across the desk of Bach Industries. He didn't give a rat's ass about Germany, only the family *konzern*. A strong Germany meant a healthy Bach Industries, and a healthy Bach Industries, profit for Egon Bach. His venal eye rendered Seyss's love of country a rube's fantasy.

And as Seyss walked across the room and replaced the dossier on the mantelpiece, he felt a cold hand settle on his shoulder. *Sächlichkeit.*

"You know, Egon, you're right. I wouldn't dream of asking you for anything else. The information you've provided is top-notch. The rest is up to me."

Egon smiled confidently. "I'm glad you think so."

"Come to think of it, I don't think we need ever speak to each other again."

It was true. He had everything he needed. Moreover, *he* didn't want anyone left to tie him to the murder of two world leaders, either. He had no intention of being captured or killed. He was, after all, a Brandenburger.

Sensing his intentions, Egon lost the self-assured grin. "Erich, don't be rash."

"I'm not, Egon. Just smart."

"This is ridiculous. Why, we're practically family." But even as he spoke, his right hand was delving inside his jacket, fumbling for an all-too-conspicuous bulge.

Seyss found his holster, unsnapped the leather flap, and withdrew the Colt .45, all in single fluid motion. Family? With a Jew? As he dropped the safety and tightened his finger on the trigger, the thought made him cringe.

"I might as well be your brother," mumbled Egon, his words coming fast and loose. He had freed his pistol from his pocket, a neat little Browning 9-mm, and held it limply in front of him, his hand shaking almost as much as his voice. "Christ, I'm your boy's uncle. If that's not blood, I don't know what is."

Seyss let go the pressure on the trigger, cocking his head just the slightest. His boy's uncle? What was he talking about?

"Pardon me?"

And in that instant, Egon raised the Browning and straightened his arm to fire.

Seyss's grip hardened round the Colt. Stepping forward, he depressed the trigger even as he raised the pistol. A split second passed, no more, but to Seyss it was all the time in the world. As a sprinter, he had learned to measure the world in halves of seconds, in quarters, in eighths. Somehow, he could see things more clearly when he was moving. Motion brought clarity, and clarity, understanding. Where others saw a blur, he saw an outline. Where others saw a shadow, he saw a form and could discern its intent. And so he knew he had won.

Squeezing off a round, he drilled a hole dead center in Egon Bach's forehead.

Some people had no business touching firearms.

CHAPTER

47

—

IT WAS RAINING WHEN JUDGE left Ingrid's apartment the next morning. The sky huddled low, a gray umbrella leaking fat drops that tasted like dirt and gasoline. Bilgewater, he thought, from the bottom of a sinking ship. He walked down Eichstrasse to the first main thoroughfare and turned right, heading west. Ingrid's apartment was in the Mitte district of Berlin, on the western edge of the Russian zone. The area was a wreck, a maze of crumbling matchboxes. One building stood for every two knocked down. The place brought to mind a middleweight journeyman beaten to within an inch of his life and hanging on only by dumb tenacity.

He continued a block or two, then ducked under the striped awning of a stubborn grocer. The stalls were bare of fruits and vegetables. The shelves held a dozen cans of beans, corned beef, and sweet potatoes. All American. Still, the grocer stood behind the counter, apron secured around his sizable girth, hair a pomade lake, offering his customers a smile meant for a better day. Judge nodded and turned his attention back to the street.

No cars traversed the wide boulevard. No trucks. No motorcycles. In fact, he couldn't see a motorized vehicle of any size or shape. The only things moving at seven o'clock Wednesday morning were horses and pedestrians and both were hauling wagons and litters piled high with debris. He'd stepped back in time. It was 1900 and his mother was due to leave on the SS *Bremerhaven* sailing from Hamburg for New York on the morning tide.

The rain stopped and Judge ventured out into the street, craning his neck in either direction. Not good, he thought to himself. How could he expect to get around Berlin without a car? A streetcar passed, trundling along at a jolly five miles per hour. He could walk faster. A squad of Red Army soldiers shuffled by and in his nervousness, he waved hello to them. Slowly, the city came to life. A jeep zoomed past, then a truck with a red star painted on its hood. Another jeep, another truck. This went on for five minutes, interrupted only by the hacking cough of some ancient German sedans jury-rigged to run off a wood-burning fire.

Two motorbikes zipped by in close succession, hardly more than beat-up Schwinns with a scrappy little motor bolted to their chassis. But Judge couldn't care less about the size of their engines. Anything that could get him around the city at a decent rate was okay by him. His scavenger's eye fell instead to the twin black saddlebags hanging over the bike's rear wheel. Emblazoned in gold were a huntsman's circular horn and the initials DBP. Deutsche Bundespost. The German postal authority.

Judge had his answer.

A LAST MOTORBIKE WAS PARKED in the courtyard behind the stalwart stone premises of the Berlin Mitte post office. It looked even older and more beat up than the others, its tires bald, more than a few spokes bent, broken, or missing. The gas tank was dented and the seat ripped, so that even from his position twenty yards away, he could see a spring or two protruding. Still, the bike had a license plate affixed to its front tire guard and the requisite black saddlebags.

Judge hid himself in a recessed doorway halfway up the alley leading to the post office and for ten minutes watched the postmen come and go. From the scant activity, it was clear that mail service was only just being restored. He considered bribing a carrier for his bike or simply asking for a ride, but discarded both possibilities without real consideration. He needed the bike and he needed it now, without argument, discussion, or disagreement. Like it or not, there was only one surefire way. "The strong-arm stuff," Spanner Mullins liked to say, and for once, he didn't disagree.

Running back to the street, he wrestled a sturdy length of two-by-four free from a pile of debris. He returned to his spot just as an engine sprang to life. A glance revealed the courier to be an elderly man dressed in an army sergeant's field gray tunic. Taking a breath, Judge gripped the plank in his hand like a Louisville Slugger and brought it to rest on his right shoulder. And as the cycle crossed the threshold of his vision, he stepped into the alley and swung for the bleachers.

It was another man who struck the mailman, a stranger who chucked him off the bike and gave him a swift kick in the gut for good measure. Better the postman concentrate on regaining his wind than giving chase.

Climbing onto the bike, Judge tested the throttle with a few tentative strokes. The chassis might be gone to crap, but the fiesty engine growled magnificently. He steered the bike onto Blumenstrasse, accelerating wildly until the post office was far behind him. He had the criminal's "high" going—the fast-beating heart, the clarity of vision, the sense of invincibility—and God help any man who tried to stop him. Yet even in the crystalline delirium of theft, part of him knew he'd hit rock bottom. Brawling with General Carswell at Jake's Joint, beating up Bauer, and now, committing what amounted to armed robbery. He'd been on a downward spiral since setting foot in the country and now he'd reached his final refuge: the lawless and wholly unrepentant landscape of his youth.

It was necessary, a rational voice preached. *You didn't have any other choice.*

Stow it, his old self answered. The time for arguing was long gone.

At the next street, Judge veered left and didn't slow until he'd reached Unter den Linden. Ingrid had drawn a crude map of Berlin in the cloak of dust that layered her vanity table. If he ever got lost, all he had to do was motor north or south—depending upon where he was in the city—and he would hit the grand boulevard that in the western part of town was called the East–West Axis, and in the east, past the Brandenburg Gate, became Unter den Linden. Once on this street, he could orient himself.

Little sign remained of the storied linden trees his mother used to describe so fondly. The few standing were nothing but charred stumps. Passing beneath the Brandenburg Gate, Judge slowed the motorbike to a crawl. A hundred yards away sprawled the Reichstag, Germany's House and Senate rolled into one. The massive building had been at the center of the fight for Berlin and it had paid the hangman his wages. A gargantuan web of twisted steel and crumbled walls erupted from a rubble island an entire city block in length. Ahead lay the East–West Axis, eight lanes across, and on either side, the Tiergarten, Berlin's Central Park, a sprawling lot denuded of all vegetation. A mile along, the Victory Column rose from the center of the boulevard, a soaring iron pillar one hundred feet tall, fashioned from sword and cannon captured by the first Kaiser at Sedan in 1870 and topped by a statue of Samothrace, goddess of victory. Four flags flew from its summit: the French Tricolor, the Union Jack, the Stars and Stripes, and the Hammer and Sickle. American tanks, self-propelled guns, and artillery were drawing up on either side of the street, cannons to the fore. He had little question about Truman's route.

Driving, Judge began to check the faces of the men he passed. He was looking for a particular pair of eyes, brazen, too confident by half, a hard-stamped jaw, and a cruel mouth. But if he knew the face he was looking for, he didn't know the nationality. Russian, German, Hungarian, British? No, he decided. None of the above.

Seyss needed to move about freely through Berlin. He required a maximum of freedom that was accorded only one person these days: an American soldier. An officer, to be sure. For his grand finale, Seyss wouldn't have it any other way.

Judge steered the bike left at the Victory Column, but soon found himself disoriented. Pulling over to the sidewalk, he waved down a neatly dressed gentleman—the only one around with a clean shirt, pressed trousers, and hair combed in a part. In his best colloquial German, he explained he was new in the city and that he needed directions to Wannsee. The man didn't question his story and obliged gladly, going so far as to quiz Judge afterward on the route. When Judge had passed the impromptu exam, he asked whether the man had any idea where the American president was expected later that day.

"*Ja, natürlich,*" came the enthusiastic reply. "The Air Defense building on Kronprinzenallee. Just around the corner. All their greatest generals will be there. Patton, Bradley, even Eisenhower, himself. It was on Radio Berlin yesterday evening."

Judge scooted forward a foot, the bike's scrappy engine sputtering in time to his own agitated heart. The entire high command present at one occasion. He had little doubt Seyss would attend.

Confident now that he possessed at least a rudimentary idea of the cityscape, Judge set out to find three addresses. The first belonged to Rosenheim, Alfred Bach's urban oasis, the others to close friends of the Bach family with whom Ingrid had proposed they might stay, the Gesslers and the Schmundts.

The western section of Berlin had escaped the war with only minor damage. Some houses were in disrepair. Shutters hung askew. Lawns grew untended, while whole facades screamed for a fresh coat of paint. The majority, however, appeared in good enough shape: narrow Wilhelmine row houses fronted by gardens of roses and petunias and surrounded by quaint brick walls.

A jeep was parked at the corner of Schopenhauerstrasse and Matterhornstrasse. Judge slowed his motorcycle, and as he passed, granted the two MPs on watch an officious nod. Instead of crossing through the intersection, though, he turned right onto Schopenhauerstrasse itself. He kept his speed down, the wheels bouncing over the uneven cobblestones. He slowed further as he passed number 83, glancing to his right long enough to spot a steel helmet framed in the second-floor window. Whether it was Honey or Mahoney waiting for him, they were being obvious about it. A second jeep waited at the end of the block. Two more policemen in front and a field radio in back.

The family Gessler occupied a Teutonic castle shrunken to scale on the half island Schwanenwerder. No jeeps this time. No policemen playing at surveillance. But the lack of military presence only heightened Judge's anxiety. Spanner Mullin's first law of surveillance was to cover not just a suspect's home but the homes or gathering points of all known associates. According to Ingrid, the Gesslers had been the Bachs' clos-est friends for more than thirty years. Jacob Gessler was her godfather. If Patton was interested enough in Judge's capture to station a squad of MPs at Rosenheim, why hadn't he put a soul here?

Judge brought the bike to a halt in front of an imposing wrought-iron gate. A black Mercedes sedan was parked in the forecourt. The car was covered with grime; its windshield a slab of mud. It hadn't been driven for a month. His eyes fell to a puddle of oil on the forecourt not far from the front door. Nearing the gate, a section of asphalt had been washed away from the driveway. The earth was still damp from the morning showers and a single set of tire tracks was clearly visible in the mud. The tracks bled onto the main road before fading a few yards far-ther on. Had the master of the house gone for a morning drive or had his guest?

Climbing from the motorbike, Judge unbuckled a saddlebag and withdrew a few letters, then pushed open the fence and walked up the drive. The front door opened before he had a chance to knock.

"*Kann ich Ihnen behilflich sein?* Can I help you?" The man was short and gray-haired with a clerk's wispy mustache and a banker's distrustful gaze. Seventy if a day, but none the weaker for it. At home on a warm summer's day, he wore a three-piece suit of navy serge.

"Special delivery. I have a letter for your guest."

"I beg your pardon?"

"Personal, Herr Gessler," said Judge, guessing. "For Herr Seyss."

Gessler stepped onto the front steps and shut the door behind him. "Who are you? I don't know what you're talking about."

"A message from the Americans," Judge continued, his suspicions writing the script. "It is imperative I reach him."

Gessler's eyes opened wide. "Herr General Patton?"

Judge nodded. "*Jawohl.*"

Gessler stepped closer, whispering in his ear. "Herr Egon has gone to meet the Sturmbannführer at Schmundt's home. Grossen Wannsee twenty-four." *Schmundt, another of Ingrid's friends!*

"Herr Bach is here in Berlin?"

Gessler had gone red with excitement. "But you must hurry. He left an hour ago."

Judge ran to the motorcycle, kick started the engine, and rode like hell for the suburb of Wannsee. It was a fifteen-minute trek along the lake of the same name. Flicking his wrist, he checked his watch. Eleven o'clock.

Seyss is here. Seyss is in Berlin.

He repeated the words over and over, as if until now he hadn't quite believed his own suppositions. He crossed the S-bahn tracks, and then a small bridge, slowing to read the street sign. Grossen Wannsee.

The single-lane road wound right, then left, climbing and descending a series of rolling hills. Giant oaks lined the way, a centuries-old honor guard. Judge passed through their meandering shadows as if they were reminders of his own conscience. He'd had Seyss and let him escape. He wanted to believe he'd been frustrated by his adopted humanity, that his reflexes had been blunted by the certainty—or was it just a wish?—that reason must vanquish force. More likely, it was nerves. Either way, nine men and four women were dead as a result of a moment's hesitation. And his brother's killer left to run wild with no telling what devastation he might yet wreak.

Judge eased up on the throttle, stealing glances at the august homes lining the road. Number 16. Number 18. The bike sped round a corner and suddenly, he was there. Number 24. A blue-and-white plaque screwed onto a moss-encrusted gatepost showed the numeral in a quaint curlicued script. A car was pulling out of the driveway. A sleek black roadster, and it braked as its front tires crept onto the main road. Judge caught only a glimpse of the driver. Khaki jacket, tanned face, dark hair.

Wearing the uniform of an officer in the United States Army was Erich Siegfried Seyss.

48

THE LOBBY OF THE BRISTOL HOTEL was an oasis of shade and calm. Ivory linoleum floor, black marble counters, and a ceiling fan spinning fast enough to rustle the leaves of the Egyptian palms that stood in every corner. Ingrid presented herself to the concierge and asked if any of the reporters covering the conference in Potsdam were guests of the hotel, and if so, where she might find them. The question was hardly a shot in the dark. Only two hotels were open for business in the American sector, the Bristol and the Excelsior. Judge had promised her the reporters would be at one of them. The concierge directed a hand toward the dining room. "A few are presently lunching, madam."

Ingrid thanked him and walked in the direction he had pointed. Instead of entering the dining room, however, she continued to the women's loo. Her hair was mussed, her face sweaty, her shoes speckled with dust. Standing in front of the mirror, she tried to repair the damage, but her palsied hand only made it worse. *Sit down*, she ordered herself. *Relax.* She smiled, and the smile was like the first crack in a pane of glass. She could feel the fissure splintering inside of her, its veins shooting off in every direction. It was only a matter of time until she shattered.

The trip to the hotel had left her a wreck. She'd seen plenty of bombed-out houses, streets cratered from one end to the other, even entire city blocks razed to the ground. But nothing compared to the marsh of ruins through which she now walked. It was a bog of char and decay and rubble. Block after block blackened and leveled. Streets buckled open. Torn sewers spitting effluent. She'd felt as if she were descending into a nightmare one step at a time. And everywhere, people. Old men hauling wheelbarrows loaded with wood and pipe. Women carrying buckets of water. Mothers pushing perambulators crammed with their worldly possessions, leading their children by the hand. Other children—whole packs of them!—wandering on their own. All of them gaunt, dirty, and forlorn. A festival of the damned.

Stranger still—what really drove her batty—was the quiet. Berlin was nothing if not noisy: an exuberant symphony of horns and bells and shouts and squawks. Where had it gone? The silence that accompanied the squalor was unnatural. Walking, she would lift herself onto the balls of her feet, as if straining to catch a remark. All she heard was the constant *tap-tap-tap* of the trümmerfrauen; forlorn women chipping away a lifetime of mortar from an eternity of brick.

But all of it was bearable until she came upon the horse.

It was on the Ku'damm, just past Kranzler's. A bulldozer had been by to clear the boulevard, plowing drifts of mortar and stone onto the sidewalks. Every twenty meters someone had carved a passageway to cross the street and it was through one of these crumbling couloirs that she'd spotted it. The animal lay still on the ground, surrounded by a small crowd. A wagon loaded with brick rested a few feet behind. The horse was terribly thin, stained black by its own sweat. Its fetlocks were tapered yet muscular, more jumper than draft horse. A lovingly braided mane hung limply on its neck. Obviously, the beauty had dropped from exhaustion.

Ingrid's first instinct was to rush toward it, though she knew she could do little to aid the poor creature. Before she could reach the circle of onlookers, a man cried "*Achtung!*" and she heard a ghastly whinny as something heavy and not quite sharp struck the horse. Another blow cut short the animal's cry.

There followed another *thwack*, and another. And a moment later, the horse's rear haunch was handed through the crowd, passing from one person to the next, before being laid atop the wagon. A stream of blood curled between her feet, beckoning to her like an accusing finger.

"Saw!" cried the brusque voice, and she'd fled.

Brushing an errant strand of hair from her face, Ingrid leaned close to the mirror as if proximity to her reflection would help her sort out her feelings. She decided she'd been foolish to accompany Devlin Judge to Berlin. To abandon her child to join in another man's crusade. Already she'd forgotten why she'd come. Was it to redeem her inaction during the war? Or to satisfy her long-simmering and silently fought feud with Erich Seyss? No one left Ingrid Bach until she said so! Was it this, then—her desire to be loved, to be attended to, to be found attractive—that had hastened her departure? Or robbed of a man's presence for so long, had she mistaken Judge's attention for something more lasting?

The arrival of Judge onto her mental stage softened her damning tirade and for a few moments she comforted herself with memories of their night together. But soon, her unsated guilt demanded that Judge, too, be accounted for and dismissed. What could he feel for her? She, the daughter of a war criminal, the lover of the man who had killed his brother? She was a whore who showed her breasts for a few days' meals, a harlot who danced on a general's arm to win his good favor. She still didn't know what might have happened had she not seen Judge Friday night at Jake's Joint. It was a question she refused to answer.

Whatever her intentions, she knew her motivations were ultimately selfish. By accompanying Judge, she'd cast herself as victim—of love, of war, it didn't really matter—and again absolved herself of her responsibilities. To her country, her family, and, ultimately, to herself.

When would she finally summon the courage to stand alone?

THE REPORTERS WERE EASY TO spot. They sat gathered round a long table, six restless men in civilian garb among a placid sea of olive and khaki. They eyed her like starving dogs spotting the day's only meal. Why shouldn't they? She was the only woman in the room.

Ingrid decided that it was too crowded to approach them immediately. She didn't want to attract more notice than she had already. She asked the maître d' for a table and was shown to a banquette in the rear of the restaurant where she ordered canned ham with tomatoes and a Coca-Cola. She was very hungry. A breakfast of a hard roll and Hershey bar didn't carry one far. Her meal arrived and she ate quickly, aware that all eyes were on her. Several times she heard hoots of laughter and looked over to see the newsmen observing her unabashedly. They'd finished eating before she'd arrived and looked to have settled into a long afternoon of drink. She waited until the room had cleared, then with some trepidation, rose and crossed the floor to speak with them.

Six eager faces turned up to her in welcome.

"I was wondering if I might ask a favor of you gentlemen," she began.

"I was thinking the same thing, myself," one of them shot back. He was a sweaty little man with a salt-and-pepper goatee and the name Rossi on his press pass.

Ingrid smiled and let go an easy laugh to let them know she could take a joke. Oddly, the chubby man's rude remarks relaxed her. She had, after all, grown up with four brothers.

"It concerns one of the president's associates," she went on. "He's my cousin, in fact. Chip DeHaven. Are any of you acquainted with him?"

"Yeah," answered Rossi, "we're fellow members of the Harvard Club, can't you tell?"

"Actually," Ingrid pointed out, "he attended Yale."

Rossi flushed as his colleagues pounded him with acerbic laughter. The man next to him—slim, gray hair, and a ghost's tan—chimed in. "Excuse me, ma'am, but we saw you talking to the concierge. We couldn't help but overhear you speaking kraut. I didn't know Carroll DeHaven had any German relations."

Ingrid damned herself for her carelessness. Judge had told her to only speak English but the journey to the hotel had left her too flustered to remember. She considered denying the fact but wanted no more made of her nationality. "Carroll DeHaven *is* my cousin," she said evenly, "on my mother's side, if you must know, and I'm anxious to reach him. Would any of you be going out to Potsdam this afternoon? I've a letter that I'd like delivered to him."

The lot of them shook their heads. Then Rossi jumped in, "Tell you what, sister. Come on upstairs, we can *sprechen Sie* a little, then you can tell me all about you and Chippie boy and Yale. You want him to get a letter, mail it!"

More laughter.

Ingrid shook her head, fed up with Mr. Rossi's coarse behavior. She'd spent enough time chatting with the GIs guarding Papa at Sonnenbrücke to pick up some of their lingo. Finally, she'd been given an occasion to use it. Circling the table, she knelt close beside the obnoxious lout and brushed her most seductive finger along the underside of his bristly chin.

"Mr. Rossi, is it?"

"Hal."

Ingrid flashed her eyes. "*Hal* . . . If I thought for a second that you knew the first thing about pleasing a woman, you know—how to make her really hum and purr—I just might consider it. But I can spot a limp-dicked paddywacker when I see one and I don't care to waste my time with you. Terribly sorry . . . *Hal*."

The table erupted in a gale of laughter. And to his credit, so did Rossi. When the commotion died down, he said, "Okay, okay, I apologize. Listen, lady, there are over two hundred of us reporters in town for the big show. Only two are allowed to attend the conference each day. The rest of us are stuck here twiddling our thumbs. I'm sorry, but if you want to talk to your cousin, you should go see Colonel Howley. He runs things in the American part of town. Frank Howley. Maybe he can help."

Ingrid thanked the table and stood to go.

"And if he can't, *schatzi*," Rossi shouted after her, "don't forget my offer."

The table burst out all over again in boisterous laughter.

INGRID WAS PASSING THE FRONT desk when Rossi caught up to her.

"Hey, sister, you want that letter to get to DeHaven, maybe I can help."

She kept walking. "I doubt that."

"A few of the guys are heading out to the Little White House tonight for a small shindig. Strictly on the q.t. A little poker, some booze, anything to get out of Berlin. Maybe we'll see old Chippie."

Ingrid realized she had no choice but to take the offer seriously. Stopping, she turned to face him. "Are you asking me to come with you?"

"If you can stand an hour's car ride with a classy guy like me, why not? We're leaving from the Excelsior around seven. Come by for a drink first."

"The Excelsior at seven. Deal."

Suddenly Rossi frowned, stroking his whiskers. "There's just one thing I gotta ask you."

Ingrid eyed him dubiously. "What?"

"Serious now. This letter, it's not gonna get me into any trouble?"

Ingrid smiled. "Mr. Rossi, if you can get me to Potsdam, this letter of mine just might make for the biggest story of your career."

Rossi shrugged, unimpressed. "Lady, if a dame like you goes out to a party with me, that's the biggest story of my career."

"THE FLAG THAT WE ARE TO RAISE today over the capital of a defeated Germany has been raised in Rome, North Africa, and Paris," declared President Harry S. Truman from the steps of the Air Defense building. "It is the same flag that was flying over the White House when Pearl Harbor was bombed nearly four years ago, and one day soon, it will fly over Tokyo. This flag symbolizes our nation's hopes for a better world, a peaceful world, a world in which all the people will have an opportunity to enjoy the good things in life and not just a few at the top."

Seyss was only half listening to the words. It was bad enough having to stomach your own country's propaganda; just plain nauseating trying to swallow someone else's. Inching forward through the crowd of American soldiers, he was more concerned with the men on the stairs than with what they had to say. Truman was a particularly unimposing figure. Standing before the microphone, straw hat in hand, he wore a light summer suit, wire-rimmed spectacles, and two-tone shoes that would do a salesman proud. Behind him and to his right stood Dwight Eisenhower, Omar Bradley, and, finally, George Patton. *A true friend of Germany*, Egon had said. A regimental band was off to the left, brass horns held at the ready.

Seyss kept his chin raised, his eyes glazed over with that proper mix of rapture, respect, and naïveté that the Americans reserved for their president. A few hundred soldiers had assembled for the flag raising and together with Seyss they had bunched themselves into the modest courtyard. Look at their faces. Such hope. Such faith. Such trust. How was it that their war taught them the opposite of his?

Step by step, ever so slowly, Seyss neared the president. He was careful not to jostle. Never did he push. If the men around him were aware of his movement, they didn't mind it. A bead of sweat fell from beneath the brim of his cap, stinging his eye. He glanced up. The sun was at its highest, not a cloud to deflect its powerful rays. The day hot and sticky. Still, it was more than the heat causing him to perspire.

Pulling a handkerchief from his pocket, he lifted his cap and wiped his brow. He had the itchy neck, the twitching muscles, the flighty stomach, that came with the proximity to action. Twenty feet away, Truman droned on and on. Standing on his tiptoes, Seyss sighted a clear line of fire. The .45 rode high against his hip. The Browning he'd taken from Egon scratched the small of his back. Were he to draw his pistol and fire, he'd get off three shots, four at most. He'd kill the president, and if he was lucky, Eisenhower. But then what? The Horsch was parked three blocks away. A cordon of military police surrounded the gathering and a dozen heroes-in-waiting tugged at his elbow. He wouldn't get far.

"We are not fighting for conquest," Truman was saying. "There is not one piece of territory or one thing of a monetary nature that we want out of this war. We want peace and prosperity for the world as a whole. We want to see the time come when we can do the things in peace that we have been able to do in war."

Truman stepped from the microphone and the crowd of soldiers broke into an enthusiastic cheer. Behind them, a few hundred Berliners had gathered. With dismay, Seyss noted that the locals were as fervent in their applause as the Americans. They'd clapped the same way when Hitler announced the retaking of the Rhineland and the Anschluss with Austria. When Paris fell, they'd gone absolutely crazy.

The cheering grew and grew, causing Seyss to wince with discomfort. Now was the time to act. The noise of gunfire would be swallowed by the boisterous ovation. He'd have a second more to get off an extra shot or two. In the ensuing confusion, he might even escape.

Still, there remained the bigger question: Would killing Truman, or even Eisenhower, "make the cauldron boil," as Egon demanded? Would it spark a war between the Ivans and the Yanks? A conflict grave enough to bring in Germany on the Allied side? Of course not. Egon had been right all along. A Russian must be seen to kill the president. A Russian must kill Churchill, too. A Princeps for modern times, with Berlin, not the Balkans, the powder keg of Europe.

Seyss's own eyes had borne out the Circle of Fire's most outrageous claims. Day after day, Germany was being stripped of her machinery, her industry, her very means of survival. Two weeks after the Russians had moved out of western Berlin, their barges still traveled the Havel and Spree laden with disassembled machinery. The Americans were doing nothing to stop them. Hell, they were probably doing the same with their share of the pie.

In a few months, a few years, a decade at most, the Amis would be gone, leaving Stalin and his monstrous hordes poised from Danzig to the Danube. And when the Russians advanced, how was an agrarian state to stop them? With a commando force of holsteins and Herefords?

No, Seyss decided, he wouldn't waste his life killing Truman alone.

Why write a footnote to history when he could write an entire chapter?

Just then the orchestra burst into the Star Spangled Banner and the crowd surged forward. All voices joined as one, heads tilted back as the flag was raised over the new headquarters of the United States occupational government of Berlin. God bless America!

JUDGE HAD LOST SEYSS. One second he had him, the next the crowd was driving forward and he was gone. One uniform among hundreds. Shoving his way through the mass of Germans, Judge neared the line of GIs meant to keep the citizens of Berlin a safe distance from their American masters. He shuffled to the right and stood on his toes, keeping his eyes pinned to the spot where, until a moment ago, Seyss had been standing. A news camera set on an elevated tripod blocked his view. He shuffled to the left and met the fierce gaze of a military policeman. Damning his luck, Judge lowered his head and retreated into the recesses of the crowd.

It had been near impossible to keep up with Seyss on the way to the ceremony. A three-stroke motorbike was no match for a twelve-cylinder Horsch, and several times Judge lost sight of him altogether. Only Seyss's arrogance had saved him. The unmistakable black silhouette provided sharp contrast to the dull and ruined cityscape, standing out clearly from a quarter mile or better. And in those anxious seconds when the Horsch's sleek profile was no longer in view, Judge steeled himself to act at the earliest instance.

Frantically, he'd asked himself what could he do? Shoot Seyss? He didn't have a gun. Stab him? He didn't have a knife. All he had were his bare hands and his will. But that, he determined, was enough. The sight of a filthy kraut grappling with an American officer would bring soldiers running in a hurry and give Judge ample opportunity to declare in his best Brooklyn accent that Seyss was an impostor, an escaped Nazi war criminal intent on harming the president of the United States. It was an accusation no one could lightly dismiss.

But when Judge had arrived at Kronprinzenallee, Seyss was already walking from his parked car, and in seconds, he had disappeared into the ranks of the gathered soldiers.

Abruptly, the ceremony ended. The flag fluttered in a light breeze atop the Air Defense Command. The orchestra played a Souza march. The assembled dignitaries shook hands with one another and slowly made their way from the podium. A hive of officers swarmed at the base of the steps, waiting to greet the president and the former supreme Allied commander. Despite his average height, Truman was easily visible. His pale straw hat stood in marked contrast both in color and shape to the olive military covers. An easy target. Judge cut through the crowd moving in a course parallel to Truman's. He thought feverishly of what kind of diversion he could create. Something that would alert the president to the danger he was in. All he could think of was to yell what he shouted at opposing pitchers when they'd struck out Pee Wee Reese or Pete Reiser. "Get lost, you bum." He looked around for something to throw. A bump on the head would hasten his departure, that was for sure. He found nothing. Naturally, the grounds had been cleared of debris for the ceremony.

By now, a picket of soldiers had formed around the president. Truman's automobile drew up and he climbed in, followed by Ike and Omar Bradley, the two ranking generals present. Watching the sedan pull away, Judge breathed easier. Only Patton remained on the podium. His stiff posture belied some interior strain, either physical or mental. Judge eyed him, thinking, *You sonuvabitch. You're helping Seyss. You're a part of this.*

An officer mounted the podium and addressed himself to Patton. He stood toe to toe with the general, shaking his hand exuberantly. Patton colored visibly and looked in either direction, but the officer did not release his hand. Only as he leaned forward to whisper something in Patton's ear did Judge catch the tan skin, the arrogant jaw, and the flashing blue eyes.

"GENERAL, I BELIEVE IT'S TIME we finally met."

"The pleasure's all mine, Captain. Did you serve under my command?"

"You might say that. Actually, I'm serving under it now."

"Then you're off-limits, son. My Third Army doesn't grant R and R in Berlin. Which unit are you with?"

"A very special one. We call ourselves the Circle of Fire. My name is Seyss. Erich Seyss. Once I was a major."

George Patton flinched, his normally ruddy mien flushing an exquisite plum. It wasn't often a major could make the equivalent of a field marshal squirm and Seyss was enjoying the moment immensely. He leaned closer to Patton, whispering in his ear. "I wanted to thank you personally for the dossier on Terminal. I wouldn't have a chance without it. But it's hardly enough. Not if I'm to do a proper job and get out in one piece."

"Spit it out, man," Patton said through clenched teeth. "You've got your credentials, what else is it you need?"

"Be at the entry of the Cecilienhof tomorrow at eleven. Keep yourself visible. The fourth plenary session is scheduled to start at eleven-thirty. I'll be accompanying you into the main hall, and if things go as planned, out again as well." When Patton didn't answer, he added, "Otherwise, I can't promise what will happen to the dossier. It might be hard to explain how a man under house arrest got his hands on such sensitive material or how he got *here*, for that matter."

"Egon Bach is indispensable to the rebuilding of Germany," blustered Patton.

"You mean he *was*." Seyss smiled, and before Patton could ask him what he meant, fired off a salute. "I look forward to seeing you tomorrow morning at eleven. Good day, General. It is an honor. Truly."

Returning to the car, Seyss focused his mind on the task at hand. Tomorrow morning at ten he'd report to the Bristol Hotel for a ride out to Potsdam. He'd need some civilian clothes before then and some time to study Egon's dossier. For all the information the papers gave him, it couldn't begin to give him a picture of the setup of the place—the placement of security guards, who sat where, where the leaders lunched, the layout of the Cecilienhof itself. All that he must learn for himself.

Seyss sneaked through the crowd, finally breaking free of it at the corner of Wilhelmstrasse and Prinz Albrechstrasse. Spotting the Horsch, he picked up his heels and walked a little quicker. It was a beautiful machine. The registration said it belonged to Karl Heinz Gessler. Now, there was a name from the past. During Ingrid's time as a student at Humboldt University, the two had dined regularly at the Gesslers. The cuisine was terrible, as he recalled. Nothing but overcooked sauerbraten and lumpy spätzle.

The thought of Ingrid brought back Egon's odd words. "Christ, I'm your boy's uncle." Seyss wanted to dismiss the remark as a ploy, an almost successful effort at distraction, but the words stayed with him. He wondered if Ingrid was the reason Egon had come to Berlin. Egon had stated that Judge had enlisted her help to track down her onetime fiancé. Brother and sister had never gotten along, but he'd always suspected that Egon was secretly mad about her. Maybe too mad.

More likely, it was Judge, Bauer's capture and the subsequent call to Patton giving Egon ample reason to believe the American intended to travel to Berlin. *Judge!* Every time he heard the American's name he felt a dread chill. Instinctively, he turned and scanned the street behind him. He saw the usual mishmash of city folk. A pair of trümmerfrauen hard at work. A one-legged veteran begging. A postman fiddling with his motorbike. Nothing to worry about. Calmer, he realized he'd half expected to see the fiery-eyed American bearing down on him. Nerves.

Unlocking the Horsch, he climbed into the driver's seat and keyed the ignition. Over the velvet growl of the twelve-cylinder engine, he asked himself where in Berlin he might hide if he were traveling with Ingrid Bach and two days absent without leave? The answer came at once, and he smiled. Why not have a look? He needed a quiet spot to spend the afternoon, someplace sufficiently private where he could delve into Patton's dossier without interruption. Who knew? He might find an old set of clothing.

Even better, he might find Judge.

KNEELING ALONGSIDE THE PURLOINED MOTORBIKE, Judge observed Erich Seyss slide into the sleek roadster. Whatever ideas he'd harbored about jumping him and screaming bloody murder he canned the moment he saw the German speaking to Patton. As far as Judge knew, any MP around the place might be one of Patton's henchmen. Waiting for a puff of smoke to shoot from the exhaust, Judge swung a leg over the ripped seat and kick-started the engine. The Horsch pulled away from the curb and crept up the street. Judge allowed it a fifty-yard head start, then angled the bike into the center of the road and gave chase.

The black sports car traveled north along Wilhelmstrasse, slowing to cross Unter den Linden, then accelerating wildly when it reached the other side. Judge threaded his way through a gaggle of pedestrians, almost losing Seyss as the automobile made a sharp right turn around a devastated street corner. Opening up the throttle, Judge ducked low and cut the corner only to see Seyss turn again, this time left. Pylons of debris six feet high cluttered the road. He thanked God for the mess. One extended straightaway and Seyss would be out of sight.

Even so, Judge had to struggle to keep up. The Horsch was just too fast. Eyes tearing from the wind, he came to an abrupt and unpleasant realization. Continuing surveillance on Seyss was futile. It would be no use trying to arrest Seyss and impossible to catch him in the act. If he wanted to stop him, he had to kill him. And soon.

At some point, the two crossed into the Russian zone. Dozens of Red Army soldiers patrolled the street, but given their lackluster posture it was difficult to tell if they were on duty or off. The Horsch turned right onto a broad boulevard teeming with horses, pushcarts, and pedestrians. Blumenstrasse read a street sign posted on a scarred row house. Judge recognized the name. The post office where he'd stolen the motorcycle was located somewhere along this street.

Seyss had pulled away again. Judge worked the throttle, not wanting too large a distance to grow between them. The bike shot forward, and at that instant a pushcart piled high with fractured porcelain nosed into his path. The road was blocked. Braking madly, he threw the handlebars to the left. A grunt and the bald tires slid out from under him.

He came to rest two feet from the pushcart. His pants were torn, his knees and elbows bloodied. The bike was a wreck, front tire folded back on itself, chain broken and splayed like a three-foot worm. Ignoring the halfhearted queries of passersby, he skirted the pushcart, desperate to catch sight of the Horsch. He spotted it, a hundred yards up the road. As if in sympathy, it had stopped to allow an oncoming streetcar to pass before negotiating a sharp left turn. With a sigh of infinite frustration, he watched Erich Seyss disappear up the narrow street, a shimmering shadow under the midday sun.

Then his eye came to rest upon the striped awning of a stubborn grocer. And above it a street sign. Eichstrasse.

And he ran.

50

THE DOOR SLAMMED AND INGRID RUSHED from the bathroom.

"Devlin, I have some wonderful news. You'll never guess what—"

He stood in the doorway, dressed in the uniform of an American officer, blue folder tucked under one arm. His face was harder than she remembered, shorn of youth's innocent disguise. His cheeks were hollow. His jaw thicker, more resolute. New lines advanced from the corners of his eyes. He was the only man the war had made more handsome.

"The uniform," said Erich Seyss, touching the lapel of his jacket. "Strange, I know. I'm still getting used to it myself. It's the only way to get around town without too many questions."

Ingrid stared at him for a few seconds, not knowing what to say. Her skill at making conversation had fled, along with the air from her lungs, and for a moment, she couldn't decide how to comport herself—whether to act the maiden betrayed, the resourceful mother, or the secret accomplice come to aid in his capture.

He decided for her. Closing the door, he crossed the short distance between them and took her in his arms. He stroked her hair, and for a few seconds, her heart fluttered as it had six years ago. Here he was, then, the long-lost object of her adoration. The man whose actions had shredded her every belief in herself. The source of her strength and her misery. The father of her only child.

She held him for as long as it took to realize she no longer loved him, then let him go. "Hello, Erich."

"Ingrid."

She raised a hand to his cheek, wanting to touch him. It was a reflex, a remembrance of an intimacy lost. And she stopped herself just shy of his burnished skin.

Seyss looked her up and down, nodding his head. "Now I know I wasn't a fool to let you ruin my career."

Ingrid broke from his embrace and walked to the vanity, needing the distance to make sense of his words. "I beg your pardon?"

"I came back for you," he said, following her every step. "Two years ago, it was, in March. We'd lost Stalingrad. Everyone knew the war was over. It was just of question of when. Suddenly, I decided that you were more important than the party or some bureaucrat's idiotic rules. I didn't have a pass, but I left anyway. I took a sleeper to Munich, then drove to Sonnenbrücke. You were gone. To a friend's somewhere for the week."

"But I was married. Surely you knew."

"Of course," he answered, standing at her shoulder like a stubborn suitor. "Foolish of me, but I thought I could lure you away."

Ingrid stood preternaturally still, her eyes fastening upon every detail of the apartment's hard-won cleanliness. The floor she'd mopped with a moth-eaten sweater, the furniture she'd dusted with a lace dress, the duvet plumped up after airing for an hour. Her surprise was not rooted in disappointment or regret. Not for an instant did she ask herself "what if." She was captured, instead, by her immunity to his words. And at that moment, she realized she was truly free of him.

"No one told me."

"Only Herbert knew." Seyss smirked. "Glad to know someone can keep their oaths." He laid a hand on her shoulder and turned her around so they were standing close to each other. Uncomfortably close, by Ingrid's reckoning. Smiling mawkishly, he took her hands in his. "Ever since, I've wondered what would have happened if I'd arrived a day earlier. I've asked myself the same question again and again."

"It's in the past, Erich. We're different people now."

"Would you have divorced Wilimovsky? Would you have married me?"

Ingrid tried to avert her eyes, but couldn't. His unwavering gaze didn't belong to a spurned lover but a betrayed commander. It was his pride, not his heart, that had been wounded. "No."

"And now that he's dead?"

Finally, she looked away, her eyes coming to rest on their intertwined hands. "For the longest time after you left, I kept track of your whereabouts. I'd call my brothers and ask if they'd seen you, if you were safe. Sometimes I swear I wanted to hear that you'd been killed. The hardest thing I ever did was to stop caring for you."

"I'm sorry."

She pulled her hands free. "It's too late for apologies, Erich. Six years. These days, that's a lifetime."

"When did you stop?"

"Stop what?"

"When did you stop caring?"

"I don't know," she said. "What does it matter?"

Grasping her arms, he gave her a violent jolt. "When?"

She stared at him before answering, keenly aware that despite his lovelorn words he was not here to pay a social call. "Long before you 'ruined your career for me.' I didn't have the strength to hate you anymore."

Turning her shoulders, she forced herself from his embrace. She was frightened by his coarse behavior. Never had he been pushy or demonstrative. If anything, he was the opposite. Cool to the point of indifference. "*Sächlichkeit*," he'd called it, and when she used to say that it was just a soldier's ruse to get out of an argument, he'd simply smile at her and give a shake of his blond head.

A queer expression crossed Seyss's face, a rare current of indecision, and for a moment his lips moved as if he was going to ask her something. But just as suddenly, his hesitation vanished. Pivoting, he walked to the window, and right away she saw that his bearing had changed. The spine had stiffened. The shoulders fallen back. He was the soldier again, the time for reminiscences done and discarded. And she knew she'd been right to feel afraid when he'd first walked through her door.

"How did you know I would be here?"

Pulling back a lace curtain, Seyss craned his head outside and peered up and down the street. The windows were simply wooden frames, the glass blown out during the battle for the city. "I didn't, really," he said, pulling his head back into the apartment. "Egon mentioned you might be in town. He told me all about your crusade with Major Judge. Actually, I was looking for a place to go to ground for a few hours. Tell me, *schatz*, when is he due back?"

Ingrid approached him, laying a hand on his shoulder. "Erich, please go. I won't tell him you've been here. I give you my word."

He shot her a bemused look, as if her suggestion was ridiculous, then returned his eyes to Eichstrasse. "Soon, I take it. Or do you wear that perfume all day long?" He sniffed at the air. "Joy. It was my favorite. I suppose I should be jealous."

Ingrid took a step back, her cheeks flushing with shame. She'd picked up a *petit flacon* of the perfume at the open-air market in the Tiergarten, a token to celebrate her finding a way to visit her cousin. Now her victory was in tatters, and she had to find some means of alerting Devlin to Erich's presence.

"It's madness, Erich. Whatever you're trying to do, stop it. Just leave now. Leave the apartment. Get out of the country."

Seyss might not have heard. His only response was a dry laugh, followed by a hunching of the shoulders that signaled an increased concentration. "Where has he been all day?"

Ingrid was careful in choosing her words, wanting to be cooperative so long as it didn't endanger Devlin. "Looking for you."

"Thank God Berlin is a big city."

Seyss moved away from the window and set out on a tour of the apartment. Two strides took him to the door, which he latched with a turn of his wrist. Grunting, he returned to the windows, drawing the lace curtains over each—she supposed to prevent anyone from seeing in. His last stop was the bathroom. A window above the tub led to a rusted fire escape at the rear of the building. Using both hands, he wrenched open the window, brushing away a smattering of broken glass. Taking one of the buckets, he set it precariously on the rail of the fire escape.

The softest step on the escape would send it clattering to the ground three stories below.

"And when did he leave?" Seyss asked, retreating from the bathroom.

"Just after seven."

"What did you say he was wearing?"

Ingrid detested his smugness. "His uniform, of course," she said, gathering the courage to lie. "Just like yours."

SEYSS HAD ENVISIONED IT DIFFERENTLY. She would rush into his arms. They would hug, and in her long-denied joy she would forgive him his transgression. Naturally, they would fall onto the nearest bed and make love, and it would be a loud, sweaty, earthy affair. The imaginery scene had taken place in a dozen familiar locales—Villa Ludwig, Sonnenbrücke, even here, in their lovers' hideaway on Eichstrasse—and a thousand exotic ones, too. Six years' fodder for a soldier's dreams.

And like a storybook it had almost come to pass: the unexpected meeting, the hushed voices, the tender embrace as his fingers caressed her hair, still the same vixen's blond that he'd adored. Even the mention of Judge's Christian name and the piercing note of her perfume had failed to dim his hope. She had wanted that pleasure for herself. One word and his carefully constructed palace had crumbled to the ground. "No."

Seyss sat down on the bed, motioning for Ingrid to take a seat on the couch across the room. He took out the .45, checked to see that a round was chambered, then set it beside him. Six years had passed. He sighed. People changed. Smelling her florid scent, his jaw suddenly clenched. *Sächlichkeit*, he ordered himself. *You don't know this woman any longer.*

"*Schatz*, I must ask you another question. No more pleasantries, all right? Very important." He waited until her eyes were fully on his. "What news did you want to tell Judge?"

Ingrid lifted her shoulders and smiled. "Nothing that concerns you. Just that the water is running again."

Seyss could still hear the expectant lilt to her voice. *Devlin, I have some wonderful news. You'll never guess what.* "No," he said. "That wasn't it. You were too proud of yourself. Your cheeks were glowing. What was it?"

"I've already told you. We have water again. Go check for yourself. The concierge was here before you came."

It was a game attempt, he'd give her that.

"Judge, he's here now, but one day he'll leave, and it will just be us again. Come, *schatz*, what were you going to tell him?"

Ingrid opened her mouth, her lips forming around some unfinished words, but said nothing. Seyss rose from the bed and knelt in front of her, placing a hand on one knee. "You never were a gifted liar. Truth was always your strong suit. It was your honesty, your exuberance, that I loved about you. So, *schatz*, before we go any further, let me be honest, too." And just then, he gave her leg a very firm, very carefully placed squeeze so that she sucked in her breath and whimpered. "There is nothing you know that I cannot find out. *Verstehst du?*"

Biting her lip, Ingrid nodded reluctantly, and he could see a tear forming in her eye.

"What, then, did you wish to tell our friend, Devlin Judge?"

Ingrid remained silent, her knees buckled together and her arms fastened around her.

It was a pity, thought Seyss, that people could be so unreasonable. He slapped her cheek and Ingrid's head caromed to the left. A little something to get her attention. Her eyes glared at him wildly, and from nowhere, she threw a punch. He deflected it, yanking her off the couch and tossing her onto the floor. The sight of her lying there angered him—he hated nothing so much as disobedience—so he kicked her in the stomach.

"Darling, don't do this to yourself," he said, picking up the pistol. "Think of our boy. Would he like to see his parents fighting this way?"

Ingrid's eyes squinted in disbelief. "You knew?"

"I'm touched." He offered a hand to help her up and she knocked it away. "Not until now."

"Don't be, Erich. You just fucked me. You may be his father, but you're not his parent."

Seyss struck out blindly with his boot, catching her squarely in the sternum, lifting her a few inches off the ground. He was angry at her impudence and her courage, angry at his own predilection for sentiment. He felt no kinship because of their shared offspring. Instead, he felt disgusted and foolish, her rejection of his affection tempering his willingness to overlook her Jewish heritage.

Ingrid squirmed on the carpet for a minute, coughing, making pathetic gurgling noises. Slowly, she gathered her breath and drew herself to a sitting position. Her defiance was ebbing visibly. To make sure of it, he jumped as if to kick her again. She threw out an arm to block the feigned blow, then shrank to the carpet, crying. Bending down, he helped her onto the couch and offered his handkerchief. It was the least a gentleman could do.

"As you were saying . . ."

"I'm going to Potsdam this evening," she whispered.

"Louder!"

Ingrid cleared her throat, lifting her voice. "My cousin is a member of the presidential delegation. Chip DeHaven. Stalin is throwing a soiree for Truman and those left behind are giving a small party at the Little White House. We're meeting at the Excelsior at seven."

Seyss nodded. The Little White House. Kaiserstrasse 2. A map in the dossier showed its location and floor plan, another that of Stalin's villa on the Havel. He'd study both after he killed Judge. "Who invited you?"

"An American reporter. His name is Rossi."

Seyss sat next to her, placing an arm around her shoulders. "Why didn't you just tell me in the first place? So foolish of you to bring this on yourself. All to do a job the Americans should be taking care of themselves."

He pulled her close and kissed her hair. She was noticeably thinner than when he'd last seen her—cheekbones more pronounced, eyes that much larger, waist without the least fat—but her slender figure served only to make her more alluring than she'd been. Maturity had added the final strokes to an unfinished masterpiece. Seeing that she didn't resist, he kissed her again, this time on her cheek. Slipping his arm lower, he turned her waist so that she faced him more directly. "So we have a boy," he said. "Smile. Be happy his father is alive. No boy should grow up without his papa. We're together again. As it should be."

"Never," she said, and he felt the venom in her words.

Tossing her shoulders, she tried to stand up but a firm arm locked around her back defeated her struggles. He slid down the couch and moved his head toward hers. Her lips were dry and chapped. Feeling her shift, he tightened his grip and placed a hand on her breast. She was always sensitive there, he recalled. He pressed his body into hers so that she might feel his attraction, then snuck in two fingers to unbutton his pants.

Just then the bucket clanked and clattered down three flights of stairs.

Startled, Ingrid gasped and held him tighter. Seyss shook her loose and jumped to his feet, grabbing the pistol and running into the bathroom. The fire escape groaned as someone mounted the steps. Jutting his head out the window, he caught sight of a mop of dark hair climbing the rusted stairs. He brought the pistol to bear and cocked the hammer. It was a man and he was coming up fast, but where was the uniform Ingrid had mentioned? Seyss waited, knowing a shot would ricochet off the scaffolding. He didn't want to fire. A gunshot would bring unwelcome attention. The figure rounded the stairs. A head popped from the sea of metal slats, looking expectantly upward and Seyss was staring at the dirt-smeared face of a teenage boy.

"He paid me. He paid me," the boy was yelling, hand raised to ward off Seyss's bullet.

Seyss didn't hear him.

By then, the door to Ingrid's flat had crashed open and Devlin Judge was rushing across the room, a jagged section of pipe in hand.

"RAUS! RAUS!"

Devlin Judge charged across the room, brandishing a heavy lead pipe. He yelled for Ingrid to get out of the apartment but she stood as if frozen. His rusc had brought them a few seconds, no more, and it was only through speed and surprise that they could take advantage of them.

Seyss dashed from the bathroom, a look of incomprehension heating to anger, then resolve. His hand rose sharply and he brought the muzzle of the Colt to bear. Before he could fire, Ingrid was upon him, hands working to free the pistol from his grasp. Judge leaped onto the coffee table and launched himself at the German. The gun bucked once, twice. The noise was excruciatingly loud, clotting his ears with an unbearable ringing. Gunpowder from the muzzle blast scalded his cheek and the next instant he collided with Seyss, his head spearing the German in the ribs. The momentum of flight propelled both men into the wall. With a thud, they landed in a confused heap.

Judge cleared his left forearm and pinned Seyss to the ground. Staring into his callous, confident face, he suffered every bitter emotion of the past ten days. His humiliation at being bested at Lindenstrasse, his frustration at allowing Seyss to escape from the armory, and his unspoken anger and will to revenge on behalf of his brother, Francis

Xavier. These feelings and a hundred more for which he had no name came to an instant, uncontrollable boil inside him. Cocking his free arm, he delivered two quick downward jabs. The first blow connected solidly with Seyss's cheek. The second glanced off his chin and scraped the floor, causing Judge to lose his balance. And in that instant Seyss's fist erupted like a coiled spring, a freight train on a vertical track catching his jaw square on. Judge's sight darkened and his vision collapsed to a narrow band of light, grainy and unfocused. He tumbled to the floor and his head struck something hard and uneven. Stunned, he thrust his hand behind him and his fingers danced across the cool metal of Seyss's pistol. The discovery and its concomitant prospect of revenge most sweet enlivened him.

Scrambling to his feet, Judge noted with dismay that Seyss had risen, too, and was propelling Ingrid toward the door. Judge took aim at the plane of Seyss's back. The trigger caressed his finger like lips to his ear, begging him to fire. He hesitated. A shot at such close range might easily pass through Seyss and kill Ingrid, too. He yelled for the two to stop, but even as he spoke, Seyss twirled, shunting Ingrid in front of him. He had another gun in his hand—and as Judge threw himself behind the sofa, it exploded. The bullet struck the wall behind him, misting the air with vaporized plaster. Ingrid screamed, and when he raised his head, the apartment was empty.

Judge ran to the door and popped his head into the hallway. Two more shots came his way but neither was close. Seyss was buying time, executing a retreating action to the Horsch with Ingrid, a flesh-and-blood shield. Judge slid down the stairs, his back to the wall. He was desperate to stop Seyss, but prudence forced him to pause at the top of each landing, to advance inch by inch until he could be certain the next flight was clear.

Reaching the street, he wasn't surprised to see that Seyss had trundled Ingrid into the black roadster. She was half inside the sports car, her flailing arms providing a scrappy if ineffective resistance. Seyss jabbed the pistol into her ribs, hard enough to make Judge wince. He shouted for her to calm down, to do as he said, and she stopped fighting. He shoved her head into the tight compartment and climbed in beside her.

Twenty yards separated Judge from the car. Twenty yards from the woman he cared for and the man he wanted to kill. Keeping his body hidden inside the building's entry, he released the cartridge and ran a thumb over the bullets. Five shells plus one in the snout. He imagined himself bursting from the protection of the building and blasting his way to the car, saw the spent brass casings, spitting from the Colt as he emptied the gun into Seyss's torso. It was craziness. Seyss would take him the moment he showed himself. An idea came to him. The tires, he thought. Shoot the goddammed tires!

Arm extended, Judge peeked from the building. A young couple walking hand in hand interrupted his line of fire. Seeing his pistol, they turned and fled down the street. Just then, the Horsch's engine spat brusquely and revved. Judge stepped from his hiding place and began firing. One, two, three shots. All misses. The Horsch screeched from the sidewalk, shuddering as it executed a 180-degree turn. Judge ran after it, firing wildly at the tires, praying no strays would violate the gas tank. He didn't dare risk a shot at the tightly bunched silhouette inside the cockpit. Suddenly, he heard a fat bang, louder even than the gunshots and the left rear tire exploded.

INGRID FELT RATHER THAN HEARD the tire blow. It was as if someone had kicked the car, knocking a leg out from under it. The Horsch veered left and Erich flung both hands onto the wheel to correct the vehicle's course, letting the gun fall onto the floorboard at his feet. Spotting her moment, Ingrid sprang. Her ribs were very sore where he'd prodded her with the pistol, but she managed to twist and lunge across the armrests and make a grab for the wheel. Clutching the circle of polished wood, she yanked it right and held on for dear life. The car lurched into the curb, bounced off, then climbed onto the sidewalk. Seyss rose in his seat and delivered a vicious elbow to her chest. Crying out, she released the wheel and fell against the door. He thrust the wheel to the left, but by then it was too late. Traveling at forty miles per hour, the Horsch struck an elderly man, then careened through the plywood façade of an electrical goods store. Ingrid brought both arms in front of her face, wanting to scream but finding fear had lodged her cry deep in her throat. It didn't matter. By then, the world was screaming for her—the splintered wood breaking upon the car, the furious engine howling in protest, the tires seeking purchase on the slick cement, and above it all, Erich yelling for the car to stop, stop, stop. Sliding across the deserted showroom, the Horsch slammed into the back wall and came to an abrupt halt.

SEYSS SAW THE COLLISION APPROACHING. Bracing one arm against the steering column, the other on the handbrake, he let the shock roll through him. He waited for a moment after the car had come to a stop, taking a deep breath, then making an inventory of his body's complaints. His forearm ached. His chest was sore (from the collision with Judge) and his ankle throbbed curiously. He hoped it wasn't broken. He raised a hand to his forehead, expecting to see blood, but it came away clean. Amazingly, the windscreen had not shattered.

He glanced at Ingrid. She was dazed and unmoving, but apparently unhurt. He remembered her ridiculous attempt at bravado, saw her grasping the wheel, tugging at it like a hellion, and he grew enraged. All of this was her fault. Running a hand across the floor, he found the Browning, then turned to face her.

"I'm sorry, *schatz*," he said. "But really, I can't have you messing up my life any further."

Without further ado, he placed the barrel of the pistol against Ingrid's forehead and pulled the trigger.

Nothing happened.

Ejecting the cartridge, he saw he was out of bullets. *Shit.*

Ignoring Ingrid, Seyss tried to start the car. He turned the ignition time and time again, but after a few wounded coughs the engine died altogether. Ingrid laughed but made no move toward him. The door was frozen solid, so he pulled himself out the open window. His first steps were tentative. A sharp pain stabbed at his ankle. A sprain, nothing worse. Reaching the sidewalk, he saw Judge in full flight running up the street. He'd never make it as a sprinter, but his form wasn't bad. And with that gun he didn't need to win, a close second would do.

Seyss unbuttoned his jacket and began to jog up the road. The motion flooded his wrenched joint with blood and for a few steps, he thought he might faint. Lengthening his stride, he was pleased to feel the pain subside. A crowd of onlookers had gathered round the entrance to the store. Burnt-out tanks and flak-torn aircraft were old hat, but an American officer crashing a Horsch roadster into a neighborhood store . . . that was a novel sight. Judge met his eye, then broke off the chase and ran into the store. *Idiot!* He actually cared for the girl. Ingrid must have freed herself, for a second later, Judge was back, rejoining his pursuit with a new vigor. Forty yards separated them. Putting additional weight on his weakened limb, Seyss was pleased to find it accept the exertion. He ran faster and the distance between them quickly grew.

And as he ran, he became aware of the curious stares thrown his way from the local gentry. It wasn't usual to see an American fleeing a German. Not in Berlin, at least. Turning this observation over in his mind, Seyss discovered a neat solution to his problem. A nifty way to end this ridiculous charade once and for all.

Coming to the next corner, he turned left and headed west. Eichstrasse was practically on the border of the American zone of occupation. It was just a matter of time before he came upon an American installation. The sun shone high on the yardarm and soon he was sweating, his shirt damp and his jacket tight across the shoulders. Not wanting Judge exhausted, he slowed, allowing him to gain some ground. Judge rounded the corner a second later. He had settled into a steady stride and though perspiring heavily, looked ready to run another five kilometers. At his shoulder was Ingrid Bach. When had she turned into such an athlete?

Remembering the pistol, Seyss stoked his tempo. He heard Judge yell "Stop!" and not a second later a bullet whizzed overhead, sounding in its proximity like a drunken bumblebee. Then he saw it. A block up the road, an American flag flew from the balcony of a white stucco building—a *gemeindehaus*, or district governmental office. He smiled at the red and white stripes curling in the soft breeze. It wasn't a flag he'd ever wanted to salute, but it was one he had surrendered to willingly. Prisoners on the eastern front couldn't expect Hershey bars, Budweisers, or Lucky Strikes as part of their daily regimen. He stumbled purposely, wanting Judge to gain a few feet and the thought came to him that he was a fisherman and that he was reeling in a big catch foot by foot. Nearing the American flag, he yelled in his loudest voice.

"Get me some help quick. Crazy Nazi bastard's trying to kill me. Will someone get down here?"

A moment passed. No one responded and Seyss felt a chill pass through his body. It was Wednesday afternoon. Maybe like German schools, the Americans closed their doors after twelve o'clock midweek. Just as quickly, though, his fears were put to rest. The doors to the stucco building burst open and four GIs peeled downstairs, each carrying an M-1 rifle.

JUDGE SAW THE AMERICAN FLAG and smiled. He would catch Seyss. He would explain everything to the CO and that would be that. The White Lion was finished. Just a few more steps. Tucking in his chin, he ignored the fire that had engulfed his lungs three blocks back and urged his knees higher, his legs faster. Seyss had stopped running and was waving the squad of GIs in his direction, saying something about "a crazy Nazi" and "war criminals" and "a murder." In his overheated state, Judge couldn't make it all out.

"I'm an American officer," he shouted when he was within spitting distance of the soldiers. "That man is an escaped war criminal." But he was too out of breath to make himself understood. His ragged rebuttal sounded more like, "offzer," "awrcrimnal." He sounded just like the rabid Nazi Seyss claimed he was. The GIs were all around him now, and he didn't like how they were eyeing him. Seyss stood behind them, ten feet away.

Judge raised a hand to get a breath, panting, "I'm an Ameri—"

A rifle butt crunched into the back of his neck and he didn't say anything else.

CHAPTER

52

THE EXCELSIOR HOTEL. SEVEN O'CLOCK. The bar.

Arriving at the appointed hour, Erich Seyss sauntered into the dimly lit lounge and shouldered his way through the dense, boisterous crowd. Their bubbly chatter had the relentless quality of an incoming tide, ebbing and flowing, growing ever louder. It was the sound of men and women getting drunk and not giving a damn. He took a seat at the far end of the mahogany bar and ordered a beer—a Hacker-Pschorr, thank you. Only his favorite would do tonight. If he were in Munich he'd ask for a plate of pretzels and a little mustard, too, but this was Berlin— *American Berlin*—so he settled for a bowl of stale peanuts.

The beer came and he took a great big draft. Eyes closed, he savored the frosty suds coasting down his throat, cooling his belly. He took a deep breath and tried to relax for a minute or two. It was anxious time. The time between heats. The time to keep his muscles warm. The time to concentrate on the final event.

It was impossible. Too much had happened during the day. Too much was yet to come.

He'd stayed at the *gemeindehaus* in Wedding long enough to see a groggy Judge carted away in handcuffs and Ingrid taken into custody with him. She'd made the mistake of screaming that Judge was an American while insisting with equal vigor that Seyss was a German, a war criminal, and an assassin who wanted to kill the president, to boot. The soldiers had looked at her as if she were crazy, but a minute later, one produced a flyer bearing Judge's photograph stating that he was wanted by the provost marshal for desertion and obstruction of justice. Maybe she wasn't so crazy after all. Regardless, Judge would be held in custody for a minimum of twenty-four hours. Thanks to darling Ingrid, that was all the time Seyss needed.

Finishing his beer, he slammed the mug onto the counter, snapped his fingers, and made his way into the hubbub. Time to move. He was looking for a portly little American with a beer belly and goatee, a reporter named Rossi. Great, he thought, another Italian, and wondered if there were any left in Sicily. The men in the crowd were half military, half civilian, but they were all talking about the same thing: Stalin, the goddammed Russians, and how they had better watch who they were pushing around.

Adopting a friendly attitude, he coasted through the throng, tapping the odd forearm and asking its owner if he'd seen Rossi around. The third man he approached fit Ingrid's description to a *T.* "I'm Hal Rossi. Who's looking?"

Seyss disliked him immediately. The greasy smile, the dancing eyes. He was too glib by half. "Dan Gavin," he replied in a voice loud enough to make any self-respecting German cringe. "I understand you ran into my friend Ingrid Bach this afternoon."

"Yeah, yeah, I sure did," said Rossi. "She's a lovely gal. Coming soon, is she? We're due to leave anytime."

Seyss gave an earnest shake of the head. "I'm afraid she won't be joining you this evening. She took ill around five. Something she ate. What do they call it? Berlin tummy."

Rossi looked as if his mother had dropped dead while kissing him good-night. "No. Really? Jeez, I'm sorry to hear that. Make sure you give her my best wishes for a speedy recovery."

Seyss promised to give her the message. "Listen, Hal," he added before the forlorn Ami could get away. "Ingrid wondered if I might go in her place. I'm sure she told you she had something important to tell

Chip DeHaven. I've known Chip forever and I don't want to let Ingrid down. It would mean so much to her. Got room for another body?"

Rossi tapped his forearm, signaling to come closer. "Is it all that serious?" he whispered, "Ingrid was pretty worked up about having to see DeHaven. She said it might make a decent story."

Seyss looked this way and that, as if afraid of prying ears. "Without being too dramatic, I have to admit it is. But hardly anything newsworthy. A family matter, actually."

"Figures." Rossi shrugged, pepping up a second later as he rediscovered some spark of inner cheer. "Well, Danny boy, you're not as pretty as Ingrid, but if I'm lucky, after you talk to Chip you'll spot me a hand or two of five-card stud."

Seyss smiled inwardly. To hell with Patton and the rendezvous at the Cecilienhof tomorrow morning at eleven. He was going to Potsdam tonight. "Kind of you to take me along, Hal, but that might be asking too much."

And together they headed to the bar to cement their new friendship.

Seyss had just one question: What the hell was five-card stud?

THE FORD CARRYING ERICH SEYSS, Hal Rossi, and three other half-soused American newshounds pulled into the drive of Kaiserstrasse 2 at nine fifteen. If they were an hour late, at least they'd made good use of the time. Five better chums weren't to be found anywhere in Germany. A quartet of soldiers surrounded the car, opening the doors on cue. Climbing from the sedan, Seyss saluted the ranking officer and followed Rossi and the others into the house.

The Little White House was an ungainly toad of a home; an unsmiling three-story palace painted a tepid mustard with narrow windows and a sloping red shingle roof. Sitting on a broad knoll overlooking the Wannsee, it did, however, have a wonderful lake view.

Seyss paused on the front landing, wanting to survey the grounds. A dozen soldiers milled around the courtyard chatting with the newly arrived chauffeurs. A pair of Russian sentries stood at the gate, their rigid posture attesting to a largely ceremonial role. No threat there. But nearby in the lavender twilight waited Stalin's crack troops, patrolling the wooded hills and dales of Babelsberg and its adjacent community, Potsdam.

Crossing the border into Potsdam, Seyss had been amazed at the sheer number of Red Army troops Stalin had shipped in to provide security for Terminal. The entire route to the Little White House was lined with pea green. Yet his searching eye hadn't stopped at the side of the road. He was quick to discern bands of soldiers roaming the wooded hills. He'd read a note in Patton's dossier stating that "Stalin promises to have a man behind every tree." The author might have added "and a submachine gun, too."

Inside, the party was in full swing. Lights blazed from the main salon and Seyss could see a group of gray-haired men sitting round a card table engrossed in their hands. Someone was playing the piano badly and singing even worse. He let his companions lead the way down the corridor, making sure he stayed comfortably to the rear. His first order of business was to get out of the house. Leave immediately and he'd have ten or fifteen minutes until one of his new cronies remarked upon his absence. If luck was with him, they'd be either too tight or too involved with a good hand of cards to notice.

God forbid he see Chip DeHaven. He had no idea what the man looked like, whether he was young or old, fat or thin. How to explain his fraud did not bear imagining. No words could gild his suspect presence. Someone would ask to see his identification or his orders and all he could provide was the dog tag of a GI killed nine months ago in France. It was a situation from which there would be no escape. No, he decided, he could not see Chip DeHaven.

Mumbling something about needing the commode, he backtracked to the foyer and ran upstairs. He found a bathroom halfway down the hall and locked the door behind him. Moving to the sink, he washed his face with cold water, willing away the effects of the alcohol he'd drunk. He raised a hand in front of him, trying to hold it steady. Its reflection in the mirror betrayed a tremor, and suddenly, he could feel his heart pounding inside of his chest as if it were straining to break free of its mooring. He took several deep breaths and the palsy disappeared. *Stand straighter,* he told himself. *Chin up. You're in your element. Behind the lines in another man's uniform. A Brandenburger.*

And as he stared at his countenance, daring himself to accept this final challenge, he began setting forth his plan to reach Ringstrasse 2, Stalin's private residence no more than five kilometers away, where this evening the grand marshal of the Soviet Union was entertaining Winston Churchill, Harry Truman, and their highest advisors. No doubt it was a fete of some opulence. Seyss had attended a similar dinner three years earlier, when Hitler had feted Mussolini in Berlin upon the latter's daring escape from Gran Sasso, and he knew that it would be a ritzy affair—vodka, caviar, music, the works. No one had an inferiority complex like the Bolshies. More importantly, he knew that security would not just be tight, it would be impossible. A formal guest list would exist and no matter the emergency no one not properly vetted would be admitted. An unknown American, therefore, would have no chance of gaining entry. The right Russian, though, might make it.

Seyss's attention fell to his pocket, where he held between his fingers a rough-hewn piece of paper the size of a passport. Removing it, he read over the name and the unit designation. Colonel Ivan Truchin, Fifty-fifth Police Division, NKVD. Born August 2, 1915, Stalingrad. For two months in the summer of '43, he'd posed as the great Truchin, defender of Stalingrad, parading up and down the streets of Minsk, offering the district commander his advice on the proper placement of artillery, tanks, and troops in defense of the coming German attack. He had come unannounced with neither orders nor adjutant, just an unquestioned confidence the equivalent of divine right. Move everything to the north, he had said. The Nazi warlords will surely concentrate their attack there in hopes of capturing the bridges intact. And they had listened. Was it not the NKVD who, fearing mass desertion during the battle for Stalingrad, lined up every platoon, every company, every battalion, and shot every tenth man in the head to teach a stern but much-needed lesson? If they don't get you, we will. Was it not the NKVD who liquidated the entire officer corps in the purges of '36 and '37? One million or two, who was counting? Was not Lavrenti Beria, chief of the NKVD, Stalin's closest confidant? One ignored a colonel of the Soviet Secret Police at his peril—his very great peril.

So, then, Truchin it would be.

He gave himself a final looking over in the mirror.

"Live dangerously," he whispered, and smiling grimly, left the bathroom.

IN THE COURTYARD, HE COLLARED Sergeant Schneider, the chauffeur who'd driven them from Berlin.

"Get in the car," he said. "I've got to get back to town. General Patton phoned. He needs me right away."

Schneider was a bluff country boy from the mountains of Vermont, a "Green Mountain Raider," he'd said proudly, who'd arrived in Germany only the month before. Not one to question an officer's orders, he fired off a salute and opened the rear door.

Seyss climbed in, settling into the wide leather banquette. When Schneider had guided the automobile out of the gates and onto Kaiserstrasse, he leaned forward and tapped him on the shoulder.

"Change of plan, sport. We're headed to Stalin's house. I've got a message for President Truman."

Schneider beamed with excitement, his eyes darting to the rearview mirror. "But you're a public affairs officer, aren't you? I mean, that's what I heard you telling everyone on the way out."

Apparently, Schneider listened as well as he talked.

"Don't believe everything you hear," said Seyss, with just the right mixture of pride and uninterest. "Ringstrasse two. Know where it is? President's waiting on me."

"Yessir."

As Schneider accelerated the Buick along the winding road, Seyss peered from the window into the shadowy hills, searching for signs of increased security. He saw them immediately. Whole platoons of infantry resting to the side of the road. A sudden profusion of armored personnel carriers. A bounty of barbed wire strung at fifteen-foot intervals along the ground. They were getting close. Very close.

Cresting a rise, they came upon a guardhouse and a candy-striped pole barring the path. Three soldiers snapped to attention as an officer rushed from the temporary booth. Seyss did not want him to speak with

Sergeant Schneider. Flinging open the door, he leaped out of the car and intercepted the stocky man at the front bumper.

"Good evening, Colonel," he said, spying the golden laurel that decorated the Russian officer's epaulets and noting the blue stripe that indicated he was a member of the secret police. "My name is Gavin. Daniel Gavin. I have an urgent message for President Truman. Eyes only."

"I'm sorry, Captain. No uninvited guests are permitted beyond this point. If you'd like I can phone and allow you to speak to one of your president's security detachment. Perhaps Mr. Cahill? If necessary, he can come and fetch you."

The Russian gestured to the guardhouse and smiled obligingly. Black hair cut to a stubble, pronounced cheekbones, and a single bristly eyebrow forming an uninterrupted hedgerow above his eyes, he was every bit the Mongol warrior. A descendant of Genghis Khan indeed. But his English was flawless and unaccented. Delivered in an unctuous voice the product of Moscow's finest diplomatic school, it was every bit as fluent as Seyss's.

"That's very kind of you," said Seyss. "I take it you have a direct line."

"This way."

Seyss followed him to the hut, but before the colonel could pick up the phone, he leaned close and spoke to him in the earthy Russian of a native Georgian. "Evening, *tovarich*. I commend you on your English. Impeccable. I only wish you had the same control over your men. Are you aware that a mile back a few of them have a cozy little bonfire going just out of sight of the main road? You should see them, smoking American cigarettes and giggling like a bunch of maidens."

Before the colonel could ask a question or voice his disagreement, Seyss handed him the identification card carrying Truchin's name. As the colonel studied it, Seyss continued speaking. "I lost enough men at Stalingrad not to give two shits about this petty bullshit. But humor me. Send a man back to clear it up, won't you, Colonel . . ."

"Klimt."

"General Kissin wouldn't be too happy to discover his men were loafing. Tiger is one for discipline, isn't he?"

Seyss handed Klimt the telephone. He could only pray that the information concerning Russian security measures in Patton's dossier was correct, and that Kissin was indeed the commanding officer. "Now. Please."

A worried cast came over Klimt's face. Dereliction of duty was punished with a bullet to the back of the neck for suspects and their commanding officers alike. The colonel dialed a number, then barked out some orders to send a patrol to Dingelstrasse double time. Hanging up, he retained a suspicious scowl that suggested he was only half won over. "May I inquire, Comrade General, what you are doing in an American uniform?"

Seyss lit a Lucky Strike and handed the colonel the pack. "Someone must tell Comrade Stalin what the American president is up to. With your English, I'm surprised you weren't selected."

Klimt chuckled as he took a cigarette. "Alas, no such luck."

"And you, you're from where? Kiev?"

Klimt brightened. "Yes, you've a good ear. I thought I got rid of my accent a long time ago."

But Seyss was no longer listening. He walked to the Buick and with an open hand banged it on the hood. "Okay, Schneider. Everything's hunky-dory from here. Colonel Klimt has graciously consented to take me the last little way. Go home."

Seyss walked around the crossing pole, not once looking behind him. A moment later, he heard a pair of boots thumping behind him. Klimt appeared at his side, red-faced with frustration and indecision.

"Well?" asked Seyss. "Get the fucking car, you miserable pissant. Do you think I came just to tell you about your worthless troopers? I have an urgent message for Comrade Stalin."

Whatever doubt Klimt had retained was excised by Seyss's derisive voice. Only a proper Russian could insult another so thoroughly. "*Da*, Comrade Colonel Truchin. Right away."

Watching the Russian colonel rush to retrieve his car, Seyss permitted himself only a blush of satisfaction. Getting in was the easy part. It was getting out that had him worried.

CHAPTER
53

THE ROOM WAS OPPRESSIVELY SMALL, six by eight, windowless, its sole decoration a three-legged stool, a naked bulb dangling from the ceiling, and the ripe and all-pervasive stink of ruptured plumbing. Judge paced its length, holding his cuffed hands to his chest, a forsaken pilgrim beseeching the Almighty. His knees were scabbing; so were his elbows. His cheek tingled as a thousand grains of gunpowder worked their way from his dermis. His head throbbed from the malicious vim of an eager MP. But his physical discomfort was more blessing than curse, an oft-repeating canticle keeping his mind alert, focused. To acknowledge the pain, to moan, even to grimace, was to admit defeat. "No," he whispered under his breath. "Seyss won't make it."

Hope, he realized, had become his last weapon.

They'd been locked up at 3:45 and he wasn't sure how much time had passed since. An hour. Two. Maybe more. With no watch and no means of seeing the outside world, he had only his thirst to keep the time. A little while ago, a guard had thrown in a mess kit with some chipped beef on toast. Shit on a shingle. Neither he nor Ingrid had touched it.

A welter of voices in the surrounding rooms captured his attention. Judge stopped his zealot's pacing as the door swung open. A late-afternoon glare flooded the room, forcing him to squint to make out the formidable silhouette filling the doorway.

"There's my boy. Got himself all banged up again. Look at you. No better than Jerry himself, and smelling just as bad."

Whatever surprise Judge felt at seeing Spanner Mullins was outweighed by his relief.

"He's here, Spanner. He's in Berlin."

"So I gathered, lad. So I gathered." Mullins stepped into the room, patting a hand softly against the air in a motion for his former charge to keep quiet. Under his breath, he added, "You can give me the details when we're alone. And you," he said, once more the bluff copper, addressing Ingrid, "Miss Bach, I take it? Greetings, ma'am. Just you relax. Everything will be fine. I'll have you both out of here presently."

"Thank you. That's very kind." Ingrid hauled herself to her feet and Judge could see the worry melt from her face. Mullins was just the dulcet-voiced, big-boned authority her imagination had called on to set the record straight.

In the space of ten minutes, he'd ordered the cuffs off Judge, signed for their release, and gotten them a drink of water and a bologna sandwich. Outside the district garrison, he shepherded them into a four-door Buick, its black paint speaking of police rather than military use.

"The Excelsior," Judge called from the rear seat. "He'll be there at seven."

"How do you know?" Mullins queried.

"It's my fault," said Ingrid. "I was terribly weak. He only—"

"Just get us the hell there," Judge cut in, keyed up by his unexpected release. "I'll explain on the way."

"The Excelsior, Tom," Mullins told his driver, a crew-cut bullet-headed sergeant even bigger than he was. "You've got exactly fourteen minutes to get us there."

"Be there in ten," ordered Judge.

Tom turned to give Judge and Ingrid his best knucklehead's grin. "Yessir."

The Buick navigated the streets at an uneven clip, nowhere as fast as Judge would have liked. For every open avenue, there was an alley clogged with debris. For every headlong sprint, a stomach-churning deceleration. The sun was beginning its descent, its unobstructed rays gifting vehicles and crushed buildings with a gilded edge, setting eddies of dust asparkle and lending the beleaguered city, if only for a few minutes, a golden patina.

Judge tried the window, but found it wouldn't go down. The doors were probably locked, too. A cop's car, what did he expect? Settling into his seat, he pictured himself flying into the bar of the Excelsior Hotel, getting the drop on Seyss. But the fantasy lacked an ending. He couldn't decide whether to shoot him on sight or go for the arrest.

"Now, lad," said Mullins, swiveling to drape an arm over the top of the seat. "Mind telling me how you got here? George Patton's got half the United States Army looking for you."

Judge sat forward. "Only way I could figure. I got myself dressed up as a German and gave myself up. Three hours later I was on a transport to Berlin. I should ask you the same question."

"What? Not happy to see me?" Mullins's glassy eyes narrowed ruefully. "I flew up this morning. You're lucky I didn't let you rot in that cell and take your punishment—the strings I pulled with the general to get your transfer extended by twenty-four hours and you going AWOL on me. By the bye, you can kiss your slot with the IMT good-bye. I had Justice Jackson on the phone with me this morning, didn't I? Asking all kinds of questions about why you weren't in Luxembourg at that very instant talking nice to Mr. Hermann Goering."

"Stopping Seyss is a helluva lot more important than a second-rate slot on the IMT."

"If I didn't agree with you, I wouldn't be here." Mullins shot the driver a nasty glance. "Would you hurry it up, Tommy boy? We don't have all day." Then back to Judge. "I was worried when you didn't show at up Bad Toelz like you promised. When I heard the ghastly news about the girls in Heidelberg, I phoned the hospital to see if you'd been by. Why didn't you call me then, lad? It's me gets you out of the tight scrapes, remember?"

"Yeah," Judge said, "I remember." And a sliver of shame pricked at him for having distrusted the man who'd done so much to shape his life. "Does Patton know you're here?"

"Patton? Are you daft, boy?" Mullins drew his brow together in earnest disbelief. "He'll probably throw my fanny in the can straight after he gets you. No, sir, I'm here on my own. It's my ass on the line right next to yours. I came to clear both our names."

What could be more typical? Mullins helping Judge to help himself. Anything to ensure his career against further collateral damage.

"And you're sure he's at the Excelsior?" Mullins asked.

"You can bet on it." Judge explained about Ingrid's date with the American reporter, stating his belief that Seyss was certain to take her place to secure a ride to Potsdam. His question was not whether they would capture Seyss—they would, *they had to*—but what to do afterward? "Seyss isn't alone in this, you know."

"Do I?"

"He's being backed by Patton and by Ingrid's brother, Egon. Some kind of cabal. The same people who got Seyss out of the armory, killed von Luck, and came after us in Heidelberg."

But Mullins wasn't buying it. "If it's a German you want to tie to Mr. Seyss, be my guest. But don't be dragging Georgie Patton's name into this."

"He brought his own name into it. Don't go blaming me."

Judge went on to tell Mullins about his late-night call to Patton, Patton's promise to bring him to Berlin, and the subsequent wolf pack sent to arrest him. But even as he explained, a part of his mind ventured off, imagining what would happen if Seyss had his way. A Russian shooting Truman and Churchill on Russian-occupied soil. It would be war for certain.

And picturing the renewed conflagration, he finally saw where Egon Bach fit in. Faced with a superior foe, the Americans would have no choice but to call up and rearm the German Wehrmacht. In days, Bach Industries would be back in action, spewing out bullets, artillery shells, and most important, at least to Egon Bach, profits. This whole thing was about greed. Greed for glory and greed for financial gain.

"Blarney," retorted Mullins. "You're talking about George Patton, not some hooligan from the Bowery. I won't hear any more of it."

"It's not blarney," Judge shot back. "And I don't give a damn if you believe me or not. I'll take care of things from here on out."

"Enough!" roared Mullins.

Judge raised an arm to object, but caught his tongue. Sitting back, he saw that Ingrid had gone white. Instinctively, he grabbed her hand and squeezed it, offering a comforting smile. "Fine, Spanner. I don't want to argue about it. Let's get Seyss, then we'll talk about next steps."

Mullins didn't answer for a second, his all-seeing eyes fastened upon their joined hands. For a moment his face hung limp, cheeks drooping like a mainsail becalmed, and Judge saw that Mullins had grown old beyond his years. A second later, he perked up and the mouth rose into a smile. "That's more like it, lad. Let's concentrate on the matter at hand and keep our fanciful notions to ourselves."

But Judge couldn't get the look out of his mind. He'd never seen Mullins so surprised.

Just then, Ingrid tapped Judge on the arm, speaking softly to him in German. "We just missed the turn to the Excelsior."

"Bist du sicher?" he asked, sotto voce. "You're sure? It's probably a detour."

"The Kurfürstendamm is clear. I walked it today."

"What's that, you two?" asked Mullins, his eyes trading surprise for suspicion.

Judge released Ingrid's hand and scooted forward on his seat. "You sure we're going the right way?"

"How the hell should I know? Never set foot in this town until last night."

"I thought you flew up this morning."

Mullins coughed. "Yeah, this morning. It was still dark when we landed."

"Ingrid says this isn't the way to the hotel."

"That's correct, Colonel," she said. "We should have turned right on the East–West Axis. It's the fastest way to the Kurfürstendamm."

Mullins glanced at his driver. "That right, Tommy? You're not getting us lost, are you?"

"No sir. We're right on track."

And then Judge saw it. The shitty little grin that Tommy shot Mullins as he shrugged his shoulders and said "Not to worry," that he knew exactly where they were headed. It was a grin reeking of complicity and disdain and, Judge thought, hate.

"What's going on, Spanner?" he asked.

"Nothing, lad. Tommy's taking us his way. Been in Berlin two weeks. Practically a native. Just sit back and relax yourself."

But there was nothing relaxing about Mullins's voice. It had taken on a servile edge, its tone smug and insincere. Judge had heard the voice a hundred times before, Mullins talking down a difficult suspect, dismissing an irksome complainant. It wasn't Mullins talking; it was the force. The power behind the shield, or in this case, the uniform.

It was, Judge realized with dread dismay, Patton.

"All right," he said, "but tell him to hurry."

He kept his voice easy, his shoulders relaxed, while inside he cursed himself for his willful ignorance. His surprise at seeing Mullins, followed upon by his impatience to get moving, had distracted him from closely scrutinizing the provost marshal's presence in Berlin. Christ, but the signs were obvious: his coasting through formalities to obtain Judge's and Ingrid's release, the official car and driver, the gaffe about when he'd arrived. But none was more telling than the mere fact of Mullins's bodily presence.

Mullins had never disobeyed an order in his life. The thought that, of his own volition, he'd defy Patton and jump a flight to Berlin was ludicrous, even if, as he'd claimed, he'd wanted to clear his own name. It was a leap of faith Stanley Mullins was incapable of taking.

Judge's fear came and went. His only route was to play this out to the end, try to keep a measure of dignity. He looked at his watch, returned to him when he left American custody. "Christ, it's five of."

Dropping his fingers to the door handle, he gave it a slow hitch north. Locked, as he'd thought. "Hey, Spanner, I'll need a pistol when we hit the hotel. What can you give me?"

"We've got a couple pistols in the trunk," said Tommy. "We'll pull over up ahead. Get you all fitted out. That all right, Major?"

"Yeah, that's good."

Judge nodded enthusiastically, but he knew he wasn't fooling Mullins for a second. He looked over at Ingrid, who smiled back, wholly unaware of their predicament. He decided it was better she didn't know. Her ignorance might gain them a second or two. A glance out the rear window revealed the street to be empty save a jeep trailing a hundred yards back. Probably Mullins's backup.

The Buick made a sharp and sudden turn right, bouncing madly as it advanced down an alley of torn-up flagstone and brick. Shadows drenched the car and Judge saw they had driven into an abandoned courtyard or *hof*. Half-wrecked buildings rose all around them; crumbling witnesses four stories high, weeping redbrick.

Ingrid laid a hand on Judge's leg, sitting up abruptly, her flashing blue eyes sensing trouble. "Why have we stopped? It's nearly seven, Colonel. We must get to the hotel."

Judge gripped her hands, his eyes never leaving Mullins. "You want to tell her, Spanner?"

"Go ahead, lad. You were always the silver-tongued one."

"Colonel Mullins doesn't have any intention of helping us find Erich Seyss," he said, an iron collar keeping the sorrow and anger from his voice. "He's part of it. One of Patton's boys. Isn't that right?"

Ingrid looked from Judge to Mullins, half gasping as the words found their way home.

"The lad's correct, Miss Bach. My apologies for having allowed him to drag you into this. Your problem, Dev, is that you're always asking questions when you should be following orders. You don't know when to forget being the lawyer and remember to be a soldier."

Judge kicked at the door, once, twice, ramming his heels against the chassis. The door didn't budge. As quickly, his rage passed and he sat back.

Tommy pivoted in his seat, bringing his right arm over the banquette. He had a tough's beady eyes to go with his bullet head and crew cut, and a scuffed-up Luger in his hand. But Judge's eyes weren't on the pistol. They'd found something more interesting on Tommy's uniform. A ribbon of red, white, and blue, with a star in its center, pasted on his olive tunic. The Silver Star. And clearly visible a quarter inch above it, a clean tear in the fabric where General Oliver von Luck's protesting hand had ripped the original decoration off.

"You tipped off Sawyer," said Judge. "You set out the wire for us in Heidelberg?"

Mullin's eyes twinkled, and he sighed tiredly. "All right, Tommy."

Judge threw a protective arm across Ingrid, shielding her with his body. "Jesus, Spanner, can't you even do this yourself?"

And for a split second, Judge felt removed from himself, queer and floaty, as if all of this weren't quite happening. Staring into Mullins's ruddy face, he saw the two of them walking out of a Brooklyn courthouse in the summer of '25, Patrolman Mullins and his charge, Devlin Parnell Judge; he felt the pressure of Mullins's hand the day he'd pinned his policeman's shield to his chest, and four years later when he'd exchanged it for the gold badge of a plainclothes detective.

"Why?" he asked.

Mullins dug something out of his pocket and stuck a hand over the seat. "Two reasons, if you have to know. One for each shoulder." Resting in his palm was a small jewel box displaying a pair of silver five-pointed stars. "I'm not going to have any snot-nosed punk talking down at me when I'm back Stateside. The way I see it, the mayor will be more than happy to appoint a brigadier general who served under Georgie Patton commissioner of police for the five boroughs."

"You're going to help Patton start another war just to get a lousy promotion?"

Mullins colored, rising in his seat. "Look around you, lad. If it's not now, it'll be later. Why not get the job done when our boys are still here? You think Mr. Stalin's going to sit still in Berlin? The Poles and the Czechs, why, they're done for already. They're greedy bastards, the Commies are. George Patton knows that. He's the only fellow brave enough to take steps while we can do something about it. You were a decent fighter once. I'd thought you'd understand."

"Yeah," said Judge, shaking his head. "Your own Jimmy Sullivan."

Mullins snapped the box closed, giving Judge a doleful smile. "Sorry, lad, but you've left me no other way." And shifting in his seat, he nodded to his driver. "All right, Tommy. Let's get it over."

"No!" shouted Judge.

A hailstorm of glass exploded into the car, a battery of gunshots blowing out the windows, spraying crystal splinters over Judge and Ingrid. One, two, three. The blistering reports came close on one another, melding into a terrific earsplitting roar. Somewhere inside the blizzard, the side of Tommy's face dissolved into a frothing red mass. Ingrid buried herself in the car leather, mouth frozen in a silent scream, blood freckling her delicate features. Mullins shouted "What the he—" The next instant his skull caromed from the dashboard to the window, his voice died, and his shoulders slumped against the door. White smoke choked the car, cordite from the spent casings.

Silence.

Rivulets of glass tinkled onto the dashboard.

Judge pulled his hands from his ears, releasing his breath. Ingrid stared at him in shock, her eyes blinking wildly. Tommy was dead. Spanner Mullins twitched, gasped, then was still.

Suddenly, the door behind Judge was flung open. A GI brandishing a smoking pistol peered into the automobile. Judge recognized the cornflower-blue eyes, the shock of brown hair, the open and trusting face, but the Texan's shit-eating grin was nowhere to be seen.

"Welcome to Berlin, Major Judge," said Darren Honey. "About time I found you."

54

SEYSS WAS IN.

A grand foyer greeted him, squeaky wooden floors waxed to an immaculate shine, rich yellow walls, and a gargantuan crystal chandelier bathing the circular hall in an unflattering light. The entry was packed with security men: the Americans in their double-breasted summer suits, Brits sweating in wool serge, and, of course, his fellow members of the Russian secret police, the NKVD, dressed to a man in identical boxy gray suits.

Arms behind his back, lips pursed in polite but stoic greeting, Seyss crossed the foyer. He nodded his hellos and received a few in return. No brows were raised in suspicion. No one questioned his function. No one even asked his name. His mere presence at Ringstrasse 2 bespoke his right to be there.

Behind him were two police checkpoints, a long chat with the head of perimeter security, Gregor Vlassik, and a cordon of Cossack cavalrymen, spit-shined boots and gleaming sabers on proud display. Farther back was Colonel Klimt, who could be found at this instant lying naked in the dirt with a lead slug in his temple. It had been a clean shot, barrel pressed to skin so as not to risk bloodying the uniform. Rushing to change into Klimt's pea-green smock and jodhpurs, he'd been thrown back to his days as a recruit at the academy in Bad Toelz. Inspections were often held in the middle of the night and these spur-of-the-moment affairs became known as "masquerade balls." The cadets were lined up naked in front of their beds then ordered to dress for a specific activity—a full-gear march, a formal company banquet, even a football match. The first two cadets properly attired were permitted to go back to bed. The rest went at it again and again, until at dawn, the last two standing were ordered to run ten kilometers in full combat dress.

The door closed behind him and he caught the hum of a party in progress, like the drone of distant bombers. A corridor ran the width of the house. A red carpet softened the tread of his cavalry boots, candle sconces lit the way. Seyss moved purposefully through the hall, his fore-knowledge of the house's layout, its security measures, easing his anxieties and lending his step a confident, unimpeachable gait.

He knew, for example, that Vlassik had an office at the west end of the hall, and that next to it was the radio room. He also knew that there was only a single bathroom on the ground floor, so that during the evening guests in need would have occasion to traipse upstairs in search of another. What interested him most, however, lay at the end of the hall: the formal dining room where tonight the three leaders of the Western World were gathered to celebrate the defeat, rape, and pillage of the greater German Reich.

Ahead, the French doors to the dining room swung open, spitting out a tuxedo-clad maître d'. Spotting Seyss, the man raised an inquiring finger and rushed over.

"No uniforms!" he hissed under his breath. "The *vozhd* has expressly requested that all officers not invited to the formal dinner parties remain in the service area. Comrade, this way."

Seyss stood rock still, appraising the officious man with an insolent gaze. A feeling of utter invincibility had come over him. He was no longer Erich Seyss. No longer a German officer impersonating a Russian officer. He was the colonel himself. He was Ivan Truchin, hero of Stalingrad, and no one, not even the *vozhd*—or supreme leader, as Stalin liked to call himself—would be permitted to show him disrespect.

"Very well," he answered a moment later, his dignity satisfied. "Lead the way."

The kitchen was a hive of activity. Waiters, chefs, sauciers, sous-chefs, patissiers all scurrying this way and that. Two broad tables ran the length of the room. On them were a dizzying array of dishes. Smoked herring, whitefish, fruit, vegetables, cold duck. A giant tureen of caviar four feet across sat half-eaten near the trash, a veritable mountain of the precious black roe. The second course was being served: a lovely borscht with dollops of sour cream. An enticing aroma wafted from the ovens: roasted venison. Stacked in the corner were crates of liquor: red wine, white wine, cognac, Champagne. It was more food and drink than the average Russian would see in a lifetime.

And supervising it all, the meddlesome prick who'd shepherded him into the kitchen.

Seyss pulled aside a passing waiter, pointing at the maître d'. "Who is that?"

"You mean Comrade Pushkin?"

"Pushkin the author?"

The waiter laughed, then realizing he was laughing at a colonel of the secret police, frowned. "No, sir, Dimitri Pushkin, the maître d'hotel of the Restaurant Georgia in Moscow, Comrade Stalin's favorite."

"Ah."

Seyss followed the waiter to the service door and watched him deliver his tray of steaming borscht. Stalin, Truman, and Churchill were seated at the same table, separated from one another by their closest advisors. Churchill looked sullen and morose, more interested in devouring the monstrous whiskey in his hand than chatting with his dinner partners. Truman and Stalin were deep in conversation, clearly enjoying each other's company. Stalin banged his good hand on the table and Truman tossed his head back, cackling. Bottles were produced. Vodka for the American, white wine for Stalin. A toast was made. *Nastrovya!*

Seyss didn't know who he hated worse. Truman for being so weak. Or Stalin for being so strong.

There was not a single security officer inside the dining room. Just the eight round tables, each seating between seven and ten guests, all male. Twenty-five feet separated Seyss from the head table. Truman was seated sideways to him and Churchill at the far side, facing him. Seyss's problem was obvious: There were too many bodies in his line of fire. He couldn't nail two head shots at this distance. Not with any certainty.

Or maybe he was looking for excuses.

For the first time, he wondered if he'd been naïve to factor escape into his plans.

Dismissing the notion, Seyss resumed his study of the room. A grand piano was set off to one side, its lid raised. Apparently, there was to be entertainment. Four sets of curtained French doors gave onto a flagstone terrace, and beyond that a broad lawn sloping to the banks of the river Havel. Another look around the place convinced him. He needed his men outside.

Retreating from the doorway, Seyss walked the length of the kitchen searching for the exit to the terrace. A chef was pulling the venison from the oven, basting it in its own warm juices. Pots boiling to overflow were eased from the stove, steaming string beans poured into a sieve. A flurry of pops spoke of wine being uncorked and decanted. Sliding past this well-rehearsed chaos, Seyss noticed his heart beating faster, his stomach grown flighty. A bead of sweat escaped his brow and traced a slow course across his forehead. His earlier sangfroid was nowhere to be found. He smiled at his sudden distress, recognizing the familiar sensation. Nerves. It was always this way before a race.

He found the back door in an alcove past the pantry. Standing next to it were two men and two women, all clad in evening dress, talking brightly to one another. The women were typical Bolshies: fat, ugly, and in need of a good wash. Both held violins to their ears, plucking the strings, bowing a few notes, tuning their instruments. Their conversation halted the moment they saw Seyss.

But Colonel Truchin was in an ebullient mood. Mixing among them, he opened the door and tucked his head outside. The sky had darkened to a dusky azure. The temperature was pleasant, not a cloud to be seen. He smiled, relaxing a notch.

"A beautiful evening, yes?"

The musicians responded merrily. "Wonderful. Gorgeous. A pity not to play *al fresco*."

Seyss inclined his head at the suggestion. "Yes," he agreed. "A pity." The best ideas were always the simplest.

JUDGE SAT IN THE FRONT of the jeep, hand on the windscreen, leaning to the right so that his head captured the brunt of the passing wind. He kept his eyes open, allowing them to tear. He'd decided he preferred a moist, unfocused landscape to the stark and desolate one Darren Honey had just revealed.

Darren Honey, captain attached to the Organization of Strategic Services.

The OSS had known about Patton for the last three months—his growing psychosis, his hatred of the Russians, his admiration for all things German. Judge had come along at the right time, the investigation into Seyss's escape a perfect medium to insert an agent into Patton's command. No one had any idea at the beginning that Seyss would be linked to Patton so directly. They'd only wanted to see to what extent Patton abetted or interfered with the investigation. Serendipity, Bill Donovan had called it. To paraphrase a famous general, he'd rather be lucky than good.

Judge thought there was more but Honey wasn't talking, except to say he was sorry for allowing Mullins to beat him to the *gemeindehaus* in Wedding. Just as well, though. It saved them from having to deal with Mullins later.

They'd crossed the Glienickes Bridge five minutes ago. Officially they were now in Potsdam. The road rose and fell, carving its way through sparsely forested foothills. Russian soldiers lined their path like a green picket fence. And though it was high summer and the trees thick with leaves, there was a smokiness to the air, the spicy scent of smothered embers and burning wood that made him think of fall.

Honey's walkie-talkie gargled and he held it to his ear. A voice spat out some words in a foreign language. Honey answered back in the same tongue.

"The Russians found one of their men in a drainage ditch not far from Ringstrasse. Dead." Honey hesitated, then added, "His uniform was missing."

Ingrid shot forward from the backseat. "Quick. You must ring the president. Call Stalin. Warn them Erich is here."

Honey spoke a few more words into the walkie-talkie, then set it down. "Taken care of."

"That's it?" Judge asked. "Where are the sirens? Why isn't every one of these soldiers picking up his gear and moving his ass to Stalin's place?"

"Taken care of," Honey repeated, and Judge knew he was no longer in charge.

They passed through two checkpoints, stopping each time for ten excruciating minutes as Honey's papers were meticulously scrutinized and phone calls were made up the chain of command. Judge asked for a pistol and Honey shook his head. One hothead with a gun running around Stalin's residence was enough. Judge was only there in case they couldn't find Seyss. Same went for Ingrid. They were the only two who knew his face close up.

The road had assumed a long, steady curve and the Havel was visible in the cuts between the houses, a calm blue expanse framed by sloping grass bank. Cresting a rise, they came upon a black Mercedes parked on the side of the road. Honey braked hard and pulled the jeep over. A man was already running toward them, pale and thin with lank dark hair and a drooping mustache. He was dressed in a gray suit and carried a bundle of clothing under one arm.

"For you, Major Judge, please to put on. Quickly." He handed over a blue blazer and white shirt, then ran back to the black sedan.

"Do as he says," ordered Honey. "And hurry up about it." Putting the jeep into first gear he followed the Mercedes up the hill.

"Who was it?" asked Judge, slipping on the clean dress shirt and blazer.

"A friend."

"But he's Russian," Ingrid protested.

"I hope so," Honey retorted. "I don't know how else you expected to slip into a state dinner given by Marshal Stalin."

Judge was as curious as Ingrid about the man's identity, wondering why the hell he knew his name. *A friend*. He had a good idea what that meant. "Who was it?" he asked again, and this time held Honey's gaze until he answered.

"Vlassik. General Gregor Vlassik. Head of compound security during the marshal's stay. It's his neck if anything happens. Like I said, a friend."

They pulled back onto the road and followed the Mercedes for three minutes. Number 2 Ringstrasse was a gated stucco mansion painted the color of rust, with a mansard roof and dormer windows. Truman's bodyguard was parked on the main road, a bevy of G-men in pinstripes and fedoras toting Thompson submachine guns. Churchill's escort was more discreet, lounging in a half dozen Bentleys. Vlassik waved off a brace of sentries and both cars coasted through the open gates, parking in a covered court to the left of the front door.

The Russian was out of the Mercedes in a flash, ushering his three guests into the service entrance. From the moment he stepped inside, it was apparent something was wrong. The mansion was deadly quiet, the kitchen half deserted. Vlassik rushed to a lone waiter who sat smoking a cigarette, perusing a Moscow newspaper.

"Where is everyone?" Though he spoke Russian, the gist of his question was obvious.

The waiter shrugged, pointing toward the rear of the houses with his cigarette. "Outside on the terrace. I believe they are performing some Tchaikovsky. Perhaps the Violin Concerto in D minor."

Judge grabbed Vlassik's sleeve. "I take it Tchaikovsky on the terrace wasn't part of the program."

Vlassik blanched and shook his head. "No, comrade, it was not."

Judge turned to Honey, hand extended, palm open. "Give me a goddamned gun and give it to me right now."

Vlassik beat him to the punch, drawing a heavy revolver from his boot and slapping it into Judge's hand. "A Smith and Wesson thirty-eight. Standard police issue, *nyet*? If you are to see this man Seyss, please to kill him."

Judge flicked open the cylinder, checked for rounds, then slapped it home. "You've got my word."

THE MUSICIANS WERE REALLY QUITE good, though Seyss would have preferred something more somber for the occasion, Beethoven's Eroica, for example. The piano had been rolled outside and the two female violinists stood next to it, bowing vigorously, swooning in time to the pianist's dramatic runs.

A few words to Pushkin as to Stalin's ire that the American president found the dining room too smoky and the anxious little Muscovite had moved like the wind to reorganize the musical entertainment. No wonder he presided over the best restaurant in Moscow. He knew the first rule of catering: The guest comes first. Though, Seyss added somewhat sympathetically, after this evening, Pushkin could probably forget about returning to his post at the Restaurant Georgia. If he returned to Moscow, at all, it would be in a pine box.

Seyss stood on a fringe of lawn at the top of a gentle slope that fell away to the riverbank. Behind him the forest encroached at his back. Lining the lawn from the villa to the Havel, were members of the crack division assigned to guard the residence of their supreme leader. To a man their faces were turned to the terrace, eyes watering at the romantic musings of their own Pyotr Ilich Tchaikovsky.

From his vantage point, Seyss had a clear view of the gathering. Churchill, Truman, and Stalin stood shoulder to shoulder at the forefront of the assembled guests. He measured the distance to his targets as seventy feet. A chest shot with a pistol from this distance would be simple. A head shot, more difficult. A hand brushed his holster, thumb freeing the pistol guard. Using the last three fingers, he eased the revolver a centimeter or two from its well-oiled cradle. Once he drew the weapon, he would have to move fast. Aim and two shots, aim and two shots.

The cauldron must be made to boil.

It was time.

Raising his nose to the fragrant night air, he took a tentative step forward. His muscles itched. He felt loose and energetic. He saw himself down in the blocks, imagined the feel of the clay as his fingers danced over the starting line. This was the part he'd always liked best, the prelude to the race, sizing up himself and the competition, his uncertainty hardening to conviction. *Macht zur Sieg.* The will to victory. The memory of it all made him smile. He rolled his neck to either side, breathing deeply, his eyes focusing on the targets. Truman dressed in a charcoal suit, an appreciative grin pasted to his face. Churchill in a khaki uniform, arms drawn over his chest, liking none of it. Seyss took a deep breath and swallowed hard. His mouth was dry and suddenly he didn't want to smile anymore.

Sächlichkeit, a voice urged him, and his entire body stiffened.

One last race.

THE GUESTS HAD ASSEMBLED ON the terrace forming a large crescent around the musicians. They stood with their backs to the villa, forty men in dark suits enjoying the lively music. Judge rushed to the edge of the gathering, eyes scouring the group for the distinctive pea green of a Russian officer's uniform. He found only three or four soldiers, generals all, each above fifty.

"Shit," said Honey. "The troops are in the woods."

Dozens of Russian soldiers lined either side of the lawn, emerged from their positions to enjoy the music. Every man shouldered a machine gun, a pistol in his belt. Many more remained partially shrouded, shadowy figures inhabiting the forest's border. Any one of them had a clear, unobstructed shot at the Allied leaders.

Judge skirted the crowd. Harry Truman, Winston Churchill, and Josef Stalin stood ten feet away. Caught up in the music, they were impervious to the frantic hunt being launched around them. He saw Vlassik whispering urgently in Stalin's ear and Stalin shooing him away with an expression of grave irritation. Judge turned his eyes to the soldiers closest to the terrace, squinting to make out the features beneath their woolen caps.

"*I see him.*"

It was Ingrid and her voice was ice. She clutched at his arm, using her free hand to point toward a cluster of soldiers half hidden beneath the overhanging branches of a centuries-old pine. "There."

Still pointing, she released Judge's arm and began to jog, then run across the terrace.

"Erich!" she yelled. "Erich, don't!"

A gunshot cracked the night air and Ingrid seemed at once to stop and rise on her tiptoes. A flower had bloomed high on her back, larger than any rose Judge had ever seen, and as she collapsed, his heart fell with her.

Seyss emerged from the shadows, sprinting, pistol extended in front of him, firing in time to his step. His cap blew from his head and Judge saw his face, hard, determined, fearless.

The musicians played a few bars longer, first one violinist cutting short a bow, then the other. Finally the pianist dropped his hands from the keyboard, looking altogether mystified. The guests remained where they stood, the combined civilian and military leadership of the three most powerful countries on earth, warriors all, and not a soul among them moving.

By now, Judge was running too. Firing and running, closing the distance to the president. Honey dropped to one knee, and steadying his arm, began to blow off rounds. Somewhere in the tumult, Judge could hear the spent shells tinkling to the ground like coins from a winning slot.

Ten feet separated him from the president. A last step and he was there. Throwing himself in front of Truman, he grabbed the man's shoulders and chucked him to the ground. Then he was falling, too, spinning in time to see Seyss's gun spit fire, feeling a sudden and terrible pain spear his hip.

Seyss came nearer, his runner's stride relentless, and Judge imagined he could see his finger whitening as it tensed around the trigger. All his efforts were for naught, for Francis, for Ingrid, for himself, and now for the president. The White Lion would succeed. The thought sparked in him a terrific rage, a fury that cauterized his pain and momentarily erased his worry for Ingrid.

Raising his pistol, Judge fired twice, striking Seyss in the shoulder and the thigh. He could hear the bullets' impact, a dull and concise thud, could see filaments of his uniform waft into the air.

Still Seyss's pace did not slacken.

Judge waited a moment longer, until Seyss's body filled his entire field of vision. He yelled "Stop!" and squeezed off his final round, even as another slug knocked him to the ground.

A perfect dot appeared on Seyss's cheek as a puff of pink smoke burst from the rear of his head. His step faltered, but only for an instant. Still he ran, but his stride was looser, his mouth open, his eyes no longer focused. The gun rose in his hand, but just as quickly fell. Arms flailing, he tumbled recklessly to the ground, his pistol clattering to the flagstone.

Seyss lay a foot away from Judge. He was dead, his blue eyes frozen on the infinite distance.

Judge rested his head on the terrace and stared into the night sky. A single star twinkled above him.

"Ingrid," he shouted, his voice sandy and weak.

And waiting, he begged the star, and whatever force had made it, for an answer.

But by now every security officer in Potsdam had descended onto the terrace. The FBI men and their machine guns were pushing their way through ranks of uniformed NKVD regulars. British agents had surrounded a wholly unperturbed Winston Churchill, who Judge heard call for "a whiskey, a bloody great big one, and make it snappy." Stalin stood nearby, huddled with his top commanders.

Peering through a forest of milling legs, Judge fought for a sign of Ingrid. Then he saw her; she lay prone, her legs crossed at the ankle, her form unmoving. Clenching his stomach, he called her name through gritted teeth. "Ingrid!"

Abruptly, his view was blocked by a familiar figure kneeling at his side.

"Are you all right, young man?"

President Harry S Truman folded his jacket into a square and placed it under Judge's head.

Judge touched a hand to his hip and it came away warm and wet. The other slug had taken him in the shoulder. Curiously, his entire body was numb. The pain, he realized, would come later. He pulled himself forward an inch or two to regain sight of Ingrid Bach.

"Keep still," Truman said, his earnest features etched with concern. "We'll get a doctor here in a jif."

Suddenly Ingrid's legs twitched. General Vlassik was kneeling at her side, speaking to her. Applying a compress to her shoulder, he helped her sit up. Her face was pale, her blouse soaked through with blood, but she was alert. She was alive.

Judge closed his eyes for an instant, sure it was his Francis Xavier who had answered his prayer. "Yessir," he said.

Truman brushed his hand against Seyss's uniform. "Jesus. One of theirs. And I thought Stalin had security wrapped up damned tight."

"No," Judge protested, fighting to raise himself on an elbow. "He's not a Rus—"

A firm hand pressed him to the ground, cutting short his words. Crouching alongside the president, Darren Honey gave a discreet but unmistakable shake of the head.

"Not what?" Truman asked.

Judge looked at Honey a moment longer, then he knew. They had wanted this to happen. Honey. Vlassik. The OSS and whoever was behind it.

"Nothing," said Judge. "I wasn't sure if he was dead."

"He's dead all right, damned Communist." Harry Truman glanced over his shoulder. Seeing Stalin, his jaw hardened. His eyes shot back to Judge, but he was looking right through him. "Maybe I can't trust that sonuvabitch after all."

Judge turned his head, losing himself among the tall pines that bordered the rolling lawn. *No,* he thought to himself, *you probably can't. And maybe it's better that way. Maybe mistrust was the best form of vigilance.*

And closing his eyes, he saw himself standing on the docks of the Brooklyn Navy Yard with Francis: two brothers with their hands locked together in farewell. Curiously, he was unable to speak, unable to offer any warning about the future, even to say good-bye, and after a moment, Francis turned and disappeared into the busy crowd, leaving him only the question in his eyes and the weight of his expectations.

EPILOGUE

"DAMMIT, WOODRING," BELLOWED GEORGE PATTON, "have you got this fine example of American engineering gassed up and ready to go yet? We have ourselves a few dozen pheasants to nab for Sunday dinner. They won't wait all day, you know."

Private First Class Horace C. Woodring snapped open the rear door of the custom-made Cadillac model 75 and fired off his crispest salute. "Yessir, General. She's all set. Guns and the dog will ride up ahead with Sergeant Spruce in the jeep. If you'll just climb in, I promise I'll have you in the woods bagging those birdies inside of two hours."

Patton roared with laughter and slid into the roomy backseat. "Get in, Hap," he called to his long-time adjutant, General Hobart Gay. "I told you Woodring was the best. He's the fastest there is. Better than a Piper Cub to get you there ahead of time. Isn't that right, Woodring?"

"A private never disagrees with a general."

The cheerful driver waited for Gay to settle in next to Patton, then shut the door behind him. Sliding behind the wheel, he spent a moment adjusting the rearview mirror so that he could keep sight of Patton at all times. It was rare to see the general in such high spirits. His mood had been almost unremittingly grim since his transfer to the Fifteenth Army in early October. Losing command of his beloved Third Army had dealt him a crushing blow, though everyone agreed afterward that he'd never been cut out to be military governor of Bavaria, or any other place for that matter. Not with his mouth. Not old "Blood and Guts."

The last straw had come at a press conference in September. Before an assembly of some fifty reporters, Patton had publicly voiced his sentiments about the Nazis being no different from Republicans or Democrats, while admitting that he'd made use of many former Nazi officials to run the Bavarian government.

There was more to Eisenhower's decision to relieve Patton of his command than that. Much more. But Woodring kept those facts to himself. After all, he reminded himself, he was only a driver and not privy to such sensitive information.

Making a sweeping left turn, he powered the Cadillac onto the autobahn, his keen blue eyes searching the asphalt for signs of ice. Sunday, the ninth of December, had dawned raw and cold. At 7:00 A.M., the thermometer hanging outside the motor pool had read thirty degrees Fahrenheit. Two hours later, a timid sun had broken through the cloud cover. Expanses of newly fallen snow hugged both sides of the highway, sparkling like twin fields of diamonds.

Their route took them south from Bad Nauheim along the Kassel-Frankfurt-Mannheim autobahn toward the wild, game-rich forests of the Rhine-Palatinate. Approaching the town of Bad Homburg, Patton insisted they exit the autobahn and visit the ruins of a restored Roman outpost in the foothills of the Taunus Mountains. Woodring obliged. In his few weeks driving for the general, he'd learned to expect detours—Patton always wanted to visit this hospital or that cemetery—and had factored a little extra time into that morning's timetable.

For ten minutes, Patton slogged through the muddy ruins in his knee-high leather boots, crowing about "his friend Caesar" and "conquering Gaul" and "the glory of battle." Woodring smiled inwardly. The crazy old goat truly believed he'd fought at Julius Caesar's side.

Just before ten, the two-vehicle convoy left Bad Homburg, continuing on its southward trek. Patton sat forward in his seat, a rapt expression illuminating his dour features. They were driving over territory the Third Army had taken eight months before. Past Frankfurt. Past Darmstadt. Past Wiesbaden. Patton didn't stop talking for a moment's time, pointing out bridges his men had captured, beaming with undisguised pride at his soldiers' derring-do, and, of course, his own.

Near eleven, Woodring left the autobahn for a second time, transferring to National Route 38. In another quarter of an hour, he spotted a sign indicating that they were nearing the city of Mannheim. Soon he began to recognize familiar landmarks. A kiosk. A hotel. A police station. He'd traveled this part of the route a dozen times in the dead of night. Flashing past on their right was a marker showing that they'd entered the village of Kaefertal. The road was littered with debris: half-tracks lying upside down, charred Tiger tanks, horsecarts splintered and upended. The town looked as if the war had ended yesterday.

"Look at the derelict vehicles," Patton exclaimed, grimacing at the passing sights. "How awful war is. Think of all the waste."

"It's terrible, sir. Just terrible," answered Woodring, but his eyes were glued to the road in front of him, not on the parade of broken armor. Approaching from the opposite direction was a large two-and-a-half-ton truck, a standard army transport. Seeing it, Woodring flashed his lights once and got a flash in return.

Two hundred yards separated the vehicles. One hundred. Woodring moved the Cadillac toward the center of the road. At fifty yards, he accelerated to thirty miles per hour, raising an arm to point out a crumpled Mercedes staff car off the right-hand side of the vehicle.

"Would you look at that?" said Patton, half standing in the cabin, craning his neck to get a glimpse.

It was precisely then that the oncoming transport turned left, directly into the Cadillac's path. Woodring sat back in his seat and calmly spun the wheel to the left, waiting a half second, then braking with all his might. He heard Gay say "Sit tight," and a split second later, the two vehicles collided. With an angry scream of metal, the truck's right front fender plowed into the Cadillac's hood, crushing the radiator and releasing a geyser of steam. Patton, already leaning on the front seat, was thrown forward, his head striking the dashboard, then flung back like a rag doll into the passenger seat.

The accident was over in a second, the truck come to rest at a right angle to the Cadillac.

Woodring flung open his door and rushed to the rear of the vehicle.

Patton lay in Gay's arms, bleeding profusely from wounds to the forehead and scalp.

"Hold tight, General, we'll get an ambulance here pronto. You're going to be fine, sir."

"I believe I am paralyzed," said Patton, his gravelly voice absent any fear. "I'm having trouble in breathing. Rub my shoulders, Woodring. Work my fingers for me. Rub my hands."

Woodring did as he was told while Gay supported the general from the rear. Running a hand behind Patton's neck, he felt a distinct outcropping an inch or two below the skull.

Patton looked at him imploringly. "I said rub my hands, dammit."

Just then the truck driver stuck his head in the open door. Woodring met his gaze and nodded. Everything had gone off as planned. Patton's neck was broken at the third vertebra. It was a mortal injury. He'd linger a few days, a week at most, but there was nothing any doctor could do to save him. By Christmas, he'd be dead and buried.

George Patton was staring up at Woodring, a tear welling in his eye. "Jesus," he moaned. "This is a helluva way to die."

Woodring sighed grimly, pleased he wouldn't have to speed things along. The OSS taught a man to do almost anything. He'd killed Nazi generals while they slept on the eve of D-Day, chased a fugitive war criminal across Germany, even helped save the life of the president of the United States. Hardest, though, was getting used to being called a different name every day. Woodring. Honey. Who knew what was next? Maybe someday someone would use his real name: Honnecker.

For now, though, it was still too German.

AUTHOR'S NOTE

Many veterans of the Second World War, both American and German, offered generously of their time and recollections during the research and writing of this novel. Some I am proud to acknowledge, others have preferred to remain anonymous.

In Germany, Dr. Gunther Weber shared with me his experiences of day-to-day survival in the wreckage of postwar Germany, as well as elements of his training and duty with the 1st Parachute Division of the German army. In the course of an afternoon, over a delightful *apfelstrudel* and more than a few Pilsner Urquells, two strangers from different generations and different countries became friends.

Colonel James Scanlon (USAF ret.) related the derring-do of a nineteen-year pilot who after completing 30 missions aboard a B-17 "Flying Fortress" transferred to P-51s so he could "have a little fun."

Master Sergeant Jewel Phegley (USA ret.) was kind enough to describe his time as a "Nazi hunter" in southern Germany.

Lt. Col. James Milano (USA ret.) discussed his experience in Austria working to establish an intelligence network to spy on Soviet occupation forces. His excellent book *Soldiers, Spies, and the Rat Line* (Brassey's) revealed a good deal about the sordid dealings of the United States intelligence services with former members of the SS. Anyone interested in the subject, and Klaus Barbie, in particular, could do no better than to view the riveting documentary *Hotel Terminus*, by Marcel Ophuls.

General Thomas Ayers, (USA ret.) was kind enough to steer me through the labyrinthine animal that is the United States Army in the course of my research.

I would additionally like to thank my outstanding guides in Germany: Elizabeth Keiper in Dresden, Sarah Slenczka in Nuremberg, and Bob Woshington in Berlin.

Few figures in the annals of the Second World War are as fascinating as General George S. Patton, Jr. To be sure, he was a military leader of unsurpassed skill and vital to a timely victory in the European Theatre of Operations. Yet for a man who demanded the utmost in discipline from his men, he was often incapable of exercising a like control over himself. It is this, his flawed humanity, that makes him such an exhilarating and controversial figure.

The roots for my characterization of Patton were drawn wholly from the historical record. I can recommend without reservation two superb biographies: *Patton: A Genius for War* by Carlos D'Este and *Patton: Ordeal and Triumph* by Ladislas Farago. It is worth noting here that the OSS was well aware of Patton's leanings and in June of 1945 ordered his phone tapped. Portions of his conversations are quoted verbatim in the novel, though I must point out that his correspondent was fictitious. Patton was relieved of his command September 22, 1945, for inflammatory comments concerning his use of former Nazis in the occupational government of Bavaria. General Dwight Eisenhower said afterward that he hadn't fired Patton for what he'd said, but for what he was going to say next.

I must mention that Private First Class Horace C. Woodring had no known affiliation with the OSS. He was merely the soldier unlucky enough to be driving the car in which George Patton suffered his fatal injuries.

The rest is the author's fantasy.

As always there are many others who deserve my sincerest thanks.

Susanne Reich was a partner from the beginning, offering love, encouragement, as well as invaluable editorial advice.

Sarah Piel at Arthur Pine and Associates cast a constructive eye over early versions of the manuscript and lent her excellent judgment to subsequent revisions. Lori Andiman, also of Arthur Pine and Associates, helped spread the word across the globe.

Leslie Schnur showed the author her every faith in his talents. For her support I will be forever grateful.

Irwyn Applebaum and Nita Taublib welcomed me with open arms and pulled out all the stops, artistically and professionally.

To my editor, Mitch Hoffman, I offer my respect and thanks. His unflagging enthusiasm, deft insight, and ever diplomatic criticism made a tough job easier, and maybe even fun.

Finally, to my agent, Richard Pine, my heartfelt appreciation. Two down and a dozen to go!

GERMANY: JULY, 1945

ZONES OF OCCUPATION:
BRITISH   RUSSIAN
FRENCH   AMERICAN

0 Miles   50   100

DEN

HAMBU

BREMEN

HANOVER

Weser

HOLLAND

Rhine

ESSEN

KASSEL

COLOGNE

MARBURG

BELGIUM

BONN

MALMEDY

Rhine

FRANKFURT

WIESBADEN

LUXEMBOURG

Main

HEIDELBER

STUTTGA

PARIS

BADEN-BADEN

Rhine

FRANCE

FREIBURG

SWITZERLAND